ISLE OF GLORY

By the Same Author

ISLE
OF
GLORY

Jane Oliver (pseud.)

G. P. Putnam's Sons
New York

FOR
FATHER ANDREW, S.D.C.
in
most grateful
memory

" Et repleta es, et glorificata nimis
in corde maris. . ."
" Replenished and made very glorious
in the midst of the seas. . ."

EZEKIEL : 27 : 25

Contents

PREFACE

THE HISTORICAL NOVEL is the mongrel of the arts. The novelist may follow his fancy, the historian's business is with facts. But the historical novelist is suspect on both counts. How much of his work is fancy and how much is fact? In regard to the present book the answer is simple. No essential incident has been wholly invented. There is histcrical evidence or at least traditional ground for the whole dramatic story of Columba, and out of a list of forty chief characters, only eight unimportant fictitious individuals have been introduced, to serve as types of the passionate paganism with which any priest of the new faith must have had to deal.

The action takes place in those countries which were not yet, in the 6th century A.D., known as Scotland and Ireland, but as Alba and Erin. The colonising Romans had not undertaken the series of expensive campaigns which would have been necessary to subdue their heroic peoples, and so Alba and Erin had remained outside the immediate influence of Imperial Rome during the whole of the occupation of Southern Britain, which lasted for approximately the first four hundred years of our era. Consequently they also escaped the chaotic effects of the collapse of the entire colonial system of the Empire early in the 5th century, and the subsequent arrival of wave after wave of virile Germanic barbarians, anxious only to stake their claim to the fertile areas between forest and swamp which the Romanised Britons had cultivated, content to let grass creep across the great trunk roads of the Empire and squirrels pry into the secrets of the ruined civilisation whose cities now stood deserted, skeletal and seared by fire.

As the Romanised, luxury-softened Britons retreated westwards, the Saxons with their thunder-riding gods swept after them, to pause, as the Romans had paused, before the mountains which barred their way. But already, with the arrogance of the successful invader, they were beginning to apply the term " Waelisc " or " foreigner " to the remnant of the ancient people ot Britain which still defied them in the west. And it was in the west and north that the last spark of Christianity was cherished as the dark ages came down, from the west and the north that the challenge to the thunder-gods sounded again. Priests and scholars went constantly between Wales and Erin. David, Cadoc

and many others were teaching thousands in the monastic
schools which were sheltered by the Welsh mountains, and
thousands more were flocking to the great cultural centres which
grew up in Erin ; at Moville, under the famous Finnian, himself
a pupil of Ninian of Candida Casa in Alba, who had been taught
in his turn by Martin of Tours ; or at Clonard, whose equally
famous Abbot had been a pupil of David of Wales.

The eager, imaginative Gaels of Erin responded instinctively
to the new creed which reached them as Rome fell. Their
legendary past was already full of chivalrous stories of unworldly
splendour. Their great tradition, their profound love of beauty
and courage, their intuitive perception of spiritual truth, all made
them ready to greet the epic of the young Prince of Glory as the
fulfilment of their deepest hopes. They had always believed in
the existence of a spiritual order of reality : it mattered less
whether they called their land of heart's desire Heaven or
Tir-nan-Og, thought of its citizens as the lordly ones of the shee
or the guardian angels of God.

So, while resistance to the Germanic invaders was collapsing
in Southern Britain, in spite of all that individual heroism
(symbolised in such song-cycles as that of the semi-legendary
King Arthur and his knights) could do, the lights that the invaders
extinguished were already springing up again elsewhere. In the
5th century, Patrick was already preaching in Erin, David in
Wales, Ninian in Alba. By the second half of the 6th century,
Columba had founded his monastery on Iona, and Mungo had
returned from Wales to establish his community at Glescu, on the
river which was later to be called Clyde. The Catholic re-
conversion of Southern Britain, which had lost its religion as well
as its comforts in the Germanic tidal wave, was to be anticipated
by the Celtic conversion of the north, for it was not until the year
of Columba's death that Augustine lit the first tall candle in the
obscurity of Kent. By that time the Celtic Church had converted
the whole of Erin and most of Alba, and in the 7th century Aidan
was summoned from Iona to establish another holy isle, using
Lindisfarne as his headquarters for the conversion of all
Northumbria.

The present book concentrates on the stormy story of Columba
and the work which laid so many of the foundation stones of
Scotland. Columba came from Erin, to become, with Ninian
and Mungo, one of his adopted country's three great founder-
saints. In writing of him, I have tried to tease out some of the
tangled strands of hagiographical, traditional and historical
evidence which have, in fourteen hundred years, wound themselves

so closely about his vivid personality. To do so, I have been
obliged to make the utmost use of every slender clue I found,
building up the characters encountered from whatever indications
I could obtain.

Thus, the only descriptive epithet which seems to have been
bestowed on Columba's father in an age when most outstanding
men had descriptive nicknames, seems to have been that of
great-grandson of the famous Niall of the Nine Hostages. From
this I have ventured to deduce an atavistic, unheroic character,
living in its poverty on its past. Again, it may seem odd to
associate the quality of gaiety with a saint whose personal life
is known to have been of unparalleled austerity. But when a
devout chronicler like Adamnan uses the adjective *hilaris*,
(associated, of course, with the noun *hilaritas* and our
English hilarity) in his description of Columba, it seems to
indicate that gaiety was inherent in his very holiness. Most
people will, probably, admit that the rare quality of inner joy
is not a circumstantial thing. And the whole of this story is an
attempt to show the development of a character whose violence
and excesses were finally transmuted into the spirituality which
inspired the western world.

In a book about the 6th century almost every other phrase
seems likely to be an anachronism, and though diligent search
has eradicated many, others, still undetected, probably remain.
But one at least is deliberate. I have ventured to render the
Latin as translated by the small boys at the monastic school into
the English of our own Authorised Version, knowing that that
version was not to be written till a thousand years later. I did
this because the children's translation was actually into the Gaelic
which must have had for them a wealth of homely associations.
Such associations, I felt, could only be conveyed in English by the
technically inadmissible use of phrases which, being familiar to
most of us from childhood, have for our ears the same homely ring.

The snatches of verse attributed to Columba are my own
composite renderings of some of the Gaelic verses attributed
to or traditionally associated with him. Both Gaelic and English
versions of these are to be found in the four volumes of Gaelic
folk-lore published by Alexander Carmichael at the beginning of
this century, to whose loving work I acknowledge my great debt.

The names of most of the chief characters have been anglicised
in order to spare the reader the exasperation of having to associate
them with a collection of vague sounds. But the name Maeve
—of which the correct Gaelic spelling is Meadhbh—should
rhyme with save, Eochaidh sound something like Yochay,

and the Gaelic word for fortress, though spelt dun, should be pronounced doon. The modern provinces of Ulster, Munster, Leinster, Connaught and Meath were, in the 6th century called Ulaid, Mume, Laigen, Connachta and Mode. Scotland, in early times was, it should be remembered, known as Alba or Alban, and until the 10th century the name of Scotia seems only to have been applied to Ireland, from which the first Scots came. Incidentally the name of Erin, familiar in romantic poetry, is actually the dative case of the Gaelic name of ancient Ireland, which was Eriu, and from which the present Eire is derived, just as Alba was, strictly speaking, Albu. For this, and for much other invaluable information, I am indebted to Professor R. A. S. Macalister, Litt.D., L.L.D., F.S.A., to whom my grateful thanks are offered, not only for the erudition of his books, but also for the kindness and courtesy with which he has personally answered my many questions. The heroic associations of the word Erin, however, have become so strong that I did not care to lose them for the sake of blank exactitude. I have also rejected the suggestion that the new name given to the island after the monks' arrival was Ioua and not Iona. The fact that Columba and Iona both mean dove, in Latin and Hebrew respectively, while Ioua means (as far as I know) nothing in particular, seems too significant to be merely coincidental. But for these and for any other liberties that I may unwittingly have taken, I hope those better informed will forgive me.

I should like to thank Miss Henrietta Tayler, F.R.Hist.Soc., for most kindly reading and criticising my manuscript, Miss Lucy Menzies for introductions and the offer of books, Mr. J. Robertson of the Signet Library, Edinburgh, who found me so many new sources of information, and all the people of Iona, Donegal and Dublin, who showed me much kindness and gave me such valuable help.

A list of the chief characters is given at the beginning, and a brief bibliography at the end of the book. My chief source of information, of course, has been the unique *Vita S. Columbae*, written only a century after the saint's death by Adamnan, ninth Abbot of Iona. This is available in Dr. Reeves' famous edition of the Latin text, with exhaustive notes, and in Dr. Fowler's translation. Those familiar with Adamnan's account will, I hope, be more aware of the fidelity with which I have used the recorded facts than of the occasional temerity of my excursions beyond them. Such excursions have been primarily in search of the robuster truth which the hagiographical whitewashing of flesh-and-blood characters tends, as far as I am concerned, to obscure.

THE PEOPLE OF THE BOOK

THESE CHARACTERS are all historic, or at least strongly traditional, except where otherwise stated. They are listed in approximate order of appearance.

Nalda (fictitious character) an elderly nurse.

Phelim a nobleman of Erin, the great-grandson of Niall of the Nine Hostages, High King of Erin, who died in A.D. 405.

Eithne Phelim's wife, descendent of the royal line of Laigen (Leinster).

Colum later known as Columba in the Latin and Colum-Cille (Colum of the Church) in the Gaelic. Phelim's eldest son. Born 521. Died 597.

Cruithann a learned Christian priest in Erin: Columba's first teacher.

Maeve (fictitious character) Eithne's younger sister.

Tombul (fictitious character) Phelim's champion, professional strong man and leader of his house-company of warriors.

Gemman a bard.

Olim of the Golden Tongue (fictitious character) chief court poet of Ulaid.

Finnian of Moville scholar, traveller and saint of the Celtic Church.

Finnian of Clonard saintly abbot of the great monastery.

Molaise a recluse and saint. Columba's soul-friend or confessor.

Kenneth
Brendan } Columba's first friends at Clonard. Members of the
Comgall group known as the Apostles of Erin.

Dermot, High King of Erin between A.D. 544 and 565.

Aedh, High King of Erin in A.D. 575 (the year of the Synod of Drumceatt.).

Rus
Lugaid
Eochaidh
Torannan (Reeves has " Tochannu ")
Cobtach
Macculthan (Reeves has " Moculthemne ") } Monks who landed on Iona with Columba at Pentecost, A.D. 563.
Ernaan (later the Superior of Hinba).
Catan
Grellan (Reeves has " Grillan ")
Carnan
Oran
Scandal

Urdan (fictitious character) a boy whose speech was restored; many such miracles are recorded by Adamnan.

Two Druids who, according to tradition, posed as Christian bishops in order to persuade Columba to leave the island. (Dr. Reeves does not accept this, but the tradition is very strong.)

Melban (fictitious character) A discontented monk.

Gondal (fictitious character) A Pictish lad.

Brude, King of the Northern Picts from A.D. 554 to 584.

Broichan Arch-Druid at Pictish court.

Lorne (fictitious character) a Pictish girl.

Eogan cousin of Conall, King of the Scots in Alba. Chosen by the nobles to succeed him.

Aidan another cousin, chosen as Conall's successor by Columba.

Baithene second Abbot of Iona.

ALSO : Nobles, warriors, peasants, pagan and Christian priests, monks, fishermen, students and children.

I

Prime

" Pater noster, qui es in coelis,
Sanctificetur nomen tuum.
Veniat regnum tuum,
Fiat voluntas tua,
Sicut in coelo,
Etiam in terra . . ."

MATTHAEUS. VI 9.

CHAPTER I

THE OLD WOMAN's face was like a piece of carved oak. The firelight built up the heights of brow and cheek-bones, gouged deeper hollows round the mouth that was pursed over nearly bare gums, and stressed the fanning creases at the corners of the grey eyes that were so typical of the western land which had not yet been called Donegal.

Over the fire of turf on the central hearth of Phelim's timbered hall great cauldrons of water steamed, and serving-maids anxiously came and went in obedience to Nalda's creaking voice, while she herself, irritable with the mounting fear that threatened to outweigh the experience of a lifetime's emergencies, jerkily shook out of armfuls of white linen till they gave off a faint fragrance of the aromatic herbs with which they had been packed in Eithne's dower-chests just under a year ago.

Then Phelim abruptly opened the heavy outer door at the far end of the hall. He seemed to bring the torrential winter rain in with him as he stood there, at first too bemused to close the door, impatiently tearing loose the fastening of the cloak that hung in dripping folds about him with fingers that were clumsy from fear as well as cold. Behind him the rain sluiced down from a windless, unbroken sky that seemed as dark as the midnight world below it, and when Phelim turned to close the door at last he could see it come shuddering down in thousands of silvered rods which struck the ground so hard that it was hazed with the fine spray of their recoil. As the heavy door swung shut the desolation of the night was only partly excluded : the muted shudder of the falling rain still sounded about him, and even the high-piled fire hissed as raindrops fell on it from the central hole in the thatch through which the smoke escaped.

Phelim let his sodden, hooded cloak fall across a bench and hurried towards his wife's old nurse, his lean, swarthy face gaunt with terror in its frame of rain-sleeked black hair. He stood for an instant at her elbow, silent save for his gasping breath. Only when she made no movement could he force himself to speak, in a harsh voice that he scarcely recognised as his own.

" Well ? Any change ? "

The old woman shook her head without looking round. Her eyes were closed now, and as her lips moved, he could catch fragments of incoherent petitions, hear the names of those ancient gods whose worship had been banned from Erin for over a lifetime, though their fame lingered on, he knew, in remote corners of the officially Christian land, cherished by the imagination of those who found it hard to change old ways for new. So now, in this hour of terror, when anguish for her darling made it impossible to bear the sight of that husband who had brought her to this pass, it was not to the blessed Virgin or the kindly saints that Nalda prayed, but to Danu and Aengus, Brigit the healing goddess, Buanann and Ana, and Cleena of the fairy hill. Presently Phelim could bear the sound of it no longer. He took the old woman by the shoulder and fairly shook her in his fear.

" Is—is she still as bad as ever ? "

" Yes."

" Worse ? "

" She is no better."

Nalda rose, the warm clothes held to her breast, her narrowed grey eyes surveying Phelim inimically. It had always been her opinion that her lady Eithne could have made a better marriage than one which took her so far from her royal home in Laigen merely to enter the household of Phelim of the Hy Niall, a precious poor specimen of manhood by comparison with what was her lady's due, and no more than a king's cousin, at that. Turning a contemptuous shoulder on him, she hurried away down the hall. The timbered, barn-like building was pillared with young pine trunks that supported the beams of the roof, the outer aisles were divided by partitions into alcoves in which, huddled beneath sheepskin coverlets, on straw-bedded couches, the men of Phelim's household, tired by a day's hunting and oblivious of crisis, already slept. At the far end of the hall, granted only the privacy of the heavy leather curtain which divided the family's sleeping quarters from those of the rest of the household, Phelim's young wife had now lain in labour for two days and nearly two nights.

" Surely," said Phelim, striding beside Nalda's shuffling feet, " it cannot last much longer ? "

Old Nalda shook her head, but with terror-sharpened perception, Phelim realised that even she, the wise woman, was desperately afraid.

" How long can her strength hold out ? "

Nalda's only reply was an angry, incoherent sound.

" Can you—even you—do nothing ? " cried Phelim hoarsely.

" Everything possible is being done. Would I—I of all people —neglect her ? " The scorn in Nalda's voice made it almost a snarl.

" Can I not see her ? Even for a moment ? "

" Indeed, and you cannot."

Fiercely prohibitive, the old woman disappeared between the folds of the heavy curtain, leaving Phelim to pace up and down in the firelight, biting his nails to the quick, listening to the monotonous battering of the incessant rain, the vehement snores of his sleeping followers which seemed almost offensive in their indifference. To Phelim, married less than a year, this was a crisis that shook the foundations of the world.

As he paused by the heavy curtain Phelim could hear the fluttering whispers of frightened women, dominated by old Nalda's harsh voice, now softened to such a croon of reassurance as to be almost unrecognisable. But never a sound from Eithne. Not a whimper, not even a sigh. Was she still alive ? With his hands raised to force his way between the curtains, Phelim stood shaking in the shadows, then, letting his hands fall helplessly to his sides, he stumbled away to subside on to the stool by the central hearth from which old Nalda had risen. There he crouched, his unsteady breath coming in sighing gusts, his restless fists pounding his forehead in gestures of almost crazed despair. Could that silence mean anything but utter exhaustion ? Was Eithne going to die ? If she did, he would kill himself, too. The suspense was unbearable. Never in his whole life had he known anything like it. He had been dreading this for months, almost ever since it had become evident that she was going to bear a child. Eithne had laughed at him. She had not been in the least afraid. She had said—what was it—that God would bring her safely through the dangers of childbirth. Phelim was not to worry. He need only keep calm and pray.

Pray ? Phelim groaned. What was prayer ? He knew nothing about it. He had accepted Christianity because conversion to the new religion was expedient in a courtier once the king and the rest of his household had been baptised. With Eithne it had been different. She had received the new creed as gladly as a warrior receives a challenge, a musician hears a new melody. All that was finest in her seemed to have responded instinctively to the words of the Christian priests with their eager faces and their strangely tonsured heads. She had greeted the Christian gospel like news from the native country of her soul. Phelim might scoff, he might envy, but he could not share. Now, through the haze of terror which obscured his usual wariness, Phelim began dimly to visualise the possibility of making a bargain with Eithne's unknown God, as his pagan ancestors might have considered bargaining with their own. Frenziedly, as he sat with his head in his hands, his fingers clutching at the

locks of his thick hair, he tried to think of something he could
offer, some terms which a deity who controlled life and death—
should such a being exist—might be willing to accept.

Then, at a touch on his shoulder he sprang, trembling, to his
feet. Old Nalda was beside him, shaking her head in answer to
his instant question.

" Is it over yet ? "

" No. But she's asking for you. Can you keep quiet now, if
I let you come within ? "

" Yes—yes . . ."

He crept after the old nurse between the curtains, into what
seemed a blaze of light from the tapers which the women held
around the bed. As he appeared they withdrew discreetly into
the background, but Phelim had not even noticed they were
there. His wild eyes saw Eithne and Eithne alone as he flung
himself on his knees, tears blinding him at the sight of her pale,
sweat-streaked face and the valour of her faint smile.

" What can I do ? " babbled Phelim. " I can't bear this.
I don't know how to pray. But I'll do anything . . . offer
anything I have to your God if he'll save you. I care nothing
about . . . the rest . . . He can have the child . . . I want
you . . . If it's a boy . . . I'll give him up . . . I'll give him
to the Church . . ."

Eithne's drawn face changed, seemed to gather strength from
her amazement and delight.

" Phelim . . . do you mean that ? "

" Yes . . . yes . . . yes . . ." He laid his cheek on her
hand, sobbing. " Anything . . . your God can have anything
in the world . . ."

" I believe . . . God will accept him," Eithne whispered.
" Yes, Phelim. Remember . . . my dream . . ." She bit her
lip, stifling a sudden, involuntary cry.

Nalda took Phelim by the shoulders as he stumbled to his
feet, bundling him away from the bed. " Go now," she
said.

An hour later Phelim's son was born. They called him Colum,
and at his baptism, Phelim, still shaken by the memory of Eithne's
ordeal, solemnly ratified his promise, and the old priest, Cruithann,
who was Eithne's soul-friend or confessor, accepted the child on
behalf of the Christian Church. He himself, it was decided, would
undertake the responsibility of fosterage as soon as the boy was
old enough to leave home.

During the years that followed Phelim came to look with
discomfort at his own behaviour on the night of Colum's birth.

and to dismiss the undertaking from his mind as much as possible. As life returned to normal the memory of his panic-stricken attempt to bargain with God shamed him. He did his best to belittle it, hoping that as time went by Eithne would come to agree with him that it had been an over-generous gesture, an excess of zeal which could surely be counteracted by a token payment of some sort.

But every now and then he was reminded of it, and such reminders disturbed him more and more. He had his first quarrel with Eithne about it one autumn evening when he had come home to find the younger children already bedded and old Nalda telling stories by the hearth with Colum, half asleep, in her arms. Phelim paid no attention to his son as he strode past, shoulders hunched, towards his private quarters on the far side of the curtain, and Colum, whose interest in Nalda's stories was keener, at five years old, than his interest in his father, let him go unperceived. He was smiling up at Nalda with eyes as grey as her own, though the hair that curled thickly over his restlessly rolling head was bright as a nimbus of red-gold, a thing to wonder at among that dark-haired folk.

"Go on," he commanded imperiously. "I want more."

"And more you shall have, bless your heart," said old Nalda, gathering him close. "Time was, my lamb, when the young sea-god, Manannan, him that was beautiful as a summer morning, was riding in his chariot over the salt waves of the sea. Now, the sea that was Manannan's kingdom was never like to drown him as it would drown you or me. A gentle plain it was, covered with bright flowers——"

"Think shame of yourself, Nalda," said a reproachful voice at her side. The old woman's guilty start made Colum's heavy lids flicker, but he was too sleepy to do more than glimpse his mother, Eithne, in her bright dress and contrasting cloak, who had paused beside them like a severe young angel, her usually serene face puckered by an unhappy frown. Colum let the lids slide over his eyes. That meant she didn't like Nalda's stories. It was a pity, for they were the best of all . . .

"Nalda, Nalda," Eithne was saying, "is it of the old gods that a baptised woman like yourself should be telling that child of mine?"

Though his eyes had closed again, Colum could tell old Nalda was smiling, that she was going to wheedle and not rage. His mother couldn't be really angry, then, or Nalda would have caught the anger from her as easily as he himself had once caught a rash from one of the other children of the dun. Nalda was not usually the one to take scoldings meekly, even from his gentle mother, whom she loved. Sometimes she flared up like a fire in the gorse, but now, perhaps because she was feeling sleepy by the pleasant glow of the turf fire, she accepted Eithne's rebuke as quietly as the wolf-hounds accepted his occasional poundings that meant nothing and had no weight behind them at all.

" Indeed, my lady," Nalda was saying, " I had forgotten. Do not the old tales come more easily to me still when my thoughts wander ? And aren't they natural for any child of Erin to wonder at ? Let me be telling him something different, then, about the hosting of the shee . . ."

" Certainly not," said Eithne hastily. " That would be no better at all. Who would think it is over a hundred years since the blessed St. Patrick came to preach in Erin ? Have these years all gone by in vain ? "

Nalda sighed and shook her head. The lines on her weather-beaten face seemed to deepen with the sadness that came over it. " Alas, no, my lady. Sometimes I think he has done his work so well that the fairy hills are empty and the lordly people of the shee all gone."

" And a good riddance, too," said Eithne warmly.

Old Nalda looked up at her with a crooked smile. She could tell from the weight on her arms that Colum was asleep, blessings be upon the lovely boy that he was, and whatever her lady might have to say against the tales of the old faith, was it not such a tale that had just brought the sweet sleep to him ? But Eithne had also been her nursling, over twenty years ago, and she was troubled, Nalda knew, by the very thought of such tales. There she was, bless her heart, with her head all full of the new stories of angels. Why should she be fretting her by admitting that she herself always felt more comfortable with the old tales than the new ? Perhaps it mattered less than Eithne thought, in the end of it all, what names people gave to the kind of people of the unseen world. They'd know at least, wise as they were, that an old, ancient woman like herself couldn't change her ways as quickly as the young girls changed the ribbons in their hair. They'd understand, surely enough. But Eithne, she knew, did not. To comfort her Nalda said : " well, then, I'll sing him the lullaby of the blessed Bride that you taught me yourself if it'll make you any happier, my dear lady."

Eithne's smile drove all severity from her candid face. She said : " yes, Nalda. Please do," as eagerly as a child.

" Not that it's needed," Nalda added under her breath, with a flicker of rebellious triumph, as Eithne turned away. " Is he not sleeping like an angel in my arms already, and without a whisper out of the blessed Bride ? "

But Eithne considered that she was just far enough away to pretend that she had not heard. She hated scolding at any time, and Nalda, who never quite forgot that she had been her own nurse, was such a very difficult person to scold at all. She quickened her pace as she left the central hearth at which Nalda was sitting with Colum and went down the hall towards the leather curtain that hung across the far end. Phelim, her husband, was for once not in attendance on the king that evening. She wondered if she ought to have a word with him about the way Nalda had been going on. It would probably not do much good, of course. If there was one thing Phelim disliked more than another, it was being asked to intervene in a matter of domestic discipline. She sighed. Of course it was pleasant not to be bawled at like some of the other women who were married to famous warriors. But just sometimes she wished Phelim would use his authority a little more . . .

Beside the central hearth the old woman continued to rock and croon, her body moving rhythmically, her eyes half-closed, her thoughts straying to and fro among the events of her long life as the shadows strayed among the weapons that hung by the sleeping-places of the men of the household. Twenty-four men, her master Phelim mustered, twenty-four men whose sleeping-places were ranged round the hall in which Phelim's household ate and slept and drank and sang. Eithne's serving-maids slept, three to a wide couch, on the far side of the hall with the children, under old Nalda's own watchful eyes. Food was cooked at the central hearth and eaten at the long trestle table which took up most of the space at meal times. But afterwards it was taken down to clear the floor for the dancing that shortened the winter nights ; the juggling, cock-fighting or play-acting which brought crowds of his followers to Phelim's hall, or the arrival of some poet with his harp and retinue, who gave himself, people often thought, great airs as he accepted Phelim's hospitality as no more than his due and the household's gaping admiration as a matter of course.

Phelim himself, great-grandson of Niall of the Nine Hostages, that warrior and High King of Erin, was, in the prime of his life, only a small, worried man. In him the greatness of his ancestry seemed to sleep. He was not a king, high or low, merely the local king's cousin, holding the hereditary office of keeper of the royal chessmen. This appointment suited his precise nature admirably, and carried with it the comfortable tenure of hall and lands in return for attendance at court as required. Such an obligation was pleasant enough, for he was in good company, privileged to dine at the king's table, attending him as the Brehon Law ordained, in common with a learned judge, a physician, a bishop, a poet, an historian and a musician, each of ollave rank, the equivalent of a doctorate in their respective spheres. Behind these great men, dining in state, stood the soldiers of the king's house-company, headed by his personal champion, an immense man of valour who lounged, fully armed, about the court, prepared at a moment's notice to encounter in single-combat any stranger who might be rash enough to strike the bronze shield which hung at the entrance to the royal dun.

But Phelim himself was no warrior : he yawned behind his hand while tales of pitched battle and single combat circled the board as interminably as the goblets of spiced wine which soured his queasy stomach. Like the other nobles of the province, he was obliged to keep his own house-company, equipped and ready to go with the king on such warlike expeditions into neighbouring territory as might be considered necessary for the maintenance of his reputation. Phelim grumbled a good deal about this : he complained that his household did nothing but wrangle and gorge themselves, but on the whole they gave him less trouble than they might have done. This was perhaps due to the fact that when he became head of the household as well as keeper of the royal chessmen on his father's death, he had at once taken the precaution of engaging his own personal champion in case his precise ways and lack of physical presence failed to evoke from his followers the proper degree of respect. Tombul, Phelim's champion, was an unmarried man of his own age and rank, his foster-brother and friend, who had chosen the career of a professional champion for the sake of the freedom from domestic responsibility and the promise of excitement which it offered him. Phelim knew he could rely on Tombul's loyalty and laziness to prevent him from seeking a better position, and Tombul's personal prestige was amply sufficient to ensure good discipline among the men of his household.

So he left the organisation of his house-company gladly in Tombul's competent hands, spending most of the free time which his duties at court left him, slumped on his sleeping-couch behind the leather curtain, working out new chess problems with which to divert the king, or carving the beautiful and elaborate sets of chessmen from blocks of oak or the tusks of wild boar which the huntsmen had brought home. All manual labour was considered beneath the dignity of a noble, but Phelim's restless spirit craved the solace offered by his skilful hands. This his wife, who was baffled by so many things about him, understood. She would bring her embroidery beside him as he carved and polished his exquisite little figures by the light of a couple of rushlights that flared on the rough table in the midst of a litter of chips and tools.

He was busy at his carving that evening when Eithne came round the curtain, and did not hear her till she spoke at his elbow so unexpectedly that he drove the point of a carefully whetted bronze knife deep into his thumb. With an angry exclamation he swung round.

"What in the world makes you creep about tlike that, startling people? Look what you've made me do!" Indignantly he held out his injured thumb, on the pad of which a bead of blood slowly formed, toppled, ran across the nail and dripped on to the floor.

"I'm sorry, Phelim," said Eithne penitently. "I was anxious about Colum. And I didn't realise you hadn't seen me come in. Let me bind it up for you."

Phelim shook his head in the exasperated, shamefaced way of a man aware that he had been making too much of a small injury. "How can I carve with a bundle of cloth round my thumb?" he mumbled, putting it in his mouth and sucking it glumly. "What's the matter with the boy?"

"Nothing," Eithne said. "He's asleep."

Phelim took his thumb out of his mouth. "Well, then, what's troubling you?"

"It's Nalda," Eithne said unhappily. "I'm afraid she's a better nurse than a Christian, Phelim." She sat down on a stool and drew her embroidery frame towards her.

Phelim snapped his fingers crossly. "Surely for us," he said, "that's just as well. Her soul can be no concern of ours."

"No, but I'm thinking of Colum," Eithne said. "I caught Nalda telling him tales of the old gods. I don't like it. I've forbidden it before, but I can't make her listen. She may have been baptised, Phelim, but she's a pagan still."

"Does it matter?" asked Phelim absently, looking down at his thumb. It was smarting, and the tiny wound was a nuisance. Blood oozed from it so that he could not carve. He turned the half-finished figure about in his uninjured hand, noting impatiently all that remained to be done.

"Does it matter?" Eithne echoed him in consternation. "How can you ask such a thing? Can we let such a woman remain in charge of a boy whose life has been dedicated to the Church?"

"Oh—that." Phelim's voice showed his rising exasperation.

" We'd better forget that, my dear, don't you think ? I believe he's got the makings of a better warrior than a churchman after all."

" Phelim ! " Utter distress rang through Eithne's sharp cry. " Surely you must be joking ? "

" Why ? "

" Because you promised—you swore it on your knees——"

Phelim tried to shrug away the memory of that winter night, over five years ago now. He recalled, but could no longer feel the anguish of mind in which he had knelt beside Eithne's bed. In that hour his wife had meant everything to him, and the little crumpled bundle soon to lie in old Nalda's arms, nothing at all. Now, after six years of marriage, the ordeal of childbirth had lost much of its significance. His wife had borne him other children, but none like their first-born. She had, perhaps, come to mean less to him nowadays. His eldest son had certainly come to mean more. " I didn't know what I was saying," he mumbled. " You can't hold me to that sort of promise now."

" But, Phelim——" Eithne's embroidery had fallen from her hands, her eyes were wide with unbelieving dismay, " it wasn't like that at all. You swore a solemn oath afterwards. You swore, I tell you——"

" I would have sworn anything before any god you liked to name," said Phelim uncomfortably, " just to keep you safe. I— well, I suppose I lost my wits a little that night. Now the boy is turning out so well it seems a pity to condemn him to the religious life, doesn't it ? He might even have the makings of a champion, I believe."

For a moment Eithne looked at him in silence. When she spoke again there was scorn as well as dismay in her voice. " Never," she said coldly, " would I have thought that a member of your family would so ignobly break his pledged word."

" It cannot be held against me," said Phelim stormily. " I swore under duress. I feared that you would die."

" I would rather have died a dozen times," cried Eithne, " than take my life on the terms you offered and afterwards hear you refuse to honour your bond."

" I tell you," snarled Phelim, " I was not in my right mind."

" I cannot believe," she retorted, " that you are in your right mind now."

" Is it not right for a father to seek his son's welfare ? "

" Can his welfare be bought by a broken oath ? "

They were both standing now, facing each other across the rough table strewn with shavings and carving-tools. Caution made them keep their voices low for fear of being overheard by the members of their household on the far side of the curtain, but Phelim's voice shook with anger, and Eithne's whisper was shrill with fear.

"You are not thinking of Colum at all," she went on. "You are only thinking of yourself. You want him to be a champion because—because——"

"Well?"

She hesitated, even at such a moment, to hurt him as sorely as the words she had bitten back must have done. But Phelim, sneering, finished the sentence himself.

"Because I am so poor a creature that I must have my first-born to avenge me, eh? Was that what you dared not say?"

Eithne covered her face with her hands.

"Well, suppose it were true," Phelim said. "Could you not sacrifice one of the other brats to your jealous God?"

"Phelim, for pity's sake, do not say such things," cried Eithne frantically. "How can you suppose another child would do? It was Colum we offered, Colum, our first-born. We—you must remember—we took him to the priest together as soon as I could climb to Cruithann's little oratory on the hill. And . . . and when he baptised the babe he accepted him in the name of Almighty God. He promised to be his foster-father as soon as he was of an age to leave his own home. Phelim—please listen—he will know what a solemn oath you propose to break. How can you think any blessing will come to us or to the child, if you break the word given to God? You would be too proud to break an oath even—even to a mere man." She broke off, breathless, struggling to keep back her tears.

Phelim looked at her under his brows. The appeal to his superstitious nature had had more effect than he liked to admit. He did not care to think of living under the curse of an apostate. A broken oath among men was a terrible thing. Who knew how it might seem to a jealous God? At the back of his conscious-ness lingered the dark inheritance of centuries of pagan worship, the propitiation of powerful deities by bloody sacrifice, the long shadows that the wrath of the gods might throw across a man's whole life.

"If you must bring a curse down on your own head that is your own affair," said Eithne. "Surely you will not also doom your son?"

Phelim drummed on the board with restless fingertips. Only too clearly he remembered the ceremony at the oratory. There was no possibility of evading that undertaking, however much he might regret the folly that had made him do anything of the sort. It was now too late to withdraw from the promise he had given. Unless—indeed—he clutched at the only possibility of escape— unless the boy himself should refuse to ratify the bargain which had been made without his knowledge or consent.

" I will not break my word," he said sullenly. " You need not be afraid of that. But I suppose even you will not seek to force religion on the child against his wish ? "

Serene again, Eithne smiled.

" It will not be against his wish," she said confidently.

" As to that, we shall see," Phelim said. He tossed the unfinished chessman down on the board among the tools, and turned away, swinging back the curtain with a petulant movement which made the rings chime on the metal rod. It was dusky about the central hearth, for the autumn twilight was not far off and the fire had not yet been made up for the evening's cooking by the servants responsible for wood and turf. The hall was quiet again. Colum slept on Nalda's knee and the two younger children were snug in their alcove. Phelim stood by the curtain unobserved, watching them, his close-lipped, habitually watchful face relaxed in the protective twilight as he looked thoughtfully at his son. Every now and then a falling turf would set up a jet of flame from the heart of the fire, and the light played over the boy's bright hair till Phelim could almost have fancied, with a sudden stab of superstitious awe, that an unearthly radiance shone about it. Wryly he mocked himself, thrusting away the memory of Eithne's dream of an angelic visitation on the eve of Colum's birth, that dream which had convinced her forever that her eldest son was a child of fate.

Snapping his fingers, Phelim moved off down the hall. He had hoped all this talk of fostering by the Church had died down so that he could have his way with the boy, training him to be a warrior whose name might match that of the legendary Niall himself. Smiling crookedly, Phelim looked down at his hands, those hands that were too clever with wood, horn and ivory for a noble, too small and womanish for a man's weapons. Yes, if he had never made that impulsive promise on the night of Colum's birth his eldest son might have silenced the covert sneers of men who thought Phelim unworthy of his inheritance. For Colum had the makings of a warrior already : he was taller and sturdier than any other child of his age in the dun. He had inherited, Phelim knew, the fierce temper and proud will of many heroes. Surely these were not the qualities of which meek saints were made ? Colum did not cry when he was hurt ; his smile made every woman love him. Must he be asked to foreswear women and weapons for ever?

Outside the hall Phelim could hear the voices of the men now back from the day's hunting. Several carcases, already skinned and disembowelled, hung from the lowest branches of an oak tree, while the dogs snarled over the entrails among the projecting roots that had been worn smooth by the hands and feet of generations of clambering children. Among the trees stood the beehive huts of the families which made up the personal following who shared his enclosure. These huts were flimsy structures of thatch and daub, grouped about his own squared and timbered dwelling like satellite moons, in their turn protected by the turf-built wall with its surrounding ditch. At Gartan the whole fertile area between the bogs in the foothills and the three flag-fringed loughs across which the coracles of the home-coming fishermen still bobbed was dotted with such duns, large or small, according to the greatness of the protecting lord. Largest of all, on a knoll which dominated the surrounding countryside, was the timbered palace of Phelim's cousin, the king, and all about the fortified homesteads lay a patchwork of little, unfenced fields, communally and rather casually farmed by men whose gifts were for hunting rather than husbandry, fields now shorn of their crops and left for the cattle to clear.

The clans of Erin had lived in such duns as far back as the records of the historians went. Each clan chose the greatest man of its ruling family to be its king, and the king of the strongest clan ruled the whole province. From the rulers of the five ancient provinces was elected the Ard-Ri, the High King of Erin. So it was ordained in the ancient Brehon Laws. At the time of the High King's election the peoples of the five provinces followed their rulers in procession up the five avenues that led to the Hill of Tara from every point on the wide plain of Meath. Then from among their own number the lesser Kings of Erin, met together in council in the Hall of Synods at Tara, chose the Ard-Ri, the god-like High King of Erin, whose authority would be maintained by his warriors, sung by his poets and commemorated by his historians throughout the length and breadth of the land that he ruled from royal Tara, which became his personal residence from that moment when the inauguration rites made him in the eyes of the people less a king than a god.

Phelim had once been to Tara, and though in Christian times the place had already lost something of the ancient splendour that went with the High King's godhead, to Phelim's fancy much of that splendour lingered, making so sharp an impression on the thwarted, secret nature of a puny man fathered by giants, that he found it difficult to separate what he had seen from what he had heard in the old tales.

At Tara, Phelim knew, the strong pulse of ancient Erin had beaten for centuries. Its great timbered banqueting hall was hung with the painted shields, hide-covered, or wooden, or beaten bronze, once carried by the country's heroes. At its long tables, at the time of the national assemblies, kings by the dozen, noblemen by the hundred and champions by the score had nightly dined. In his avid imagination Phelim could still hear the chanting of the harpers, see the smoky torch-light flicker across the great assembly, gleaming on the diadems of the kings, lighting up the bronze or golden collars of the heroes, the many colours of the mantles that were stabbed into place on the wearer's shoulders with great circular brooches of gold, silver or bronze which in the rivalry of fashion had become so large that the length of their pins had to be limited by law. The diners' long hair lay on their shoulders, their tunics were of silk or satin, stiff with fringes, weighed down with embroidery, dyed crimson and saffron and blue, scarlet, purple, green, rose, russet, or mulberry. Seven colours were permitted in the garments of kings, six in those of nobles, fewer for baser men, drab only for mere serfs.

But among the gorgeous, roaring warriors sat quieter, more sinister figures. The dark-robed physicians drank little, seemed to interest themselves less in the men about them than in the death-warrant each carried in his flesh : it was their business to mark the dulling eye, the threatening flush, the yellowed skin, to cherish inordinately the pouch of remedies each carried at the belt of his furred robe. Among them, in the pre-Christian days, had sat the magicians, the white-robed, garlanded Druids, speaking little, eating less, savouring the superstitious fear that followed them everywhere, like the faint, persistent smell of blood. But every one, high or low, had laid his arms away, for no man might wound another at Tara under pain of instant death.

By night the songs of the feasting nobility had streamed out like the fires that beaconed the summit of the hill, and by day the responsive lilt of a refrain, the echo of laughter, the hand-clapped rhythm of a country dance or the applause of a juggler's audience had risen towards the kings and judges debating the administration of the complex Brehon laws in the Hall of Synods. The sacrificial stone on the summit had cooled under the ash of the dawn-fire as they talked, though the unearthly cries that had gone up at daybreak might linger in the ears of a few squeamish folk long after the victim's blood had dried on the sun-warmed stone.

The pulse of ancient Erin might still beat on at Tara, but things were bound to change still further, even there. Phelim could smell change, as a weather-wise husbandman will smell the rain that threatens his precious crops. So Phelim was aware of the change that threatened the garnered treasure of the past that was so dear to him, the past which was bound up with the heroic weapons that were beyond his strength to wield, weapons which might have gained a new lustre as they were whetted by the strong hands of his son. Now—he shivered in the dusk—who could tell? All that had belonged to the past was threatened by something incalculable, insidious, an invasion not of strong men who might be withstood with equal strength, but an infiltration of new ideas which was as subtle as the dew that rusted a man's sword while he slept.

Phelim wandered uneasily about the dusky enclosure, while before him the activity of the returned huntsmen died down, or was localised into the movements of figures outlined darkly against glowing fires. At this time Phelim was usually required to attend upon the king, as he prepared to dine, carrying the royal chessmen in their gaily decorated bag and the board in its ornate leather case. But to-night the king was to be bled by the physicians and would not keep his usual state. So Phelim was free, and in his unreckoned freedom, restless. His goings and comings were habitually so much ordered for him that without the familiar routine he felt as ungirt as a warrior without his sword.

He wandered about the dun, therefore, only remotely aware of the wolf-dogs that rushed out of dim huts to snarl at him, the strong, ravening smell of cooking meat, the sound of a knife being sharpened on a stone, the croon of a mother to her ailing child. These things were part of his experience, known and set aside as he sought now to estimate the new forces that seemed to overhang them, threatening his life with the changing rhythm of progress, that inexorable flail.

At the gateway of the dun, he paused. The mountains seemed to have folded themselves again about the area that man had wrested from their solitudes, and the loughs lay milkily at their feet, paler than the sky. Far up on the opposite slope a solitary light glimmered. Phelim looked at it malevolently. It came, he knew, from the little oratory of the priest Cruithann, who was no doubt saying the evening office with his pupils. Phelim bit his lip. The light angered him strangely. He wanted to rush upon it and trample the candles underfoot till the darkness of the primæval hillside was unbroken once more. He raged against it silently as he stood there. Yet it drew him, even against his will. Slowly, a step at a time, sometimes pausing, occasionally turning back, then changing his mind again, he crossed the causeway between the loughs, and so at last, reluctantly, began to climb the opposite hill.

The little oratory was an oblong building of unmortared stone, roofed with the same slabs that formed the walls, the only openings a small slit above the altar-stone, facing the east, and the opposite doorway, consisting merely of two stone side-posts leaning slightly inwards as they rose towards the stone lintel, which was so low that any grown man must stoop to enter, though children could run in and out at will.

Three children were in the oratory as Phelim climbed the last slope and bent his back to peer through the doorway. They were boys of ten or twelve, wearing the drab tunics of serfs, and kneeling before the altar, hands folded, palm to palm, so that their finger-tips touched their foreheads. Their bare feet were extended, side by side, in the shadows, though every now and then a restless child moved one foot to rest on the other, as if the chill of the stone floor irked his flesh.

Beside them knelt the priest, a gaunt old man whose beard and tonsured head were white against the drab of the serf's tunic he too wore in token of the poverty he had chosen. Two candles stood on the altar-stone, guttering in the draught so that the tallow ran down their sides and solidified into freakish shapes on the rough stands. One of the boys kept opening his eyes to watch the shapes as they grew, and the priest, laying a hand on the child's shoulder, checked him, though with an unexpectedly understanding smile.

They were saying the evening office together, first in the Latin which was still unfamiliar to the three children, then in the Gaelic, so that they might come to know what they were saying in the strange tongue. Phelim stooped outside the doorway, listening intently, his scalp tingling with unexplained apprehension. Inside the oratory it was very still. The children seemed to be holding their breath as they listened to the words which were slowly becoming familiar, and which, if they took them literally, must change the whole conduct of their lives.

" *Pater noster, qui es in coelis* . . ." intoned Cruithann in his old, tired voice. The breathless, uncertain trebles of the little boys repeated the words, then translated them into the homely Gaelic of their babyhood :

" Our Father, which art in Heaven . . ."

" *Sanctificetur nomen tuum* . . ."
" Hallowed be Thy Name . . ."
" *Adveniat regnum tuum* . . ."
" Thy kingdon come . . ."
" *Fiat voluntas tua* . . ."
" Thy will be done . . ."
" *Sicut in coelo, etiam in terra* . . ."
" On earth, as it is in Heaven . . ."

Phelim turned away, to blunder down the dim hillside, aware of the light behind him as of a wound between his shoulder-blades. It was not for some time that he paused to get his breath and look up again, over his shoulder, towards the oratory in which the candles still burned, then downwards, as if for reassurance, towards the friendlier lights of the scattered duns. Then he hurried on again, going hastily, so that he sometimes stumbled over a tuft of heather or a projecting root. Part of his mind, as always, seemed to remain aloof from the rest and mock at the small man who was floundering away from one old priest and three unarmed boys who were repeating their evening prayers in a huddle of stones on a dark hillside. But Phelim's intuitions were apt to penetrate further towards the heart of things than his intellect ever did. He was not fully aware of the significance of what he had seen. But he was horribly afraid.

CHAPTER II

EITHNE smiled down at her three children who were rolling contentedly in the warm sand outside the homestead, naked in the pleasant warmth of an unusually mild autumn day. Nalda was busy near them, peeling rushes, which she would afterwards dip in melted fat, patiently and repeatedly till they were thick enough to burn with the pale, clear light which was not so hard on Phelim's eyes as the blaze and splutter of a wall-torch, or the uncertain illumination of the fire that was piled high on winter nights.

It was amusing for Eithne to wonder, as she waited for Maeve, her sister, who was still indoors, braiding green ribbons into her long black hair, whether the children were going to be like Phelim or whether they showed signs of being more like the men of her own family, the royal line of Laigen. Colum, she was bound to admit, was like none of the relations she knew. Nor was he like Phelim either. He was like nobody but himself, she thought, as she watched the intense concentration of his play with the few bones he was trying to build into some sort of structure in the shifting sand which constantly frustrated him by crumbling away. Colum's fair face had begun to flush, his lower lip jutted ominously as he struggled against the limitations of his material. Eithne expected him suddenly to lose all patience and throw everything from him as he had done once before when things were too difficult. So she waited, ready to check his fury if it should involve the two solemn-eyed, younger children in a shower of sand and bones as it had done last time he lost his temper. But now Colum checked his fury without her intervention. The childishly contorted face, the frowning brows, the pouting mouth, the furious concentration, suddenly relaxed, and an astonishing smile of delighted amusement changed the childish wrath and frustration into tolerant understanding. It was a strange expression to see on the face of a child of five, and as he swept away the insecure structure over which he had been labouring with a casual hand and began patiently to build again on firmer turf Eithne turned to Maeve, now emerging from the doorway, with a face of awe.

" It was—it was as if an angel had spoken to him."

Maeve laughed, not altogether kindly. " What nonsense you talk about that child ! He is always getting into tempers, just

34

like other children. I can see nothing miraculous about that."

"It is easier to get into a temper than to get out of it, even if you are full-grown," said Eithne. "And for a child to change so, without the help of any mortal creature, is surely strange."

"Children's moods," said Maeve, "change like the lights on the hills."

"You don't know Colum," said his mother.

"I know how much nonsense is talked of him. Already," said Maeve sharply. "What it will be like by the time he has grown to be a warrior, I cannot imagine. None of us will have any peace. We shall always be listening to tales of your wonderful son."

"You know as well as I do that Colum is not to be a warrior," said Eithne. "He was dedicated to the church on the day of his birth."

Maeve laughed. "A likely churchman, that young fury," she said. Her bold black eyes met the unfaltering gaze of the child who crouched at her feet, smiling as the sand spilled pleasantly through his fingers. Half playfully she upset his pile of bones with her bare foot, laughing again as his face contorted with the wrath that was less disturbing than the steady inquiry of his grey, unchildlike eyes.

Steadying himself, the child gathered the scattered fragments together, and carefully built them up as before. Then, just as the structure was completed, Maeve's malicious toe sent them flying again. This time Colum could not check the anger that surged through him. He flung himself, crimson-faced, on Maeve, his clenched fists pounding at her knees till Eithne had to grip him by the shoulders and drag him away.

Maeve stood her ground, her laughter mocking him. "Well, well, what a temper! He is readier to strike me than to shrive me, you'll admit?"

But Eithne, gentle as she was, disliked to see her child teased. "It is not just. You upset his playthings and then if he is rude, you will expect me to make him ask your pardon. Come away. If we are to climb the hill to the oratory and be back by dinner-time, we must start at once."

Maeve allowed herself to be led away, laughing over her shoulder at the children, who had abandoned all attempt at building and were scattering bones and sand in all directions, as if seized by a mad impulse of destruction which made Nalda clap her hands and scold as the sand flew overhead.

"I do not know what it is that makes you tease them so, Maeve," said Eithne in a worried voice. "It's not as if you weren't fond of them. Nobody can be kinder than I have seen you be when Colum has cut himself or one of the others got a thorn in his foot. Why should you want to torment them at other times ? "

Maeve shook her head, flinging back the blue-black braid which fell below her waist with the gesture of an untamed young pony, impatient of the gentlest attempt to conquer or direct her rebellious will. She was several years younger than her sister, and had only made her home with her for the last few months, since their parents' death. Maeve had been married in her teens, and widowed as the result of a hunting accident before she was twenty. An air of tumult and tragedy hung about her, which Phelim said was merely due to her need of another man. The sooner she was married again the better it would be for everybody. She twanged to and fro like a mosquito, and he wished Eithne would do something about it before the winter weather brought the household into closer contact with each other. He did not wish to be answerable for the consequences of wringing his sister-in-law's pretty neck.

But then Phelim was one of the men who were not attracted by Maeve, Eithne reminded herself, as she tried to think what it would be best to say to her sister, now swinging along in front of her in her graceful way, her green gown looped up at her girdle to keep it clear of the dust. Maeve divided people into two classes. There were those who were hypnotised by her personality and those who were not, and she spent most of her time trying very skilfully to convert those in the second category into the first. Or so Phelim said, but Eithne, ruefully aware of her younger sister's manœuvres were too complex for her unpractised brain to follow, continued to think of her as a petulant child rather than a scheming woman, and to hope devoutly that Phelim might be mistaken in at least some of the things he said.

Now, however, she felt she ought to take Maeve to task as they walked across the foot of the lough and began to climb the track which led past the oratory to villages in the next valley. The track was narrow and twisting as it began to slant uphill, since it was used only by foot passengers and pack animals, and Eithne, who was inclined to plumpness after bearing her husband three children in five years of marriage, had to trot a few steps every now and then to catch up with Maeve's long stride. And Maeve, when she heard Eithne's breathless voice, walked more quickly instead of giving her sister a chance of drawing close. She disliked being questioned about her motives, partly because she did not understand them herself. So she

hurried on, aware that Eithne was running after her, gritting her
teeth against the anticipated restraint of her sister's hand on her
arm.

"But why—why do you tease the children, Maeve?" said
Eithne unhappily. "What have they done? If they have
behaved badly to you I will see that they are kept out of your
way. But—tell me, what have they done wrong?"

"Nothing." Maeve threw the word over her shoulder and
stalked on.

"Then why not leave them alone?"

"How should I know?"

"But—but you must know why you do things——"

"Must I? Do you?"

"I—I think so," said Eithne, trying to be exact. "But then
I don't do such odd things as you do. I haven't the time."

"Of course not. You are the busy wife of an important
man. You are the happy mother of a healthy family. You are
a fine lady. I am only a poor relation, a woman without a man
to fight or fend for her, an outcast, a stranger . . ." Maeve's
voice was harsh with self-pity.

"How—how can—you say such a thing?" panted Eithne,
trotting anxiously behind her sister, stray ends of her dark hair
escaping from the net which bound it, her hands grabbing at
the folds of her crimson gown which kept slipping from her
girdle and threatening to trip her up. "You know you are no
exile while we can give you a home. And as for being without a
man to fend for you, I can think of several who would ask nothing
better if you would give them leave."

"I do not care for them," said Maeve curtly.

"Perhaps," said Eithne, "you do not care for things when
they are within your reach. Why must it—be—always the
forbidden things that tempt you, Maeve?"

Maeve turned round, towering over her breathless sister as
she waited for her to catch up. "And what do you mean by
that, I wonder?" she asked slowly. "I don't like the sound of it
at all."

"Why not?" said Eithne uncomfortably.

"It sounds as if you had been listening to gossip, my dear
sister."

"Gossip? Of course, there's gossip," said Eithne unhappily.
"Isn't there always gossip about a beautiful woman who won't
look at an unmarried man? I don't have to listen to it, but when
it's as loud as this I can't help hearing it, you know."

Maeve bit her lip. "What are they saying?" she asked,

looking far over her sister's head at the remote, dreamily vague hills. " Now you've begun on this, I might as well know."

" Well . . ." Eithne began. She was aware that things were not going according to plan. She had intended to give Maeve a kind little scolding, and now she was getting the scolding herself and Maeve did not look at all kind. That was always the way things happened to Eithne. She started off all right, but because Maeve was skilful and Eithne unsure of herself the positions were apt to be reversed before Eithne knew what was happening, so that she was now on the point of apologising for being an interfering fool. This time, however, she bit back the apology.

" It's no use being angry with me, Maeve. You should behave yourself if you don't want people to talk."

" People always talk," said Maeve. " But since they seem to be talking about me, I want to know what they're saying."

" I don't like repeating gossip," said Eithne uncomfortably.

" Then you shouldn't listen to it," Maeve said.

" I wasn't listening to it. I just heard it," protested Eithne. Maeve laughed. " What's the difference ? "

" There's a lot of difference. I can't keep my fingers in my ears all day. D'you think I like knowing that my sister's talked about ? Oh, they drop their voices when they see me coming, but they don't always see. At the salting, the baking, the spinning, the washing of clothes, the dyeing of wool . . ."

" You still haven't told me," said Maeve coldly, " what they're saying, all this time."

" How can you pretend," said Eithne, " that you do not know ? "

" The victim of the dun's gossip is always the last to hear it."

" Can any one be as unwise as you have been," said Eithne, goaded into exasperation, " and try to pretend that she doesn't know that the whole dun must be talking of her ? Have you not been seen with Nordal of the Wry Neck from the King's dun so often that the very children must have noticed ? Have you no sense of decency, at least ? The man's wife is about to bear him a child."

" The child is not his," said Maeve.

" I suppose he told you so."

" Who should know better, except the sly-faced man who lay with her when Nordel was helpless from his wounds after the bull charged him ? "

" I cannot see," said Eithne in a worried voice, " what in all the world would make you seek the company of an old scarred

warrior like Nordal when there are so many fine young men who
would give hand or eye for your favour. He is——"

"He is—kind," said Maeve suddenly. Then, as if she had
revealed too much, she changed the subject abruptly. "If we
stand here much longer we shall never get our business done at
all. You who are so religious will have the sin of idle conversation
to confess besides all the others which must lie so heavy on your
soul. Silly, aren't you," she teased, "to go hurrying off with your
little faggot of misdoings and get your soul-friend to unbind them
from your back. As if they would keep hell-fire alight for the
space of a heart-beat. Now if it were me, it would be another
matter. The fires would crackle merrily over the bundle I could
offer them."

Eithne crossed herself hastily. "Be quiet, Maeve. These
are not things to speak of in jest. And, at least, though you will
not go to confession, heaven will count it to your credit that you
were willing to bear me company on the way."

Maeve looked at her with an odd smile. "Yes, indeed," she
said. "I hope so. But I should not be too sure."

They reached the oratory at last, and found the old priest on
hands and knees, scrubbing the stone floor with ashes and a brush
of heather stems, while the pupils were grinding corn outside the
wattle and daub hut behind the oratory in which they lived.
Maeve strolled over to watch them, and Eithne's last glimpse of
her, as the old priest rose and beckoned, was of her stooping over
the quern, asking some question of the boy who was pouring the
grain into the hole in the upper stone. Then Eithne followed
the priest into the oratory, while Maeve, with a nod and an
absent-minded smile at the lads who gaped at her in admiration,
drifted away from them round the corner of the track, and
disappeared among the boulders which were strewn all over the
summit of the hill.

It was quiet in the little oratory. The thick walls and stone
roof, so near their heads, shut out the sights and sounds of the
everyday world, and the unstirring presence of the priest at whose
feet she knelt was for Eithne a visible symbol of the world invisible,
a living portent of the life to come. As she began to speak with
all the simplicity of a character unfettered by pride, the barrier
which her small sins had built between her and heaven seemed
to crumble, to dwindle away, as a dam obstructing the natural
course of a stream may be broken, little by little, till life can flow
again. Her irritability with Phelim, her anxiety over the children,
her lack of charity for Maeve, her censoriousness with the gossip-
ing women of the dun, her preoccupation with the pleasant things

of the flesh, her careless neglect of the ghostly world beyond them, all these things she spoke of, drawing them out of her memory as driftwood may be drawn from the dam that checks the stream. And as the old priest began to speak in his thin, dry voice she was aware, not only of his voice and the substance of what he said, but of much more for which she could find no words, the significance of which she made no attempt to analyse, accepting it as thankfully, as humbly and unquestioningly as she accepted the light of the sun and the warmth of the fire, the comfort of food and the cantankerous loyalty of her man, knowing intuitively that the grace which surrounded her, though it might transcend, was also akin to the earthly things she loved, so that not even the least of them, no stray cat or injured bird that the children might bring to her, no, not even the furry caterpillars from the bog or the mice from the corn-bin that she shuddered at, was to be despised or forgotten, that all living things received their life as a holy gift from heaven, that all the vagrant creatures of earth, wretched and warring and angry and astray as they might be, were yet held in the compassion of God and companioned by the charity of the saints. Underneath all burdened, heart-broken, bewildered living things she felt, if only for an instant, the strength of everlasting arms.

"May God Almighty have mercy upon thee . . ." murmnred the priest.

Eithne opened her eyes on the rough, unmortared walls of the tiny oratory, blinked, and rose from her knees. The old priest went with her to the doorway. He seemed bereft now of the unearthly quality with which he had been invested a few moments ago, so that he was only an old man again, his hands distorted with rheumatism, and his eyes dim so that he blinked like an owl in the sunlight. But it was Maeve, back by the quern now, watching the boys as they carefully collected the coarse flour that spilled from between the stones, who noticed these things about him. Eithne saw only the new vividness of the unclouded sky, and the proud grin on the face of the little boy who was carrying the sack of corn that Maeve had said must be too heavy for him to lift.

"Well, child, art thou not coming to me to-day?"

"No, Father," said Maeve abruptly.

"Very well." He showed no resentment. "Thou wilt come when the grace of God brings thee, no doubt. I can wait till then."

"I think we'd better go home now," Eithne said, uneasy at the sight of Maeve's face, the thought of what she might say.

Maeve plunged off at once with a hastily muttered farewell, so that before Eithne had moved she was twenty paces down the track, swinging along as if she were unwilling to let even her thoughts catch up with her. The old priest stood at the door of the oratory, looking after them, his awkward fingers slowly smoothing the surface of his square-cut white beard. " How much simpler life is for the simple-hearted," he said aloud.

" Did you think she was beautiful, Father ? " said one of the little boys, thankful for the excuse to rest his aching arm.

" Oh, yes," said the old man. " Very beautiful, my son. God's creatures all are, each in its own way."

" Huh . . . even goats ? " whispered the boy who had lifted the heavy sack.

The old priest heard him. " Why not, my son ? They make you all laugh, do they not ? "

" Um . . ."

" And laughter is the gift of God, blessing with beauty the creature which causes it . . ."

" But she was beautiful differently, though," persisted the little boy who was rubbing his wrist. " With her green gown against the blue sky and all that black hair . . ."

" Oh, I was thinking of her sister," the old priest said. " The light is of more consequence than the lantern, son. Hast thou not nearly finished grinding the corn. It is all but time to say the noon offices."

" We've almost finished, Father."

" Come to me, then, as soon as the work is done."

Eithne and Maeve were at the bottom of the hill, where the track widened so that they could walk side by side. Eithne was tired now, and the stress of Maeve's mood was beginning to fret her. She wanted to get away, to have a chance to be alone somewhere where she could sit down and think. But Maeve would not leave her in peace. She insisted on returning to the subject of the local gossip till the words buzzed round Eithne's head like a swarm of flies.

" That's what happens," stormed Maeve. " They persecute you, with their talk and their spite and their staring, till they change things altogether. It starts by being simple and honest, just the sort of friendship that you don't mind anybody knowing about. And they whisper about you and nudge each other and stare. And you don't like it. So you have to arrange that people shan't see you. You have to cheat people and lie. It isn't your fault. It's the fault of their cruel tongues. You know it is, Eithne. You know it is."

But Eithne, who had taken refuge from Maeve's angry voice by thinking about something else, had only heard the last sentence.

" I don't know what you're talking about, Maeve," she admitted. " Tell me again any——"

" And you don't care," said Maeve violently. " As long as you and Phelim and your blessed brats are safe for a place in heaven, the rest of us can be tormented for ever."

" Maeve, don't shout like that," said Eithne uneasily. " People will hear you. They'll wonder what's gone wrong."

" Then they'll have something else to talk about," said Maeve. " Something to whisper to each other over the wash-tubs. I don't care, I tell you . . . I don't . . . care."

She flung off through the gateway, storming between the smaller huts without taking the trouble to notice where she was going, so that curs and children, lolling in the sun, fled from her hasty feet, and the women who were talking to their neighbours in the low doorways turned to watch her as she went.

Following more slowly, Eithne sighed. She saw how the women stared after her sister's violent progress. She could guess what they were whispering, though as the women saw her their expressions changed, and they smiled and nodded, saying that it was a pleasure indeed to have another summer so late in the year. But Eithne knew that the whispers would begin again behind her, as the waters close on the wake of the coracle that parts them. Maeve had rushed through the dun looking like a battle fury. It would not be forgotten. And Phelim would not be pleased.

But she was not obliged to provide him with an explanation at once, though Maeve had already stormed through the hall and huddled herself in her sleeping-place at the far end, clashing her own blue curtains across the one small corner in which she could have any privacy. At another time Phelim would certainly have insisted on hearing all about it, but he had just been unexpectedly summoned to the royal dun, and was in too much of a hurry, as he changed his clothes and collected the royal chessmen, to spare more than a glance for Maeve's impetuous entrance.

" Oh, there you are," he said as Eithne followed. " What have I done with sword-belt ? Oh, yes, there it is. But I cannot lay hands on that new brooch for which I gave two heifers only the other day. It was of the very best workmanship, and so it should be, at that price. It was here a few hours ago. Of the finest bronze, it was, with a spiral design in enamel, and pearls set in the whorls. I had it here, I tell you, here at the neck of my cloak. I remember pushing the pin through the stuff and finding it irksome, so that at least it cannot have worked loose. And the cloak has been hanging there by the wall . . . who has been here since the morning meal ? Who could have taken it ? If I find the thief I will break every bone in his body. I will have him flogged till . . ."

"Phelim, Phelim, let us make sure first that the brooch is gone," said Eithne patiently.

"Gone, of course, it is gone. I tell you I stuck it through the stuff of my cloak. Here is the cloak. Look for yourself. Is the brooch there ? Well, then . . ."

"But you have more than one cloak," Eithne said.

"Naturally. It was my crimson cloak that I wore yesterday. So, of course, it was in that cloak I fastened the brooch. It isn't here. Well, then . . ."

"But this cloak is russet, not crimson, Phelim. Look at it in the light."

"H'm . . . yes. It is russet," said Phelim unwillingly. "Then someone must have taken cloak and all. It would be easier no doubt, than to undo the brooch. It was held fast, I tell you. In the stuff."

"You came in soaked, yesterday," Eithne said. "The cloak would be spread out to dry. By the fire, perhaps, when the meal was done, and we had gone to rest. Nalda will know. I'll ask her . . ."

She came back a few moments later with the crimson cloak, over her arm. "The brooch is here, just as you said, dear. Nalda had hung it in the sunshine because it wasn't quite dry."

Phelim grinned ruefully as he turned for her to put the cloak on his shoulders. "It is a hard time you have with me, wife. How do you bear it ? "

Eithne was laughing, but her voice was gentle. "Perhaps it is harder for you to bear the suspicion and anxiety that torment you," she said.

Phelim's face suddenly crumpled into laughter. "All that fury over the wrong cloak. I'm sorry. You must laugh at me more, Eithne. It does me good."

"Sometimes," said Eithne, "it is not safe to laugh. Not when things are worst."

"Laughter is a strange thing," Phelim said. "When you make me laugh, Eithne, it is dark no longer. What happens ? " he asked wonderingly, as he stood with his hands on Eithne's shoulders, his narrow face that had been seared with suspicion and anxiety once more the fact of the man she had known, so long ago it seemed now, as he had first fallen in love with her, when he came in the king's train to visit her father's court.

" I don't know," said Eithne practically. " But I hope it will happen again."

Phelim stooped to kiss her. " Never was there a beautiful woman with so much sense. There are many beautiful women, and a number of women with sense, but rarely indeed are these two virtues found together. Now I must go. There is talk of a visit to be paid to the court of our neighbours to the south, wife. If so, I shall be gone for as long as the king pleases. But you'll all be well enough here ? Tombul will keep the men in order while Nalda scolds the women for you, I know."

" Yes, of course," said Eithne. Perhaps, she thought, as she watched him go, it was just as well, with Maeve in this odd mood. Both Phelim and Maeve were difficult enough, in their several ways, heaven knew, and when they clashed, she herself always seemed to be the buffer. But now, perhaps, Maeve would have a chance to be in a happier state of mind by the time Phelim returned.

After she had picked up some of the things Phelim had flung down Eithne went out to watch the children, still playing on the edge of the shadow which had swung across the worn turf till they had to scramble round the building to avoid it. Nalda had brought out bread and a horn of milk, and the children were clamouring for them. Eithne sat down on the grass, too, and presently Maeve, reluctantly admitting she was hungry, came wandering out.

Eithne looked apprehensively at her sullen face. How much easier it would be if Maeve could laugh too. That short, harsh cackle of hers really wasn't like laughter at all. It could no more change her state of mind than a lightning-flash reveal a pathway. Laughter . . . the helpless, aching laughter that made the tears come . . . the sort of laughter that cured Colum's worst rages, that was different, a sort of blessing. You couldn't laugh like that and at the same time be unkind, or frightened, or cross. Laughter healed the spirit. Surely, thought Eithne, in surprise at the new idea, if anything from earth could survive such glory, there must be laughter, lovely, healing laughter, in the very courts of heaven. She smiled as she sat there, drowsy, a little tired, picturing the angels freed from the terrible austerity of tradition, wiping away tears of laughter at men's antics, as the sons of God shouted for joy.

But Maeve sat by herself, tearing fragments of bread from the hunch Nalda had given her, dipping them in salt and stuffing them gloomily into her mouth, aware that the hunger which the good bread appeased was only the lesser aspect of a hunger that seemed unappeasable, a hunger that was an ache and an ache that was almost alien, as if within her body two creatures wrestled for possession of her will, exhausting, deafening, bewildering her so that she scarcely knew where to turn or what to do. She had never, in all her life, felt so alone. Tears gathered under her heavy lids, blurring the sandy grass till she blinked them angrily away, glaring round her to make sure that they had not been seen.

Colum, who had just finished his bread, was gulping down the milk which Nalda had given him. But over the edge of the drinking-horn, held laboriously in both hands, he was watching Maeve, had been watching her, unobserved, for some time. His oddly unchild-like grey eyes did not falter as she looked at him. It was Maeve whose eyes fell, Maeve who stirred restlessly, frowned down at Colum, now lowering the empty drinking-horn to reveal a white line of milk along his upper lip, then brushing the milk away with a sweep of his hand.

" Well, child, you must know what I look like by now," she said sharply.

Slowly, with unmistakable understanding, Colum smiled.

Maeve wanted to strike him, to hurt him, to hear him bawl. She snapped her fingers because she could hardly keep her hands still. She had often enjoyed the admiration in men's eyes, and she knew the sly, envious looks of other women. But now, for the first time, she had seen pity, seen it, quite intolerably, in the eyes of this strange, five year-old child.

CHAPTER III

THE BOYS of the dun had collected at the foot of the biggest oak-tree, against the gashed and weathered trunk of which the crooked old shield-maker had tied a practice-shield, its ponderous convexity bossed and ringed with beaten bronze and backed with yew. It was a good shield, dinted from many battles, too good for such rough use, the old man had grumbled, since it might well have served again. But Phelim's champion had won it from a warrior whose skull he had split in fair combat and Phelim had said it was to be used for the lads to try their strength. So there it was, lashed to the tree-trunk that was twice a man's girth, and the lads shrieking about it like a flock of seagulls following the plough.

Tombul, the champion, stood waist-deep in the hubbub, grinning down at the excited boys in their brown or saffron tunics as he took a throwing javelin from the sheaf he carried, balancing it critically in his huge hand. It was always Tombul's task to train the lads who were approaching the preliminary tests for admission to the order of knighthood, since his skill with every kind of weapon was matched by his delight in all young creatures. And to the boys he seemed as splendid as one of the ancient gods.

" My father told me to hold the javelin so. But you . . ."

" Does a bronze-headed javelin fly better than these flint-tipped things we learn with . . . ? "

" They say no one will pass the tests who cannot send a shaft over Phelim's roof-tree and beyond the limit of the dun . . ."

" Tell me . . ."

" Show us . . ."

" How many knights will sit in judgment . . . ? "

" How many shafts must we break . . ."

" May I notch a shaft so that it breaks more easily ? "

" Listen, noisy ones," said Tombul in the tremendous voice which dominated the high-pitched clamour as a roll of thunder dominates the squabbling of a flock of sparrows in the eaves. " Listen to me. There is no need for such an outcry. I have taught you all for long enough to know that most of you should do me credit. So there is no need for these shaking knees. The knights who will sit in judgment have no wish to shame you. Rather they will seek to welcome you to their company, as you take the first step towards the winning of the champion's collar . . ."

46

" Tell us how you won yours, Tombul . . ."

" Oh, yes, tell us of the time you split a man from head to foot so that neither half knew what had come to the other . . ."

" The time you smote the shield that hung outside the Red King's dun . . ."

" The duel by the ford . . ."

" Tell us how you fought with Ard of the Terrible Sword . . ."

Tombul shook his big head, grinning all over his honest, sun-tanned face. " We are here for work, not for story-telling," he reminded them. " With the tests upon us at the change of the moon we have no time to waste. There is still much to tell you, but first of all let us deal with the prime test of spear and shield. On that the choice will go. Stand back, all of you——"

They swirled back as he swung his arms, falling over each other, squabbling, punching each other's ribs, tripping each other up, laughing and protesting, while Tombul shooed them away with sweeping gestures, as if they had been a noisy flock of hens. At last they were quiet, sitting or sprawling on the wall that marked the limit of the dun, while their instructor faced them with his back to the great tree. It was summer again, a summer in which less rain had fallen than usual, so that the streams were small and bare-footed boys were bronzed to the thighs, wearing only short tunics or a length of cloth about their loins, belted with girdles of dressed thongs in faithful imitation of Tombul's sword-belt, eager for the day when they too might bear real weapons instead of the wooden swords with which they had swaggered about the dun ever since they had the strength to lift them.

In the background one or two of the older men sat watching the lads, nodding their heads as they sagely discussed Tombul's methods of instruction and compared the entrants with those of other years. Phelim was among them, though he kept silence. Eithne, he knew, did not approve of his allowing Colum to go with the other lads to Tombul's classes. Why should he, she had asked, since he was to be a religious, not a knight? But Phelim had said glibly that even a religious would be the better for knowing something of the life of an ordinary man. Besides, the lad would not be eight till nearly Christmastide. If children were not considered old enough to take the first tests for knighthood till they were seven, then that was quite soon enough for Colum to begin his apprenticeship to the Church. He should go to be fostered by the old priest when he had passed his eighth birthday. That was fair enough. The boy had been promised to the Church and Phelim was, of course, not a man to go back on his pledged word. But the lad's own will must be considered. The life of a religious was not one for the half-hearted. Let Colum also have his say, urged Phelim craftily. He would have to live on, as knight or religious, long after his parents were dead. Let him make the decision himself, therefore, with both care and thought. And till the time for that decision came let him go with the other boys, whose talk and play and thought was all of knighthood. His mother would see to it that he learnt enough of the Church. With no knowledge of any other way of life, how could he be in any position to choose ?

So Phelim had seen to it that Colum received special attention from Tombul ever since his infant rages had made Phelim cherish the hope that his first-born might make a champion after all. The story of how he had turned on Maeve after her teasing for instance, had made him chuckle and rub his hands. Here, for once, was something for which he had to thank his sister-in-law. Perhaps it was a pity that she was no longer with them. The more Colum showed his temper the less likely appeared his religious vocation, and the better his father's choice of a future for him seemed. But since Nordal's wife had died in childbirth Maeve had married him and gone to live in the king's dun. So that unexpected assistance was no longer available, and the only thing Phelim could do was to concentrate on Colum's military education, and hope that as he came to know more of the glories of the tradition of knighthood they would eclipse the pale fancy for religion which his mother was trying to foster, so that when the time came it would inevitably be to the more obvious drama of warfare and knighthood that he turned.

Eithne, too, was beginning to be afraid, as Colum grew from an infant to a sturdy little boy who was always in and out of squabbles, rage and laughter battling with each other for possession of his vivid personality, his rapidly alternating moods apparently those of any other small boy. Had she been mistaken ? Dared she still believe the dream in which an angel had come to tell her that she must be prepared to share her child with the whole Christian world, that he must leave the country of his birth to serve the Church ? She began to wish now that the choice could be delayed. If he were given time to gain maturity, she had no doubt what the result would be. But while he was so little, so nearly a baby still, how could he be expected to weigh the tangible, glittering, glorious things of this world and the subtler things of the next ? How could he learn enough of both to choose between them, with any chance of choosing well ?

"Seven ? Is that really the age of the first tests for knight-

hood ? " she asked as the time grew near. " Surely not, Phelim.
It is far too soon."

Phelim shook his head. " Since the young hero Culculainn
was seven years old when he began his training for valour at the
court of King Concobar it has been the custom to admit boys
to the first tests at the same age."

" But they are no more than babies . . ."

" If warfare is to be their way of life they should begin to
learn of it as soon as they would begin to learn the life of the
Church. Sooner, perhaps," he added, grinning at the sight of
Eithne's stricken face. " Since a warrior does not commonly live
to the ripe old age of a priest."

" Phelim . . ." Eithne did not know what to make of
Phelim these days. He evaded discussion, refused to be angry,
and never lost a chance of telling Colum the old tales of heroic
deeds. But he maintained that he was taking no unfair advantage.
Did she, too, not take every chance of telling him the tales of the
knights of heaven ?

" I was speaking in jest, my dear," he said blandly, smiling
at the sight of her anxious face. " Is not the boy promised to the
Church ? "

" But now you say he—he himself—must choose——"

" Surely. Is that not wise ? "

" How can a mere child have such wisdom ? "

" If God wishes the child to be one of his servants will he not
claim him ? "

" I do not know," said Eithne uneasily. " I cannot tell . . ."

" You mean," said Phelim inexorably, " that you yourself
wish Colum to be a priest, and because it is your will you hope
it will be God's also. But you dare not leave it in his hands. You
would like there to be no choice, so that you can be certain of
your victory. That is just like a woman. You think that I, who
am no warrior, seek a son who will give our dun the glory it has
lacked. That is true. Yet it is not the whole truth. I would seek
for Colum the life which he will lead most gladly because it will
enable him to follow his true bent. If his whole heart goes out
towards the life of religion I will say no more. What I will not
do is to sit quiet and see my eldest son turned into a priest to
satisfy the zeal of a religious woman. I say that he shall choose.
And because he must know the things between which he chooses
I would put a spear into one hand while you put a crucifix into
the other. Can you complain of that ? "

Eithne sighed. " I cannot complain," she said. Phelim was
too clever for her: she could only wait and pray.

Meanwhile, Colum, as he grew, made as much noise as any lad in the dun. Yet he had his hours of quietness, when he sat with his knees drawn up to his chain and his hands clasped round them, staring into the fire or over the loughs to the encircling hills, hours when it was his father's turn to feel uneasy and summon him back to his noisy games. Tombul had the shield-maker weave a special shield for Colum, covering the wicker with taut hide which the champion showed him how to rub with limestone like his own till it was dazzling white and gave off a cloud of dust like that of any hero in battle when Colum strutted about the dun belabouring it with his wooden sword.

Phelim, watching him, chuckled with relief and pride. But Eithne wept as she prayed. Why had God sent his angel to her with the strange vision that had come before her first child was born? She remembered it so clearly, even now, over seven years later, as if all the times she had repeated it to herself when things were going badly had fixed each detail more firmly in her mind. Of course, Phelim said that every time she went over her dream she added something to it, so that it was growing steadily, just as Colum was growing himself. But that wasn't true. Phelim had merely stroked his chin when she told him about her dream the next morning. Then he had smiled and patted her hand. She knew quite well that he thought she must be humoured, as a woman near her time. But it had been true . . . truer than any waking thing that ever happened to her. Angels did sometimes come to people in dreams. The priest said they sometimes came to people when they were awake if they had enough faith. But usually it was necessary for the infirmity of the flesh to be laid aside so that mortal beings could endure the sight of the blessed messengers who shone with the strong light of heaven.

" Colum . . . it means a dove, remember," she said one day when they had been discussing the boy's future, " the dove that is the symbol of the Holy Spirit. I have prayed ceaselessly that it should come upon him . . ."

" Have you heard his new nickname? " said Phelim dryly. Eithne shook her head.

" They are calling him The Wolf, nowadays. I heard the lads shouting for him about the dun."

" The Wolf . . ."

" Well, you know yourself that he has a terrible temper," said Phelim more gently. " Nalda has had to beat him for it every now and then."

" He will grow out of it," said Eithne.

" If he is to be a warrior, he will not need to," Phelim said.

" If he is to be a warrior . . ." Phelim, sitting on a tree-stump in the shadow of one of the huts, watched the vivid surge of children mobbing Tombul for javelins to hurl at the shield. It was easy to tell Colum from the others, for his bright head shone among so many dark ones, and he was already taller than most of the boys of his age. His high, clear voice might be lost in the hubbub, and the clean, saffron-dyed tunic which Nalda had put on him that morning already dim with dust and daubed with grease from a pile of hides on which he had been playing. But there was something so definite about him, something so different from the windmill gestures of most of his companions in the way he handled his small sword and shield in one of the single combats which Tombul had organised, between boys of equal skill, while he himself stood on a tree-stump and shouted advice to the duelling couples through the haze of summer dust. If Colum were to be a warrior, Phelim told himself, the lad would go far. He shielded his eyes with his hand and watched the boy from under forward lids.

Yes, Colum should go far. He had strength, fury and skill. Tombul could make him a champion of the dun before he left his teens. He might also have inherited some subtlety, Phelim fancied, though that mattered less. He himself had sufficient statesmanship to guide a son who could supply the beauty and stature that his father lacked. Yes, it was odd how they compli-mented each other ; body and spirit, sinew and soul. Together . . . . there would be no telling what heights they might reach. King of the community . . . king of the province . . . why not farther yet ? Phelim seemed to see again the roaring Hall of Tara in all its legendary splendour, to hear the shouts of kings and champions acclaiming Erin's Ard-Ri. Colum, High King of Ireland. Why not ? Both his parents came from ruling families of their respective provinces, and Phelim's father, Fergus, had also married a daughter of the royal house of Laigen, just as he had himself. His marriage, like Phelim's, had been a thong to bind together in peace the royal houses which had once been so ruthless in war. Had not a great king of the Hy Niall given orders that he was to be burried upright, in full battle array, with his face towards Laigen, the home of his enemies ? But now their two lands were united in peace and would march together in war. United so that their candidate at Tara might do well . . . might do very well. Their alliance should be formidable enough to draw to its protection many of their lesser neighbours.

And once Colum had been elected Ard-Ri at Tara, what might not follow ? Phelim let himself dream, as many men dream whose

warped bodies are the symbols of souls twisted by pride and
restless with ambition, perpetually seeking what lies beyond the
puny body's reach. Ard-Ri of Erin, and himself in the shadows
behind that legendary throne, unknown yet all-important,
supplying all that Colum, with his splendid body, might yet lack.
Phelim would see to it that the new faith was not allowed to dim
the glory of Colum's kingship. Christianity was no creed for
warriors, with its strange teaching of acceptance and humility.
Phelim ground his teeth together. Such ideas would be the ruin
of Erin. In them no hope of conquest or splendour, no blood-
letting in battle, no unity lay. The contemptible doctrine would
split the country into innumerable, nameless communities, living
out their wretched lives according to a law which explicitly
forbade them to enjoy the comforts of earth if they wished to
qualify for the unspecified splendours of heaven. All very well
for women . . . for Eithne. Women always looked for instruction, obedience came natural to them. It was an obvious law.
It was different for men. A man must compel obedience ; on
his wife, his environment, his enemies. Life was at its finest
and most splendid where there was most conflict, as the charcoal
the smith used to make metals malleable glowed most brightly in
the greatest draught. Men thrived on conflict, Phelim reflected,
excitement rising in him as he listened to the din of the boys'
wooden swords pounding the taut hide of their wicker-backed
shields.

" So . . ." roared Tombul. " Strike less wildly, Moldan.
Hold the shield over your heart : do not brandish it in the air . . .
Well struck, Diarmit. But do not let him recover. After him
while he still staggers. Leave him now, Colum. He has lost his
sword and your blade is at his throat . . . let him be, now. Let
him be."

Laughingly he reached through the crowd and picked the
furiously flailing Colum off a bigger boy whose weapons he had
scattered, before flinging him to the ground. " There, that
will do, young wolf." Still grinning, he tossed the excited child
on to the grassy bank, where he lay sprawling, his face bewildered
by the bitterness of the conflict between habitual laughter and
the strangely violent rage within him. " Up, then, Grellan, and
find your sword."

" He has broken it, I think," whimpered Colum's victim.

" Then pick up a stick. Do not lie there howling, unarmed."
Tombul had no mercy on weaklings. Any lad who could not stand
the drastic process of his instruction, he maintained, would never
succeed as a warrior. As a teacher he might be rough and pitiless,

but he was their friend and their hero. What they could not endure from him, who meant them well, they would certainly not be able to endure from an enemy, to whom they were strangers, who might be both deceitful and merciless, because he wished them ill.

At last Tombul clapped his hands. " That will do, that will do. Sit down where you are."

Gaspingly glad of the respite, they flung themselves down, so that the space in front of the oak-tree was strewn with recumbent figures who lay with their heads on their arms and their weapons scattered about them, while the dust of their encounters still misted the summer air.

" You have done well enough," Tombul told them judicially. " You should win through, when it comes to the tests, if you remember what I have tried to tell you. Moldan, you wave that shield of yours as if it were a flower you were offering to your sweetheart, not a protection for your own head and heart. Diarmit, you are too slow. Colum . . . try to remember that anger is a better servant than a master, even in battle. Grellan, if you give up for lost every time a skilful fighter trips you, your head will soon be added to the pile of the slain."

" He . . . he was like someone demented . . . " whimpered Grellan.

" All the more need to get quickly back on your feet," said Tombul inflexibly. " If you have not the stomach for warfare, it is better to say so now. There are other opportunities. One may do well enough as keeper of the cattle, or swineherd to the king."

The boys sniggered, and Grellan rolled sullenly over till he lay on his face in the sand. He was an only son, who had been much petted, and his parents were only too willing for him to wait a while before taking valour. Yet, he could not, for very shame.

" Very well, then. Anybody who needs extra instruction may come to me between now and the change of the moon, which is in three days' time. On that day I will submit you all to the judgment of the knights of the dun. Each entrant is to wear leather cap and shoes, he must gird himself with a belt for his weapons, and his shield must be freshly painted or limed white. Each must have sword, spear, and dagger. The javelins for hurling I will bring. In that way I shall make sure that none has been already weakened so that it will break more easily when it is flung at the shield. That is all. You may go."

In twos and threes the lads began to scatter, most of them

making for the lough in which to cool themselves, or for a water-skin at which they could ease their dry throats. Colum was escorted by an admiring company, who flung their arms about his shoulders as they led him away for a bathe. Phelim, as he strolled towards Tombul, could hear their voices.

" Well done, little red-head. Did you hear Grellan bawl? . . . You trounced him properly. I am glad it was not me you were sitting on when Tombul stopped you. Well fought, Wolf. Well fought, Wolf ! "

Phelim smiled grimly as they led his son away. Colum was no longer angry. He was laughing and light-heartedly cuffing the boys nearest him, big lads of nine or ten, many of them, as Phelim knew. As they passed by he called out : " Well done, boy. Now go for a swim to cool your fire."

Grave for an instant, Colum looked up, as the boys fell back respectfully at the sound of Phelim's voice. Colum's face was daubed with dirt, tracked with sweat and trickles of blood from a dozen scratches, the tunic was half torn from his back, and the hair that fell to his shoulders tangled and caked with dirt. Phelim fancied, too, that he noticed an expression of anxiety on his son's blurred face. Uneasily he met the grey eyes, aware that they held some sort of unformulated appeal for help. Then hastily he denied the implication. Against what should his triumphant son need help? He brought his hand down on Colum's shoulder in a friendly way, nodded dismissal, then turned abruptly away.

Tombul was collecting javelins from the foot of the oak-tree and prising others from its deeply pocked bark. He nodded as Phelim came up. " I thought you were watching. Well, were you pleased ? "

" I was," Phelim said. " A fine lot of lads you've got there. They should do you credit this year."

" Most of them," Tombul agreed. " Grellan is a weakling, Diarmit a dreamer. Colum . . ."

Phelim chuckled. " Colum is a wolf, they say."

Tombul frowned. " I am not happy about Colum . . ."

Phelim was startled. " Colum ? Was he not the best of them all ? He is a furious fighter . . ."

Tombul carefully levered loose a javelin which had been thrown so hard that it had gone deep into the tree's trunk. " Too furious, perhaps. He fights blind, Phelim. I have tried again and again to steady him. He is an odd child. Sometimes I think he is like no other I have ever taught. Most lads fight well or fight badly, but they fight—well, as you'd expect. They fight with what is in them. Colum is different. It is as if, sometimes, a fury takes hold of him and drives him to do its bidding. He does not fight like a child, even an angry child. Sometimes—I don't know why—I'm afraid for him, Phelim. He may come to harm."

Phelim stared. " Harm ? But so may any man who fights. So surely the more dangerous he is as a fighter the better. Then he inflicts the harm instead of receiving it."

Tombul ruffled up his thick hair, which he wore shorter than most men, in a gesture of helplessness. " I know what I mean, Phelim. But I doubt if I can ever explain. Perhaps it's something I have not the right to say. You will not thank me for it. As your champion I am paid to defend your home and keep order in your household. As your son's instructor it is my duty to teach him the use of weapons. But I am not only your champion, Phelim. I am your foster-brother too, and I have the greatest respect and admiration for Eithne, as you know. I can tell what store you both set by this lad. And so, if I am troubled about him, I cannot stop saying so just because it makes you angry."

" At least you must be prepared to tell me why you are troubled." Phelim's voice was cold.

Tombul looked wildly about him, as if imploring inspiration from the sky and the oak-tree and all the powers of the round world. " It is—it is only that fighting men get to know about some things that are beyond the spear-thrust of men who are in other ways wiser, but who do not fight for a living. We know that the spirit of man is usually as snug inside the body as a foot in a well-made shoe, so that it takes death to prise him from it. But there are others that the battle-furies batten on, men of great gifts, either for good or ill. Their spirits do not sit so close in their bodies that only death will shift them. Madness may give their bodies to Neit and Nemon before it is time for them to leave this world and go elsewhere."

Phelim frowned as Tombul spoke of the malignant pagan deities of battle. " Dangerous words for a baptised man," he said.

Tombul nodded. " What do names matter ? The Christian priest knows that there are demons in earth and sea and air. They may sit on a man's book or lurk in a milk-pail. Some prey more readily on the housewife, and some on the learned judge, just as some men suffer more from phlegm and others from weakness of the bowels. I do not know why these things should be. I cannot say all that is in my mind. But I know that the battle-furies hover round your son already. I do not like it. He would be better in some other trade."

Phelim looked at him in amazement. " You mean that ? "

Tombul nodded emphatically. " I most surely do."

" Yet you yourself say that Colum is one of the best pupils you have ever had ? "

Tombul nodded, drawing a sinewy forearm across his brow. " Even so . . . " He had begun to sweat with the discomfort of attempting an explanation of something he merely felt, wordlessly, and could not possibly explain coherently in the face of Phelim's cold, analytical scorn.

Angrily Phelim pounded his fist on his open palm. " It is fantasy. I do not believe a word of it. I have seen with my own eyes that the boy fought brilliantly. I do not set any store by this superstitious talk of madness and demons. The boy should have a great career before him. Anyway—what do you expect me to do ? "

Tombul licked his dry lips. " I—I should suggest you withdraw him from the tests, Phelim, as his mother wishes."

For a few seconds Phelim hesitated. With sudden compunction he remembered Eithne's pleading, her pale face dashed with tears. Then the towering, cloud-land picture of Colum as Ard-Ri of Erin enthroned in the restored glory of Tara, under the protection of her ancient gods, swept the fainter memory away.

" I will do no such thing," he said. And Tombul could only shake his big head and look sadly after Phelim as he stalked away.

Eithne remained alone on the day Colum was to be tested. The entire household, men and women, even old Nalda and the two young children, had gone with Colum and his father to the testing-ground, leaving Eithne on her knees beside the carved wood cradle of the recently born baby, abstractedly rocking and singing to it in a voice shaken by weeping, between bouts of desperate prayer.

As a last resort she had gone to the priest the day before and begged him to forbid Colum to fight. But the old man had refused to speak either to the boy or to see Phelim, until the result of the tests should be known. For the first time she had been disturbed by his detachment, his formal, archaic turn of phrase.

" He is not like other boys," Eithne had pleaded. " His future lies in the Church. This is a distraction. It comes from the devil. For him it means terrible danger . . ."

" There is always danger," said the old priest. " The greater the gift entrusted to a soul, the greater the danger of its misuse."

" But Father—you could speak to him——"

" Where God is silent, what have I to say ? "

" But Father, you could command———"

" Where God waits, shall I show less courtesy ? "

" The child is dedicated to the Church———"

" What use has the Church for unwilling servants ? "

" Then I can do nothing—nothing———? " Eithne's voice had been broken, shrill with despair. The old priest still sat motionless, thumbing his square beard.

" Thou canst do all that is necessary."

" But . . ."

" Thou canst love him and pray for him. No mortal creature need or can do more." The level voice became gentler. " Go home and wait, my child. There is no need for this misery. Thou wilt help Colum more by doing as I have told thee."

And now she was trying to do as he had told her, breaking off her incoherent petitions to sing a tremulous little thread of song which did not soothe the baby in the slightest, since it caught the singer's state of mind and not the words, her fear infecting it till it set up a desolate howl. At last, Eithne gave up trying to pray for Colum and comfort her baby at the same time. Yielding to the more immediate urgency she rose from her knees and lifted the baby from the cradle to comfort her in her arms. Little by little the child's furious crying dwindled to a wail, to a whimper, to a croon, and in some way that she did not understand Eithne's terror subsided with it, till she sat watching the sleeping child's still face with a secret little smile of love and pity which were perhaps the symbols of a far truer prayer.

Phelim held his head high as he led Colum to the testing-ground, and Colum himself was elated. He had not yet given much thought to the future, pushing it away from him because it was something his father and mother argued about, and he liked peace to be between them. Vaguely he knew he had been promised to the Church, but as he stalked beside his father at the head of the household he could not help responding to this foretaste of a hero's life.

It pleased Phelim to see that the other boys, also marching beside their fathers, were whispering and pointing Colum out to their parents, hoping perhaps that they would not be matched against him when the single combats began. These were the last of the tests, and much could turn on them, since no boy who was habitually defeated would ever be received by the assembled knights as one of their company, yet if he had defended himself bravely it would tell in his favour, even if he had not broken many of the javelins he hurled at the shield or shown himself outstanding in the running and jumping tests which went before.

So Phelim felt reasonably confident as he took his place among the other knights who were already sitting on the turf wall or leaning over it from outside the dun. They were gravely judicial, yet Phelim noticed many anxious faces. Most of those about him were presenting at least one son. Tombul had a great reputation as an instructor, so that boys came from a considerable distance for his teaching, and many of the knights who had come to adjudicate belonged to other duns. It was an important occasion, and the boys who crowded round Tombul were nervously silent as they listened to his final words of instruction, wiping on the backs of their thighs the palms of hands too slippery with sweat to grip their miniature spears.

The first drill with weapons was purely formal. It was evident that all the boys knew how to handle their weapons in theory, however the crisis of combat might affect their skill. The watching knights nodded approval, but Phelim, rigid with impatience for the real testing, sat silent and motionless. After the running and jumping he was still impassive, but after the javelin-throwing he smiled a little. Colum had done well. Every javelin he hurled at the shield had broken against its brazen surface, and on its impact the shield had sent out a deep and satisfying clang. Other javelins had gone wide of the mark, burying themselves in the tree-trunk or sailing past it to scatter the less important spectators. Others, thrown with too little strength, had merely tapped the shield. Sometimes the knights had murmured, shaking ominous heads. But Colum's javelins had all been splintered to fragments, and now it was time for the single-combat at which he was sure to excel.

Colum was feeling slightly dizzy as he stepped out on to the testing-ground again. The horizon wavered a little in the heat, and he wriggled to free his back from the soaked folds of his sleeveless tunic as he adjusted the handles of his shield on his left forearm, and settled the long carrying-thong about his neck as he had been taught. He took a firmer grip of his sword, then stood waiting, one foot advanced, on guard. The hilt of his sword had been carved by his father, and his shield had been decorated by one of the men of the household with a ferociously realistic wolf's head on the newly-whitened ground.

Tombul had told him to keep calm, and Colum was trying to obey him, as he faced his opponent, a tall, rather oafish boy from another dun. Tombul had said he must use his wits more in fighting, not let himself be carried away with excitement. But it was all very well for Tombul, who was kind anyway, thought Colum, as he watched his instructor mount the tree-stump which was his usual vantage point, his sword held high as he looked round the waiting couples. Desperately Colum tried to grasp at the quietness of that moment, to take it with him into the pandemonium which was about to begin.

Then Tombul dropped his sword, and nothing mattered but defending himself against the boy from the other dun who was pressing the attack with confidence, seeing an easy victim in the smaller boy. Colum fought at first with great deliberation, his grey eyes wide and wary, his mouth compressed into a resolute line. He must keep calm, he must use his head, he must not get angry, Tombul had said. Only an hour ago, Tombul had repeated these things very gravely, almost as if he were afraid that if Colum lost his temper something might go wrong.

Column did not mean to lose his temper. He tried only to defend himself, as Tombul had advised, till he had taken the measure of his opponent. He fought so carefully, so moderately that Phelim snapped his fingers in a typical gesture of impatience. What was the matter with the boy? He was fighting like any of the others, without genius or fire. But Tombul sighed with relief. If Column could only maintain his skilful defence every one would be satisfied, except that old vulture, Phelim, of course. And his own responsibility as an instructor would be over. What happened to the boy afterwards would be only indirectly his concern. Soon he would be able to strike the blow on the shield which would stop the scuffling and pounding. The tests would be over—over for another year.

Then the boy matched with Colum managed to get in a shrewd blow which ripped the flesh of Colum's forearm with the point of his sword. In that instant of sudden pain something seemed to come down on Colum like a bird of darkness, so that he no longer saw the familiar world, but only a blood-streaked chaos filled with the stupid, angry, red face of an enemy he must utterly destroy. A great roaring dominated the familiar sounds of swords thudding harmlessly on shields as he sprang forward, goaded by the other boy's gaping astonishment, careless of any blows he might receive himself as he sprang, like a wolf, straight for his enemy's throat.

The older boy's screams rose high above the sounds of mock combat, and Tombul hastily struck a great blow on the bronze shield. The struggling boys fell back, panting, as he strode between them towards the furious Colum, who was crouching across his terrified and weeping enemy, his face set in a mask of almost insane anger as he slashed with his dagger at the boy's already bleeding throat.

Many of the knights, too, had vaulted over the wall and run towards them, so that in an instant a circle of curious spectators closed in, though only a few of them were near enough to see how hard Tombul had to shake and cuff Colum to make him loosen his grip. Once more on his feet, Colum seemed dazed, as if he had been suddenly awakened from a nightmare. He glared blankly around, his eyes wide, with distended pupils which turned them almost black. Vaguely he seemed to notice Tombul, the murmuring stir of knights. Last of all he saw the terrified, sobbing boy on the ground.

"What—what has happened?" he asked.

"Nothing," said Tombul gravely. "Nothing—yet."

"Then—what's he doing there?" Colum asked, looking down in amazement that slowly deepened into consternation as he stared. Dimly he remembered being matched against such a boy in single combat . . . Then . . . What had happened . . . ?"

"You should know." Tombul's voice was grim. Over Colum's head Phelim refused to meet his accusing eyes.

"You mean—I've hurt him?"

Tombul nodded. Before he could speak again the applause of the knights broke over them in an oddly animal, inarticulately ferocious roar of mingled praise and blame, from which stray phrases emerged here and there, as those most anxious to be on good terms with Phelim raised their voices above those of his rivals to make their meaning clear.

"Well fought, boy . . ."

"There goes a future champion . . ."

"At his first testing to draw blood . . ."

"To kill, maybe . . ."

"Is the other lad dead, then?"

"Likely enough. His throat is torn as if by a wolf . . ."

Colum blinked round him, slowly comprehending, appalled. Convulsively, he began to tremble. His dim memory of what had happened was overshadowed by the darkness which had come down on him like a bird of prey, the suggestion of an alien, sickeningly evil presence which befouled him with its lust to kill. Now he seemed lost in a wilderness out of reach of sunshine, sanity or laughter, surrounded by strangers who either praised him noisily or murmured against him as a murderer, whose eyes were horrible, whose very lips smacked of blood and gloated over violent deeds.

He shrank back looking wildly about him as he stood there at bay. The dagger he had used so fiercely slipped from his limp fingers. Defensively he crooked his arms about his head as if to ward off an expected blow. He was no longer a future warrior as he shrank from the men about him, only a child who had ventured into a world that had proved too strange. For a little longer he endured their staring eyes, then, quite suddenly, with a loud howl of utter misery, he ducked forward, butting through the crowd till he was clear of them, running furiously between the huts, his grotesquely decorated shield still bouncing about on his back, held by its long carrying thong, as he fled. A few moments later he burst sobbing through the doorway of his home to throw himself at his mother's knees.

Eithne put the baby gently back in the cradle, then stooped, murmuring consolation, to loosen Colum's convulsive grip and gather him into her arms.

"Why, my precious, my darling, what have they done to you?"

The face Colum raised to her was childishly tear-stained, but as his shaking lips struggled to shape the words that would express his anguish, Eithne saw that his eyes were wide with the sort of horror that spoke of a glimpse into the very pit of hell, something far beyond the capacity of a child to express by means of any words he knew.

"There now, there now, it's all over," she whispered, as she might have consoled a child after the terror of a bad dream. Yet still Colum clung to her, shaking, his whole face convulsed by the effort to explain the horror that had overwhelmed him. But he knew no words which would express the crux of his desolation, the pit of perdition he had glimpsed within his own vulnerable soul. He could only grip his mother's arms till his fingers bruised her flesh, shuddering and gasping between sobs, " I can't bear it . . . I can't bear it . . . What shall I do?"

CHAPTER IV

PHELIM AND TOMBUL came in soon afterwards. Phelim looked bleakly elated, but Tombul's broad face was grave as he swept the leather curtains across the hall to shut out the men and women of the household who were now returing from the tests, then stood with his back against it as if to defend the family he served from the inquisitive inquiry of the whole world.

" Well, now, what's all this? " Phelim said brusquely. " Snivelling, eh? What's the matter, boy? "

" Phelim, what happened at the tests? " said Eithne, as Colum merely clung closer. " Whatever can have gone wrong? "

" Wrong? " Phelim said. " I don't know what you mean. Colum was acclaimed as a future champion. He fought magnificently. The likeliest lad of the lot, the judges thought him. He's just a bit overwrought after the tests, dear. That's all."

Eithne looked anxiously up at her husband. Between his narrowed lids she could scarcely see his eyes, but she could tell he was glancing here and there all the time instead of looking at her steadily. If he were not lying, she guessed that he was keeping something back.

" There's something you're not telling me."

" No," Phelim said jauntily. " No, indeed. No."

" Was he beaten? "

" Certainly not. He passed every test. I've just told you."

" Then—did he kill any one? " It was a chance suggestion, but as she spoke she could feel Colum gasp. So—that was it. Worse, much worse than being defeated, much worse for Colum. She could guess at his revulsion from himself, the sick, imprisoned horror of guilt and darkness from which an inarticulate child could find no refuge, see no daylight glimmer of escape.

" No, no, of course not," Phelim said. Tombul stood silently behind him, his face blank with discomfort, shuffling his feet on the earthen floor.

" Tombul, what happened? " Eithne said.

But Phelim answered before Tombul could do more than look up unhappily, frowning as he cleared his throat.

" My dear, there is nothing to make such a fuss about. Colum has the makings of a future champion. He fought like a fury——"

Tombul opened his lips. But he did not interrupt.

" The other boy was no match for him. I admit he was injured, but there seems no reason to suppose he will die. The physicians are with him. He was a stranger, a boy from one of the duns beyond the lough, I believe——"

" I see," Eithne said fiercely. " Between you, you want to make the boy a murderer, an assassin——"

" That is not true," Phelim said. " He fought as he had been taught, according to the rules of single-combat. We should be proud——"

" Very proud, no doubt," said Eithne passionately. " Not content with killing our enemies in battle we must learn to kill our friends and neighbours, even when we are at peace. It is most praiseworthy, provided we do it according to the rules. Will it comfort that other child's mother to learn it was strictly according to rules that her boy was maimed by mine ? "

Phelim snapped his fingers. " Are you trying to tell me that there should not be tests for knighthood ? Are no fires to be kindled for fear some fool should singe his beard ? "

Eithne sighed. " What would be the use of trying to change men's ways ? They will not cease to fight till God teaches them better. But all men need not be warriors. Colum has been promised to the Church——"

Phelim smiled crookedly. " Even churchmen fight on occasion," he reminded her. " I have heard of holy monks who so far forgot their holiness as to fight their fellow Christians for the possession of a piece of land. Perhaps it is as well that Colum is now to be a warrior——"

" He is to be trained as a priest. You swore it, Phelim. You also swore that you would not go back on your word."

" What I undertook finally and in my right mind, I think," said Phelim deliberately, " was that the boy should choose. I abide by that. If he is fool enough to give up the chance of becoming a champion, just when he has shown his skill to all the knights of the dun, then I have no more to say to him now, and never will."

" Are you listening, Colum ? " Eithne cried.

" But he is in no fit state to choose at present," said Phelim quickly. " I can see how overwrought he is. Leave him now. Let him be. In a few weeks time, perhaps, he will be ready to make the choice. He will have had time to realise what the life of a warrior offers. Give him food and drink now and let him rest. Why should we force a decision upon him ? The future will wait."

So Colum was put to bed, unprotesting, while the sun still

shone, and the voices of the children playing with the wolf-dogs round the huts sounded all over the dun, with the chime of bridles as horses were saddled up by men about to go in search of strayed cattle, and the horns of the hunters echoed each other faintly among the hills.

He slept to his mother's surprise, for the rest of the day, unstirring, waking only at night to drink a bowl of milk and then fall back again into sleep so deep that it seemed to take him far beyond dreams. It was Eithne who stayed awake most of the night, restlessly wakeful in the warm darkness, waiting for the screams of a nightmare or a storm of terrified tears.

Next morning he seemed to have forgotten, or at least to have deliberately put from his mind all the drama of the day before. He went fishing with the other boys as usual, though when at home he was strangely quiet. Eithne made no attempt to force his confidence, and Phelim behaved as if nothing of importance had occurred. Only Tombul looked troubled, as he hung about the place, patching a rent in his shield with a carefully chosen piece of hide, whetting his weapons, making excuses to stay indoors. He looked anxiously from Phelim to Eithne every now and then, as if there were many things he would like to have told Colum's mother if only his father were out of the way.

But Phelim, for once, did not appear inclined to leave his household. He had arranged for another noble to attend the king instead of himself, he refused invitations to fish or hunt, and sat all day long at the bench in the private living-place behind the leather curtain, his narrowed eyes missing nothing, his quick ears hearing everything, his alert brain recording and analysing all that went on. He was quite content to wait till the shock of Colum's experience at the tests should have subsided. If the boy had chosen at once he knew very well what the choice would have been. Later—he thought it would be otherwise. He would ask the king's chief poet to visit the dun presently ; for the boy was imaginative enough to respond to the tales of the legendary warriors whose glory rang down the centuries, especially when these songs were sung by one of the finest living performers on harp strings, whose voice could make the most cynical old women and the toughest battle-scarred warriors weep.

Meanwhile, he would keep the boy away from his mother as much as possible. Away from Tombul, too, after what the foolish fellow had said. Though the choice must appear to be free, everything should be done to stress the splendours of martial valour. He would invite the king's champion to visit them, planned Phelim. He would ask the royal historian to bring his most impressive records to the dun. He would take Colum to the king's court, where he would hear the talk of men of learning and culture, who lived with dignity and splendour among worldly things. Colum had been long enough among the women. He must be weaned from dependence on his mother. She would make a weakling of him if she got a chance, praying and crooning over him as if he were feeble-minded. After all, he was the boy's father. It was high time he had his way.

During the weeks that followed the tests Colum appeared to have changed completely from the gay, spontaneous child he had once been. Some profound shock seemed to have driven him back into the recesses of his own nature, like a snail into its shell. He was quiet, grave, docile, apparently without animation or will. Obediently he took his place beside Phelim at the board round which many strangers gathered, as the summer days gave way to the storms of autumn, and then to the darkness of the long winter nights.

Colum's birthday and Christmas approached again. Phelim still made no effort to force a decision. On the contrary, he took infinite trouble to lull the child into forgetting that any decision was near. The men he invited were not only warriors, whose boasting might be too loud, just at present, their anecdotes too crude for a squeamish child's ear. Most of the talk Colum heard was that of learned judges, physicians, poets and historians ; thoughtful men, who took trouble sometimes, to pause in their conversation to explain a point to the silent, wide-eyed boy.

" Well, lad, have you taken in all we've been saying ? " asked a formidable old man with a thin nose, who was, Colum knew, the local king's chief brehon or learned judge. He smiled as he spoke, but it was a smile that was almost more alarming than his usual portentous gravity, a mere folding back of almost colourless lips to reveal brownish, irregular teeth. Colum, staring in a bemused way, did not hear the question, and when it was repeated, he mutely shook his head.

" Let me tell you a story then," said the learned judge, who was feeling rather more mellow than usual, thanks to Phelim's generosity with the mulled wine. " What would you say was the first duty of a brehon ? "

" Surely—to—to give judgment," Colum said.

" Exactly. But what is the right judgment ? It is not easy to say. In every case the circumstances may be different. The law as it is recorded can only tell what has been done in this case or that. Justice is greater than law. A man must give his life to serve it. Even then——" He paused, indicating inadequacy by a fluttering gesture of long hands appearing from furred sleeves.

Watching his son, Phelim saw the boy's interest kindle. Adminstration of the law was part of the duty of any ruler and Colum must be carefully instructed. He would do well to spend some time, perhaps, in a brehon school. Over the heads of his guests he looked at Eithne, sitting among her women in the shadows. She and her priests . . . the boy was not such a fool . . .

" When Cormac MacArt was a boy," said the learned judge, " he lived in disguise at Tara, where the usurper MacCon sat on the throne and pretended to rule Erin. As custom was, the people brought their complaints to their supposed king as he sat in the supreme court surrounded by his judges. But because he was a usurper he wished to show that he could give judgment without their assistance. And it was in this way that he lost his throne. The love of justice, boy, is very close to the heart of the people of Erin."

Colum nodded. It was already very close to his own.

" It came about that one day the sheep of a woman who kept an inn had tresspassed on the land which belonged to the queen, and the queen brought the complaint that the sheep had eaten up her crop of woad. Now the usurper saw the chance of enriching his lady at the expense of the woman who kept the inn. That was natural, for had he not cared more for gain than for justice he would not have dared to sit on another man's throne. Because of the damage they had done he declared the sheep to be forfeit. Do you call that a right judgment, boy ? "

" No," Colum said. It was the answer which was obviously expected of him, but the learned judge's face was again gashed with his mirthless smile, and he brought a heavily ringed hand quite painfully down on Colum's bright head.

" Well done. You speak like a judge already. Indeed it was not a right judgment. It was so false that young Cormac, hidden among the spectators, could not let it go by. " Not so," he cried. ' The cropping of the sheep should be sufficient. Let the wool pay for the woad. Both will grow again.' "

" What happened then ? " cried Colum, eager now.

" Then the people cried out that such a judgment could only be given by one who had wisdom within him, as a true king must. The usurper was driven from his throne and Cormac reigned in his place. That was the justice of Tara, lad. There is no purer source of justice than the supreme court of Erin over which the High King presides."

Colum nodded. He would remember. He would remember everything that the great men told him. After they had gone he turned over all they had said in his oddly mature, occasionally childish mind, which let those things which were beyond its scope pass through its meshes, yet retained much more, perhaps, than any of the great men realised. He learnt that the land, in theory, belonged to the people, and not to individuals, though in practice the king had his portion, or mensal land, assigned to him, while the rest was occupied by the tribesmen according to rank. He heard of land which passed from one man to another by tanistry or by gavelkind, of the rights of freemen and the rightlessness of serfs. He heard of procedure by distress or by fasting, the rules of eric or compensation, the laws of evidence by which a woman might be heard against her husband and a boy's evidence was accepted as soon as he was of an age to grow a beard. He listened while the experts argued till he was bewildered, but much of the fine tradition of justice in Erin sank deep into his mind.

From the historians in their turn he heard the great tales of past splendour which it was their business to record. Here was something that captured his imagination more than the exquisite precision of legal thought ever could. He heard of the onslaught on Ulaid led by the turbulent warrior Queen of Connaught and her husband Alill ; of the hero, Cuculainn, who alone fought the battles of his enfeebled people, defending every ford that lay in the path of the advancing army single-handed, since by the laws of ancient chivalry the outcome of such a combat must be recognised as if it had been the defeat of an entire army. He heard of the Red Branch Knights of the first Christian century, who fought from racing chariots, built tremendous fortresses, and performed prodigies of valour in the service of the local kings, of the elegant, scornful Fena, whose fame was at its height two hundred years later, who had neither fortresses nor chariots, preferring to fight on foot and billet themselves on the admiring population, and who insisted on cultural as well as athletic accomplishments before accepting any recruit to their exclusive order of knighthood.

Great names went to and fro above Colum's dizzy head as the guests reminded each other of the triumphs of Laegaire the Victorious, Keltar of the Battles, Cethern of the Brilliant Deeds, Art Aenfer the Solitary, or Conor of the Red Brows. The ancient records of Erin were drawn up from the well of the past as he listened, in long chains of glory whose links were the names of legendary kings.

But it was the poets whose art most nearly captured Colum. The lawgivers awed him, the historians amazed him, but the bards bewitched him with the beauty of their words, and the sound of harp strings they plucked so skilfully seemed to wring and twist something so deep in his body that he could scarcely bear to listen to them nor endure that they should stop. Lesser poets, at that time, earned most of their living by going round the various duns in which they had learned by experience that they would be welcome at meal-times, so Colum had plenty of opportunities of hearing the music which was so dear to the people of his country that they were accustomed to include it with housing, fire, and food as one of the necessities for which they prayed.

All the other great men of the court had been so kind that it was disappointing to find that Olim, the Chief Maker of the King's Music, was such an unapproachable person that it was extremely unlikely that he would allow himself to be aware of Colum's existence at all. Having spent twelve years in perfecting his art in one of the most famous poetic schools of Erin, he had emerged with the title of ollave, and seemed unwilling that others should forget it, even for an instant. Ollave rank, the doctorate of the various branches of learning, was more highly valued by the poets than by the members of any other profession. All those attending the king, the brehons, physicians, bishops and smiths in gold, iron or bronze, were ollaves of their particular craft, but the court poets were already claiming a unique dignity for their doctorate which was beginning to turn people against them and was to lead to their drastic humiliation in years to come. But they were at that time still at the peak of their arrogant greatness.

Olim of the Golden Tongue wore clothes of as many colours as the king himself, sat at his right hand at banquets, let his hair grow longer and scented it more strongly than any other courtier. He merely stared blankly at people whose questions he did not wish to answer, till his attendants tweaked at the questioners' sleeves and explained that the master was saving his throat. As Chief Poet, Olim carried the golden branch, set with a number of little chiming bells—the accepted token of a poetical doctorate—on all occasions, even when not actually in attendance on the king.

He, of course, could scarcely be expected to visit Phelim's dun except as an act of the greatest condecension, though after prolonged deliberation he announced his intention of coming to recite one of his less well-known poems to Phelim's household and collect the lavish presents which were usual on such occasions.

Phelim complained a good deal at the terms which had been indicated to him by one of the Chief Poet's retinue, since naturally no artist of Olim's quality could be expected to concern himself with such sordid details.

" Where other members of the royal household have been glad to come for the sake of good company and a well-cooked meal," he grumbled to a vagrant poet who had just humbly asked for a night's lodging, " I must needs accept a scroll bearing one of Olim's less popular compositions for which I have not asked and present him with a couple of heifers and a bag of meal in exchange. People will not stand so very much more from these court poets. Why can they not behave as unlettered bards like yourself do ? You are made welcome enough, and you don't grudge us a song."

" I suppose a man may take to poetry for as many reasons as he takes to anything," Gemman said. He was a rough-looking man, well known as a landless bard who was often in their district and thankful to be given a night's lodging for the price of a song. He had arrived at Phelim's dun just before sunset that evening, as he often did, his small, eight-stringed harp slung in a worn leather bag across his shoulder as a warrior would have slung his shield. He never went to court, wore a threadbare old patched cloak and tunic, seemed interested in everybody and everything, and was happiest when he was allowed to sit in a corner near the fire, stroking his harp strings till they murmured gently as the household gathered round to tell him all that had happened since he had last been there.

" It is easy enough to guess Olim's motives," Phelim said.

" Oh, yes," Gemman agreed. " But they were probably very mixed, like most people's, you know. He is not without gifts. He was considered one of the most promising students in his class at the bardic school."

" H'm, was he ? And how did you know that ? "

" Because we were there together," said Gemman placidly.

Phelim's brows rose. " You, at a bardic school ? "

" Why not ? " asked Gemman pleasantly.

And all those years you've been to the dun, wearing clothes that look as if they grew about you, letting us think you unlettered . . ."

" Why not ? " said Gemman. " Provided my playing pleased you, what more was there to mind ? "

" Did you do well at the school ? " Phelim probed. " I doubt if they held you long, you wanderer. Were you a son of learning, or whatever they call their students in the first year ? Had you

the patience to stay longer? I forget what they call men in the
second year at those places . . ."

"Oh, I became an ollave eventually," Gemman admitted
with indifference.

"An ollave?" Phelim was amazed. Such nonchalance was
beyond his comprehension. "You could shake a golden branch
with Olim? You could claim all the honours you chose? Then,
why not? Stay here then, till Olim comes with all his retinue.
Let me confront him with you. I'll arrange a contest. It would
please me enormously."

But Gemman laid his cheek to the smooth, willow-wood
surface of his little harp without even troubling to refuse. "I'll
be no party to your niggling political devilments," he chuckled,
fumbling at his girdle for his tuning-key. "Olim has chosen to
use his gift to gain celebrity. That is his affair. Why should I
challenge him? He has the right to live his life his own way. I
will not use my music to humiliate him. Besides," he added, with
a shrewd grin. "It might not end in his humiliation. He may
be a vain man, but he is a gifted one, too."

Colum crept closer as Gemman tuned the little harp, watching
the skilled sensitive fingers as they moved across the brass strings,
the deft movements which altered the tension and changed the
sound. He was enthralled as much by the man, as by the music.
There was something about his self-chosen poverty, his detachment, his serenity, which were the echoes of something deeply
familiar, beloved, yet hard to name.

"Verse-making pleases you, doesn't it, son?" the poet said,
with one of his keen, friendly glances.

"Yes."

"Want to learn?"

"I—don't know."

"I could teach you. Don't go to the schools. They stuff
you full of rubbish for the sake of calling yourself an ollave and
being admired by fools. If you love words I can teach you to use
them. That's all that matters. At least, it's all that matters to
me. What are they going to make of you, eh?"

Colum said warily: "I don't know yet."

"Well, if you want to learn how to make verses, come to me.
If you want to get rich on them, you'll have to go elsewhere.
Remember that, will you?"

"I'll remember," Colum promised.

Gemman said no more on the subject, but his eyes sometimes
rested thoughtfully on the boy who crouched near his feet as he
began to sing. He had chosen one of the most tragic tales of

heroic friendship in the legends of Erin, the two knights compelled by their conflicting loyalties to fight each other to the death, in spite of a lifetime's friendship. The poet's voice, rising and falling against the golden background of the harp strings, seemed to reach beyond the limits of the story which told of men whose loyalty to their pledged word must oppose but could not destroy their lifetime's love for each other, so that as he sang he seemed to be searching, not only for the answer to their perplexity, but for the answer to humanity's eternal problem, the resolution of opposing allegiances which threaten to tear apart spirit and flesh.

To the back of the listening circle crept other men and women of the household, men and women from the huts which surrounded Phelim's larger home, children on tiptoe after their parents, wolf-dogs lured by the light and warmth that the open door promised, till the poet was surrounded by a solidly massed audience drawn from every corner of the dun.

Into the song he poured all the wealth of his life's experience to describe the anguish of conflict, and the astonishment of tenderness that followed it, for when each day's duel was over the heroes threw their arms about each other with tears. Every night Cuculainn sent his doctor to bind Ferdiad's wounds, before allowing him to attend to his own. And every night Ferdiad sent to Cuculainn the best of his food and wine before he had tasted them. As the poet paused the silence was absolute, and the sorrow that swept through him when at last Cuculainn flung himself in despair across the dead body of his friend was shared by all who listened, till the bonds which restrained each solitary personality were dissolved in pity, and for that instant of exultation each was no more alone, but fused, blended and made one with all the rest of that company, ennobled while the spell of Gemman's voice still held them by such grief and tenderness as would have been beyond individual capacity to endure. But together, and with the guidance of the poet's illuminated imagination, they were admitted into a visionary state which took them far past the limits of normal existence, purging them of all subtler alienations as it made them forgetful of the aches and infirmities of their bodies, lifting them up, as if on the summit of human experience, to receive a glimpse of the infinite ranges that lay beyond it, glorious in a sunrise splendour that was almost more than they could bear.

Then it was over. They stirred, were aware of each other, of their several selves again, of the splutter of a falling brand on the hearth, the yelp of a dog trodden on, the shrill protest of a child. Of the illumination, the enchantment, nothing remained, except, for nearly every one, an ache at the heart which was like that of a wanderer waking among alien mountains who has for a timeless moment seen the doorway of his home in a dream.

Then someone clapped his hands, and immediately the whole place crackled with the anti-climax of their applause. But Colum, taken unawares by tears and shaken beyond bearing, was already kicking and cuffing his way towards the door, dodging between legs and round the bodies of people sitting on the ground, tripping over dogs and pushing his way past staring children, till at last he ran out into the darkness, sobbing as he went.

For some time he paid no attention to where he was going: it was only important that he should outdistance the desperate pain within him which he could neither endure nor understand. Pain of the body was bad, but it was ordinary. A tooth ached when another was coming and pushed its way up from below. He knew all about that. A foot ached when a thorn had been run into it, when he had cut or grazed it by falling down. The body felt pain when someone struck it. His stomach was disturbed when he had eaten something that was bad and must be got rid of. His head ached when he knocked it against something, or after he had sat too long in the sun. There were also times when his body came out in a rash of spots and he had to lie all day in his sleeping-place eating nothing and drinking only water till the fire within him had died down.

But this was different, this was something far worse than toothache or fever or bruises because it was not localised to a pounding point of pain or an area of itching, angry skin. When he had been ill or injured he had seemed to lose consciousness of everything except the affected part, as if all his life were occupied in trying to bear it, so that apart from his aching tooth or head or knee the rest of him scarcely lived. But now . . . he was aware of himself acutely, dreadfully, with a sudden enlargement of understanding for which he had been utterly unprepared, which had flooded through him as he crouched by the hearth listening to Gemman, and had not ebbed from him as from the others when the general emotion had died down.

On the contrary, it had remained upon him so strongly that the change of mood in the hall had been more than he could stand. When he had felt the strange beauty fade from the people about him he had been compelled to rush out into the darkness, since for all its anguish, it had struck him most with a shock, not of strangeness, but of unexpected familiarity, so that in his newly sensitised awareness he longed for the fulfilment of its promise with the desperation of an exile, yet because he did not know what he was looking for he pursued it wildly, exhausting himself physically in the search for something that was not physical at all.

Mature as the rough-and-tumble life in the dun had made him in some ways, Colum's development had inevitably been lop-sided. His upbringing had laid great stress on physical strength and independence, but his active mind had been left to make its own discoveries, except for the Christian teaching which his mother had tried to give him, and to which, boylike, he had not listened much. There were so many more interesting things to engross him, in the stables, the cow-sheds, on the loughs and among the hills. He had grown fast, eaten enormously, wondered and speculated and watched the people and beasts around him. Sometimes he had understood far more than the average child of his age and time, and, now and then, less. He had a profound native innocence, so that many coarse allusions went by him on the wind. But spiritual experience had only recently come upon him, come in a series of shocks which had flung him off his balance and left him to struggle stubbornly but inarticulately to regain it.

First had come the horrible experience of the tests, and now he had been confronted by an experience which had been just as overwhelming in a different way. At the tests Colum had learned something of the horror of isolating darkness in which evil had sought to impress its own nightmare shape upon his unwary spirit. Now, as he listened to Gemman, he had become aware that even the most perverse and far-strayed of light-craving creatures may yet receive his birthright again. He was too young, too inarticulate to try to express either the violence of his revulsion from the alien misery of evil, or the delight of his return to what seemed his native state of joy. He could only blunder about among ideas and emotions as he was blundering on the hillside, neither knowing what was happening to his wakening, distracted spirit nor where his feet would carry him next.

The winter night was not very cold, nor was it continuously dark, for a gibbous moon was scudding between the cloud-banks, from which, every now and then, came heavy showers of rain which drenched and bewildered Colum, as he slithered and scrambled, instinctively trying, like any other distracted creature, to exhaust himself, to obliterate in sleep the memory of emotional experiences whose significance he could not comprehend.

Strong as he was, the hillside was steep, and he had thrown himself at it without attempting to find any track. Though spiritually he seemed to have covered vast distances and left all familiar landmarks far behind him, it was not very long, in terms of space and time, before he was breathless, so that he had to stop, clinging to a large boulder as he blinked the rain out of his eyes and wondered what to do.

Without knowing it, he had struggled round the shoulder of the hill, so that the lights of the plain below were hidden from him by a surge of rock and heather which was itself only visible occasionally as the clouds shreded away from the face of the moon which appeared to be racing through a chaotic sea of shadows, taking the hillside on which he stood with it, so that there seemed to be nothing stable or steadfast, either in heaven or on earth.

As his breath came more easily and the pain in his side died down, Colum began to look about him, and to think of those more prosaic aspects of life which he had forgotten ever since he heard Gemman's song. He was hungry again, and the warmth of the climb was beginning to leave him. His tunic was clammily heavy on his shoulders, and his hair hung limp in a mass from which streams ran into his eyes. Colum shivered. What was he doing here, out on the hills in the middle of the night ? Why had he come ? And then, more urgently, how was he to find his way back ?

Looking anxiously round, he could see no lights below him, not even the water of the nearest lough, which should surely have shown up as a pale shield lying on the dark plain. Stiffly he turned his head to look upwards. There, at least, was a light, a steady light, that might well come from a shepherd's hut. His feet were sore, after climbing so wildly without shoes, but he limped hopefully on, since the light at least meant a human being of some sort who could help and direct him. At last he came out on a little plateau, which, even in the dark, was vaguely familiar. On it was a low stone building, backed by a few wattled huts. The light came through the open door of the building, and Colum, approaching it doubtfully, looked into the oratory as once, years before, his own father had done.

An old man in a long, shabby, lichen-grey tunic, whom Colum seemed to remember as if from dreams in which his mother asked this old man's blessing, was sitting at a small desk which had been roughly made from hand-dressed logs. He had a feather in his hand, the end of which he dipped now and then into a horn which was attached to the edge of the desk, and then made marks with it on some sort of pale, stretched stuff which was lying in front of him. Colum remembered that the lawyers had shown each other scrolls covered with just such marks, and the old man looked kindly, even familiar, though he himself was too tired to remember when he had seen him before. He raised his hand, hesitated an instant, and then knocked.

The old priest Cruithann laid down the quill with which he was transcribing one of the Psalms, took up the rushlight which stood on the far side of the desk from the ink-horn, and went to the door. Seeing nothing at first, he held the light higher, shielding it with his other hand as he peered in astonishment at a soaked, exhausted child.

" Why, who art thou, son, and why art thou out so late ? "

Colum felt oddly comforted by the gentle voice, strangely though the stately, archaic phrasing that came from the use of much Latin sounded to his unaccustomed ears. He took a step over the well-worn door-sill.

" I am Colum, sir, son of Phelim and Eithne of the loughside dun. And I—I have lost my way home."

The old man smiled as he stood aside for the boy to pass him, then closed the door upon the searching, gusty wind.

" Lost the way home ? " he said slowly. " Nay Columba, I think thou hast found it, my son."

II

Terce

" *Ego sum pastor ille bonus, et agnosco meas,
et agnoscor a meis. . .*"

JOANNES : X : 14

CHAPTER V

THE DAY after Colum left the dun Maeve returned to it. She carried her few personal possessions in a bundle, and her face was cynically amused as she drew aside the leather curtain and waited for the questions to begin. But Phelim and Eithne, facing each other across the rough table, seemed scarcely aware of her. The tears that slid down Eithne's frightened face fell fast on her clasped hands, and Phelim was drumming on the scarred wood in front of him with the blade of his sheath-knife.

" Why, what's the matter with you both ? " Maeve demanded, her voice edged with disappointment at the failure of her dramatic entry. She had been prepared for scolding, horror, and dismay. But she had not expected to be ignored, and it was in her character to endure anger, reproaches, or any sort of emotional storm more easily than indifference.

" Oh, Maeve, Colum's gone . . ."

" Gone ? Gone where ? " Maeve set down her bundle and flung back her cloak. She was flushed with indignation and fast walking, her clothes were old and mud-stained, and there were bruise-marks on the upper arms that the short-sleeved gown left bare. Phelim surveyed her gloomily, the existence of a new crisis slowly impressing itself on his mind, but denied precision by preoccupation with his own.

" We don't know where he's gone. He was here last night, listening to the singing. No one's seen him since."

Maeve tossed her head till her long hair, heavy in its braids, swung across her back. " He's gone off with a friend to torment you. There's nothing in that. Boys are all alike. When have they ever taken the trouble to say where they're going when they rush out of the homestead on their own affairs ? "

" We have asked every one," Eithne said. " He is not in the dun."

" Nor in any other within five miles," said Phelim. " I sent messengers at daybreak. I have had men searching the loughs, tracing the streams, scouring the hills. What do you suppose ? "

" I suppose," said Maeve tartly, " that Colum is hiding somewhere, just to give you a fright. You must be crazed to raise the countryside for the sake of one naughty child. I should get a belt ready and be prepared to welcome him home warmly when it suits him to appear ! "

" I have questioned Gemman," said Phelim, as if he had not heard her. The monotonous sound of his knife-blade on the table was like the drumming of rain on a shield. " He can tell me nothing. He spoke to the boy during the evening, and noticed how intently he was listening to his songs. He did not see him again."

" Who is this Gemman ? "

" A wandering singer."

" Did Colum run off after him ? "

" No. I thought of that. After Gemman left this morning I had him brought back for questioning. He said he knew nothing and I believed him."

" Believed him ? A vagrant ? He may have bewitched the boy with his singing and be holding him concealed against future needs. Your eldest son would make a useful hostage for one of the southern clans, Phelim." Maeve was obviously enjoying the prospect of drama. Better any excitement than none, even though her own adventures might have to wait for the telling.

" No," Phelim said.

" Why not ? "

" This man was an ollave, a doctor of poetry, a great artist without the flicker of an eye towards gain . . ."

" An ollave ? You said he was a vagrant ? "

" That too."

Maeve raised her hands in a gesture of bewilderment. " A great man and a vagrant ? The two things do not go together. They curdle each other as the juice of a cow's stomach curdles its own milk. What has happened, then ? "

" I have just told you," said Phelim harshly, " that I do not know. We are waiting for the return of the men from the loughs and the mountains. If he wandered far from the dun in the darkness anything may have happened. There have been wolves about, after the flocks . . ."

Eithne shuddered. " Phelim, you don't think—you can't mean——"

" I don't know what to think," said Phelim curtly. Then he turned abruptly on his sister-in-law. " What brings you back so soon ? " he demanded, more in the hope of distracting Eithne's attention than because he cared to know. What Eithne would do if any harm had come to Colum he could not imagine. Women had no fortitude when it came to their children. He himself . . . had learned to take things as they came. But all his own fear was in his voice as he questioned Maeve.

She stood with her hands on her hips and her lip curling.

" Soon ? It is all but three years since I left your dun, Phelim."

" It has not seemed so long," said Phelim rudely. " Late or soon, what brings you back ? "

" I was thrown out of Nordal's hut," she said simply.

" I'm not surprised."

" I did not expect you to be." Her anger blazed up, like a moor fire that has been smouldering for a long time, only needing a little wind to urge it into flame. " I would not have come to you except that your dun lay in my path homewards."

" Homewards ? "

" I am going back to Laigen."

" To Laigen ? "

" To my parents' home. My cousin is king there to-day, king since my father's death. He will be interested to hear what sort of treatment I have received from the Hy Niall. Very interested, I believe, Phelim. I think they will be kinder to me in Laigen than you have been. And afterwards . . . perhaps Laigen's warriors may be less kind to you."

Phelim threw down his knife and spread out his fingers on the table, groping towards the cracks in the wood as if he were reaching for harp strings. He looked up at Maeve under his brows. So that was what was in her mind. It would not be the first time war had been kindled by a woman. But war with Laigen would mean trouble for him. The king of the Hy Niall did not wish that old wound to break out again.

" You need not go," he said.

" That is kind indeed," Maeve mocked him. " But I am already on my way."

Phelim brought clenched fists down on the board. " You shall not go," he shouted suddenly.

Maeve gave him a crooked smile. " Ah, now we know where we are," she said.

" I do not care what you say," roared Phelim furiously. " You shall obey me. That is all I care about. You will stay here till I have time to find out the rights and wrongs of this."

" I will tell you myself," Maeve said blandly.

Phelim snapped his fingers.

" You need not be so impatient," Maeve said. " I shall not lie. Why should I ? People lie when they are afraid and I am not afraid of any man. There is no sense in telling lies. One might as well be dumb like the beasts. Ask what you want to know, Phelim. I shall tell you."

She stood there in her faded gown and loosened cloak, hands on hips, swinging slightly from side to side like a dancer,

smiling down at him, teasing at his anger, offering him the truth
as if she were holding a bone high for a dog so that he must
jump and snatch for it. Phelim's hands, spread out on the table,
clutched suddenly like talons. Maeve laughed.

"You would like to beat me, wouldn't you, Phelim? You
would like to hurt me till I cried for mercy. I know. Let me tell
you now that you would be wasting your time. I would let you
tear the flesh from my bones before I uttered one cry. Put that
idea away, dear and gentle brother. I promise you that it would
be most disappointingly dull."

"Stop talking," said Phelim abruptly, appalled by the surge
of wrath and lust that something about Maeve's very presence
roused in him. "Tell me what happened. What made you come
here?"

"I told you," said Maeve indifferently. "Nordal beat me.
Then he threw me out of his hut, and the few things that were
mine he threw after me. So I picked them up and set off on my
way home to Laigen."

"You are not going to Laigen," said Phelim, grating the
words between his teeth.

"You will keep me in fetters?"

"If need be. Why did Nordal beat you?"

"Because he said I received other men while he was at the
hunt."

"And was it true?"

"Oh, yes," said Maeve tonelessly.

"True? You admit it? Have you no shame? Why did
you do such a thing?"

Meave yawned. "It was dull."

"Dull? So the Hy Niall are to go to war with the men of
Laigen just because time passes too slowly for an idle woman?"

Maeve shrugged. "You do not know what it is to be a
woman, Phelim. Especially a woman whose man is so jealous
that he will not let her stir across the threshold or even admit
other women in his absence to help her grind the corn. It—it is
not good for me to be alone."

"Indeed, so it seems."

"I would not have been so rash if I had not been so lonely,"
said Maeve, and her voice was suddenly both sincere and piteous.
"You can sneer if you like, Phelim. That is true."

"True or false, it puts me in a most awkward position,"
Phelim grumbled. "I shall have to take advice. I must lay the
whole question before the king. It may affect my position at
court. It will probably mean——"

" It will mean nothing to your disadvantage," said Maeve
disdainful again. " Nordal can do no more. The people concerned
are too important. If he had only kept quiet I should have been
most useful to him. His stupid jealousy has spoiled everything.
Just because he could not go and break some of the most important heads in Ulaid, he tried to wring my neck. There are the
marks."

" H'm," said Phelim, glancing without interest at Meave's
dramatically   bared   throat.   " That's   rather   different,
perhaps . . ."

" Quite different," agreed Maeve scornfully. " Well, now
I've set your mind at rest, Phelim, I think I'll be going . . ."

" I've told you already," said Phelim viciously, " that you're
to stay where you are. Have I to put the chains of a hostage on
you to make you see reason ? "

" No, thank you," Maeve said. " Nordal did that, you know.
My wrists are still seared with his fetters. You can see those
marks too. And . . . others, if you care to look for them . . ."

" I don't," said Phelim hastily. " If you do what you're told
you will be kindly treated here. For here you shall stay."

" Is that your wish, Phelim ? "

" It is my command."

" So I am to stay here because you command it ? I have
not taken refuge in your dun ? On the contrary, I have been
kept here against my will ? Is that correct, Phelim ? "

" That is correct," snapped Phelim. " I did not ask you to
return. I do not want you here. But since you've come for
purposes of your own, here you shall stay, for mine."

" Very well, Phelim," said Meave submissively. It was odd,
she was thinking, how stupid men were, even those who thought
themselves cleverest. How easy it had been to get Phelim to make
her stay. In actual fact she had never had any intention of going
further. Laigen was far away, and the cousin who was king there
had disliked her from a child. She yawned as she turned away.
Now she had got her own way she was bored again.

" Eithne . . . I wanted to ask you . . ." she began, suddenly
remembering the existence of her sister. But she stopped in
mid-sentence, for the place opposite Phelim was empty. While
they had been absorbed in their argument Eithne had slipped
unobtrusively away. " I never knew such a place," said Maeve,
good-tempered again now that she had got her way, " everybody
seems to be disappearing. Where's she gone, Phelim ? "

But Phelim was still angry. He was also vaguely uncom-
fortable, aware that in some way Maeve seemed to consider that

she had got the better of him. She needn't be so sure. He'd have
a hostage's fetters on her if she tried any little tricks like slipping
away. As for Eithne, she was probably trailing about the dun
asking every one she met for news of Colum that they hadn't got.
Women . . .

"How do I know where anybody is ? " he said huffily.

Colum did not remember much after his arrival at the
oratory. Dreamily he had submitted to being wrapped in a dry
cloak and given a bowl filled with goat's milk and a crust of
bread. Then he had rolled himself up in the cloak and let himself
slip into sleep so deep that neither the sound of the wind that beat
against the frail mud-daubed hut at the back of the oratory nor
the whispers of the other boys who shared it with him had done
more than ripple its surface with inconsequent dreams. It was
broad daylight when he stirred, for the priest had said he was
not to be roused for the first office, and the pupils had already
done their morning tasks when Colum at last unrolled himself
from the cloak and emerged from the hut.

His surroundings were entirely strange to him. He could not
make out how or why he had come there. The little settlement
consisted of several bee-hive huts, woven of wicker and wind-
proofed with clay or turf. These huddled among the rocks as if
for shelter, while the little dry-stone oratory, its walls and roof
of carefully placed layers of stones which converged towards a
ridge-pole apex, stood against the full force of any winds that
blew. Ashes of a fire still glowed in the open space or were dusted
about in the eddies of the light breeze to which the gale had died
down. Piles of turf for thatching were stacked against one of the
huts and a quern for grinding corn stood outside another. Firewood was heaped against the oratory's sheltering wall.

As Colum stood staring about him a bigger boy came out of
the oratory and beckoned. "Come here, you," he commanded.

Still in a daze, Colum obeyed him. As he turned the corner
by the oratory he saw the familiar loughs, far below, shining in
the pale sunshine. Now he knew where he was. He had sometimes been brought to the oratory by his mother, and she had
often told him that soon he would live there all the time. Perhaps
. . . that was why he had come . . . he couldn't quite make it
out. It had all been so dark and blurred. He could only remember
the lovely, piercing-sweetness of Gemman's voice hurting him so
desperately that he had tried to escape from it by running . . .
somewhere . . . anywhere . . . so long as he got away. He
could remember climbing, climbing, in the dimness of cloud-
blurred moonlight, not knowing where to go, and yet being sure,

in some way, that he must keep on. It was all very strange. He felt utterly bewildered. His life, which had been at first like a sunlit stream idling between flowering meadows, had lately been flung about between precipices and rocks. It had all been frightening and confused. Suddenly he wanted his mother. His throat stiffened and constricted as he blinked away ignominious tears.

The big boy in the rough tunic shut the door behind them, then took Colum by the elbow and guided him forward to where about a dozen other boys were kneeling before the old priest. Colum knelt down beside them, puzzled but obedient. The priest was intoning words in a strange language, and the boys repeating them afterwards in the Gaelic that they understood. At first Colum heard scarcely anything, for in his bemused state the words were no more than a buzz. But little by little, they began to hold meaning for him, and with that gradual realisation came a slow sense of uncomprehended but infinite comfort, blessing his frightened spirit with homecoming and peace.

" *Ego sum pastor ille bonus . . .*" said the priest.

" I am the good shepherd . . ." whispered the children.

" *Et agnosco meas, et agnoscor a meis . . .*"

" I know my sheep . . . and am known of mine . . ."

It was more of a lesson than a service, for every now and then the priest would pause to correct his pupils over the pronunciation of an unfamiliar word, or to explain the meaning of an unexpected phrase. The boys had no books, but it seemed that they knew most of the chapter by heart, for there were few mistakes. Colum began to picture this shepherd, comparing him with the herdsmen of the dun, whose business it was to keep the sheep and swine off the standing crops ; mostly boys who had not the stomach for soldiering, or old men who had been crippled by their wounds and were glad to pick up a living by guarding the local herds. They were hardly reliable, for they were apt to spend a good deal of time dozing in the lee of a convenient rock, and when there was danger they usually fled howling. His father was continually trouncing them and complaining that they were more trouble than they were worth. Hirelings, he grumbled, were all alike.

" *Mercenarius autem fugit, quia mercenarius est, et non est illi cura ovium . . .*"

" The hireling fleeth because he is an hireling, and careth not . . ."

But this other shepherd, it seemed, was different. Colum wondered what his father would say about someone who fought like a champion instead of drowsing and yelling like a herd.

"*Animam meam depono pro ovibus. . . .*"

"I lay down my life for the sheep."

A wave of memory swept over Colum. He was back again in the timbered hall of his home, listening to Gemman's heart-breaking lovely voice, as he sang of the two friends who had kept their pledged word though the keeping of it broke their hearts. Again he felt the emotion of the people round him, lifting him, child though he was, into a plane of experience far beyond anything he had ever known, as if to a pinnacle from which, on the far horizon, rose the ramparts of another world. Dimly he realised how closely the feeling roused in him by the bard's song was akin to what he was experiencing now. Both hurt him almost unbearably, so that he felt as if he were being torn apart, both brought with them the same promise of intangible things about which there were hints everywhere, as of a dearer reality that lay just beyond the hoizon of the familiar world. It was also in the legends that Nalda had whispered to him of the shee, the strange, beautiful people whose hosting was like the movement of the wind across the corn's innumerable spears. It was in all that the historians had told him of the god-like heroes of the past, in all the poets had ever sung of Tir-nan-Og, the Land of the Young. It was, he dimly felt, in much that the judges had told him of the yearning of even the most ordinary people for justice and truth. It was here too, here more than ever, though as he listened, crouching in his dim corner with the pebbles in the mud floor patterning his aching knees, he could not yet say how or why.

"*Alias etiam oves habeo, quae non sunt ex hac caula . . .*"

"Other sheep I have, which are not of this fold. Them also I must bring . . ."

Floundering among unfamiliar sensations, grasping elusive ideas at random, as he had often grasped at the silvery-bellied minnows in the leaf-patterned shallows of lough or stream, Colum only heard words here and there ; strange, sonorous words which had a solemn grandeur like the altar-fires of the old faith that Nalda had told him were kindled on the hill-tops on certain nights of the year. But afterwards the boys repeated them in their homely Gaelic, and it made them comfortingly familiar, like the fire at dusk that lit up the timber walls of his own home. Colum rocked back on his heels to rest his knees a little, while the voices went on telling their strange story of the shepherd who foretold his own death and promised to return from the dead, and how people who tried to stone him because he had said he was a God.

"*Oves illae meae vocem meam audiunt . . . et ego vitam aeternam do eis . . .*"

"My sheep hear my voice and . . . I give unto them eternal life ; and they shall never perish, neither shall any man pluck them out of my hand . . ."

"*Ego et Pater unum sumus.*"

"I and my Father are one. Then the Jews took up stones again to stone him . . ."

Colum's eyes widened with distress. Why was it that lovely things were always sad ? Gemman's friends, weeping over each other's wounds, this shepherd who promised that his sheep should never perish, and seemed likely to be stoned to death . . . why was it ? Why did the clash of weapons, the thud of stones, the sound of weeping always divide people from the things they longed for most ? Was it because it was useless to long for them, or was it because the things of one world tugged against those of another, threatening to tear people apart as he had seen two puppies tearing his father's leather battle-coat ? It had been very funny watching the puppies, but there hadn't been much left of the coat.

Colum felt happier when he had remembered the puppies. The lovely things drew him always, but he did not like being sad. Instinctively, without being able to put the shape of his thought into words, he knew that happiness was a right thing, like sunlight, that when it was taken away from him he felt that something had gone wrong. If it was the tug between two sets of ideas that made for unhappiness, then surely it would be better to let one set of ideas go. The battle-coat would not have been torn if one of the dogs had given up the struggle and sat down to scratch for fleas.

If it was necessary to give up one set of ideas he would do it, because he couldn't bear to go on being torn apart. But which should he give up ? He couldn't bear to lose the lovely things that haunted him from the background of Gemman's songs, and Nalda's secretly whispered stories, and the old priest's words. But if any one gave up all the good things of ordinary life, how could he enjoy being alive ?

While he was still puzzling things out, the priest dismissed the boys who had been repeating the Gospel with him. He made a sign in the air above them, said something in the strange language, nodded and turned away. The boys made the same sign in the air, rose and stood in a line before him, ducked their heads, then turned and walked out. While they were still going towards the door Colum noticed that their faces were grave and their hands clasped before them, but once the door had banged shut behind the smallest boy who came at the end of the decorous line he could hear scuffles and shouts outside. Colum rose uncertainly, wondering whether the priest had forgotten him, and what he ought to do. But the old man was smiling quite kindly as he came and sat down near the door, on a stool.

"Well, Columba, thou hast been quiet as a mouse in the thatch all through our lesson. Now it is thy turn. Tell me, have they taught thee anything at home?"

"Oh, yes, sir. A great deal," said Colum proudly.

"They call me father here," said the old priest mildly. "These are my foster-children, whom I must teach, cherish and clothe as if they were my own. Tell me, Columba, what have they taught thee? Thy letters?"

"No, Father. But Tombul taught me to break a javelin on a shield at twenty paces . . ."

"Indeed . . ."

"I can ride a horse bareback if he is not too fat for my knees to grip him. I can swim and manage a boat . . ."

"Yes, that is always useful . . ."

"I—I can use shield, dagger and sword," said Colum hopefully, though with the memory of the tests came the memory of horror and blood and darkness, so that he frowned, shaking his head as if to get rid of a stinging cloud of gnats.

"And wert thou happy as a warrior, Columba?"

"I—I don't know. At first it was exciting. Tombul had taught us all, you see. I knew it all well. I am very strong and big for my age, sir. They said I fought well. But . . . that time . . . I don't know what happened . . . it was awful . . ."

"Tell me what happened, my son."

"Well . . ." said Colum. "Something seemed to rush on me like darkness . . . something that was outside me, weighing me down. But it was inside my head as well . . ."

Crossing himself, the old priest nodded. Colum, once started on the account of something he had never meant to think of again, found the words come more easily, felt the remembered darkness, which had seemed thick about him again as he began to talk of it, slowly thin away, with its horror and stench and solitude, till he was once more in the blessed daylight, sweating and shivering, as if he had come through a gruesome conflict, but quiet again, free, and amazed at the difference that the telling of his story had made.

"Is there anything more that thou wouldst feel the lighter for having told me?" asked the old priest.

Colum tried to remember.

"I was angry with Maeve once. I hit her. I'd have bitten

her if I could. That felt bad, but only for a little while. Someone made me laugh and the darkness left me."

The old priest bowed his head. "Yes, such laughter is from heaven. Remember that, Columba, when evil anger comes upon thee. Is there anything more?"

"I—I have been angry with my brothers and beaten them. But they had taken away things which were mine."

"Hast thou felt worse hatred against any creature?"

"No—at least—only Maeve, perhaps. She is my mother's sister who used to live with us. But she is gone now to live in another dun. So that does not matter," said Colum thankfully.

The priest hid a smile with his long fingers. "Well . . ."

"I can never hate people for long," said Colum candidly. "I can hate them terribly when they spoil the things I want to do. But then I forget all about it."

"Perhaps that is something to begin on. One day, I hope thou wilt be unable to hate any creature, anywhere, at all."

Colum's eyes were round as he shook his head. "I don't think that's possible, Father. I don't think I could ever be like that if I lived for a hundred years."

"Well, son, we shall see. And now," the old priest added, more briskly, "we must think of nearer things. Now thou hast come, we must waste no more time, for there is everything to learn yet before thee. Thou art the youngest here by more than two years. I will teach thee thy letters, and the beginning of scribing, and thou shalt hear us say the offices. More, at first, would be beyond thee. Thou wilt take thy turn to fetch wood and grind corn and bring water, Doeg will show thee such things. And now . . ."

He broke off at the sound of hasty footsteps. Hands were fumbling at the fastening of the door. Slowly, he rose from the low stool which had cramped his limbs and went to raise the latch which had stuck fast when the boys slammed it. Eithne, breathless and tear-streaked, was standing outside.

"Well, my child, what brings thee here in such haste?" he asked mildly. "What can have gone wrong so soon?"

"Oh, Father, it's Colum. I don't know where to look . . . he's gone . . . the men of the dun have searched everywhere . . ."

"The child is here," said the old man.

"Here . . . ?" Eithne gazed round the oratory in amazement. "Colum . . . here?"

"Did you not send him, then?"

"Send him? No . . . he ran from us last night . . . Colum, how could you do it? We have searched high and low for you.

Your father has had the men out since daylight. They have netted the lough and followed the streams and been out on the mountains. Every stranger had been questioned, every dun has had messengers . . ."

The old man stroked his beard and waited calmly till she paused for breath, as if, like so many other tumults, he had let this commotion pass him by.

" But child, he was always to be my fosterling," he said at last. " If he was not at home, where else should you look for him to be ? "

CHAPTER VI

WHERE HE WAS, there he remained. Phelim's imagination had been so inflamed by fantasies of malignant enemies or devouring wolves that he had ceased to believe that his son might still be alive. So Eithne's return, radiant with the news of her discovery, rescued him from such a pit of brooding that he received the news itself with relief. As for Colum's future, it seemed to have slid out of his hands. He had promised that the boy should have a free choice : he could not now go back on his word. Admittedly he had done his utmost to weight the scales in the direction of his own ambitions, but having failed, as he admitted with cynical philosophy, he could do no more.

Maeve, established in the dun again, watched both Colum's parents in her secret way. It amused her to think that they were planning to make a saint out of the child she had so often teased till he lost his temper. Sanctity was not something Maeve had often encountered. She had no knowledge of its nature, only of its counterfeits and symbols, all of which roused in her an angry impatience, further increased by jealousy of her sister who sat there so contentedly, a little smile curving her lips as she thought, Maeve knew, of her darling who had been saved from the wickedness of the world. The sight infuriated Maeve, childless and solitary as she was, out of all reason. Why they set such store by the brat to begin with, she could not imagine. He was like any other ; noisy, dirty and foolish most of the time, and when he was different she liked him still less. A saint, they meant him to be. Maeve smiled a small, secret smile as she bent her head over her embroidery. It would not be her fault if he did not prove a sinner.

But there was time enough for that, yes, plenty of time. It

would amuse her to wait, to let him sail along with his silly head among the stars. And then . . . and then . . . Maeve jabbed her needle savagely among the bright colours, wincing as she pricked her finger, drawing blood. Her smile had become merely a twisted, wry gesture of the lips, holding less mirth than guile.

"So he has gone from us, has he, our little churchman, our valiant Colum-Cille?" she said at last.

"Oh, no," Eithne said. "We shall see him often, I hope. He isn't far away, and the priest knows that little boys can be heartsick when they leave home. At first, he said, we would be wiser to leave him in their keeping, in case it should make it harder if we went to see him too much. We must give him time to settle. Then it will do him no harm to see us. He may even come to see us if he wishes, now and then."

"Perhaps, now he has become so holy, he will not want to come back among us sinners," Maeve teased.

Phelim looked up at her angrily, checking a sharp comment. But Eithne merely smiled, as she paused to choose thread of another colour. "Well, we shall see."

Colum's departure caused quite a sensation in the dun. His performance at the tests was still remembered by the women who wondered what would happen to their sons if they came to be matched against him, the older men could scarcely believe that Phelim should allow his son to abandon such a promising career, and the lads who had played and trained with him gaped in amazement at the idea of Colum giving up the exciting life of a warrior for the drab existence of a priest.

The nickname that Maeve had given him was taken up by every one who heard it. So Colum the warrior had become Colum-Cille, Colum of the Church, had he? Well, well, well . . . sometimes Maeve's own derisive giggle went with it, and sometimes Eithne's loving air of awe, when other mothers came to discuss their children's future with her. Tombul used it with undisguised relief on the one occasion he ventured to bring the matter up with Phelim, but the asperity with which Phelim told him to mind his own business was enough to discourage him from ever mentioning Colum and his career again.

Colum himself was unaware of these conflicting currents of opinion. Like most small boys spending more than a few hours away from home, the strangeness of his new environment engrossed his entire attention. It was a period of assimilation, rather than one of progress, a time for the reception of new things, the acceptance of knowledge, ideas, sensations, above all of that mysterious gift of grace, the spiritual sunlight

which nourishes a growing soul. As the youngest and newest
pupil, he spent hours with the old priest in the oratory, learning
to make his letters with a stump of charcoal on a smoothed
board which was washed and dried between lessons, to repeat the
Paternoster and the Gloria, the Tersanctus and the Canon of the
Mass. With a child's receptive memory and a poet's appreciation
of beautiful words, these things came easily to him. But his
heritage of legend and story made him always glad when the
more academic part of his instruction was over, for then the old
priest would tell him of the coming of Heaven's young Prince of
Glory, speaking with the same wonder with which Nalda told
stories of the Land of the Young or Manannan the Beautiful.
The old priest showed no hostility to the earlier hierarchy,
benevolent or malignant, the company of the semi-divine heroes
and the unearthly loveliness of the shee. Far from telling Colum
that he must no longer believe in the legends of his babyhood he
used them for the grounding of a soul already apt to wonder, to
whom he hoped to offer the heaven-lit paradoxes of the strangest
story of them all.

He was a good teacher, wise from long years of ministering to
children whose future lay among religious mysteries, and would
afterwards be sent among men and women as poets rather than
preachers, as torches kindled in heaven to catch the imagination
of a people awed by the beauties of earth. Doctrine his children
would learn when they went on to the great monastic schools
of Clonard or Moville. Disputation might eventually be useful
to some. But without illumination none of them would be fit to
serve the people at all. Doctrine and dogma might be necessary
to man, but the vision itself came from God. It was difficult
sometimes, to remember exactly what he had told them, as they
knelt round him in the oratory, fidgeting a little, as was the nature
of young creatures, nudging each other and whispering when
they thought he did not notice, drooping a little wearily now and
then. He only knew that he was seeking with all his strength,
with his concentrated and transmuted will, with all the warmth
of a deep and quiet love for the beings entrusted to him, with all
the simplicity of his own child-like, child-comprehending soul,
to give them the treasure of inner vision with which he himself
had been blessed.

Sometimes he wondered how much of what he had tried to
teach remained with them when they ran shouting about in the
sunshine, reacting inevitably from the strain of memorisation and
repetition imposed on them. It was difficult to guess. Their
faces were docile and blank. Columba was different. Columba's

expression changed like the colours of an April hillside when the cloud-shadows chased each other across it. He knew that Columba would accept all he could offer in great gulps, like a greedy puppy which is aware of its own hunger, but has no knowledge of the most suitable food, for which responsibility lies on the man who feeds it.

The old priest treated all his pupils with the grave courtesy proper to illustrious guests, but he often found himself watching Columba with special interest, as if aware that in this child a spirit of unusual quality had been entrusted to him. It was difficult to give precise, intellectualised reasons for this impression. Logical reasoning was not an habitual occupation with the old man. Unlike the fishermen who waded thigh-deep in the shallower waters of the loughs by night with spears and torches in their hands, their feet planted securely on the mud and pebbles of its bed, he had come to abandon the limitations and restrictions of the intellect and throw himself upon the greater resources of the spirit as a swimmer throws himself upon the surface of the sea.

In the days which followed Columba's arrival he pondered a good deal about the boy. It was not only his ardour, his eager brain, his gaiety, which drew the old man's attention, but something less easy to define, yet impossible to miss, something that made his bright head shine sometimes, he fancied, among the shadows, so that it seemed darker in the oratory when the boy had gone. Was it an illusion, sent to mislead a presumptuous old fool? Or was it, perhaps, a token that the hand of heaven had already been laid upon this young child? The old priest shook his head as he crossed himself. He could not tell.

Nor could Columba tell why the new, arduous, frugal life made him so happy. He received it all, wide-armed, and hugged it to him with delight; church services, Latin repetitions, shared tasks of all kinds, the cheerful companionship of his friends and the occasional head-cuffings of bigger boys. The lessons fed his receptive brain, the companionship comforted the child's ache for his mother's gentleness. He accepted it all; the squabbling and rivalry, the painful scribing of his first chapter of the Gospel on an old, stained skin which someone had already spoiled and discarded, with ink that lumped and gouted, and a badly split quill that spat. Slowly, with daily repetition, the incomprehensible Latin words became familiar, and, as the old priest explained the first principles of grammar, their vagaries began to take some sort of shape. Poet as he was to be, the sound of words already had the power to move him far more strongly than the loveliest harping that was wordless. The repetition of the Gospels, which occupied some part of each day, made so deep an impression on him that the Latin words and their homelier translation were to remain interwoven in his memory all his life long. In spite of the familiarity with the Latin text which was to come in later years from infinitely painstaking study and endless transcription, Columba was always to recall the sonorous phrases as they were echoed in the Gaelic of his childhood by the just-breaking voices of his first friends.

Day succeeded day so uneventfully that he sometimes felt he had spent scarcely more than a few hours at the oratory, and sometimes that he had been there since the beginning of time. But in some strange way the seasons appeared to gain speed as they followed each other, until, before it seemed possible, he had been a pupil of the kind old priest for seven whole years.

He was growing fast now, but taking his strength with him so that he remained sturdy as he grew tall. The simplicity of the life suited him : he asked nothing better than the bread, porridge, eggs, fish and milk on which they lived. Strict fasting was considered beyond the strength of children, but on Wednesdays and Fridays there was bread and milk only, and the old priest ate nothing till the evening. The manual work of the settlement was graded to their strength, but something was expected of everybody. Fishing, harvesting and husbandry in general were supervised by two lay-brothers and done by the boys in turn.

The humbler tasks had at first been as new to Columba as the Latin version of his name. Like any other nobleman's son he had already been instructed in archery, swimming and chess playing, the use of sword and spear and the management of a horse. But at the oratory Columba had learned to herd swine, milk cattle and shear sheep, to sow, reap and kiln-dry the corn which in wet seasons would have rotted if it had been left out in the settlement's small fields. He had learned in his seven years' apprenticeship to the religious life how to split wood, cure skins, prepare vellum for the making of books and satchels for keeping them in. More than this, since there were no women in the settlement, he had taken his turn at grinding corn, kneading dough, and patching clothes. It had been an active, exacting, varied existence which he had shared as vigorously as he had shared the routine of his father's dun. Yet the religious way of life, as he had soon realised, was based on an ideal so different that the two environments might have belonged to two different worlds.

It was with a certain bewilderment, therefore, like someone

wakened from sleep, that he greeted his mother when she came to see him, as she did every month or two, bringing some small present of food, or a tunic she had made for him, knowing that he was growing so fast that his last would be skimpy already, anxious to feel that though the time would soon come when she must surrender him entirely, these little necessities still made him at least partly her own, even now he was a great lad, all but fifteen.

"Why son, you are as tall as I am now, and strong as a tree! How you have grown! No, now you are cheating, up on your tiptoes. Put your heels down . . ."

Columba grinned, standing before her, his thumbs twisted into the cord that girdled his tunic, his bare toes scrabbling at the warm dust of the courtyard, suddenly shy as his mother looked him up and down, keenly and lovingly, noting each rent in his tunic, every trifling scar.

"You're still happy, son?" Unlike Phelim, who had abandoned his eldest son so completely that he now scarcely spoke of him, Eithne still missed him constantly, and found it impossible to solace herself with her younger children, of whom there were now five, tumbling and shouting about the dun with healthy abandon, showing no spiritual inclinations whatever, but only the keenest interest in all Phelim had to tell them of hunting and warfare, rank and display. Sometimes, in the midst of her noisy, cheerful family, Eithne felt, these days, very much alone.

"Yes, yes, of course I'm happy, mother. You know I am. I've always said so. This place is—well——" Columba broke off, finding it difficult to explain what he felt about the oratory. He always meant to tell his mother so many things, when he heard she was coming, about his friends Cawdor and Orchy, sons of a smith and a swineherd, who handled their coracles so skilfully on the lough, and Medor, who could draw such beautiful animals in the curves of the capital letters of the manuscripts he was learning to copy in the Latin. And there was Doeg, the lay-brother, who knew the call of every beast and bird and could make them all come to eat out of his hand. But for some reason, though the thought of them was still in his heart, he could not speak of them now. His mother, gentle as she was, belonged to the other world, in which his father would have been angry with him with making friends with the sons of a smith and a herd. Here, that sort of thing existed no longer. Their heroes were villagers who worked with their hands; as fishermen, shepherd or carpenter.

"D'you realise that I've had to come here to see you ever

since you left us?" said Eithne one day. "You've never once been home, though it's so near."

"Yes, I know," said Columba uncomfortably. "But I'll come the next time I'm sent fishing." He was repentant, aware of always being glad to see her, of having too easily forgotten her after she had gone.

"Will that be soon? It will give great pleasure to your father as well as to me, Colum. He will want to hear all your news."

"Will he?" asked Columba doubtfully.

"Yes, of course. You needn't be afraid. He isn't angry any longer."

"Oh, I'm not afraid," Columba said.

"You'll come, then? You won't forget."

"I won't forget, Mother," he said.

So the next time they went down to the lough he asked permission to go on to the dun to see his family, and the old priest agreed. Some of his fosterlings came from remote villages, so that they saw their parents seldom, but since Columba lived so near he had guessed that only trouble at home prevented him from wanting to return. But since his mother saw him whenever she came to the oratory it had not seemed necessary to interfere.

It was odd, Columba thought, to be crossing the logs that bridged the ditch again, and walking on a fine spring morning between the huts towards his father's door. It all felt quite unreal, not alarming, just unreal. And there seemed to be nobody about the place, nobody at all. He walked slowly, as if he were making his way through a dream, held back by invisible obstacles rather than by his own reluctantly consenting will. He stepped over the threshold, then stood gripping the doorposts and staring, remembered panic threatened to grip him again as he thought of Gemman and the way he had sung there, years ago. At last he forced himself to walk down the long room, looking about him at the weapons on their racks above the empty sleeping couches, the leather curtain half drawn at the far end, the ashes of the fire lying softly on the big hearth-stone, flanked by turf-baskets, in the centre of the hall.

Nobody seemed to be about. It was not yet noon, the men were evidently out hunting, and the wolf-dogs had gone with them, all except one old bitch who lay dozing by the fire. But she knew Columba, and merely thumped her tail on the earth floor.

For some reason he could not make himself call out to his father and mother. He merely moved down the deserted hall to stand beside the old bitch, looking round him and recognising the devices on the shields and thinking how much smaller it all seemed now. In some way that made him feel sad. He stooped to pat the old bitch, which rose stiffly and followed him as he went forward to where the curtain hung. It clinked on its rings as he pushed it further back, expecting to see his parents look up at the sound. But nobody was there. His mother's embroidery was tumbled on the table. His father's knife lay beside a pile of chips. Though they had only just left, or would be shortly returning, he felt defrauded, almost angry that they should not be there now. They should have greeted him at that most important instant of his first return. Why should they leave him to stand there, among the remnants of his childhood, unwelcomed and alone?

A voice from the doorway startled him, and he swung round in consternation, for it was a voice he had hoped never to hear again, even though, just at that moment, it might be almost better than none.

" Well, so it's our valiant Colum-Cille," said Maeve. " Colum the churchman, come to give us his blessing. Well, well, well." She came down the hall towards him, laughing, her black hair blown into tendrils about her flushed face by the midsummer wind.

Seven years, it seemed, had changed Maeve very little. The beauty of her face had not yet been irrevocably marred by discontent, and at the sight of Columba the familiar malice flickered impishly in her eyes again. Threatened by her teasing, his face grew obstinate and his voice was sullen.

" I was looking for my mother," he said.

" Of course. I didn't imagine you'd come in search of me," Maeve agreed. " I can see just how much more surprised than pleased you are to find me here again."

" Where are the others?" Columba asked uneasily.

" If you'll stop looking at me as if I were a banshee I'll tell you," Maeve said. " Smile first, though. Smile . . ."

Columba's lower jaw jutted out as it always did when some-one goaded him. Maeve smiled herself, then she took a pace forward and flicked a forefinger under his chin, jerking it up so that he bit his own tongue. The sharp pain made him flush. Angry tears came into his eyes. He clenched his fists. It was years since he had felt like this. He had thought the overwhelming darkness, the fierce tongues of fire, had been left behind in the shadow of childhood. Now they had come upon him again in such strength that the serenity he had learned from the old priest gave way before the onslaught. He stood there sweating, his finger-nails marking his palms, his lower lip caught between his teeth as he struggled against invading anger, feeling as if fire itself were lapping about him, while he fought desperately for self-control.

"Your father," Maeve said cheerfully, "has gone off with the hunters after a wild boar. The women and children are all out at the woad-picking, and your mother has just been sent for because someone's child is ill. There . . ."

She stretched her long arms above her head and yawned gracefully. It was a gesture which showed off every line of her body under her green gown, a sensuous, lazy movement, like a cat flexing its limbs before a meal. She was enjoying herself. Life had been unreasonably dull lately, and she never could abide the long days when she was supposed to help the other women in the fields. She had made the excuse of an aching head which had served all women like herself since time began. It had been specially fortunate, for she had come back to find the family wonder-child just arriving home. Here, at last, was the chance of amusement; a new subject but a situation she knew well. She sat down at the table, pushing Eithne's sewing aside and cupping her chin on her hands.

"Don't be so angry, Colum," she said. "I was only teasing you. Why do you mind?"

Her voice was no longer sharp and malicious. The edge had gone from it, the danger was hidden in softness, as a cat's subtle velvet sometimes hides its claws. Columba felt the change without knowing its purpose, and something within him responded, as if her new mood were so nearly akin to the anger that dominated him, that it could influence it, transmute it into something that was as fiery, as avid, as violent and even more cruel, yet in some way unrecognised and new to him. New . . . and strange . . .

"Look at me, Colum . . ." Maeve murmured.

Slowly, unwillingly, in response to that overwhelming compulsion, Columba raised the lids of his heavy eyes. He had been looking at the floor, at his own tanned and calloused feet, at the chips from his father's whittling that lay all round the stool on which he usually sat, as if he sought to grasp at any excuse that would keep him from seeing Maeve's now smiling face. He felt himself, instinctively, to be in danger, without knowing what the danger was, just as an animal may stand shuddering on the verge of a bog, sensing its treachery and yet drawn by the scent and promise of fair pastures beyond. So he stood, child no longer, tall and sturdy as a young oak, the first down of manhood dusting jaw and upper lip, aware of sensations

that were as appalling as anger, and even more overwhelming,
subtle and deadly sweet like the beguiling songs of the shee that
Nalda had so often sung to him under her breath.

" Look at me, Colum . . ." Meave said again.

Slowly, helplessly, he raised his eyes. She was smiling at him
as he had never seen anybody smile before. Her slow, lingering
sweetness enticed him like the scent of a flaunting flower. It
seemed to reach out and envelop him, as if her arms were already
about him, pinioning him, holding him fast. He struggled against
a sort of faintness that was almost nausea, aware that the compulsion she had for him was oddly, but distortedly familiar, as
if its beauty was that of some candid flower of heaven that had
been nurtured and perverted in the underworld of hell.

" Why, you're a great lad now, Colum," Maeve was saying.
" And there was I taking you for a child still. Strong, too, aren't
you ? "

Columba nodded dumbly.

Maeve held out a hand, the other still cupping her chin, her
head a little on one side, the heavy braids of hair falling over her
shoulders, her voice coming lazily between scarcely parted lips.
" Yes, you look strong, terribly strong . . . You could twist my
arm as if you were wringing a skein of yarn, couldn't you, Colum.
Would you like to try ? "

Columba ran his tongue across his dry lips. His voice died
in his throat. When he could speak at last it was only a mumble.
" Perhaps, I would," he said unwillingly.

Maeve pulled back her sleeve to the shoulder. " I'm strong
for a woman, you know," she said. " You'd be surprised. Try
then . . . try and see."

" No," Columba said abruptly.

Maeve raised her arched brows and something of the laziness
went out of her voice. " Why not, Colum ? "

" I don't know," Columba said. He scarcely realised that he
had spoken, nor why. He only knew that as he stood there,
darkened and yielding despairingly, like the animal about to ignore
all its warning instincts and step from solid ground into the
bog, some shaft of light had reached him, brief yet unmistakable,
as if his name had echoed towards heaven from some vantage-
point of prayer. And immediately everything was changed. The
blessed faculty of laughter came back to him, making it appear
unutterably absurd to think of Maeve's bared arm as a boneless
hank of yarn that smelt atrociously of the sheep from which it
came. Her face, which had seemed to swim towards him on a
hot, unfathomable tide of yearning, now slid back into its place.

Her beckoning arm had no more power over him than the skein itself might have had. The miasma which had been suffocating him shredded away like an early mist at sunrise. The whole business became, not sordid, or vicious, but infinitely, deliciously absurd. Unexpectedly, he giggled.

The sound angered Maeve as nothing else could have done. Her lazy, beckoning pose changed to rigid defiance and indignation. So might a cat, toying pleasantly with a helpless little creature that its teeth had already half disabled, spring suddenly to the defensive at the approach of a more formidable foe. A flush deeper than Columba's darkened her face and neck, she sprang up and faced him, forgetting that she could tower over him no longer. No seduction, only sheer naked malice was left in her voice now.

"I had taken you for a grown man. What a fool! You're just a silly, sniggering child!"

"I'm sorry," Columba said, smiling still. "I didn't mean to be rude . . . it just suddenly seemed so . . . funny." His voice still shook. He was aching with unspent laughter. It swept through him in great waves that were tipped with glory. There was no longer any darkness. He could feel neither anger nor fear, as one of his moments of vision came upon him, and the mind of another creature became briefly known to him as it is perpetually known in heaven, in all its desperation and its loneliness, its passion and its pain. In that instant he looked past Maeve's beauty, past her pretty feline graces, into the shadowed desolation of her being, a being astray and despairing in darkness, yet created for happiness as a flower is created for the sun.

"I'm sorry, Maeve," he said again. His voice held all the pity, the understanding, the nascent wisdom of a maturing spirit, was quite unlike the casual apology of a child. For the second time in his fifteen years his unwanted compassion taunted her. Calmly, with deliberate intention, she stepped forward and slapped him. Her open hand stung sharply against his cheek, making him gasp with astonishment and pain. With the indrawn breath a new emotion, akin to anger in its savagery, yet strange in its violent desire, seemed to surge in upon him. Taken unawares in what seemed a moment of security, he floundered desperately in the roaring flood-tide of flame-lit darkness again, groping in vain for the lost sanity which had so recently blessed him, clutching wildly at the last traces of laughter and peace.

As they eluded him he plunged forward, his face suffused with the mottled flush of uncontrollable fury, the fiend voices yelling in his ears as he took Maeve by the shoulders with a strength that astonished her. She was still smiling as he gripped her, forcing her back against the wall, his teeth showing between lips drawn back in a wolfish snarl. As he began to beat her head against the knotted timbers her smile disappeared and her sensuously provocative face was contorted with real terror. She opened her mouth to scream, but the sound died in her throat as his fingers tightened to a stranglehold about her neck.

"Colum . . . Colum . . . for heaven's sake . . . have you gone mad?"

His mother's horrified voice pierced through the roaring darkness about him. Eithne had run the length of the hall and was tugging at his wrists, sobbing with terror. Abruptly Columba let Maeve go. She sagged, limp and breathless, against the uneven wall. Then he turned slowly towards his mother, shaking convulsively as the memory of an earlier fury came upon him, sickening him with its nightmare fear. Once again, only a timely intervention had saved him from having blood upon his soul. Next time . . . next time . . . what would happen if no one intervened?

CHAPTER VII

COLUMBA might not yet have enough worldly knowledge to know why Maeve had provoked him into attacking her. He did not associate the recent scene with the whispered conversations which went on occasionally among the older boys at the oratory. But he was wretchedly aware that he or part of him had literally intended to kill her, and that knowledge, as well as his mother's horror, darkened the rest of the visit to the dun. He was glad when it was time to join the fishing-party returning from the lough and climb with them the steep path which wound up and round the shoulder of the hill, hiding his home from sight.

But the memory of Maeve's twisted face, and the fiercely clashing anger, invitation and fear that played across it, remained with him, haunting his days and waking him sobbing from terrible nightmares, the meaning of which he did not understand. It was a relief to tell the old priest about it when next he went to confession, and a comfort to find that the old man had such definite advice to give.

"Thou art a great lad now, Columba," the priest said, "and hast learnt all that I have to teach thee. I can say, I think, that thou hast done well. Thy scribing is still uneven because of too

much haste, yet it already shows the beginnings of a fair hand.
Thou knowest the Gospels, the daily offices, and many of the
Psalms. Doeg tells me thou canst swing an axe with the mighty,
sow, reap, thresh and grind. Also that thou hast a knowledge of
cattle, art skilful in a boat and wise in the way of fishes. It is
time, friend, that thou shouldst go up higher." He laid a hand
on the kneeling boy's shoulder, smiling at his dismay.

"You want me to leave here, Father?"

The old man nodded. "Surely it is no surprise? We have
always talked of the great school of Moville for thee. And many
of thy friends here have already gone there. I will speak to thy
parents. It would be well for thee to go as soon as it can be
arranged."

"You mean—because of Maeve?" Columba's face was
troubled. Had he done something so wrong that he was to be
sent into exile? The priest shook his head.

"Not only because of her. The thing has been long in my
mind. Thou hast done no wrong. It is not wrong in itself for a
man to desire a woman, or for a woman to long for a man. The
love that blossoms between them is a holy and a blessed thing,
foul though the weeds may be that come when it is not tended.
All love is one, as the sun's light bears the same blessing for all,
though the response of the living things that need it may vary, as
love varies between lovers and parents, children and friends."
He paused, as if carefully searching for the words that would best
express something that must not be misunderstood. Columba
watched him anxiously, but the old man sat so still that he might
scarcely have been breathing, one hand laid, palm upward, on
each knee, as if in mute prayer for wisdom, his half-closed eyes
fixed on a point on the wall behind the boy's head. "Canst
thou follow me?"

"Yes, Father," Columba said.

"That blessing is available for all men, in their homes, in
their work, in the world. We of the Church deny ourselves some
of these things, and if you are to be a churchman you must know
why. It is not because we think them evil. They are not. But
those who seek Tir nan Og must not linger among the flowering
meadows of Erin, and we who are strangers upon earth dare not
take too much thought for the flowers by the wayside if we are
to guide others on the long way towards heaven. Maybe it is
not clear to thee what all this has to do with thy going to Moville?"
the old man concluded with his gentle smile.

"Not quite," Columba admitted.

"This is but a little place of beginnings," said the old priest.

" Moville is different. Thou wilt find students from all over
Erin, lads like thyself by the hundred, and many older men.
There thou wilt see the work of the Church in all its contrasting
splendour and privation, its poverty in this world and its rich
store of treasures elsewhere. I cannot command thee to forsake
the consolations of earthly love, the companionship of wife and
the joy of children, in order to save thy strength for the ghostly
battle. I can only say that such a battle is best fought single-
handed, like the champions of the old bards' tales. Thou must
choose for thyself, Columba. But not yet. First thou must know
more of the choice."

So, in due course, Columba set out on the long journey to
Moville, the great monastic school which had gathered itself
round the remarkable personality of Finnian the scholar, priest
and traveller. Finnian had returned to Erin from Candida Casa
in Alba, where he had studied under the great missionary
Ninian, who had his Christianity from Rome under the guidance
of the heroic Martin of Tours. Columba did not travel alone,
but waited till a party had been made up in the neighbourhood,
containing not only lads like himself, but also a couple of middle-
aged, travel-wise monks who made nothing of the journey through
the bogs and forests and mountains which lay between Gartan and
Moville. They trudged on, staff in hand, rough tunics girded
above their bony knees, from sunrise till sundown without haste
or respite, long after the more impetuous boys had begun to limp
and tire.

Columba was amazed by his first sight of Moville. Years at
the oratory had not accustomed him to crowds, and there seemed
to be no end to the students, both young and old, who were
grouped round their teachers in the timber-built churches, of
which there were several on the meadows by the broad estuary,
or, more frequently, crowded about the lecturers in the open
air. Some of the students lived with the local inhabitants, paying
for their keep in corn and cattle if their fathers were wealthy,
or giving their domestic services in exchange for board and lodging
if they were poor. Ambitious students had combined to build
themselves huts of timber and thatch, and sometimes they
employed humbler students to wait on them and do the cooking,
so that their own time might be free for discussion and study.
Many of the young men, independent yet not wealthy, knocked up
little bothies of branches roofed with turf, so that the whole plain
was dotted with a variety of structures, some expertly and others
more casually made, both those they had built themselves and
those they had taken over from the people of Moville. For the

original village had been as completely blotted out by the
invasion of eager, noisy, argumentative young men who had
descended upon them, as a stubble field is blotted out by a flock
of hungry birds. The villagers grumbled at the students,
but on the whole they did well enough by them. And because of
the reputation of the great Finnian, the competition for a chance
to learn from him was so great that hardly a householder in
Moville was without as many young men as he could find room for
within his mud walls.

As Phelim's son, Columba came with certain advantages. His
father had no patience with the monastic ideal of poverty, and
did not consider it suitable that the son of a nobleman should
be meanly lodged. So as a condition of his son's departure he
had insisted on making arrangements for him to board with a
nobleman of his acquaintance whose dun was on the verge of the
mushroom crop of huts and bothies. He had also made arrangements, unknown to Columba, for him to be brought to the notice
of the principal himself soon after his arrival. If Colum must
take to religion, Phelim had said to Eithne with an air of resignation, at least the instruction he received might as well be of
the best.

And so, after a little unobtrusive work on the part of his host,
who had been gratified by the presents Phelim had sent on
behalf of his son, Columba joined the circle of boys and men
sitting at the feet of the great Finnian, who lectured in the timber
hall which adjoined the church, in which students were always to
be seen busy at their desks with vellum and ink-horns and pigments, diligently copying the well-worn texts of Gospels or
Psalms.

The principal of Moville was a very different character from
the old priest whose oratory Columba had just left. He was a
traveller, a scholar and a martinet. His tall, gaunt form in his
drab habit, the narrow head, fiercely aquiline and domed by the
frontal tonsure behind which white hair swept nearly to his
shoulders, was unforgettable. So was his voice, which had a
great range and variety of expression. He could be inspiring,
appalling, commanding and illuminating. Most of his students
were terrified of him, but Columba, who was not accustomed to
being terrified by anybody, found him as invigorating as an east
wind. And Finnian soon picked out Columba from the rabble
of new students who were sent to him for their first instruction.
With his bright head, eager intelligence and promise of scholarship, he was not to be easily missed.

"Your Latin : better than I expect from beginners," Finnian

shot at him one morning, pausing suddenly in his restless pacing to and fro in front of his nervous class. " Name ? "

Columba grinned boldly back at Finnian as he gave it.

" Who sent you ? "

Columba's reply was swift as an answering sword-stroke.

Finnian looked at him with interest. Like many men whose nervous irascibility make them much feared, he welcomed and respected any boy with the courage to stand up to him. From the moment of their first encounter Finnian marked down Columba as a student likely to do him credit, which meant that he came in for fiercer criticism, more gruelling tasks and scantier praise than his less gifted companions, who stumbled through grammar or translation and could neither sing the Latin Psalms nor remember the sequence of the Gospels. To Columba, with his careful grounding in Psalter and Testament, his keen wits and excellent memory, these things presented no difficulty. His voice, which had been high and sweet at the oratory, had broken now, and was already steadying into a bass of tremendous range and power which, taken together with his great stature and increasing strength, made strangers take him for several years older than he actually was.

But the quality above all others which attracted most people was the happiness which seemed literally radiant about him, as if the delight he felt in the mere fact of being alive went from him like the rays of another sun. Every aspect of life at Moville excited in him an immediate response, whether it was a lecture on the writings of the Early Fathers, the translation of some obscure passage which had baffled scholars, the study of illumination, then just beginning to beautify the work of the scribes with the variety of design and colour which their Celtic natures craved, a violent discussion with a group of fiery disputants of his own age, or a race across the ruffled waters of the estuary in frail craft of wicker, waterproofed with sewn hides.

When he first came to Moville from the oratory Columba had been still blessed by the direct, intuitive perception proper to the childhood from which he was emerging, so that he accepted mystery, paradox and marvel as his spiritual birthright. But as he grew, the limitations of his reasoning brain began in due course to offer resistance to the free movement of his imagination, and the conflict between them produced a state of acute irritation which resolved itself from time to time in violent quarrels with those whose opinions differed from his own.

Between these outbreaks, however, the theologian in Columba tended to dominate for a time the dreamer and the poet, so that he turned for companionship towards the more intellectual members of the great university, associating with brilliant young men who gathered in secluded corners to thrash out questions of disputed renderings, expressed doubts of the authenticity of the Gospels, aired all the fashionable heresies, and considered themselves rather better informed than their teachers. At one stage Columba had agreed with them. But as he listened, he became rather less sure. He was seventeen now, superbly healthy and immensely strong, just ordained deacon, and anxious, like all other young men about him, to make up his mind about his future.

" You know, I am not altogether sure that I shall enter the priesthood, after all," one of his friends declared during an evening's argument. " I can't help thinking that it is merely becoming a refuge for mediocre minds. Now, I——"

" I can think of a lot of things about Finnian that I don't care for," Columba protested, " but I'd never have accused him of having a mediocre mind."

" Finnian is getting old, my friend. We have to think of the future——"

" When we come to rely on the past and its traditions we shall be getting old ourselves," somone added.

" I believe I should do better in a secular capacity," drawled a handsome, rebellious student from Connachta. " The life of a historian makes a considerable appeal to me. A man is free to develop his gifts as he pleases, without being at the beck and call of some superior who gratifies himself by ordering better men about."

" I fancy I should find myself well suited as a judge. The law offers a man liberty from every obligation except that of meting out justice——"

" A physician has considerable opportunities for advancement and study——"

" A chronicler is not expected to abandon his common sense and obey instructions blindly——"

" Nor, as a matter of fact, to live in conditions of such bestial discomfort——"

" Do you ever think of anything except your own advantage ? " asked Columba suddenly.

They turned on him the cold, speculative stare of people who have been subjected to a vulgar intrusion. " Ah, it's our young firebrand from the wilds again," someone said eventually. " I shouldn't let that sort of question disturb you, my friend. If one does not occasionally bring one's feet back to earth one is apt to lose one's way among the rosy clouds of heaven. Time enough for that, if you ask me, when we're summoned by the angels. Meanwhile, perhaps you'll forgive us if we discuss the possibilities of a useful residence on earth ? "

" You can discuss them without me," said Columba, abruptly, antagonized by such talk among men whose presence at Moville had seemed to indicate their freedom from mere worldly desires. Angrily he flung out of the hut in which the discussion was in progress, hearing their amusement rise raucously behind him as he plunged through the dark expanse of huts and bothies, the dim shapes of which were dominated here and there by the looming bulk of lecture hall or timber-built church. Without any special purpose he found himself entering the church in which he did his share of transcribing the Scriptures. Two or three young men were still writing, but behind a pillar he noticed a vacant desk.

His anger and bewilderment subsided as he slid on to the high stool. The rushlight burned on the reading-stand, the quill lay, gouted with ink, where the last student had tossed it down. Columba picked it up listlessly. If his friends were right, he was wasting his time in religion. He too could perhaps use his gifts better in one of the secular professions, as historian, physician, or poet. Look, they had said contemptuously, at the mendicant position of a monk. And then consider the dignity and importance of an ollave poet.

Columba sighed as the struggle within him flared up again. There seemed to be no peace anywhere. Now, in an instant, he was torn and battered by conflicting duties and possibilities, as a coracle caught by a winter's storm is swept out of sight of land. Between the darkness of the sky and the darkness of the sea were only the bared teeth of the ferocious waves, by whose fury the frail craft seemed likely to be assaulted till it sank. Sometimes, Columba thought, the conflict between the two sides of his nature seemed as if it must overset the balance of his mind.

Moodily he returned to the work before him. His eyes sought the Gospel beside him on its stand. The copy had been begun by some diligent and accurate scribe, for all the letters hung exactly from the fine lines which his stylus had incised, without the slightest deviation between the size of one character and the next. A fortunate fellow, thought Columba. Untroubled by a single wandering thought. He had stopped writing in the middle of a sentence. Yes, indeed, so he would. What he had written he had written, like Pilate. The conclusion of a phrase could be another man's affair. Smiling in spite of himself, at the lack of imagination in the fellow, Columba scanned the beginning of the interrupted sentence and began to write on, his brain recording, his numbed spirit slowly responding to the momentous words :

"*Ego sum resurrectio et vita ; qui credit in me, etiamse mortuus fuerit, vivet . . .*"

Into the quiet church, where the only sound was now the scratching of another student's quill on the surface of an uneven sheet of vellum, seemed to come the remembered voices of the boys at the oratory, years ago, kneeling at the feet of the old priest to translate the Gospel of St. John, and learn the words by heart.

" I am the resurrection and the life : he that believeth in me, though he were dead, yet shall he live . . .''

One by one the other students blew out their rushlights and went out of the church, leaving ghostly little twirls of acrid smoke that lingered above their vacant desks. Columba's light became the one small pool of illumination in a sea of shadows as he wrote on, absorbed in his work, his restlessness soothed by the rhythmical movement, his imagination caught by the tremendous drama of the raising of Lazarus.

" *Nonne dixi tibi, fore, si credideris, ut videas gloriam Dei ?* "

" Said I not unto thee," murmured Columba under his breath, in the habit of earlier days, " that if thou wouldst believe, thou shouldst see the glory of God ? "

The words struck so strongly at his consciousness that they might well have been spoken aloud, and it was with a shock of sudden awe that he became aware of a tall figure watching him from the shadows just beyond his rushlight's glow. The quill fell from his hand, he gripped the edge of the desk, half rising.

" Well, Columba. Startled you, eh ? " said Finnian.

" A—a little, sir," Columba said.

" Working late, aren't you ? Long past the supper hour."

" I didn't know." Columba made an apologetic gesture. " I wanted to get away——"

" Too much talking. I know. Young people are all alike. Round and round like the pony at the mill. But much less useful. Talk gets you nowhere. What do you mean to do ? "

" That was what was troubling me," Columba admitted.

" Knew this was coming," said Finnian. His aquiline profile as he turned to stare into the darkness was mellowed to the colour of old parchment by the gentle light, and the thick white hair that sprang back from the frontal tonsure backed the lean scholar's face like a nimbus of pale fire. Here was no dreamer like the old priest of Columba's early days, but a man whose life was fiercely consecrated to an ideal before which every other consideration must give way, who would no more have counselled one of his followers to seek a compromise in order to avoid martyrdom than he would have contemplated such an ignoble possibility himself. " This was bound to happen," he said crisply. " To you."

" To me, sir ? Why ? " Columba was surprised. He had not know that Finnian, from the lofty pinnacle of his great learning and absolute power at the head of the university of Moville, would have found time to watch the progress of a junior student. But he did not yet know Finnian, who prided himself on his ability to assess the promise of every young man who came before him, who never forgot a face and seldom made a mistake.

" You've got a good brain and a bad temper. You rely too much on the one and make no attempt to harness the other. Your friends flatter you. You like to sit about and shout each other down, you and the other young fools who think they can wrangle themselves into the kingdom that is to come. Expect they're telling each other that they'd be wasting their talents in the Church. Eh ? "

Columba grinned.

" Believed them, didn't you ? " Finnian's grim face came closer, his dark eyes seemed to bore through Columba's skull in search of the truth he might be trying to hide. But Columba did not intend to hide anything. He was not secretive by nature, and even now, he was not afraid.

" Sometimes I did believe them," he said.

" Pah ! " said Finnian. " Worst of these clever young men is that they think cleverness is important. They want to make terms, to bargain for places on the right hand and the left. Can't be done. The life of religion isn't a career. Careers belong to the world. Those who want them can stay there. Religion offers first to teach a man humility. Without that fundamental quality he can learn no other. As a rebel against authority this may seem unwelcome. As a poet, it should mean something to you."

" It does, sir," Columba said. " And yet——"

" And yet you prefer rebellion ? "

" Freedom perhaps," Columba said.

A hint of hostility, of powerful forces equally matched, flashed for an instant between them. Then it was gone. Teacher faced pupil again as Finnian made an abrupt gesture of negation. " Freedom is not circumstantial. What happens to a man matters little. What happens within him matters much. Freedom is a spiritual state. Few of us achieve it. We have too little courage."

" I realise that."

" Your intellectual materialist does not. He knows only what he stands to lose. Considers his self-sufficiency too valuable to be sacrificed. You have glimpses of what you're offered in exchange. Understand me ? "

" Oh, yes," said Columba wearily, " I understand. But what must I do ? "

Finnian drew his thin brows together, concentrating all his tremendous power of thought on the boy before him. An intellectual himself, he was unsparing in his condemnation of intellectual methods. A martinet, he lashed those who coveted riches or power. It was, thought Columba, watching him also, as if Satan sought to cast out Satan from the older man's soul. With a sudden premonitory shiver, he hoped that he might never be matched against Finnian on an issue of any importance. He liked him, he respected him, but he knew that he would be utterly ruthless if occasion served.

" Do ? " said Finnian curtly. " You must learn to control yourself. And you must make up your mind."

" Yes, I know. But——"

" You have been long enough here, now," said Finnian, as the old priest had said, once before. " We have taught you much. Now you will do better elsewhere. There is too much discussion here, too many gifted young men wondering on what profession they will bestow their gifts. You must have action, not words. Work, not wrangling, is the thing for you. The question is, what work ? "

" What had you in mind for me, sir ? "

" I would have sent you to Clonard, the new monastery under its missionary Abbot whose name is the same as mine. There your work would have begun, the work of kindling in others the flame that your own life bears. But now——"

" But now, sir ? "

" I am not sure. It may be that the wood is too green to burn. The things of this world may hold you too strongly. Only you can tell. Now . . ." he paused, frowning down at Columba, assessing him inexorably, " I would still say : leave Moville. But I would advise you to go off alone, where you like, for as long as may be necessary for you to know the trend of your soul. If a worldly career attracts you, remain in the world. Your father has great ambitions for you . . ."

" How—how do you know ? " said Columba in surprise. He had fancied that was all over and done with. It seemed strange that his father should still seek to control him, that Finnian should know.

Finnian shrugged. " Never mind. I do know. And if in your heart you would rather be great as this world counts greatness, you must say so now. The time for looking back is before your hand is laid to the plough."

Columba nodded without speaking. He felt as if a great weight had come down on his shoulders, as if under the burden of this choice, so clarified by Finnian, all his native gaiety was quenched. The thought of all he must forsake lay heavy upon him. Perhaps Finnian was right. He was not worthy to put his hand to such a plough.

" Don't decide now," said Finnian. " Take as long as you like. A year, if need be. Go where you will. Come and tell me when you know what you must do."

" Shall I ever know ? " said Columba, with all the violence of a young man's sudden, abysmal despair.

" You will know," said Finnian. With one of those abrupt, unconvincing smiles which crossed his austere face like a gleam of wintry sunlight on ice, he turned and left the church. And soon afterwards Columba blew out his rushlight, slid down from his stool and groped his way to the door. His movements, which were usually so sure, even precipitate, were for once tentative and uncertain, and he went slowly, as if he had lost his way between reality, vision and dream.

So he was to leave Moville. The command saddened him. Next morning he collected the only things he could take with him, his own laboriously-made Latin copy of the Gospels in its leather satchel, the axe he would carry on his shoulder. He dawdled, because he did not know where to go, and the only thing he wished to avoid was a return to his father's dun. He pictured his father, carving chessmen and telling him of the fine positions he might have for the asking : his mother, saying nothing, though her eyes pleaded with him against the blandishments of the world. Maeve would be there too, he remembered, looking at him sidelong and taunting him with her bitter tongue because the spice of danger in their dealings with each other pleased her. All his childhood's memories would be thick about him, tugging him back towards raging, remembered darkness. No, he would not go home.

Where, then ? Southwards, through Laigen ? He remembered that his mother's family had been its ruling house, and one of the other students had himself come from the south of the province. His mother's kinsmen, it seemed, were still great people there. Columba questioned the boy from Laigen again, and was told that the journey was easy enough in summer-time. He had no wish for a king's court, but he was feeling lonely. To find his mother's home might in some way comfort him for abandoning his own. At least the search gave him an objective. And so, on the morning after his talk with Finnian, when the spring green had begun to blur the winter outline of the trees that stood about Moville, Columba set out for the south.

Finnian might have sent him away to make up his mind, but during the days that followed, while he made his way through forest and bogland and across occasional stretches of boulder-strewn, barren moor, Columba was not consciously using his mind at all. The problem of his future seemed to have withdrawn itself : his consciousness was entirely preoccupied with the present need to cover mile after mile on narrow, twisting tracks made by villagers or cattle, to defend himself, if need be, from wolf or wild boar, to beg hospitality from the peasants who courteously received him, offering him gladly a place at their tables and a corner in which to sleep. As he went he found himself thinking less of his own problems than of those of the people who had received him into their huts and wished him godspeed in the morning.   Occasionally, too, scenes from his childhood floated, unbidden, through his mind. He pictured his mother at her embroidery, his father whittling restlessly at his little figures of ivory or wood as he listened to some story-teller or bard. He remembered Gemman, singing so beautifully to the music of his small harp. Gemman . . .

Suddenly his journey achieved the possibility of purpose. Gemman, the bard . . . if such a wanderer as Gemman could be said to have a home, it was somewhere in Laigen, people had said. Gemman had sung at his father's dun on the night he had run away. Gemman had been kind, not haughty and unapproachable like the court poets. Gemman had promised to teach him if he wanted to learn the rules of poetry. Perhaps Gemman would help him now . . . On the other hand, he might be at the other end of Erin. He might even be dead. It was ten years since he had sung at Gartan, and though Columba realised that as a child he had had no clear idea of grown-up ages, the poet had seemed to be an old man then. But at least, though he might not be able to find him, he could always try.

When Columba asked for news of Gemman he was directed to him at once. It was unbelievable that anything should be so simple. Events seemed to fall into place as if they belonged to some pattern that had already been long ago laid down. Gemman lived, it seemed, in a hut deep in the forest, a hut which he had built for himself. He was actually there, when Columba went in search of him, sitting by a stream with his harp across his knees. His hair and beard were greyer than Columba remembered them, but otherwise he had scarcely changed. He greeted Columba courteously, nodding as the boy mentioned his name.

" I thought you would come, sooner or later," he said.

" Will you teach me ? " Columba asked abruptly.

" All that I know, my son," Gemman said.

The months that followed made Moville, with its crowds of hurrying, busy, argumentative students, seem strange as a feverish dream. Gemman did not argue. He taught an art as something beyond dispute. Carefully, quietly, he explained to Columba the complex verse-forms used by Irish poets, the richness of rhyme and rhythm, the questions of stress and the choice of words. To Columba Gemman's teaching came as a godsend, nourishing and developing the artistic side of his nature which both the devout old priest and the scholarly Finnian had left untouched. As he listened to the bard's beautiful voice the limitations of the logical, deliberate, consciously reasoning brain were transcended by a faculty which was timeless and without limitation, bearing him beyond the possibility of doubt and questioning, towards a quiet certainty which was in itself a prayer.

After a while Gemman persuaded Columba to produce his own verses and showed him how to pick out the accompaniment he wanted on the bard's small harp. At first Columba's voice was husky with embarrassment, then deep and strong and grave as he forgot that anybody was listening, and sang because the ideas flowed so urgently through his mind that they gave him no peace till they had found their way between his lips. And like all young creatures, it was of the bewildering anguish of life that he sang :

> " Why is there pain
> At the heart of a song,
> Beauty thàt bleeds
> In the sweep of a hand
> On the strings of a harp ?
> Why do I search
> Always in vain
> For the home of my soul ?
> Under the sun
> Dark is my way.
> Under the moon
> Haunted I go

By the longing that cries
From the heart of a song,
The sorrow that pleads
From an old man's eyes . . ."

Gemman nodded his head slowly when Columba had finished.

"Yes, you have the sure hand and the seeing eye and the heart that clenches with pity for the trouble in the world," said the old bard. "When your ear is trained, Colum, you should go far."

"I am to be a priest, sir," Colum said doubtfully.

"A priest, eh? H'm," Gemman said. "Yes, I remember now. Colum-Cille, they were calling you at Gartan when I went there last. Colum of the Church. Well, why not?"

"What has heaven to do with poetry?" said Columba.

"Everything, maybe," said the old bard. "What has a stream to do with its source or a mirror of steel with the sun that kindles it?"

"At Moville," Columba objected, "we used to argue all day long about the attributes of the Holy Trinity and the sinless nature of our blessed Lady, and the order of precedence among the warriors of the heavenly host. But nothing ever seemed to come of it all . . ."

Gemman yawned. "I should think not."

"But here I never want to argue at all."

"Poets need not argue," said Gemman superbly. "They know."

Columba, kneeling at his feet, looked up eagerly. "Sir, tell me what you know."

Gemman smiled. "Ah, that's another matter, son. It won't go into words. At least, not the sort of words that can be used in broad daylight between you and me. But listen—I'll try to tell you in another way . . ."

He reached for his harp and ran his fingers over the strings. Then he began to sing. It was an ancient, haunting, pagan ballad of the hosting of the shee, but through it went such a nostalgic awareness of man's homeward destiny that Columba began, as he listened, slowly to understand many things that his reasoning brain had been unable to grasp, from the realisation of which anger and impatience had driven his emotions astray. But now he knew, as Gemman blended hand and ear and voice into a single instrument for the interpretation of beauty, that so the faculties of his own insurgent nature must be blended too, till the poet in him kindled the priest and the priest guided the poet, and the scholar served both in humility as the brazen strings of the harp served the bard.

Each without the other, the several aspects of his nature would always be inadequate. Warring, they must tear his life apart. But blended, kindled, dedicated, they might achieve unity in an enterprise which would sweep him far beyond the limitations of pride or power, a pilgrimage which must take him, hot-foot, over the rim of the apprehensible world. Now, as never before, the possibility of a life so unified obsessed him with such passion that every intellectual objection seemed to melt away, leaving him confronted by a vision so splendid that his eyes filled with tears.

" *Ut tristes, semper tamen gaudentes* . . ."

" As sorrowful, yet always rejoicing ; as poor, yet making many rich ; as having nothing, yet possessing all things . . ."

Without realising it, he had spoken aloud as he rose to his feet, his eyes wide and unseeing as he took a few tentative steps.

" Going, son ? " Gemman said tranquilly.

" Yes," Columba brought his attention back with difficulty to the visible world. " D'you mind ? Had you more to tell me ? "

" Not now. You are going home ? "

Columba shook his head. " No. To Clonard," he said.

CHAPTER VIII

COLUMBA reached the great monastery, which had been built only twenty years before and, like Moville, on an estuary, just at sunset. His first impression, as he paused on the edge of the woods that backed it, was not of many and variously important buildings as at Morville, but of an immense expanse of unassuming little bothies grouped about a more impressive timber church than he had yet seen. The last rays of the sun sent the shadows far across the threadbare turf and the tingling of handbells carried by priests on their way to vespers rose above the lowing of the cattle which were being herded from their pastures. Presently from the church came the sound of men's voices chanting their evening prayer.

There seemed, just then, to be very few people about. Columba wondered what to do next. His arrival at Clonard, unknown and unexpected, was very different from his arrival at Moville, where his father had made such elaborate arrangements for his

reception. But the orderly arrival of a drove of cows showed
that someone must be driving them, and Columba waited till
the animals had passed by, their breath sweet about him,
the white dust hovering waist-high in a soft cloud. Behind
them came someone rather older than himself, but dark-haired
and more slightly built. He was a gentle looking boy, already
wearing the priest's frontal tonsure, but there was, Columba
fancied, something unexpectedly strong about the curves of the
sensitive mouth.

" Can you direct me ? I am a stranger here," said Columba,
as the boy paused beside him, smiling and shielding his eyes from
the sun's level rays.

" God bless you, stranger. My name is Kenneth," the older
boy said.

" And mine is Columba." He held out his hand. Kenneth
took it in his own, a hand which was leaner and gripped harder
than anybody casually looking at him would have suspected. The
two boys took stock of each other. Columba, in his patched and
faded tunic, girded well above his bare, bramble-scarred legs,
stood with his axe across his shoulder, bare feet planted squarely
astride in the white dust, and looked hard at Kenneth, taller
than he but not so broad, who leant on his staff and looked back
at him out of wide-set, honest eyes that were brown as those of the
cows he was herding, not fierce and grey like his own. They
smiled at each other, but warily, as young men do whose
immensely contrasting characters make each seem odd to the other.
It was the first meeting of two life-long friends.

"Welcome, Columba. I will gladly guide you," said Kenneth.
" You cannot see the Abbot yet a while, for he is in church, like
all those who have not got evening work to do. When did you
eat last ? "

" I have eaten well early this morning," said Columba,
swinging his axe from his shoulder and grounding it at his feet.
" But I would be glad of food presently. Tell me, where must I
build my hut ? "

" Since you are a stranger, you had better build it close by
the church," said Kenneth. " The Abbot likes to have the new
students near him. But there is no need to start felling trees at
sundown. You can share my hut for the night, break bread with
me and go in the morning to see the Abbot. That will be time
enough."

" Will it ? Good," said Columba, raising a hand to check
a prodigious yawn. " I have been walking since daybreak."

" Come, then," said Kenneth, lifting his staff to tap a dawdling heifer on the flank. "Once we've got these beasts penned for the night I'll take you with me. Help me collect them up from among the huts, Columba. They've strayed in all directions as we talked. Up, then ! Come up, will you ? Mind that wily old animal, friend. She's trying to dodge back to the pasture. We dare not leave them there at night for fear of wolves."

Together the two boys guided and intimidated the herd of obstinate, scary creatures to the pen which had been built for them in the middle of the extensive settlement. Then Kenneth led Columba to his own hut near the river-bank for the night. It was Kenneth, too, who took him next morning to see the Abbot, a shrewd old man who ruled the great monastery of Clonard with the skill of a priest whose genuine love of the young gave him understanding, an understanding which was entirely un-contaminated by any desire for power.

He received Columba with a sort of piercing kindness, questioning him about what he had learned at Moville, his reasons for proposing to join the priesthood, the lectures he had attended and the degree of learning he had attained. Columba answered him simply, contrasting the kind, rubicund, rather bulky old man with the austere Finnian whose cold irony had terrorised the students of Moville. Here at Clonard the Abbot kept no particular state. The room in which he received students was as plain as a peasant's hut, and he slept in a corner of it on a couple of boards covered with a hide.

"Yes, you will find it rather different here," said the Abbot, twinkling suddenly at Columba so that he flushed at having his thoughts so quickly detected. "Moville is a great international centre, to which students go because of the learning and reputa-tion of its principal. Finnian of Moville is a scholar who is known far beyond the coasts of Erin. You said he taught you, I think ? "

"Yes, indeed, Father," Columba said.

The Abbot chuckled. "He deserves his reputation. He has earned it. He has been to Rome, even to the Holy Land, I believe, and as a scholar there is nobody to touch him. It is said that he is, perhaps, just a little jealous of his learning. I would not like, for instance, to be the man who attempts to deprive him of the credit for any of his remarkable achievements. I doubt if that would be wise. Not wise at all. Still, none of us here are ever likely to try to do that, are we, Kenneth ? " He chuckled at the thought. "This is not a college but a monastery, Columba, and our business is less the achievement of personal sanctity than the encouragement of sanctity in others. You have satisfied the examiners at Moville in regard to your intellectual progress. Do you require further time for meditation, or are you ready for me to prepare you to take your priest's vows ? "

Columba hesitated no longer. Hesitation did not seem possible at Clonard. " I am ready, Father," he said.

" Good. Let me see, you must also have a soul-friend. I shall send you . . ." He paused, and his kindly face grew grave as he looked thoughtfully at Columba. " . . . yes, I shall send you to Molaise. He lives apart from the rest of the community, but Kenneth here will tell you how to find him. He will guide you more wisely than any one I know."

" Yes, Father," Columba said. Already he felt happier for the decision he had just taken, and for the prospect of life at Clonard. He was aware of warmth, understanding and humour in the relationship between Abbot and monks. At Moville the strenuous intellectual ambition of Finnian had expressed itself in the bitter rivalry and conflicting ideals of his brilliant students. Here, the benign influence of the Abbot lay across the whole place like the blessing of autumn sunshine on orchard and harvest field.

" You must go now, Columba. I have other people to see," the Abbot said presently. " But remember, I am always here. Never be afraid to ask to see me. If I can receive you immediately, I will. If not, I will keep you waiting no longer than I must. Now, Kenneth, take him away."

As they left the Abbot's presence it seemed to Columba that life at Clonard might almost have belonged to another world from Moville. At Moville the vital pulse of all activity had throbbed through Finnian's lecture hall, echoed more faintly in the lecture-groups of minor men. Here at Clonard it was not the lecture halls but the tall church, in the morning shadow of which Kenneth was now helping Columba to build his hut, that lay at the heart of every enterprise, whether undertaken by Abbot or monk, deacon, lay-brother or serving-lad. At Clonard, too, for the first time, instead of making his confession to his immediate superior, as at the oratory, or to any available priest, as at Moville, it had been decreed that he was to have a permanent soul-friend, or confessor. And Kenneth spoke with veneration of the sanctity of Molaise. So Columba arranged to go regularly and see the old man, who lived in a hut he had himself built on the edge of the bay. He was in due course to find his new confessor's gentleness more formidable than Finnian's cold eyes.

As the two young men hewed branches, bent willow wands and cut turf for Columba's hut, Kenneth told him something of what the crusading church of Clonard symbolised in all their lives. The first monks of Clonard had built it themselves, rearing great tree trunks heavenwards to support the lofty roof, deliberately dedicating to the new faith the splendid aisles of the forests in which the pagan Druids had performed strange rites and evoked their uncouth gods. Between the ranked wooden pillars stood the desks of the scribes and illuminators, already beginning to grope towards the art which was later to make Erin famous. Even now, colour and design had begun to blossom from the sombre pages of black-lettered vellum, and the curls and scrolls which grew from the extremities of the tall capital letters were tending to shape themselves into the wondering faces of little beasts and fabulous birds. For the love the scribes of Clonard felt for their work and their companions spilt over into love of all the other created things, that were also of the household of God.

Kenneth took Columba into the church and showed him the way in which the pillars were carved, each one differently, in bold sweeping designs of great beauty and strength, as if the monks had also wished to bring into their church the fretwork of symmetry in leaf and branch and glimpses of sky, which, in lopping off the lesser branches, they had been obliged to leave behind. Here, too, from every odd nook and cranny, beneath leaf or interlacing scroll, peered the furry faces of mouse or rabbit, stag, squirrel or doe. High under the eaves hovered a cornice of carved birds, so that the great figures of the angels which stood sentinel behind the stone slab of the altar were accompanied by a multitude of lesser wings.

Watching Columba, Kenneth was reassured by the change that came over his face, by his vehement nod of comprehension, by his sudden tears. He had not missed the beauty and tenderness of the work that had been done by so many people, he could picture the smiles on the faces of carver or scribe as he worked the creatures of the woods into the pattern of his prayers. Together they went from pillar to pillar, from this piece of carving to that, pausing to watch a student at work on the new copy he was making from a tattered and worn book of the Gospels, or the transcription of another version of a much-used Psalter on vellum which he had himself prepared and ruled.

"We need so many copies," Kenneth explained. "When we send people out into the wilds to found new churches each must take his books with him, and we try to make them as beautiful as may be so that he shall be comforted as he reads them, remembering Clonard."

"A man might do anything with this behind him," said Columba, still shaken by the impact of so much beauty, stirred as he had been on the night he had first heard Gemman sing. Strange, he thought, how profoundly a man might be moved by beauty, how laughter seemed to speak to him in the native language he had learned in heaven, while the most erudite disputations of the intellectuals merely stirred up the dust of the earth. At Moville he had been furiously restless, rebellious and unsatisfied by all the brilliance of the finest brains of the age. They had illuminated only as lightning illuminates, without comfort, continuity or warmth. At Moville they had spoken with the tongues of men and of angels. But here at Clonard there was charity. Charity that bore all things, believed all things, hoped all things . . . " *Charitas . . . omnia tegit, omnia credit, omnia sperat, omnia tolerat* . . ."

Columba sighed with relief. " It is good to be here."

" At Clonard," Kenneth agreed, " a man feels he is near home."

Kenneth was the first of Columba's friends, but soon others gathered round them. They formed a little band of ardent spirits who derived from the life at Clonard a zest which urged them on, inspired by the sight of life at its most beautiful, as if they could not rest until they had carried its candles to the very ends of the darkened world. In them, as Gemman had shown Columba, the poet kindled the priest and the priest guided the poet, and the beauty of their vision obsessed them, glorifying all they did.

" This is Brendan," Kenneth had said, one day. " He spends all his spare time in boats, and talks of Happy Isles beyond the sea till we no longer listen. He'll be glad of a new pair of ears."

Columba liked the look of the huge young man with the restless hands and the blue eyes that seemed always to be scanning horizons, but could be so surprisingly gentle when he brought them back to dwell for an instant on the faces of his friends.

" Glad, indeed," said Brendan. " He doesn't understand, Columba. But I can't help feeling there's something at the back of all the legends. Maybe one or two could be discounted, but I've studied all the old texts I could lay my hands on or get the historians to translate for me, and they speak of them all the time. You look as if you'd have the stomach for adventure——"

Columba grinned. " I have," he said.

" Well, then, this is what's always in my mind. Those Happy Isles, they might be the same place as they call Tir nan Og, that's the Land of the Young, as you know. It seems to lie somewhere far out to the west. I keep thinking it may be another name for the Earthly Paradise—the Garden of Eden that we lost with Adam—at the Fall——"

"Well," Columba said. "I'd never thought of that."

"Nobody has except me," Brendan said simply. "But if we could find it again, think what a haven we could offer the world——"

"What about the angel?" objected Kenneth. "He'll still be guarding the entrance with his flaming sword."

"Perhaps he'd let Christians in," said Brendan. "And anyway, I wouldn't expect to stay there myself. It's the voyage I want, and the discovery. I'd leave the new country for the people who're so tired that they need to rest there while I went on looking for other lands. You'd come with me, wouldn't you?"

"I might," Columba said. "But perhaps we'd better build our first churches within reach of Clonard."

Brendan sighed. "The sea wind is in my hair and the gulls call me. I'm weary and stale . . ."

Columba's face went blank as he listened. For an instant the sunshine dimmed about him and the faces of the young men disappeared in a whirl of grey skies and moaning wind. His feet seemed to rock as if a boat were beneath them. He heard the crack of a sail as the wind filled it and the craft heeled over. A waste of waves across which cormorants plunged between the crests was before him, and in a patch of sunlight lay an island like a jewel girdled by rocks, a brooch in an iron setting, where water green as grass went whispering over milk-white sand. Bemusedly he drew his hand across his eyes as the inner vision vanished. Brendan was still finishing his sentence.

". . . and stale on dry land."

Vivid as the impression had been it had not occupied even an instant of time as perceived by the surrounding world. Its significance had been part of another order which was at odds, apparently, with that external world in which he lived and moved and had his being. Strange . . .

"Yes, one day perhaps I will sail as you do, Brendan," he said. "In search of one of your Happy Isles."

A few days later Columba encountered Comgall, the skilful scribe who was already making daring innovations in the infant art of textual illumination, always experimenting with pigments and dyes. Colour was his passion, as the sea was Brendan's, and Kenneth's the healing of disease. Columba was first aware of him when he passed his desk in the church and saw how he had made his page of the Gospel blaze. Comgall, small and quiet-faced, looked up with a smile as he heard Columba's gasp of pleasure.

"You like it, friend?"

"I do, indeed." One of the things that drew people to

Columba was the immense interest he took in all their doings, his genuine and immediate delight in all their gifts. As he bent over the desk at which Comgall was working, asking eagerly how he got this colour or that, the sympathy that went between them created a bond which was not to be broken for the rest of their lives.

" I see things always in colour," Comgall explained. " When they sing in church it reaches me in great waves of light, and when I read the Gospels the words have colour too. I want to put some of the light and colour on these pages so that others may see it too. But I cannot . . . I cannot . . ." all the artist's despairing frustration rang through his voice, " put down what I see."

" Any more than I can put it into my poems," agreed Columba. " It is always the best that escapes. But you have captured so much of the beauty. These colours here . . ."

" I grind them myself," Comgall said. " Some of the plants give good dyes, and that purple comes from the mussels that Brendan brings me from the sea. I have a fine strong red, and the green is the best I can make, but the blue is poor, so it will come no better. You write poems, do you ? In Latin or Gaelic ? "

" In both."

" I would copy them out fair for you if you could find me the vellum."

" Would you ? " said Columba gratefully. " Could you spare the time ? "

" Of course. I would do them at night, when my task here is done."

" It would give me great pleasure to see them written down," Columba admitted.

" It would delight me to do it," Comgall said.

The two young men looked happily at each other, warmed into kinship by appreciation of each other's skill. In that moment Comgall became one of the company of enthusiasts who were gathering round Columba, caught by the quality of leadership which was beginning to be evident in him even in these early days when he had just entered the priesthood and taken his first vows. His bright hair, tonsured back from his high forehead, curled almost like flames about his splendid head. He could cut down a sapling with a sweep of his axe, out-row Brendan on the broad river, sing like one of the choir of heaven, and grind his share of the corn given out to the students so fast that Kenneth swore one of the angels must have helped him. Above all, he bore about him a sort of heavenly gaiety, a quality of happiness towards which the others turned as naturally as they might have turned towards the sun. It was this, more than any consciously assumed authority, which brought the young monks who had also recently made their profession round him, roused their love for him and for each other in a way that no amount of exhortation could have done. In Columba's presence they were aware of the possibility of reaching towards another plane of existence, as if, without overt exposition, the beacon of his kindled spirit made many hidden things clear.

But Columba himself knew only that people came to him, people whom he loved and received gladly, with whom it was possible to work out immense schemes for the conversion of the farthest corners of Erin to the creed which offered truths so great that they could only be expressed in terms of paradox, truths that sounded above the clamour of intellectual argument like the trumpets of the conquering host before which the walls of Jericho fell down.

They spent hours working out what they should do. They did not debate much as to what they should say. Somehow, that seemed to matter less now.

"We did nothing but talk at Moville," Columba said. "And it got us nowhere. We just went round and round in circles and ended up where we began. Or else we all got too angry to listen to each other any longer and it broke up because we all talked at once."

"The truth won't go into words," said Comgall. "Not angry words, anyway. Sometimes you catch some of it in your poems, Columba . . ."

"Just enough to know how much more has escaped," Columba said.

"Words are a wide-meshed net," said Brendan. "Music is better."

"We shall have music too," said Columba. "Kenneth shall make our melodies, and we can all sing. Comgall must bring his colours, so that our churches are as gay as a summer meadow strewn with flowers. People will come to us because we talk to them of happiness and freedom. We shall cut down the Druid groves and let the sunshine bless the little fields. We shall offer them laughter and hope instead of fear and darkness. We shall show them the way home. The great question as I see it, is how best we can do these things. We all know what it is we want to do."

Their plans matured under the benevolent guidance of the Abbot, who recognised in them the ardent, adventurous temperament of men capable of converting others, not by argument or proof or discussion, but from sheer contagion of a faith which bore in itself the proof of its own reality ; a contagion which would infect the most recalcitrant people of Erin with new hope, whatever their resistance to theological argument, and however deep their grounding in paganism might be.

" So far, so good," he told Columba, " but there is yet much to do. A missionary community must not forget the needs of men's bodies while ministering to the rebirth of their souls. Have you a priest who is also skilled in medcine and the decoction of herbs ? Do you know anything of monastic organisation among unconverted strangers ? Have you musicians, singers, scribes ? Has any one set about making the copies of the Gospels and the Psalms which you will need before starting new churches ? And what of your rank as a leader ? It might be wiser to wait until you can be consecrated as a bishop, perhaps."

Columba ran his hands through his hair in a gesture of distraction. " You have thought of all the things which might have escaped me, Father. But I will try to answer you. We have two men who are skilled with herbs, though Comgall uses them only for the colourings which can be pressed from them. But Kenneth is also going with us, and as you know, he has been blessed with healing hands. We have singers and scribes, and the copies of Gospels and Psalms have been already started. As for the question of authority, I had not meant to claim any, beyond what my friends wish to give me because of what I can do for love of them. Need I have more ? "

" You must consult your soul-friend on that matter, my son," the Abbot said.

" Yes, Father. I will go to-day."

" As for the matter of organisation," said the Abbot, " I advise you to go and see how monasteries are run elsewhere."

" I cannot think," said Columba, " that I would find a monastery whose rule I would put before that of Clonard."

The Abbot smiled. " Yet it might be wise to see others, if only to learn what it would be best to avoid and what to perpetuate, even among the things you find here. But let your soul-friend advise you from his greater knowledge of your needs. It is to Molaise you go for confession, is it not ? "

" Yes, Father."

" You could find no man better qualified to advise you now," the Abbot said.

Columba found his confessor as usual near his hut on the lonely promontory, where he could meditate in a peace unbroken by the comings and goings of the young men of the monastery. Molaise, like so many of the early saints of Erin, felt a need for solitude more urgent than his need for sleep or food. His contacts with the hidden life of reality seemed to begin at the point where his physical body was most quiescent, when, subdued by wakefulness and fasting, it yielded priority to the heavenward-turning soul. When Columba came striding along behind him, he was sitting on the shore, his eyes wide and blank, his hands folded, his face towards the blurred line of horizon which stretched like a taut bowstring between sky and sea.

Without moving he greeted Columba. " I have been waiting, my son."

" It is I, Columba——"

" Yes, I know."

" You knew, Father? But how? " Columba stood with his hair blown back from his head by the sea wind, towering over the small man who had not yet looked at him. His own face was awed. Molaise never seemed to be aware of anything that went on about him, and yet, as now, he was not to be taken by surprise.

" There is nothing strange in that knowledge, Columba," said Molaise dryly. " No man in the community storms his way along the shingle with such impatient strides. Had I not been aware that you had been sent to me, I should have guessed from the way you announced yourself in a hail of small spurned stones."

" Indeed, I had forgotten to curb myself," said Columba, penitently. " But it was because I wanted to waste no time——"

" I know your zeal, my son," said Molaise. " It delights me. Yet there is some danger in it. Action is good, since we are to be known by our works. But patience is also necessary for anybody who is to become a leader of men."

" How shall I learn patience? " sighed Columba. " It is hard to make oneself take time and wait when there is so much to be done, Father. Life is so short for a man's work."

" A man's work is completed in eternity," said Molaise. " Why then should you spoil it because of a little loss of time? How old are you, Columba? Twenty-five? I know you, and the dangers that lie about you because of your very zeal. It is essential that you school yourself, that you learn humility——"

" Humility, Father? " Startled, Columba was stung to incredulity.

" Humility, my son. It is the essential virtue that you lack."

" I—I—I did not think myself proud. Surely the rule of Clonard does not leave a man much chance of arrogance——"

" Humility comes easily among friends. It is also necessary to learn it in the presence of enemies."

" Yes, Father," said Columba tonelessly.

The old man shook his head. " Your voice is obedient, but there is still rebellion in your heart."

" I will do my best, Father."

Molaise sighed. That may not be enough. I cannot teach until you wish to learn. If you cannot learn from me you must learn from life. But that will be harder, you know."

Columba looked troubled. " What do you mean, Father ? "

" God is not mocked," said Molaise. " The gifts he has entrusted to you are not lightly to be tossed aside. You will remember what I have said, perhaps too late to save yourself pain. For you must learn, my son."

" How shall I learn most quickly, Father ? " Columba asked, trying to beat down the hot, prickling sensation of resentment which threatened to dominate his obedience, uncomfortably proving the truth of what the old man had just said.

" Understand men before you seek to lead them," said Molaise. " Become a meeker priest before you presume to be a bishop. Then go and live alone that you may learn more of the ways of God before you teach others to follow them. Compel patience upon yourself. If your plans are good they will mature and become better. Now go, but come back to me again."

As he turned his face once more to the sea Molaise listened to the retreating footsteps of the resentful, perplexed and crestfallen young man, who was returning to the monastery so much more slowly than he had left it. Molaise smiled, as he crossed himself, and his thought shaped itself into a prayer for this child who had so much greatness in him that it would be worth the devil's while to seek to destroy him utterly, perhaps by over-intoxicating him with the possibilities of his own powers.

CHAPTER IX

THE MEMORY of his confessor's warning lay heavily on Columba's spirit during the days that followed his visit to Molaise. To be accused of pride, that most deadly sin, when he had thought with a certain satisfaction (when he thought about it at all) that had surely given up sufficiently bright prospects for there to be no doubt of his humility, was hard. Labouring to impose obedience on his revolting spirit, he was still aware of the smoulder of resentment, the sullen heave of resistance to an accusation which seemed unjust.

He was the eldest son of a family which claimed direct descent from the High Kings of Erin. His father, he knew, had even believed it possible that he, Columba, might have been himself a High King. Admittedly, he had never wanted such distinction. To surrender the career of a champion, the authority of a noble, the possibility of kingship, had cost him so little that it had scarcely seemed surrender at all. The call of other-worldly things had sounded in his ears from infancy, whether they echoed from the stories that old Nalda had told him between devouter Paternosters, haunted Gemman's songs and the records of the historians, or rang, clear as a bell, through the Gospel narratives. Was it not enough to have forsaken all the carnal world could offer in answer to the call of the ghostly one? Could a man be called proud when he wore coarse linen when he might have worn silks, went barefooted and bareheaded when he might have worn the great crown of Erin, washed the feet of his friends when he might have seen his nobles kneeling at his own, fasted and laboured when he might have caroused at Tara and been forbidden on account of his grandeur to labour at all? As for the leadership his friends offered him, he had not sought it. It was by no choice of his that crowds gathered when he spoke or sang, that something within him that he did not understand seemed to kindle in the hearts of the people who listened to him the same flame that blazed in his own. Molaise had said he had been so gifted by God. Was he to refuse to use, then, the eloquence, the leadership that he had been given?

Kneeling on the hard floor of the church in a dark corner where he would be unnoticed by the scribes who were busy with their quills and pigments and ink-horns, Columba angrily welcomed the ache in his back and knees, compelling himself to repeat prayer after prayer. But the familiar words seemed unable to rouse in him any inkling of that presence, that blessing, of which he was at other times so vividly, so joyously aware. Leadenly his petitions recoiled on his own spirit. Resentful and bewildered, he sank slowly into the despairing depths with which he paid occasional penalty for the gaiety which habitually raised him to the heights. He was not yet wise enough to recognise the elements in the struggle. Physical pride had been easily conquered : his increasing awareness of the things of the spirit quite naturally diverted all the forces of his urgent nature from the things of the world. But it had not occurred to him, until the recent warning, that the faults proper to his qualities might be diverted in that direction, too. Nor did he realise how much more terrible an ordeal must precede the elimination of spiritual pride. And so, though he had compelled himself to the letter of obedience, there still remained in him a hard core of intractable rebellion, even when, after an entire night's vigil, he at last rose stiffly from his knees.

Molaise had said he must renounce ambition : he went to the Abbot and said that he would prefer to remain a mere presbyter rather than be consecrated as a bishop. Molaise had advised him to learn more of men before he sought to lead them : he asked permission to go to other monasteries where he would be a stranger. Molaise had advised him to live for a time alone in order to purge the hubbub of the temporal world from his ears ; he would make his home for the time on one of the remotest islands of the west. Surely his obedience must now be proven beyond doubt ?

"And after these journeys, what then, my son ? " the Abbot said.

Columba stood before him with clasped hands and downcast eyes. "I do not know, Father. But no doubt God does."

The Abbot raised his sandy eyebrows. Here was his brightest torch most strangely quenched. Perhaps Molaise, for all his insight, had been too hard on him. The lad was a poet as well as a priest, subject to the violent emotional contradictions of his gifts as well as those of his race. He spoke gently. "Tell me, son, what is in your own heart ? "

Columba's dejected attitude changed slowly, yielding to the return of enthusiasm that swept over him as the returning light sweeps over a countryside that has been lost in low cloud. His grey eyes rested on the Abbot without seeing him, the pupils contracting as if he were looking towards a bright light. Slowly his arms rose from his sides in the gesture of a man lifting a chalice and holding it high before an altar. His voice was low and dreamy, his remote eyes smiled.

"In my heart, Father, are the unbuilt monasteries of Erin, the sanctuaries of Derry and Durrow and Kells. I hear the axes ring as my companions lay them to the tree trunks, and the voices of many people singing to the glory of God. I see the dawn breaking over the forests of Erin, shredding away the memory of nightmare and magic and despair. I see the sweetness of the land, the beauty of the wild creatures and the loveliness of its peoples, visible and invisible, gathered together like an offering that is held up to the smile of God. I see the faces of the saints, our fellow-countrymen, gathered to bless our altars, I see the quiet eyes, the pitying hands of Mary, patron of all despised mothers, I see the blessed shepherd leaving ninety and nine folded sheep for the sake of one gone obstinately astray."

Then suddenly his face went blank. He covered his eyes with his hands. "Darkness has come down on me. I can see no more." He was shivering. His face was strained now, tracked with little rivulets of sweat. The Abbot laid a hand on his shoulder, gentling him as he would have gentled a shying horse. Instinct told him that the young man's inner vision had encountered something at which his conscious self dared not look.

"Go to the church, my son, and steady yourself by copying out a chapter of one of the Gospels. St. Matthew, I think. You are in no state to bear the revelations granted to St. John. Work for a while, but not too long. Stop when your rushlight is burned to the socket. Then eat. And afterwards sleep."

"Yes, Father," Columba said.

"If you would indeed learn more of men and how to govern them, I will send you to Mobhi at Glasnevin." He sighed. "I know that when you leave us many will demand to go with you, so that Clonard will be the poorer for their loss. But since the zeal has come upon you I will not seek to keep you here. Now, go to the church and write."

Columba bowed his head and went. He was aware of a mounting urgency within him that surged against the possibility of delay or restriction like a spring tide. He wanted to gather them all together; Kenneth, Comgall, Brendan, and the rest; to tell them to take up their axes and follow him in that very hour, singing as they set out to build homing-places for the lost children of the household of God. "*Pater noster, qui es in coelis . . . venait regnum tuum . . .*" Now, now, in that instant, might the kingdom come! Why had Molaise commanded him to learn patience? Had any of the blessed saints, he wondered, also known how hard it was to wait?

The next few years, full of contrasting activities as they were, had indeed their share of waiting, for Columba forced himself to withdraw even from the dedicated activities of a monastic community and retire, as Molaise had advised, to a remote island off the west coast of Erin. Molaise himself had by then also withdrawn almost entirely from the world to the western isle of Innismurray, so that when Columba went to confession he had to take a coracle and paddle out to the fortress-like plateau of red sandstone which rose high out of the water between the great ocean and Erin's western mountain range.

But the contemplative life, which offered Molaise the fulfilment of his native genius, was still a pennance to Columba. Now over thirty, he still craved for action. The imaginative genius of his race, the fine scholarship derived from years of study, the compassionate understanding of the priest, and the strange visionary quality which was his own particular gift, were all beginning to blend now, making the towering man with the head of bright hair and the voice that could be heard above a gale the sort of influence which drew men and women from every corner of his native land.

They demanded his leadership. He could not refuse much longer. Round him had gathered the inner circle of his devoted friends, mostly men of his own age, who, like himself, had been so obsessed by the paradoxical immensities of Christianity that they could not rest among the banalities of temporal prosperity and power. Their response sustained Columba's purpose. He went up and down the land, with axe on shoulder and Gospel-satchel slung on his back. He was radiant, tireless, compulsively magnetic. People began to say that angels accompanied him. Of the other presence, the dark shadow of his old enemy, that destroying rage which he believed to have been purged out of him since his visit to Molaise at Clonard, they were unaware, and Columba himself, engrossed by the sheer joy of his chosen work, had entirely forgotten it.

Wherever he went, young men's voices called people together by the sheer beauty of their singing. Axes rang, churches rose, monasteries were formed and left in charge of one of the young priests, to shine out like tapers kindled among shadows, while Columba and the rest of his company passed on. And so, as the years went by, the glimpse of the future he had seen at Clonard became translated into terms of timber and wattle, monastery, school and church. Derry was his first foundation, built on high

land by the river which bordered his native province, winding
inland between those oak groves which Columba loved. He and
his friends had come to Derry from Glasnevin, where Mobhi and
many of his monks had recently died of the yellow plague. After
Derry, came Durrow, Raphoe, Kells . . . Columba strode along
the winding tracks of Erin, his habit kilted about his bare
knees, his voice ringing over woodland or moor as he sang the
poems he made up on his journeys, covering the miles at a pace
which made even his sturdy companions sometimes wilt. Among
all the monasteries he founded with his friends, up and down Erin,
Columba never forgot his first foundation, Derry on its knoll
above the northern river. And it was of Derry that he most
often sang :

> " Derry of the angels
> And the flowering thorns,
> Derry of the quietness . . .
> Mirrored are the wings
> Of the gulls in burnished waters.
> And the great arms of the oaks
> Rise to heaven as if in blessing
> When my boat returns from sea.
> Dear is Swords and dear is Durrow,
> Dear to me Raphoe and Kells,
> Ah, but dearer still is Derry,
> Derry, white with angels' wings . . ."

As they went, the gospellers exchanged their news of the
Kingdom of Heaven for the smaller change of events on earth. So
from time to time Columba heard of the hardships of those Scots
from Erin who had set out, fifty years before, to found the kingdom
of Scottish Dalriada on the neighbouring island of Alba, that
northern part of Britain which had been called Caledonia by
the Romans, who had found its defenders too much for them.
They had tried to seal it off by a great wall and leave it, as they
had left Erin, outside the orbit of Imperial Rome. But though
the wall still stood, the Romans had been overwhelmed in their
own country, so that that part of Britain which had been their
colony lay desolate and overrun, men said, by the kinsmen of the
ferocious Germanic pagans who had sacked the very city of
Rome.

So the Scots from Erin were not confronted by the disciplined
legions of the Empire, but by the veteran warriors of the Picts
who were natives of Alba itself, and were as furiously opposed to

the Scottish invasion as they had been to the Roman one. Yet in spite of constant Pictish opposition the settlers from Erin still clung to a portion of the country that was later to be called Scotland after them, winning their first foothold on the rugged land which projected westwards into the ceaselessly striving waves that had crumbled away all but the hardest granite. Their courage and their hardships caught at Columba's imagination as he went about among their kinsmen of Erin, but at that time it seemed unlikely that he would be called upon to offer more. Urgent matters lay nearer at hand.

It was when the group of men who had begun to be called the twelve apostles of Ireland were preaching near Moville that the first news of Finnian's return from Rome reached them. Comgall brought it back from Moville where he had gone that day in search of pigments for his illuminative work on the capitals of the Gospel copy he was making.

" Finnian is back from his great journey," he told Columba, as he unpacked his satchel in the hut which they used as a refectory.

" I did not know that he had intended to be back so soon," said Columba. " All the way from Rome——"

" He came back with in haste a great treasure," Comgall said.

" Treasure? Finnian? He cares for nothing earthly save his books."

" It is a book he has brought," said Comgall. " A translation of the Gospels, made by a certain Jerome. He talks of nothing else. Apparently it is a superb rendering into the Latin——"

" Did you get a sight of it ? "

Comgall grimaced. " I did not. He is as jealous of it as a cat is of its first kittens. It is kept in the church, under lock and key, and nobody is permitted as much as a glimpse of its binding. The students are clustered round Finnian like flies, but he waves them away, and will not trust them alone with it. He is a strange man, Columba. Why should he bring Jerome's translation back to Erin over a long road thick with dangers—they say he slept each night with the book for a pillow and a sword in his hand—if he is to deny it to the Church of Erin now he has brought it here ? "

Columba shook his head. " Perhaps he thinks less of the gift than of his privilege as the giver."

" But why ? " objected Comgall. " Is our Father in Heaven niggardly with his gifts of sun and air ? "

"All men have their faults," said Columba. "Finnian is a great scholar, with a precise mind that is faithful to the least comma in Gospel or Psalm. It is natural, perhaps, that he should be over-scrupulous in the matter of deciding where credit is due."

"But if he keeps his new translation under lock and key and pores over it alone at night-time, as they say he does, what use is the gift to Erin?" Comgall said indignantly.

"None," said Columba. "As far as I can see." He took his lower lip thoughtfully between finger and thumb. "How much I long to have a look at it. I wonder . . . yes, I wonder if by any chance he would grant such a privilege to me . . ."

"To you, if to any one," said Comgall.

"Perhaps . . ." Columba had begun to pace about the hut, his heavy brows drawn together, his mouth grim. "Well, we shall see . . ."

Next day he went to Moville. He had no difficulty in obtaining an interview with Finnian, for the younger man's fame had reached his former principal before him, and Finnian left his lecture hall to greet his now distinguished pupil, hands outstretched, and genuine cordiality illuminating the lean face which was now yellower, more fiercely aquiline than ever, and seamed with new lines of fatigue and pain. Yet the voice which greeted Columba had all the old rasping abruptness which had frightened so many students, to which Columba responded with the same unintimidated grin.

"Well, I'm glad you came," he said when Columba had followed him to his own dwelling. "You've done great things, I hear. Half the country seems to be talking of you. Nonsense, much of what they say. Miracles, they're attributing to you, I believe. Shouldn't let that sort of talk get about, you know. Leave magic to the Druids. Their speciality."

"I've done nothing out of the ordinary," said Columba frankly. "But some strange things have been done by God."

"H'm," said Finnian, looking severely at his former pupil. He was tall, but Columba was now taller. It was unpleasant to have to look up to the lad. Undignified. "Sit down," said Finnian, pointing to a stool.

Columba obeyed. His face was grave, but his grey eyes amused. He allowed Finnian to tower over him, to impress on him the need for discretion in leadership, for resistance to popular clamour lest magic and miracle should cheapen the message he brought.

Diplomatically he let himself be admonished. He was biding

his time. It would be easier to obtain a concession once he had
let his former principal establish his intellectual superiority.
Columba was not interested in intellectual supremacy over the
people of Erin who flocked about him, nor did he make the
mistake of supposing that it was for himself that they came.
When he spoke he was aware that his words were carried forward
on a wave of light and eloquence which had its origin far beyond
him, offering the listening people an experience which owed
its illumination and its beauty to the source of that light alone.
He was no more than its bearer : his fidelity could add nothing
to the glory nor his failure take a fraction of it away.

It was some time before he could steer Finnian from the
discussion of miracles to the question of the translation he
had brought from Rome, but eventually he succeeded. " Yes, I
should be glad to show it to you," Finnian said eventually.
" Mind you, I would not show it to most people. It is the only
thing of its kind in the whole of Erin. Jerome completed his
translation long before you were born, but this is the first copy
to be transcribed for Erin."

" I should appreciate the privilege," Columba said.

" I know you would," said Finnian. " As a matter of fact
there are one or two points I would like to discuss with you.
You were never a fool, and now I hear they consider you an
exceptional Latin scholar——"

" I have too little time for scholarship these days," Columba
said.

" No doubt, no doubt. An itinerant preacher usually has,"
said Finnian. " It might do you good to take time off your
gospelling to study here. Restore the balance. A man gets to
think too highly of himself when he is worshipped by the
illiterate——"

" I would like nothing more than the chance of spending
some time here," said Columba. " I cannot imagine greater
fortune than the opportunity to study Jerome's translation while
it still remains in your hands——"

" Still remains ? " questioned Finnian sharply. " I intend
to retain its custody, I assure you."

" You do not mean to have it copied and sent to all the
churches of Erin ? "

" Why should I cast such a pearl before these swine ? Have I
not risked my life to bring it home with me in order that a select
few of Erin's scholars may study it ? By my permission, of course."

" The people of Erin would welcome it, sir. They have so
little, only a few copies of the Gospels which through constant

copyings, each adding its mistakes, have become sadly marred. It would be a treasure beyond price for each church to have its copy of this new translation made by one of the finest scholars in the world."

"A treasure which is much too good for them," snapped Finnian. "You must leave me to judge of those fit to receive such things. The common people are as children to be fed from the hands of those with better judgment. I will show you the translation, as I have promised. But it is a privilege. And for you alone."

Columba bowed his head.

"Come to the church," said Finnian. "It is kept there."

The church seemed small and dark by comparison with the beautiful building at Clonard, dwarfed by the lecture halls which had sprung up round it as the fame of Finnian and his great school spread. It was high noon, but only spear-heads of restricted light blunted themselves on the earthen floor from the narrow window slits. The desks of the copyists were vacant, and the church had an indefinable air of having lost some of its significance, standing there empty while the lecture-halls were full. Columba looked uneasily round him while Finnian unlocked the door of a cupboard in the little sacristy which had been built on to the main aisle.

"You must come in here," he said. "I will not bring it out into the church. Any one might come by. Are your hands clean?"

"Yes, sir," said Columba. But he wiped his fingers on the rough wool of his habit as Finnian jealously laid the heavy book on the desk which stood near the cupboard from which he had taken the precious thing. As he came closer to Finnian, stooping to look at it, he felt huge and clumsy and his heart thundered against his chest wall. Here, from the city of the martyrs, some of whom might actually have set mortal eyes on their risen Lord, was the new translation which brought the very words that Christ had spoken nearer to succeeding generations, peering back through the centuries in search of a gesture, a smile, a turn of phrase ; bemusedly seeking, like Thomas, for the print of the nails and the spear-thrust in the side.

"You may take it in your hands. But only for a moment," Finnian said.

Columba took the book and raised it to his lips. In that instant he was no longer aware of the dim sacristy, of Finnian's twitching fingers, as he waited for his treasure to be returned to him. He saw instead the faces of the people to whom he had

preached and sung all over Erin, the common people who had
heard him also, gladly, who had recognised the words that had
been unto the Jews a stumbling-block and unto the Greeks'
foolishness as the symbols of life and truth. These were the
people to whom Finnian would deny the Gospel, hoarding it
for scholars to mumble over and students to dissect, so that in
their mumblings and disputations he himself might achieve
greater fame. Within him something revolted. This was a treasure
which should belong, not to the learned but to the simple, not to
the rich, but to the poor in spirit, not to the elect, but to the
sheep from alien folds. Aloud he only said, scarcely expecting
permission :

" Sir, might I have the great privilege of studying this book
further ? You have so little time to spare, but I have more. If
you must go, may I remain ? "

Finnian opened his mouth to refuse, considered the possible
repercussions of such a refusal when the request had been made
by such a distinguished scholar, and changed his mind. He was
not actually feeling very well. The strain of the long journey
had perhaps been too much for him. He was shivering in the
chilly sacristy. He would be quite glad to return to his own room.

" Very well," he said grudgingly. " Provided you lock the
book away securely before you leave and bring me back the key."

" I will," Columba said.

But when the door had closed behind Finnian he hid his
face in his hands, shocked by the strength of the impulse which
urged him to take advantage of this heaven-sent chance to make at
least part of Jerome's translation his own. He had asked and
received permission to study the precious book. He had not
asked if he might copy it. Such permission, he knew, would have
been violently refused. But why ? So that Finnian might achieve
greater glory as its unique owner, offering the common people
stones while he retained the bread ?

He, Columba had dedicated his life to the common people.
He had sworn to teach them, pray for them, serve them. Must
he steal for them, too ? Was this temptation or opportunity ?
He rose and began to pace about the sacristy. Uncertainty
racked him. He could not pray. After what seemed a long time
he found himself remembering that the Abbot of Clonard had
once set him copying the Gospel of St. Matthew in order to achieve
peace of mind. Perhaps, without actually taking a decision, he
might do a little copying now.

A careless student had left some sheets of vellum on his desk.
More were in the cupboard. Columba took them, finding an

inkhorn on another desk, elsewhere a quill. As he wrote the first words he was aware of an immense appeasement, as if the tension within him relaxed as the conflicting emotions within him found their way down his arm and out at his tingling fingertips. He wrote all night, his hand unwearied, his concentration undiminished, his lips moving as he murmured occasional passages aloud. When the morning light filtered through the narrow window-slits he reluctantly laid his pen down. He would have to stop, two-thirds through St. Matthew's Gospel. He had hoped at least to be able to capture some of the best-loved phrases of his favourite gospeller, St. John. But now, according to his promise, he must lock the book away and return the key to Finnian. Otherwise he must lose even what he had written. He did not know what to do next. It was possible that Finnian might let him have the key again. He could not tell. He had no plan, and was still torn with uncertainty about the rights and wrongs of what he had already done. Had the impulse which set him copying so furiously come from hell or from heaven ? If from heaven would God not send him a sign? With his incomplete copy under his cloak, he went slowly towards Finnian's timbered dwelling. As he wrote, he had not felt the slightest fatigue, but now he ached with it, and his eyelids were as ponderous as if they had been weighted with lead. A young priest met him on the threshold, holding up an admonitory hand.

" You cannot come in."

" I have business with Finnian," said Columba.

" Finnian is doing no business to-day. He is delirious. The physicians say it is a high fever caught on the journey from Rome. He can see no one, no one at all."

" I understand," Columba's voice was awed. He made the sign of the cross as he turned away, the key still in his hand, towards the house in which he had once lodged, for food and a few hours' sleep. His mind was made up now. Surely he had his sign ?

That night, and each night in succession, he returned to the church and wrote there till daylight. He carried the key of the cupboard round his neck by day and spoke of it to no one. Every morning he went to inquire for Finnian and to return the key if he should have asked for it, and afterwards, having heard that Finnian was still delirious, he offered thanks, and went to his lodging to rest before writing again.

So the work went on, verse by verse, chapter by chapter, Gospel by Gospel, till the end, that Columba had scarcely dared to hope for, was actually in sight. Every morning, when he locked up the precious book and took away the pages he had copied, before blowing out the rushlights that had burned nearly to their sockets, he was prepared to have to surrender the key and write no more. And every night he was able to return, restored by a few hours' sleep, to cover sheet after sheet of vellum with his beautiful small script. He received many invitations to be present at distinguished gatherings of illustrious scholars, and steadily refused them. His eccentricity was accepted: it was commonly supposed that he spent his nights in vigil and prayer for Finnian's soul.

So Columba wrote on, driving his way through the final chapters with a furious resolution that made his quill shriek as it scored the surface of the vellum that he had obtained from several sources so as to give no clue to the purpose he had in mind. Every night he drew the bolt behind him shortly after sundown and every morning he withdrew it soon after dawn. He had little fear of interruption since the night offices were said by the monks in their own chapel, and few of the scholars were given either to vigil or to prayer. At first his work had the urgency of desperation, but as he approached the end of his task he began, insensibly, to relax, to appreciate what he wrote, to neglect precautions. He had begun the twentieth chapter of St. John and was absorbed in the culminating drama of the resurrection when the unlooked for crisis came.

"*Nisi videro in manibus ejus vestigium clavorum . . . nequaquam credam . . . Deinde dicit Thomae: Infer digitum tuum huc, et vide manus meas, et profer manuum tuum, et immitte in latus meum . . .*"

He was murmuring the words aloud: '"Except I shall see in his hands the print of the nails . . . I will not believe . . ." Then said he to Thomas, "Reach hither thy finger and behold my hands, and reach hither thy hand and thrust it into my side: and be not faithless, but believing." And Thomas answered: "My Lord and my God."'

The rushlight flickered. Columba laid down his quill and absently kindled another to replace it. " . . . blessed are they that have not seen, and yet have believed." He flexed his stiffening fingers. Only the last chapter remained. He would finish his task before daybreak, return the key, take his treasure home . . .

Then a small sound startled him. Someone was fumbling at the outer door. Too late he realised that for once he had not bolted it. Someone was in the church. Unsteady steps were coming towards the sacristy. He sprang up, gathering newly written sheets together, on a wild impulse to restore them and the

Gospel book to the cupboard. But it was too late. In the doorway
stood Finnian, ghastly pale, but clear-headed, a cloak thrown
over his habit, a staff in one emaciated hand.

"Sir . . . what are you doing, at this hour . . . ?"

"Say rather what are . . . you doing, Columba?" said
Finnian, in a croaking voice that slowly gathered strength. "I
gave you permission to study the translation from Rome, not to
copy it. How dared you do such a thing?"

"I claim the rights of a priest whose needs are the needs
of Erin," said Columba.

"You have broken your pledged word——"

"I gave no word——"

"You knew my wishes.——"

"I knew you were wrong——"

"How dare you——"

They were both angry now, facing each other across the desk
on which lay the precious translation and its copy, the vigorous
young priest with the violent temper and the gaunt old man in
whom fury had overwhelmed the weakness of convalescence,
whose first coherent thought had been for his precious book, so
that at dead of night he had outwitted his attendants and tottered
to the church from which the tell-tale light streamed.

"I would dare all things to do my work——"

"This is not your work, this is wicked covetousness. It is
mortal sin——"

"It is a greater sin to keep the Gospels from a Christian
people——"

"The book is mine."

"And mine the copy——"

"No," cried Finnian, his voice breaking, suddenly shrill. "I
claim both."

"You shall not have them. I have laboured to make the
copy. It is mine."

"I shall have it torn from you . . ."

"You can try!" roared Columba. He gathered the sheets of
vellum into his arms and stood there defiant, obdurate
as a cliff. It was obvious that he would yield only to
greater force, but fury drove Finnian on. He actually considered wresting the copy from the young man's arms. Forgetting his age, his rank, his recent illness, he took a step
forward. They were on the verge of a savage, degrading
struggle. Then, warned by the look of sheer murder which he
surprised in Columba's eyes, he stopped, dumbfounded. For
perhaps a dozen heart-beats they glared at each other. Finnian's

brain worked fast. He took refuge in the threat which must surely decide everything.

" I will appeal for justice to the High King."

Columba shrugged. " Do as you like. But I warn you that it will make no difference. I will give up this copy of the Gospels for no man on earth nor devil from hell."

Finnian thrust his sick eagle's face forward. " Such defiance means a death sentence."

Columba's great laugh seemed to shake the little wooden building. " I doubt it. But I have still a chapter to write. I will bring you the key in the morning. Shall I escort you back to your bed or will you go ? "

" You will regret this," snarled Finnian, beating the butt of his staff on the earthen floor. " You will regret this when you are hailed to Tara to answer for this monstrous action. Take your impious hands off me ! " he added hastily, as Columba laid the copy on the desk and advanced menacingly towards him. " I will go alone."

He shuffled painfully out of the sacristy and through the darkened church. Columba could hear him fumbling with the fastenings of the outer door, and at the uncertain, groping sound compunction suddenly overwhelmed his anger. He had been violent and undutiful. Finnian might be a parsimonious scholar and a martinet, but he also was a very weary, sick old man. Columba hurried through the church and wrenched open the heavy door which had fallen into place behind Finnian. Outside, the whole plain was washed in moonlight, through which his former principal was palely creeping like a ghost. Columba ran after him, speaking impulsively.

" Sir, I acted in haste and anger. I——"

But the face that Finnian turned on his was sharp and unforgiving as a sword's blade.

" We shall meet at Tara. I have no more to say."

CHAPTER X

THE HALL OF SYNODS at Tara was full of grave and reverend men who had spent many years of their lives debating precise points of law. They wore long dark robes, over which their white beards flowed nearly to their girdles, and attendant scribes hovered in the background of the shifting groups, alert for the instructions of each learned judge who nodded and murmured and stroked his beard among his peers. On the throne at the far end of the hall sat the High King of Erin, gorgeous in the robes of seven colours which only royalty might wear.

The High King's fierce, swarthy face was blank and proud beneath the encircling diadem, and his light eyes roved continually over the assembly, as if in search of suspected slights to his supreme majesty. Round him eddied the petitioners and their legal representatives with a continual bending of knees and bowing of heads, officials called periodically for silence, and there were whispered consultations between the High King and the illustrious judges who stood about him, consultations to which the King did not always appear to listen before pronouncing judgment in a loud, harsh voice. But afterwards all the trumpets from the corners of the great hall would sound a fanfare that set the bats astir among the smoke-blackened rafters overhead.

Columba, surrounded by his supporters, stood among the crowd. He did not understand the proceedure, but his father had taken up his cause with fervour, and undertaken to see that everything necessary was done. Phelim, who was with Columba in court, had aged a great deal in the last twenty years during which his son had become famous. He seemed, at sixty, to have lost, with youth's initial impetus, almost all his vitality. He was fretted, at home, by the presence of Maeve, who still, after all those years, kept up the pretence of being held against her will in Phelim's dun. And still, in middle-age, she bore a notorious reputation for her relationships with men so eminent that he dared not interfere. From his wife he had little comfort either. Eithne seemed to care for nothing but the nation-wide reputation of her eldest son. Phelim had felt lonely, forsaken and old until this crisis had revived his old hopes once more.

In Columba, on the other hand, the first fervour of youth seemed to have been supplemented from some deeper source of strength, so that, as a man in early middle-age, he gave the impres-

sion of immense power, of joyous though not entirely disciplined
spirituality, and the determination to let no single instant of a
lifetime pass him by unused. He was chafing, inevitably, at the
prolonged delay ; wondering, too, at the High King's indifference.
As a child, he had thought such judgments must be inspired by
Heaven. Now, quite evidently, he was not so sure. As he watched
the blank, arrogant face of the High King who was, as Phelim
kept muttering, their kinsman, but no more aware of them, in
his pride, than of the mud that gouted his shoes, as he heard the
harsh, indifferent voice give judgment according to the whisperings of the old men behind his throne. Columba found himself
remembering the story of the false judgment given by the usurper
MacCon, which had been told him long ago by the learned judge
who had been invited to dine in Phelim's hall.

Kenneth, now in charge of his own monastery, was also
waiting for the verdict. He had left his duties to his deputy in
order to be with his leader on such a momentous day. Knowing
Columba's turbulent spirit as he did his face was anxious as he
waited. It was evident that Columba had already reached the
limits of his patience, and if further demands were made on it
they might prove impossible to bear.

Phelim, too, was watching his son, but stealthily. The old,
fantastic dream of greatness had never quite left him. He welcomed the possibility of an adverse decision which would give him
the excuse to challenge the supremacy of the High King who had
been elected from the southern branch of the illustrious Niall's
descendents. There had always been keen rivalry between north
and south, and from this rivalry he now hoped much.
Phelim had been getting a little out of touch with things at court
lately, and it had been, surprisingly, Maeve who had dropped
him the hint that if the judgment went against Colum at Tara
he need not accept it, since any chance of a conflict with the
southern Hy Niall would be well received at the northern court.
He had received the information with reserve, at first, looking
up at his flamboyant sister-in-law beneath his brows.

" I suppose you know what you're talking about ? "

" Oh, yes," Maeve had said dryly. " I always do."

" And what d'you expect to get out of this for yourself ? "
he had asked bluntly.

But Maeve had only smiled. " Nothing, Phelim. I just
thought you ought to know. After all Colum-Cille is your son
first and a priest afterwards, isn't he ? "

So Phelim had grunted and had let it go at that. It must be
sheer love of stirring up trouble that prompted her to drop that

hint. After all, she was nearly twenty years older than Colum. What could he mean to her?

As he waited for the High King's judgment, Phelim was remembering Maeve's face as he had seen it then, haggard and desolate like that of a battle fury. Aggravating as she was, he thought, at times he could feel sorry for her. She was lonely, too, he told himself, as he shifted from foot to weary foot, jostled by freeholders who had come to complain of trespass, nobles with tales of unpaid revenues, husbandmen whose homesteads had been burnt down, fathers whose daughters had been enticed from home and raped, injured parties whose assailants had not paid the proper honour price. Case after case dragged on, and Columba fretted at their endlessness, while Kenneth tried to soothe him and his father to fan his rage. On the far side of the hall, towering gauntly above his scholarly supporters, Finnian also waited, his face so emaciated after his recent illness that it was like a mere yellowish parchment stretched across a skull. As the day wore on Finnian fastened his eyes on the High King with increasing intentness, as if all the will-power that had governed his entire existence was concentrated into the burning focus of this day's insistent zeal.

Then, at last, the learned men who had stood beside Finnian and Columba began to make their way unobtrusively towards the throne. The time for a decision was approaching. The elderly brehon who represented Columba came reluctantly out of the trance of profound thought in which he had been sunk, nodded, and led the way till they reached the open space which was kept clear by soldiers of the king's house-company. There they faced each other again; Finnian, who seemed so frail that only his tremendous will kept life within his emaciated body; and Columba, radiant as the sun in splendour, yet with thunder-clouds banked about him and smouldering with uneasy fire. Their names were called and the case between them was at last declared.

The High King yawned. This matter of a couple of books seemed of very little importance. He was not a subtle man and the implications of Columba's kinship with the northern ruling house as well as with his own were lost on him. He only wanted to get the matter settled so that he might go and dine. His advisers whispered. He turned his head, muttering: " what's that? Judgment for the claimant, on the grounds of . . . very well . . . I see . . ."

He rose. The officials called for silence as his blank eyes roved round the hall now packed with people who appeared to be awaiting his decision with commendable eagerness, though why it mattered so much to them he was sure he could not tell. A couple of monks and a couple of books . . . not even the fate of a hostage or a tract of land. Still . . . He cleared his throat, listening to his own voice with pleasure as the superb notes boomed out.

" Hear my words, people of Erin. As to each cow belongs her calf, so to each book belongs its copy. I give judgment for Finnian, and decree that the copy he claims shall be handed to him immediately. The court now stands adjourned in order that we may dine. Let the officers see to it that . . ."

But before he could complete his sentence Columba had surged forward, thrusting away the reverend judges with such impetuosity that they staggered indignantly aside. Scarcely knowing what he was doing, borne beyond all moderation by the thunder-darkened rage that had now and then possessed him utterly in his wild youth, he shook his fists in the High King's face and roared :

" I defy the judgment ! "

" Eh, what's that ? " The King, about to step from the throne, was startled into banality by the unexpected shout.

" It is unjust," stormed Columba. " The copy is mine, by right of the labour of my own hand."

The High King flicked his fingers. " I have spoken. Seize that noisy fellow and take him away."

" Touch him and you will regret it," said Phelim icily. He had taken the precaution of having his own house-company in attendance, and at his gesture they surrounded Columba, who was still roaring defiance over the gathering tumult, while Kenneth, clinging to his arms, was entreating submission, but in vain. In various parts of the hall other scuffles were breaking out between people who were also dissatisfied with the judgment which had been meted out to them. Women screamed, men fought, the northern tribesmen drew out the unlawful weapons they had secretly brought into the Synod Hall, as they surrounded Columba and the sardonically exultant Phelim, in a belligerent, unyielding ring.

" Judgment has been given. It will be enforced," shouted the High King.

" Not while our warriors from the north still live," answered Phelim. As he gripped Columba's hand his son was aware of a great surge of answering emotion. With tears in his eyes he responded to the loyalty of the kinsmen he had scarcely seen since childhood, who had gathered around him in his emergency. Of all that lay behind it he was unaware. His father's ambitions, Maeve's restless desire for drama and conflict, Phelim's use of

the dispute as a pretext for an insurrection : these things were
beyond his ken. All he knew was that the cherished copy of
Jerome's translation of the Gospels was still in its satchel on his
back, and if Finnian's supporters wanted it they must come and
take it not from him alone, but from the protection of armed
men.

The events of the next few hours during which Phelim's
party, with Columba amongst them, left Tara, and headed for
the north, were hazed by the anger and elation which dominated
him so that Kenneth's gentle, persistent voice was merely exasperat-
ing. Impulsively he struck him aside. " Submit ? What
nonsense is this ? "

" Columba, what madness holds you ? This means war . . ."

" I know it," Columba exulted.

" But consider . . ."

" Consider the justice of our cause . . ."

" Not justice but mercy . . ." pleaded Kenneth.

" The choice is not mine."

" It still may be. You can yield . . ."

" Never, never, never . . ." roared Columba to all the winds.

" Columba, what has come over you ? " whispered Kenneth.
He crossed himself in terror. " You speak like a stranger, drunk
with the lust of blood . . . I have never known you behave so,
never before."

" I speak as a priest. My duty is to serve the people of Erin,"
Columba said.

" But Finnian—he too is a priest—shall servants who follow
the same master wrangle among themselves ? Can you not reason
with him ? "

Columba shook his head. " Finnian's heart is closed to me.
He will not listen. I have tried."

" Even so," begged Kenneth, plodding desperately beside
Columba, outpaced at every stride, " could you not go to him
once again ? Could you not plead for understanding now, before
we are all carried into battle against our vows ? "

" I can do no more," said Columba grimly. " I tell you he
will not listen. I have the book here. If he lets me keep it there
will be no battle. But if he seeks to reclaim it we will resist.
That is all. In our hand will be the sword of the Lord and of
Gideon. Can anybody doubt the justice of our cause ? "

" Between Christians, can there ever be justification for
conflict ? " said Kenneth unhappily. He was aware that he was
saying something which went against the habits of his contemporaries, the tradition of his warlike people, the instincts of

the entire human race, which had fought its way up out of the remote mists of pre-history by means of the principle which governed the life of the animals they had first fought with : let the strongest take what he needs and hold it while he can. Yet he had long been conscious of a slowly deepening conviction that warred with that elemental principle of barbarism, a conviction which seemed to descend upon him from some as yet unknown way of life which lay far off in man's spiritual future, and already strove within him against the desire for violence which rose, like a miasma, from his animal past. In this uneasy conversion he was, he knew, almost alone. Even Columba, the greatest torch of the faith, could not understand what he took for squeamishness.

" Is it not right that the common people should be taught ? " he said.

" Why, yes," Kenneth admitted.

" And are the Gospels not necessary for their teaching ? "

" Yes, of course."

" Am I not carrying on my back the finest translation which ever reached Erin ? Is it not right that we, who teach the people, should possess this ? "

" Yes," Kenneth admitted.

" But if others seek to take it from us, how can we keep it if not by force ? "

" I do not know," said Kenneth unhappily. " Perhaps it would be better not to have it than to hold it at such a price."

" Such a price ! Are we not a nation of warriors ? Is it not better that they should use their weapons for God rather than to annex each others' goods ? "

Kenneth shook his head. He could not argue. He could never find words to express his deepest convictions. They seemed to come to him from an environment which had outworn the significance of words. He relapsed into silence, and Columba strode along beside him, singing, while the wind lifted his bright hair.

Columba was not, however, entirely happy about the business, and much of what he had been saying to Kenneth came more from the necessity of reassuring himself than of convincing his friend. He was in an odd state of mind, a sort of prolonged spiritual twilight, which had much in common with the flare-lit darkness of his early rages. It was not a dramatic enough eclipse of the spirit for him to recognise it, yet sufficiently different from his usual piercing awareness of heavenly things for him to feel bereft. But since his nature tended always to seek the resolution of his problems in action rather than contemplation, he was now forcing himself on, assuming an attitude of certainty because it seemed a necessary state of mind.

Actually, the one chief actor in the drama who had no doubts whatever was Phelim. The disputed judgment had given him exactly the opportunity he had been waiting for, and from that moment the weariness of the years seemed to fall from him, till he was again the active diplomat, the wary general, the man of affairs who gathered the threads of great events into his skilful hands. Much had already been done in the way of unobtrusive preparation before he went with Columba to Tara. It did not take long to send the runners to rouse the tribe to arms. Columba and his precious book were surrounded by a bodyguard, and before they reached the borders of their own province reinforcements were arriving daily to the encampment on the high ground near Culdremne, which the king of the north had decided to defend against the southern followers of the High King. He made no secret of his position, nor did the High King's men hide their intention of attacking it. The army of the south was also gathering fast. Spies reported its numbers, and soon the glow from scores of camp-fires could be seen on the southern horizon by night.

Columba spent the time of preparation in a strange mood of restless elation which made him disinclined for sleep, meditation or prayer. Instead, it drove him to and fro about the encampment, by night and by day. He watched the furiously working smiths beating out sword-blades and spear-heads on portable anvils, while sweating lads blew their furnaces to white heat and the sparks surrounded them like a cloud of brilliant flies. Sometimes he paused by the shield-makers, who were weaving wicker, shaping wood and stretching hides, or saw how fast the carpenters could cut new hafts for spears or fit brazen heads to sheaves of javelins. Once he caught a glimpse of Maeve, laughing wildly in the arms of a drunken chief, but she was so changed, after twenty years, that he would scarcely have known her, and the sight offended him so profoundly that he went hastily away, soon to forget it again. For excitement now ran like wine through his blood, and memories of the old tales of his childhood filled his mind. The sky seemed fuller of the ghastly forms of the battle-demons who came like vultures to the smell of slaughter, than of the quiet wings of the angels of God. Only Kenneth, alone and forgotten in busy preparations, prayed desperately for Columba, his friend still, right or wrong.

At last the opposing armies moved into position. Columba

marched with his kinsmen, the Gospel book on which they based their hopes of victory slung on his back, a stout staff in his hand. Though he meant to take no part in the struggle, the book should not be torn from him while he remained alive.

As the tribesmen passed the centre of the encampment on the summit, where the king of the northern people stood to salute them, each man brought a stone in his hand, throwing it at the king's feet as a symbol of his own life. When the battle was over, Columba knew, they would file back again, each picking up a stone. From the pile which remained could be reckoned the number of the slain. Raising his hands, he blessed them ; slingers, pikemen, swordsmen and archers, spearsmen mounted or on foot. They wore steel caps, and were girded with broad belts through which were tucked knives or daggers. Their shields, freshly whitened and painted, were dazzlingly bright in the sun. They fought barefoot, and no man wore armour : the warriors of Erin disdained it, preferring to go into battle in their finest tunics, dyed golden with saffron and heavy with embroidery, those of the noblemen often made of silk or satin which their wives had stitched so that they were as gorgeous as if bound for a feast. As they passed the king they beat their shields with their swords till the lime flew up in a white cloud from which emerged the northern battle-cry.

The battle began at first light and lasted until sundown. The men of the south defended themselves stubbornly, and Columba kept close behind the line of flailing swordsmen, shouting alternate encouragement and prayers. He was so hoarse that he could hardly speak when the final charge of the northern warriors had driven the enemy from their last hold on the foothills of the embattled summit. Dusk was draining the colours from the sky as they floundered back across the stream that scores of bodies had tainted, broke from the ruthless pursuit and fled in every direction from his kinsmen's terrible swords.

Columba followed no farther than the hillside above the stream, from which he watched the pursuit fade into the gathering dusk. Raising clenched fists above his head in a gesture of triumph, he croaked the northern battle-cry as he slid down the slippery hillside which had been churned into mud by the hundreds of feet which had fought over it all day. He wanted to shout, but he was almost voiceless, to declaim a poem to victory, but only a clash of swords echoed in his head, to thank God for deliverance, but as he stood with the sweat chilling his limbs under his mud-daubed, high-girded habit, heaven seemed unbelievably far away. Why should it be so hard to rejoice when his prayers had brought his supporters victory ?

Disturbed, uneasy, still whipping himself towards a triumph without heart in it, he went wearily on, stepping over the dead bodies that sprawled across his way till a slight movement from what he had taken to be another corpse halted him abruptly. Again the hand moved, very slightly, from the wrist. The eyes implored. Columba knelt to look more closely.

"Why, Tombul, old friend . . ."

"Has it gone well for us, Colum?" the old champion whispered.

"Well, indeed," said Columba wretchedly. "But you . . ."

"It does not matter . . ." The words could scarcely be heard now. "My body was ageing . . . though I had pleasure in it . . . still. If we have beaten those scum from . . . the south . . . I am ready to . . . go . . ."

"Do not go, Tombul. Do not leave me," pleaded Columba. He felt, in that instant, like a child again. The darkness was coming down on him, forlorn between the dying and the dead on the churned hillside. "You, who first taught me to hold shield and sword, stay with me still . . ."

But it was too late. With a faint, apologetic smile, Tombul died.

Columba crouched beside his body while the last of the exultation which had sustained him ever since the adverse judgment had been given at Tara ebbed from his spirit, as if that, too, were being drained from him to drift down the tainted stream which carried away the dead men's blood. He was bereft, bewildered, hideously alone. The shouts of the warriors still following the defeated enemy seemed to change, to become the hellish laughter of the demons who were fastening eager talons into so many violently disembodied souls. Columba covered his face with his hands. But still he could not pray. Between him and heaven there seemed to be, once again, some barrier which his horrified petitions could not pierce: impenetrable as a vast shield, it caught his prayers like a flight of javelins, deflecting them till they fell back on his own despairing soul.

The very lapping of the stream seemed to accuse him. He fancied he could hear, above the sound of the water that surged about the mounded bodies, the voices of the dead men who had been his friends.

"*Columba . . . Columba . . . life was sweet. I was married ten days ago . . .*"

"*Your father was my battle-comrade, Colum. I have held you on my knee . . .*"

"*We were schoolfellows, Colum . . .*"

"*Colum, Colum the wolf, have you forgotten Moldan?*"

"*And Luigne . . . ?*"

"*And Orc . . . ?*"

"*Columba, Columba, it is so dark here . . .*"

"*Oh, mother, mother, mother . . . I am lost and afraid . . . it was my first battle, Columba . . . the first time I had ever borne my shield in war . . .*"

"*Pray God to forgive us our sins, Columba . . .*"

"May God forgive me mine," Columba cried. He beat his face with his clenched fists, then thrust his fingers into his ears in a desperate attempt to shut out the voices. But they reached him still.

"*There is a mighty gathering here to do you honour, Columba. Three thousand men . . . three thousand men from north and south have died for you . . .*"

"*Pater noster qui es in coelis . . .*" prayed Columba desperately . . . "*demitte nobis debita nostra . . .*"

"*Three thousand of us have died for you, Columba . . .*" cried the unearthly voices round him. "*Pray for us, man of God, for we are strangers in an unknown world . . . we shall never smell the gorse in flower above Gartan again . . .*"

"*Demitte nobis debita nostra . . .*" groaned Columba. "Our trespasses . . . our trespasses . . ." He flung himself on his face among the dead, grief choking him, guilt racking him, murmuring anguished, incoherent prayers. It was quite dark now, and the returning victors passed him by unseeing in their haste to regain the encampment, haling their prisoners with them towards the smell of cooking and the welcoming glare of many high-piled fires.

Columba lay there till the first light of morning brought a gradual, ghastly clarity to the battle-field. In the grey dawn he could hear the dead men's voices no longer: he went about among the bodies of his friends, mourning because the rigor of death held them so that he could not even close the wildly staring eyes or straighten the distorted limbs. With fresh horror he saw the faces of the dead men whose voices had cried about him in the dark. There lay Tombul, the old champion, felled like the oak under which he had taught them to cast javelins . . . Moldan, who had held his shield as if it were a flower for his sweetheart . . . Luigne . . . Orc . . . As he saw them, he groaned aloud.

Too late he had remembered the warning given to him, long ago, by Molaise at Clonard. "I know the dangers that lie about you because of your very zeal," Molaise had said. "Your voice is obedient, but there is still rebellion in your heart." He had often seen the old man since, receiving much good advice from him as the burden of his own responsibilities increased with his success as a gospeller, but though Molaise had sometimes praised and often rebuked him, Columba had always felt that his confessor had something else in mind, something of which he constantly tried to warn him, something more serious than the normal blunders and temptations of an eager, adventuring soul. Molaise had been afraid for him, Columba knew. He had known something . . . something of which he himself had once or twice had glimpses . . . from which he had always turned away. It would have been better if he had looked boldly at the dark cloud on the far horizon of his inner vision. It had come upon him now, the deadly temptation, and he had not known it, under its disguise of duty, till it had driven him into mortal sin. He knew that now . . . oh, yes, he knew it now. But it was too late. The men who had been his friends were dead, and he who had sworn to do all to the glory of God had betrayed them, for his own greater glory and the confusion of Finnian. Now that it was too late, he saw it all.

In the encampment on the summit behind which the sun was rising the trumpets were sounding. His absence would soon be detected now, and men would be sent in search of him, men whom he could not face, whose dearly bought triumph he could not share.

" *Alius aliorum membra* . . ." members one of another : it was a principle he had always accepted glibly enough. But he had never experienced the consequences of defying it before. Now, in the deaths he had been instrumental in causing he felt death touch his own soul. The hands he raised to heaven seemed those of a suicide as well as a murderer. To his distraught mind it was as if he bore the halter of Judas as well as the brand of Cain.

Dry-eyed now, he blundered about the battle-field, purpose slowly taking possession of his bemused soul. Like the prodigal son, he was obsessed by the need to confess the sin that crippled him, to seek penance and absolution, if such things remained, even for him. As the light strengthened he set his face towards the west. Picking up his staff, he forded the stream and set out for the remote island in Innismurray, where he would find Molaise.

In his desperation, he was scarcely aware of the fatigues of the journey or the time he spent on the way. Moving like an automaton he walked from sunrise to sunset, eating only such bread as the peasants whose villages he reached in the evening broke off their loaves for him, cupping a few mouthfuls of water between his hands at an occasional spring. When he reached the west coast he was gaunt to the point of emaciation, and his grey eyes were dark with the accumulated anguish of a man who has long borne his grief about with him night and day. His urgency was so evident that a fisherman lent him a coracle immediately. In the mellow afternoon light he paddled out to the fortress-like isle, across a sea so still that the reflection of the red sandstone cliff with its group of low beehive huts hardly wavered on the green waters till his paddle broke it. Above him the gulls wheeled, crying incessantly like the lost souls of the pagan legends, and the tawny sails of a few fishing-boats scarcely flapped as they lay becalmed.

Molaise received him in a small hut with an entrance so low that he had to crawl through it. Within was only a shelf on which the hermit sat by day and extended himself by night. Sunlight streamed through a window-slit in a narrow beam that quivered between them, Columba fancied, like an angel's sword.

The hermit signed him with the cross.

" You are in trouble, my son ? "

" Trouble ? " cried Columba, as he crouched at the old man's feet. " I have sinned beyond forgiveness, Father . . ."

" Make your confession, my son," Molaise said. " The question of your guilt must rest with God."

But Columba could not speak at once. He knelt there shaking, incoherent with tears, his whole spirit convulsed with such self-loathing as he had never known, his knuckles white as he beat his fists on his bowed head. Quietly Molaise sat watching the mortal conflict for which he had been waiting, the inevitable crisis which must make or break this life which held greater possibilities for good or evil than any other that had ever been placed in his charge. The habitual remoteness of his face had been replaced by an overwhelming pity, lightened by a hint of something like relief that such an anticipated crisis should now at long last be at hand. He never stirred while Columba told the whole story of the coveted translation and the surreptitious copy, the judgment he had defied and the battle which had followed.

At last it was done. Quietened now, Columba waited for the penance which must precede that absolution for which he had scarcely ventured to ask. It must, he knew, be a heavy one, but when it came, he quailed under it, speechless.

" You must leave Erin, my son," Molaise had said.

As if the words had mortally wounded him, Columba crumpled at the hermit's feet, his hands gripping his own throat, his head

bowed to the very ground. " Leave Erin . . . but to leave Erin
is to die . . ."

" You must leave Erin," repeated Molaise inexorably. " For
the sin you have confessed to me I must banish you beyond the
sight of the coasts of home till you have won to-the light as many
souls as you have sent to wander in darkness. Then, and not till
then, you may return."

" Father . . ." pleaded Columba, " order me to be scourged,
to be maimed, to have the hand that offended thrust into the
fire. But do not send me from Erin . . . the home that I
love . . ."

" The men who died at Culdromne also loved their homes,"
said Molaise.

Columba bowed his head.

" How many were the dead ? " Molaise demanded.

" I believe . . . as many as three thousand . . ."

" When you have claimed three thousand lives for heaven
you may turn your boat's head for home," the old man said.
" Till then, do not pause on your journey while the peaks of Erin
rise above the sea. Do you hear me ? "

" I hear you, Father," said Columba wearily.

" Then obey me."

" I will obey."

It was very quiet in the hermit's cell, so quiet that Columba's
uneven breathing sounded louder than the crash and recoil of
the waves on the rocks below. Molaise knew well the passionate
love of his home which was part of Columba's volcanic, tumultuous nature. In exiling him he had deliberately chosen the
heaviest penalty that lay in his power, recognising this for the
crisis point at which a life must be broken so that it might be
remade. The breaking was in his hands : the course of
Columba's future depended on heaven alone.

He had been severe. Now he spoke more gently. " Lift up
your heart, my son," he said. " Your work will go on. You will
take your message with you when you sail the seas."

" I am not worthy . . ." whispered Columba.

" None of us are. Yet we are needed."

" But where . . . ? " The words held infinite desolation.
Molaise laid a thin hand on the disconsolate head.

" Wherever men are struggling against heavy odds, wherever
they are in darkness, beleaguered by the forces of this world,
forsaken, overwhelmed. I have heard," he went on, " that men
from Erin are in dire straights on Alba, where the Picts are
harrying them back towards the sea . . ."

Columba listened numbly as the shape of his new task slowly emerged from the mists that hid the remote island which had not yet been called Scotland. But he could not compel his reluctant spirit to recognise the future that lay there. Molaise did not expect an answer. He was not even looking at Columba as he spoke on. " The Scots from Erin are your fellow Christians, and Alba itself lies in darkness. Much might be done there."

" Much . . ." Columba agreed.

" Do not be afraid," said Molaise. " It is often not from those actions which seem to us most successful that most is achieved for the glory of God. ' *Vae vobis, quum bene dixerint omnes . . .* ' "

" Woe unto me, indeed, when all men praised me," Columba groaned.

" It is often from what seem our greatest failures that heaven's blessing flowers," said Molaise. " What could have seemed darker than the Friday night that fell on Golgotha ? Yet that darkness has illuminated the world. This is your darkest hour, my son, yet it is already passing, and beyond it breaks the first light of a fairer day."

" Give me your blessing, Father," said Columba hoarsely. " And I will go."

As he stood up in the bright sunlight outside the hermit's hut he was aware the oppression was slowly lifting from his spirit. He had received the heaviest penance he could ever have imagined, yet in its acceptance, a new promise shone. The barrier that had intercepted his desperate prayers had gone. He might be homeless, but once again nothing lay between him and heaven. He had never felt more desolate, yet he began to sing as he scrambled down the cliff-path to the borrowed coracle. He must find Brendan, the roving monk who was always trying to persuade people to go with him. Brendan would have no regrets at leaving Erin. How could he, thought Columba, when his own heart held all the parting-sorrow in the world ? Brendan would help him, he knew. They might even sail together, though whether in search of Tir nan Og or the Garden of Eden or to the rescue of the Scots on Alba he did not know. It scarcely mattered. The words that Molaise had spoken had not yet taken root in his soul. He only knew that he must leave Erin, and that the world was wide.

III

None

" Cognoscetis veritatem, et veritas
vos in libertatem vindicabit."

JOANNES : VIII 32,

CHAPTER XI

FOR CENTURIES the winter storms had thrashed about the island, sending great sheets of spray flying high over the ancient rocks that had been heaved above the face of the waters by the birth-pangs of the prehistoric world. Older than Alba or Erin, older than any living thing, the rocks of the island had been moulded in immeasurable antiquity, spewed to the surface of the boiling waters by subterranean fires submerged again and again during the aeons of pre-history, wrenched perhaps from the fabled Atlantean continent by the importunate seas, seared by the savage pressure of ice-sheets which bore boulders of rose-red granite from the mainland and left them with the first fertile deposits when the unthinkable cold relaxed and the ice-sheets began to slither, screaming and grinding and scarring the rocks as they abandoned them, to slide at last into the berg-filled sea.

The ages that passed over the island had individually left almost as little trace as the sheets of flying winter spray, but the deliberate processes of evolution eventually ground down the rocks and silted the hollows with soil. The first humble living things stirred again after the cataclysms that had submerged the ancient continents and raised new lands from the floor of the sea. The island, survivor of the antediluvian world, remained as a sort of bridge between measurable and immeasurable antiquity, and the legends of lost lands and forgotten peoples clung about it as the wreaths of seaweed garlanded the rocks that were perpetually flogged by the gorged but still insatiable sea.

Like a sentinel it stood off the coast of Alba, the rose-red cliffs of the larger intervening island, later to be known as Mull, matched by the rose-red boulders of granite which had been borne across the Sound by the ice-sheets. The scarred surface of the rocks was slowly hidden by soil and turf and heather, offering, on the sheltered eastern side that was nearest to the mainland of Alba, an eventual foothold for a few bushes, even an occasional tree.

Innumerable colonies of white-shelled marine creatures lived and died on the coasts of the island, and the busy waves pounded their shells into banks of astonishingly white sand, while at other points their ceaseless action on the dourly resisting granites and gneisses produced great drifts of rounded pebbles of many colours, so that as the water sleeked their surfaces, the

beaches of green, white or rose-coloured fragments were like
slopes of jewels which might have come from the treasuries of the
queens of that legendary Atlantis, which, according to the
magicians and story-tellers, had once been there or thereabouts,
its memory lingering in nostalgic tales of Tir-nan-Og and the
Land-under-Wave.

But the child collecting firewood on the beach to the south of
the island knew little of these things. He had overheard people
talking now and then, round the driftwood fires for which he and
the other children were sent to fetch fuel from the beaches, carrying their loads back to the group of beehive stone huts that
clustered on the little plateau between the towering rocks that
overlooked the southern, island-dotted sea. He knew that the
little colony of fisher-folk, who lived on what they could catch
in the Sound and the flesh of the seals which bred on a smaller
island nearby, believed everything that the few white-robed,
long-bearded magicians who virtually ruled the island told them.
The magicians did not toil like the fishermen. They remained
in the huts that had been built for them, casting spells for fair or
foul weather or studying the evidence to be found in the movements of the stars, the entrails of sacrificial victims or the flight
of certain birds. They disliked being watched at their divination
and scared the children of the settlement away with awful
threats. But they took no notice of Urdan. Urdan was dumb.

Nobody took much notice of Urdan. They knew very little
about him. He had been found wandering on the far side of the
Sound by a boatload of fishermen who had sailed along the coast
to barter their fish for the barley meal they lacked. They had
questioned him and received no answer, but being on the whole
kindly men they had taken him on board when he wept as they
prepared to leave him. When the ᵧ got back to the settlement the
magicians had looked at him without interest. A male child of
perhaps seven years old. Sturdy enough, but dumb, perhaps
from birth. It did not matter to them.

So Urdan had remained on the island, adopted by the family
of one of the fishermen, drudging over small tasks and wandering
away by himself when the restlessness came over him because of
all the ideas that boiled inside his head and the questions he was
unable to ask.

Sometimes the fisherman's wife would scold him when he did
not return, like the other children, with his load of firewood, but
more often nobody noticed when Urdan was missing for hours,
even for days. In summer-time he sometimes stole a barley
bannock or a piece of dried fish to stay his hunger and went

wandering off round the west coast of the island which perpetually drew him. It was not only on account of the beauty of its towering rocks with their streaks of green and white and sunrise red that ran through and through the seal-coloured masses that Urdan went so often to the western coast of the island, not even on account of, the gentle, wondering faces of the seals, though he loved them, and would sit for hours watching them bobbing about in the rock pools or clambering on the sun-warmed rocks. He was aware of other things which he could not name, sensations of unseen companionship which sometimes saddened and sometimes elated him, though he could not say what they were or whence they came.

He neither saw nor heard the coming and going of these presences, but another, barely developed faculty made him sure of the existence of strange creatures which seemed to belong less to the visible world in which men caught fish and women baked barley-bread and children gathered firewood than to another world which lay just this side imagination, whose citizens came and went between the island and the sea. But since he could speak to nobody of these things, even if he had wished, Urdan's experiences were unknown. To the fisherfolk of the settlement he was just a male child who was growing lanky as he neared adolescence, and was often punished by his foster-parents for coming back empty-handed or forgetting to gut the fish or carry the water-skins or mend the nets.

But no punishment ever cured Urdan of his habit of wandering. It was as if the blank which lay at the back of his childhood irked him, so that he must be continually seeking the early memories he had lost. Sometimes he felt that the clue to them was in the keeping of the sea-people, and sometimes he doubted it. He looked for it at random, as he looked for specially beautiful pebbles on the beach, because he did not even know what he was looking for. Beyond the day on which the fishermen had taken him to the island lay nothing but a blank curtain of unutterable terror, but he felt that behind it were other memories, people to whom he had spoken, days without fear. And so, one day when the gales that flogged the island all winter had dropped at last, he felt the restlessness upon him again, and slipped away from the settlement where the women were busy making bannocks with the barley the men had bartered for the first big catch of the season. And for once, this morning, he made his way, not to the west but to one of the few southern bays that offered a wide gap in the cliffs and a shingle beach that was easily accessible from the sea.

It was one of those days when the land, just released from the grip of winter, seemed almost more beautiful than he could bear. The sloping tongue of green meadow which ran down to the beach between the seal-coloured, greenishly striated rocks, was starred with tiny flowers. Among the spears of the flags the sunshine-coloured blossoms were unfurling, and primroses seemed to fill every cranny of the cliffs. As he went, Urdan smiled, skipping every few steps, hugging his arms across his chest, as if he greeted all the returning beauty of the world.

It was low tide when he reached the beach, and the safe channel of deep water which threaded its way through the treacherous rocks which would have ripped the bottom out of any coracle that ventured to pass over them, was plainly visible through the jade-green swell, while the terraced beach of variously coloured pebbles subsided, step by step, to the edge of the whispering sea.

Urdan had gone barefoot all his life, like everybody else on the island, so that the calloused soles of his feet scarcely felt the rounded stones as he picked his way to the edge of the water, where the last petulant sallies of the tide gave the pebbles it covered a fugitive, brilliant sheen. They were not dull and inert like ordinary unpolished pebbles, but seemed to hold a sort of vitality in their cloudy gleam. He had just found a specially large one and was wondering what its colour reminded him of when a sudden voice at his elbow made him jump.

" It's the colour of the underside of a wave, eh, son ? "

Urdan flung back the lank strands of dark hair which had fallen round his brown, snub face, and instinctively threw up his arm as if to ward off a blow, peering warily at the stranger from under its shelter. But the man who was smiling down at him from what seemed an immense height did not seem to be angry. He must have landed while Urdan was collecting the pebbles, for his coracle bobbed in the shallows behind him. And outside the cruel ranks of rocks a bigger boat waited, full of men who watched, resting on their oars. They were strangers . . . they might be pirates . . . memory rushed over him in a sudden flood . . . like those who had surprised his home on the mainland, cutting out his father's tongue because he would not tell them where his treasure was hidden . . . torturing him before they flung his body into the flaming shell that had been their home, and ran his mother through the body with one of their long spears . . . The scene rose up before Urdan again, in all the horror which had struck him dumb . . .

" Do not be afraid, little one," said the big man with the kind smile and the sad eyes which looked as if he, too, knew what it was to lose a home. " We will not hurt you. Tell me, what is your name ? "

Urdan opened his mouth and pointed down his throat, shaking his head at the stranger with the oddly bright hair which did not start growing till so far back on his head, and who now first held out his hands to the boy, folding both of Urdan's into one big palm while he first made a sign in the air with the other and then laid it on his head.

" *In nomine Jesu Christi* . . . may this child receive again the gift of speech . . ."

Urdan felt nothing, saw nothing out of the ordinary, heard only the kind voice asking him again : " what is your name ? "

But this time he smiled back at him and answered without hesitation : " My name is Urdan, sir."

" Good. And what is this isle ? "

" It is called Hy." (He pronounced it, in the local way, ' Eeh.') " It is a strange isle, sir." Words came pouring out now, as if, having been dammed back so long, he could scarcely use them fast enough. " They call it the isle of the magicians."

The stranger laughed. " We will make it the isle of saints."

" Will you ? I know nothing of saints. But I know all about magicians. They can do terrible things. They cast spells and cause madness and call up the dead and . . ."

The big man took his hand. " You need no longer be afraid of the magicians, child. Or of anything else. But tell me, who are these people standing behind you ? Are they your friends ? "

Urdan twisted round abruptly, still gripping that strong hand. Behind him stood a group of fishermen who had crept up in the shelter of the big knoll in the centre of the meadow that they called the fairy hill. They were naked except for the cloths they twisted round their waists when fishing, but he could see they carried stones in their hands. They did not like strangers on Hy, Urdan knew. The magicians had discouraged the traditional island hospitality. In a moment a shower of stones would be aimed at his friend who stood there alone, unarmed and entirely unconcerned. His companions in the long-boat which was now nosing its way towards the shore would be too late to help him. It was the way of the islanders to stone strangers first and investigate afterwards. Already Urdan could see arms bending, stones raised . . . He flung himself suddenly forward, arms outspread as if in protection of the tall stranger whose waist was level with his head.

" Do not harm him ! " he cried in anguish. " He is kind . . . he is good . . . please, do please listen . . ."

At the sound of his words they fell back in consternation. Did they not all know the dumb boy who could only make uncouth noises when he was beaten, who had never in the seven years since he had been brought to the island, spoken a coherent word ? Now his voice was as clear as that of any of their own sons.

" It is magic . . ."

" He has got back his voice . . ."

" They are magicians . . ."

" Then they can strike us dead . . ."

" The Druids will hear of it . . ."

" Do not anger them . . ."

A series of soft thuds on the springy turf suggested that stones had fallen from frightened hands. The stranger grinned broadly, and began to speak to them in a dialect which was very like their own.

" My friends," he said, " do not greet us with blows. We have come in peace. My companions——" he indicated the men who had now beached the long-boat, and were hauling it up the shingle out of reach of the turning tide "——have come to serve you, bringing healing for body and spirit, knowledge of medicine and husbandry, new tales for your firesides and hope of eternal life."

" How do we know these things are true ? " said the chief fisherman suspiciously. " If we let you land you may afterwards murder us all while we sleep."

" Do we look like liars and murderers ? " asked the tall stranger.

His companions had now ranged themselves behind him, weaponless, tanned by exposure to the sea air, burdened only with satchels of books, cooking-pots, craftsmen's tools, and bags of meal. They looked frankly at the islanders, who looked doubtfully back again, turning to mutter together, nodding or shaking their unkempt heads. " This is the strangest welcome I have ever had," he reproached them. " At home the poorest bondsman would have been better received. You have called us murderers and tried to stone us. Why are you so afraid ? "

" Murderers ? " clamoured Urdan, his unpractised voice uneven and shrill, " of course, they are not murderers. Murderers are different. Their faces are hard. They do not look at your eyes. They killed my father and mother. I know them . . . I know . . ."

"The boy is right," said one of the fishermen. "These men do not look evil."

"He can speak well, too . . ."

"It is magic . . ."

"Good magic, though. Better than that which brings sickness or tempest . . ."

"Our magicians could well endure a little rivalry," said an old man shrewdly. "They rule us as they will."

"Come then, strangers," said the chief fishermen doubtfully. "We will welcome you. But did you come far in that cockle-shell, alone?" he added, suddenly suspicious of the man who had first explored the landing-channel in the wicker-framed coracle now bobbing in a rock pool.

"No, indeed. There is our boat," the stranger answered, nodding casually towards the narrow, sixty-foot craft which had been hollowed out of a single tree-trunk, equipped with seats for four pairs or rowers, a central socket for a mast, and carried a neatly stowed sail. "We towed the coracle behind in case of need."

The fishermen nodded approvingly; "The lesser craft would have surely foundered in these seas." Then, abruptly: "what is your name?"

"Columba, they call me in the Latin," said the tall man, who still held Urdan's hand. "But in our own homelier tongue I am Colum-Cille."

"Colum-Cille. Huh," said the fisherman. "I never heard the name. And why did you choose our island? There are many others in the wide sea."

"I landed," said Columba, simply, "to see whether from your highest peak I could still catch a glimpse of Erin. If so, I may not stay. That bond has been laid upon me."

"So you, who work magic, are also under authority?" said one of the fishermen. His voice was surprised.

"If I come among you it will not be as a leader but as a servant," Columba said.

The fisherman sighed. "It is not so with our magicians. We hope," he added, "that you will stay."

"First I must climb the peak and see if the bond that is upon me will allow it," said Columba. He laid aside his cloak, girded his habit, and accepted the staff that one of his companions held out. They made no attempt to come with him. Even Urdan, who had taken a few dancing steps after him, fell back, though he gave no sign. There was something prohibitive about him which warned them all that he would prefer to be alone. They busied

themselves with their gear while the fishermen looked on and
Urdan ran from one to another, chattering like a jay. Columba
strode on up the green meadow. Soon it tapered into a gully and
was eventually lost among the boulders and peat-haggs of the
hillside. The little hill which was the highest point in that part
of the island was not high or hard to climb, though the going
was rough. He worked his way upwards among the heather and
scattered rocks till presently he stood on the summit and felt the
wind that must have passed over Erin blow through his worn
habit. It seemed to touch his skin like a friend. Tears filled his
eyes as the sorrow of exile gripped him. The voices of his friends,
the beauty of the church at Clonard, the scent of the bogland,
the pillared quiet of the forest oaks near Derry, all were borne
towards him on the warm west wind, so that the pain of it was
beyond bearing. He fell on his knees on the bare rock, his arms
stretched out in a gesture of uttermost longing, his tear-blinded
eyes turned as if to ask a blessing from the sun that shone also
on his lost home. His throat was thick with sobs, his knees
ached from the harsh rock of this unfriendly land where people
had brought stones to greet him. Could it be heaven's will that
he should remain ?

He forced himself to pray, as he had prayed so often, ever
since he had left Erin, for strength to bear the weight of the great
load that seemed to crush out his life, the burden which he could
not relinquish for an instant, but must perpetually carry alone,
heartsick and weary beneath the responsibility that Molaise had
laid upon him for the death of three thousand men. It was a
responsibility that he had accepted, by which as now, he seemed
sometimes likely to be overwhelemed. His soul cried out under
it ; a host of devils whispered that he need carry it no further. At
any moment he could turn the nose of his boat towards home. It
was true that a sentence of excommunication had been pronounced
on him by the national synod of priests after the battle of Culdremne, but that had been a mere formality. His influence over the
people was so great that he could afford to ignore it. As for the penance ; he alone had heard Molaise pronounce it. Only Molaise
would know of his failure if he were to return. The temptation convulsed him with its violence. He longed, unutterably to yield. It
had required all the strength of his will to compel himself to prepare
for departure, to forbid his dearest friends to come with him
because they must now be responsible for all the new monasteries
he had founded in Erin. Afterwards, perhaps, they might visit
him in his exile, but meanwhile he had chosen other companions,
skilled in various crafts, and mostly, like himself, in the middle

forties, from the scores who clamoured to go with him. And so, accepting the penance to the letter, it was with a dozen men who had neither special ties nor distinction that he had proposed to leave his home.

On the eve of departure he had returned to the dun to say good-bye. It was a sad journey, for the spring had been a wet one, the loughs were swollen and the plain a bog. The logs of the causeway squelched as he walked across them, and he was glad to find the fire piled high in Phelim's hall. This time he was expected and both his parents were there to meet him. Phelim greeted his son with all the exasperation he felt for a man who had wilfully flung his chances away for the second time ; Eithne's pride and love for him shone through the tears she could not check ; and Maeve merely stared at him moodily from her place by the hearth, her chin cupped on her hand. The excitement of battle no longer sustained her. She was bored again.

Columba did not stay long. His mother's pain at parting from him was barely concealed by her delight in all he had already accomplished, her awe at the unexpected fulfilment of her never-forgotten dream. For the first time, as he kissed her, he saw that she was getting old. It was as if the other world, for which she longed, already drew her away. Maeve, on the other hand, who was only a few years younger, seemed to have been arrested in a sort of brassily blatant middle-age, as if the lusts of her flesh had given her body greater vitality. Her eyes were so bright above crescents of shadow that he could scarcely bear to meet them, even though he had no idea of what her part in provoking the fatal battle had been.

To his mother he said : " I shall return, my dear one. It may be soon." But to his father he merely said : " Good-bye."

They set out between Easter and Pentecost, during the forty days which the Celtic Church regarded as the holiest in the year. Columba had taken an oar himself, and as they rowed down the river he compelled himself to watch the shores of Erin slip by, the beautiful glades of blossoming hawthorn, the pillared oaks, the green pastures across which the cattle wandered, slowly diminishing in the distance as their boat slid down the widening lough from his beloved Derry towards the inexorable sea. Above him, as he rowed, circled the gulls, their harsh clamour the very voice of sorrow, a lament that must surely remain in his heart till the day he came to die. Then, as now, tears had blinded him, so that he was glad he had insisted on taking an oar with the others, who sang as they set out on their adventure, so that no one would guess that their leader wept instead.

They had been well received by Columba's cousin Conall, who ruled the nearest settlement of Scots in Alba, though the news he had to give of Scottish progress was bad. The Picts from the north and east harried them incessantly, and they had been compelled to surrender, foot by foot, much of the ground which, during the last fifty years, they had so hardly won. Here, during his first visit to the mainland of Alba, Columba heard a good deal about the northern Picts whose headquarters were far beyond the mountains which formed the backbone of the country, at the Druid-ridden court of their King Brude. Conall was thankful to see Columba ; for he maintained that the position of his people in Alba might be very different if a Christian missionary could eliminate the influence of the Druids in Alba as it had already been eliminated in Erin.

The interests of the Druids, as magicians, were vested in the paganism of the established order, so that the best attack on them, he argued, would be made by attempting the conversion of King Brude. Conall had been anxious, in fact, to keep Columba with him at his court in western Alba, but Columba had refused to stay. He must go further, for the hills of Erin were still visible on the western skyline, and he must find an isle from which they could not be seen. Once he had established his headquarters on some such remoter isle, his monks would be reasonably safe. He must make sure of that, he explained, before personally undertaking any missionary expeditions and leaving them to continue the routine work. It was Conall who had suggested landing on Hy. There were a few Druids there, he admitted, and the island had a sinister reputation, but no doubt his fiery cousin would feel that these things only made it more necessary for him to take possession. Columba had smiled, and agreed.

But now he had reached the island, he felt very differently. All the forces of darkness seemed to have combined to attack him, from the moment he went inland, cunningly using his desperate nostalgia as the best point of assault on an otherwise well-defended soul. As he crouched on the hilltop, the very air seemed dark with demons, and the agony of his homesickness was doubled and redoubled as the loneliness of the sorely tempted came down upon him. Round him he seemed to hear voices crying : " *Return . . . return . . . you can do nothing here.*"
" *Glory and honour and success wait for you in Erin . . .*"
" *Leave this barren isle and the handful of fisher-folk who tried to stone you . . .*"
" They sought also to stone my master," Columba groaned.
" *Dare you compare your trials with his ? Such pride is a sin . . .*

a deadly sin . . . deadly sin . . ." The words beat on his ears as
if the very gulls echoed them.

" *Ne nos inducas in tentationem . . ."* prayed Columba in agony.
" *Sed libera nos a malo . . ."*

He raised his eyes, from which the tears had dried, as if in
the heat of the conflict, to peer towards the western horizon,
beyond which the mountains of his own beloved land lay. But
there was nothing ; not a peak, not a headland, not a single
smudge blurred the smooth meeting-line of sky and sea. Only the
clouds that sailed there, tinged already with the warmth of the
westering sun, suggested the smooth pastures and softly rolling
hills of his lost home. Shading his eyes with his hand he stared
westward till the strain made him blink. Nothing lay to the west
but the baseless hills of heaven. He dropped heavy arms to his
sides. Here was his place of exile, the first land from which he
could no longer see Erin. Here he must stay.

This barren isle . . . was this to be his home ? Crouched
on the bleak summit he looked at the meagre slopes of green visible
in the saddle-shaped depression that crossed the centre of the
island between the rocky outcrops which rose to the north and
south. Even there the rocks showed through the turf as the bones
of a starving beast show through the skin. Beyond, to the north,
the burgeoning of the ancient lava formations below the single
peak was lit and shadowed in the level light till it gave him for an
instant the illusion of oak-groves, bordering the thread-bare
pastures to the verge of the drifts of startlingly white sand and the
banks of many-coloured pebbles by the edge of the western sea.
For an instant his heart beat with the strength of new hope as he
seemed to recognise, in the unfamiliar desolation, one of the
dearest beauties of his own land. For an instant only, then it
sickened as he looked again. The springing hope was dashed to
death against the barren surfaces of ancient, volcanic rock. Life,
on this forlorn outcrop, seemed like a final condemnation from
which his spirit shrank as a man's strong body shrinks from
violent death. The oak-groves of Derry, the singing monks
chanting their way through flowering pastures, the eager welcome
of the people, the sound of axes and saws as the new churches
rose ; such memories haunted him till the air seemed full of wist-
ful shadows, and the voices of his tempters rasped about his
ears with redoubled fury.

" *To come here is to bury yourself alive . . ."*
" *To live here is to hide your talent in a napkin . . ."*
" *This penance may save your own soul . . . but what of all those
who need you in Erin . . . ? "*

" *Molaise is but one old man . . .*"
" *His wits are going . . .*"
" *Rebel . . .*"
" *Defy him . . .*"
" *Return to your work . . .*"
" *What can you do here ? Preach to the seals ?* "
" *You will break your heart to no purpose . . .*"
" *There is nothing but rock . . . barren rock . . . no seed can grow . . .*"
" *You will drown your soul in darkness . . .*"

Columba flung himself on the ground, while over him broke such waves of despair that he gasped for breath beneath their onslaught. The whole world seemed to heave about him, to become a wilderness, in a night without star. The purpose of his life mocked him with its absurdity. Disillusionment seared him, the gulls that screamed about him echoed the voices of the demons who plucked at his spirit. The sacrifice asked of him was more than he could bear ; the choice one he was unable to make. Strain as he would, he could not regain the blessed state of peace in which all things were made plain. Even his inner vision had deserted him. He could not see what lay beyond the desolation of that place and hour. Words broke from him of which he was scarcely aware, echoing from the cataclysm which had once threatened to engulf the very light of the world. Now, in his own outer darkness, their echoes brought the first hint of companionship, a morning freshness to the sullen air.

" ' *Abba, Pater, omnia fieri abs te possunt . . . transfer a me istud poculum . . .* ' "

The sky might be still full of jeering, triumphant voices . . . the wind had risen and was tossing the gulls high above the summit, was tugging at his habit, chilling his limbs with its breath. But in the west the sinking sun had dyed the company of little clouds till they seemed like the very gates of glory that opened in the fabled land.

Columba lay motionless, shivering with exhaustion, while round him the fiend voices seemed to diminish, the tumult to die. At last, scarcely above a whisper, he spoke again.

" ' *. . . verum non quid ego velim, sed quid tu . . .* ' "

On the words he fell asleep, the short, profound sleep of utter spiritual exhaustion, to wake again before the last traces of the sunset had faded, calm now, and beyond the possibility of further doubt. Taking up his staff, he retied his girdle more tightly, and made his way among the boulders and heather, down the hill.

CHAPTER XII

THEY LAY that night in the lee of the little hill in the centre of the landing-place, wrapped in their cloaks, the copies of the Psalms and the Gospels, which were their most precious possessions under Columba's head for safe keeping. The Gospel book was an old, battered copy which had journeyed about Erin with Columba for the last twenty years, lent now to this new monastery now to that, so that as his head touched the satchel which contained it, Columba felt at once nearer to the places that he loved, for all the careful hands which had transcribed so faithfully the copies which were to be the age-long treasures of Derry and Durrow and Kells. He was glad that they had brought the much loved old book with them on their journey, instead of Finnian's version which had caused so much bloodshed. This had been left behind in Erin, to become the battle trophy of his kinsmen, who had begged to keep it in token of their victory, since Columba, sick at heart, felt he never wished to see the fated thing again.

Morning came early, for darkness scarcely touched the island in summer-time, dipping down upon it only with the light touch of a great wing, then lifting again, when the blaze of the sunset seemed barely to have faded, to disclose the pearly pallor of a northern summer dawn. Columba, who had scarcely slept, saw the sunshine touch the desolate summit of his ordeal, then steal down the bouldered slope towards them, transfiguring the bleak hillside like the blessing of God. Leaving his sleeping companions, still muffled in their cloaks against the dawn-chill, he walked up the slope to meet the rays of the sun, beyond the limit of the retreating shadow which still held the little bay, where small pearly waves lipped at the shingle and rolled back with a faint purring sound. Already, Columba fancied, the sun's rays had warmth. As he entered the area which it had illuminated he seemed to enter a different world, to be seeing rather, the significance of a temporal world eternally renewed.

The night before the bare rocks had bruised him. Now, in every crevice, he saw clustering flowers. The night before the sea had surrounded him like the limits of his prison. Now he saw for the first time the changing colours that swept across it to the rose-red cliffs of Mull. Then, apart from his twelve followers, he had seemed solitary. Now he could smile at the wrangles of the seagulls, watch with affection the bobbing, whiskered head of an inquisitive seal. Where he had seen nothing but the bleakness of the rocky island, Columba now saw for the first time, its elusive beauty, a beauty which owed less to its configuration than to the constantly changing quality of the light in which it lay. The night before it had seemed indeed an island of ancient, sinister magic. Now it might still be, to his poet's intuition, enchanted ; but the enchanted creatures had their own quality, an innocence which belonged to the morning of the world when all things had been made new. Raising his hand he blessed them all, visible and invisible, circling gulls and nimble sheep, shadowless people of the shee, strange creatures from the sea and the drowned western lands ; fishermen and magicians, children, pack-horses and cattle, small beasts and birds, with that sign of the cross whose saving arms reached to the ends of the world. Then, because the happiness which had come upon him was too great to be restrained, he threw back his head and began to sing. So it was that the first sounds his followers heard were those of a psalm of triumph, and their first sight as they lifted their heads from their cloaks on the morning after their arrival on the island was Columba himself, coming towards them down the sunlit slope among the tiny flowers that patterned the rabbit-cropped turf, his arms flung wide and his face that like of a man who sees heaven open before him, his deep voice rolling ahead of him in tremendous waves of joy.

Reassured, they knelt at his feet for his blessing. They, too, had been afraid the night before, at the sight of their leader's haggard face, still seared with the traces of lonely struggle. But now, in the morning light, all things seemed possible, and Columba's eyes rested lovingly on them, as he allocated their several tasks, and blessed them each by name.

" We must go further to-day," he said, " and begin to build our home. Last night I saw the whole of the island. The most fertile land is in the centre, but most shelter is to be had on the east. We shall build our church at the nearest point to the mainland, and round it our mill and barns and granary shall rise. Catan, Grellan, Eochaidh, you are our husbandmen. Keep our few tools in your hands. You shall decide where grain is to be sown, what stocks we must keep, what we may use for bread." He smiled affectionately at the three strong men he had named. " I put you also in charge of the sacks of grain and meal. Is this within your strength ? "

" Yes, Father," they all said.

" Rus, the red-head, you are our smith. Get Scandal to help

you with the tools and Carnan to blow your fire. Lugaid, you
have skill in cooking food and kindling fires. I leave the preparation of our meals in your charge, with Ernaan, who is the
oldest of us all, to do the lighter tasks. Torannan, you have a
kindly way with beasts. When we have obtained cows, you shall
care for them. Macculthan, Cobtach, I leave to you the boats
and the nets needed for fishing. Oran . . . I will put no burdens
on you at present . . ."

" But Father, I would wish to do my share. I am well enough.
It is only the sea, and my queasy stomach . . ."

Columba looked compassionately at the white-faced man with
the anxious, dark-ringed eyes. " You shall indeed do your share,
Oran. But not yet. Let the others bear the burdens for the
present. Come with me."

He led the sick man to the shelter of the central rock and made
him rest there while Lugaid, who had been put in charge of the
provisions, handed to each of his companions a carefully measured
portion of bread and the goat's milk cheese which had been
given them by their kinsmen in Alba. Oran would not eat, but
he drank thirstily from the skin water-bottle which Lugaid
brought them afterwards. Then Cobtach and Macculthan, the
tall men responsible for the boats and fishing-tackle, came to
Columba to ask whether they should approach the eastern shore
of the island by land or by sea. Columba thought for a while
before answering.

" The tide is out so that we can see the rocks that lie in wait
for us," he said at last. " Also, we have many burdens and
inland the going is rough. We will take to the sea again. I will
go ahead in the coracle while you follow in the long-boat. Let
us lose no time," he added, looking shrewdly to windward. " A
storm will reach the island presently."

" A storm, Father ? " asked red-headed Rus in astonishment.
" Surely this is the fairest morning the world has seen ? "

" Nevertheless, a storm will come," said Columba. " A
storm raised by those who would like to see the end of us. But
there will be time to reach the northern sands before it if we do
not delay."

They were soon at sea, to the dismay of young Urdan, who
had made his escape from the fishing village and reached the
bay just too late. He even plunged into the water to his waist
in his desire to reach them, holding out his arms and imploring
them to return. But Columba waved and pointed, his gestures
indicating that they were only going to make a circuit of the
coast. Urdan seemed to understand, for he set off, leaping from

rock to rock like a young goat, to follow Columba's coracle to the northern sands.

The coast of the island was almost continuously fanged with reefs and rocks, so that an unwary stranger ran a great risk of dashing himself and his craft to pieces. Here and there were little inlets, floored with the white sand which had silted into every hollow, so that the tides, flowing to and fro above it, took on the colour of translucent jade, shadowed to blue and purple where seaweed waved below the surface or under-water reefs ran out from the coast, or turned almost crimson above the out-crops of rose-red granite from Mull. A semi-lunar bay rimmed with white sand, opposite the mainland, offered one obvious landing-place, but Columba passed it by, prospecting other possibilities in the coracle which he manœuvred among the rocks with all his strength and skill, while the heavily-laden long-boat followed at a wary distance, under the guidance of Cobtach and Macculthan, one at the tiller and the other ready in the bow with a pole to fend their craft off the hidden rocks among which Columba skimmed unconcerned.

He gave the signal to land at last, turning his little craft towards the northern stretch of white sands on which the red-legged seabirds stalked and clamoured. After the fatigue of rowing, the uncertainty of their adventuring, the men in the long-boat were thankful to feel its keel jar at last and with a certain finality on the firm white sand. Here, at least, was some hope of permanence, for beyond the sand-dunes they could see gentle slopes which the imagination of Catan, Grellan and Eochaidh had already clothed with young green barley, and Torannan pictured as kindly pastures for the cows they would soon possess. Rus, the impetuous, was planning the foundations for church, refectory and dwelling-huts on the smooth green, and Lugaid had selected a great rock in the lee of which he would kindle his first cooking-fire. They were cheerful and excited as they brought their small stock of possessions ashore, and Columba, watching them, shared their enthusiasm. They were at the beginning of an enterprise which, if God prospered it, might grow beyond the scope of human imagination. As he sat on a rock with the exhausted Oran at his feet, the group of busy young men wading through the shallows seemed to become shadowy, to yield place to a company which he could not number : strangers from many lands and centuries, diverse in all things except the instinct that brought them there.

He saw boats hung with black from which mourning warriors unloaded the coffins which held the bodies of their rulers, for burial in ground which had become holy, others hung with brighter stuffs which brought great men in state, lesser people in the rough habit of pilgrims, holiday-makers in short bright garments who were also pilgrims from the later centuries, often without knowing it themselves, though Columba, with his quickened inner vision, saw them for what they were, saw the hidden desire for holiness in a successful man of the world, the sin that troubled a great prelate, the pure beauty of a weather-beaten drab, the greed of a frustrated leader, the worldly longings of a sad-faced nun. Time, which for his companions was like a band which flowed past them with the turning of the world, had changed its quality for Columba, as if often did, so that he looked, not merely at the point on the time-band which at that instant confronted him, but through it to the other times which lay beyond it in the future, layer upon layer, simultaneously evident to him as all the rings which mark the growth of an oak-tree would be evident to an observer whose vision could pierce their substance from a vantage point near the central core.

He saw, in that moment of revelation, some sights which saddened and others which delighted him ; saw the successors of their small company setting out to enlighten the western world from the monastery which was not yet built. He saw their journeys through furious flood and tempest, he saw schism and disputes at home, watched the forces of heaven encountering the legions of darkness in unlikely places, knowing that the community, the family, or even the character of a potential saint might be divided against itself, striking blindly first for one side and then the other, the finest purposes somehow blunted, the most ignoble occasionally exalted, the balance continually shifting, on the island, as in the whole world of which it had always been, in some way that was not yet clear to him, a focus point, a plexus of vast spiritual power, which might be used disastrously for man's own ends or blessedly as men learnt to make themselves available for the ends of God. Above all, he saw that his arrival was no accident, not even merely part of a personal expiation. For the larger scheme, the ultimate purpose, it was good that he should be there.

" Strangers, we have come to ask you to leave the island." The harsh voice by his side recalled Columba from the contemplation of timeless immensities. He saw again his bare-legged companions man-handling the long-boat through the shallows, the red-legged seabirds which they had disturbed wheeling fretfully above the rocks, the translucent green water whispering across the white sand. Then he turned to the two long-bearded men in white habits that fell to their heels. They had trudged unnoticed towards him among the sand-dunes while his thoughts had been elsewhere. At his feet Oran, who had been asleep, now stirred.

"You do not come to welcome us?" asked Columba.

"You·are not welcome," the older stranger said.

"Indeed? Why not?" Columba seemed amused.

"We do not care to receive strangers here," said the younger man.

"That is already clear," Columba agreed. "I asked you why?"

"We are the priests of this island. No doubt you are needed by some less fortunate land. We do not wish you to waste your labours on people for whom guides are already provided. Therefore we suggest that you replace your goods and sail onwards. There are other isles."

"And if we refuse?"

"We will be obliged to use the forces at our command against you," said the older priest. He looked coldly round the group of men who had now ceased unloading the boat and gathered round, frankly listening. "We would be loth to do this, since we are very powerful. Some of these—yokels—might be hurt."

Columba looked at them with unshaken good-humour. "On whose behalf do you speak?" he asked.

The taller priest drew himself to his full height. "We are Christian bishops," he said glibly, "who have been sent long before you to convert the isle. Therefore, if you have come here in search of converts, it would be better for you to go elsewhere. This land is in our charge."

Columba sighed, then stooped and drew a circle in the sand. "My friends," he said concisely, "that is not so. You are, I think, not Christians but Druid priests. Nevertheless, let us talk in peace. Here is the mystic circle with which you symbolise the movement of the sun in heaven. I have not come to strike that sign from heaven, but to complete it." He stooped again and cut the circle twice with the sign of the cross. "See, I have not erased the symbol of your worship. Instead I have added another. The path of the sun in heaven glorifies the head of the Son of God."

"We know nothing of this," they said harshly, exasperated but unabashed by the failure of their masquerade.

Columba smiled candidly up at them. "Nor do I know much of the movements of the stars. If I teach you of the young Prince of Glory I shall be ready to hear of other things. The truth is too great for any one man to grasp. Part of it may lie in my hand, another in yours. Shall we not share our knowledge ? "

The two Druids looked furtively at each other. They had expected stubborn bigotry, perhaps magical trials of skill. They had received an offer of understanding, encountered such tolerance that they were at a loss. Something about Columba's bearing told them that such an offer was not made out of weakness, but from the vantage-point of unsuspected strength. The people of the island were infinitely credulous, and the Christians might have new and better magic. Perhaps it might be as well, meanwhile, to avoid putting things to the test. Better merely to make life seem difficult for these strangers, to persuade them, of their own accord, to leave.

"We shall have to consider your offer," said the senior Druid. "As custodians of the ancient mysteries, we may not part with them except to those who are worthy."

"As a priest of Christ I am commanded to offer his Gospel to the despised and the rejected," Columba said.

"Our skill and erudition are reserved for the elect."

"The compassion of God is offered to the whole world."

"Only the strongest can bear the impact of our knowledge."

"The greatest truths of our faith are revealed to the lover and the child."

"I see you are no initiate," sneered the senior Druid.

Columba smiled as he shook his head. "Merely an ordinary man obsessed by the love of God."

"I doubt," said the senior Druid, "whether we shall have much in common, strangers." He had flushed uneasily at the thought that the newcomer might be in some way deriding him. "It scarcely seems likely that we shall find ground for profitable discussion."

"And yet," said Columba blandly, "will it not be interesting to explore such ground as there may be ? "

They looked darkly at him, their humourless faces creased into expressions of suspicion and distaste, their eyes smouldering with indignant pride. Columba's attitude was, they felt, unpardonable. He had presumed to suggest that they, custodians of the ancient wisdom, were merely the equals of a handful of vulgarians who seemed to have a slight knowledge of popular magic, but no culture, no tradition, no aptitude or glimmering of erudition at all.

"Such discussion could lead nowhere," said the senior Druid.

" Our lives are dedicated to the pursuit of wisdom. What can your new-fangled creed have to offer us ? "

" Nothing," said Columba, " if you have already all you desire. Before a man's eyes can be opened it is first necessary for him to know that he is blind."

" Admittedly," said the younger Druid, " you have devoted some attention to popular magic of the kind used to heal those who, through their own excess or folly, are now sick. Such healing may provide its practitioners with a certain brief popularity, but I fear you will find such popularity remarkably short-lived. That boy, for instance, whose name I forget, who is babbling your praises all over the island——"

" Ah," said Columba, hiding a smile behind his hand. " So that is why you came. I wondered."

" ——is just as likely to throw the first stone when you fail to provide him with his diet of daily marvels, And you are liable to find that a fatiguing obligation."

" No Christian," said Columba gravely, " should need to be reminded that popular acclamation is a fickle thing. Nor was the boy's tongue loosened for our glory. If Urdan's words bring the people to listen to greater news than his, then, and then alone, it will be a blessed thing."

" Oh, it was clever enough," said the younger Druid. His grudging tone reminded Columba of one of the judges he had heard disputing legal niceties in Erin. " You could scarcely have done anything more calculated to catch the interest of a credulous people. I only warn you against starting a demand for the magical which you will presently find yourselves unable to satisfy."

" You call it magic. I would call it miracle," said Columba.

" And the difference ? " snapped the younger Druid. He thrust forward an inquisitively sharp nose.

" Magic appears to violate natural law in order to bring glory to the magician, irrespective of the welfare of his victims," said Columba slowly. " A miracle transcends the laws known by man, but to the glory of God, and with the consent of those concerned."

" You juggle with words," rasped the younger Druid. His lips curled in a sneer, but his eyes were anxious. When dealing with a rival who wished to pit magic against magic, he was fairly sure of his ground, for the Druidical training was strenuous and extensive. But this encounter presented new features. A man so dedicated to the deity he served might indeed be the recipient of supernatural power. He glanced at his companion, who had been watching them in thoughtful silence, his fingers twisting the curls of his elaborately cut beard. Now the older man took up the conversation, speaking casually, as if he had just remembered something, when on the point of turning away.

" You may not know it, but this island's soil is already holy," he said. " It has been dedicated to the most ancient faith in the world in the days before the sea swept over the great land of which these isles alone remain. Human sacrifice has been offered here. It will be demanded again. One of your company will have to buy the future from the ancient past before you can remain. I suppose you had not been told of that ? " he asked the group of listening men, thrusting his parchment-pale face towards them, his smile showing a double row of uneven teeth. Pursuing his advantage he turned away from Columba and paced towards his scared companions, pointing a long, rheumatic forefinger at each appalled face in turn.

" Ye-es, a voluntary sacrifice, too. Will you offer yourself, I wonder ? . . . Or you ? . . . Or you ? Will you lie down in the dark ground and close your eyes to the light of the sun ? Life is still pleasant, here on earth. Will you gamble it away for the promise of your fabled heaven ? "

They shrank from him, and as they shrank he followed, gaining assurance from their terror. Running a pale tongue over dry lips he taunted them again.

" I tell you, one of you must offer himself as a sacrifice, so that the island receives its tribute. The bodies of many Druids have bought our right to preach here. Can you offer as much ? Or are you too squeamish ? Eh, heh, heh," he chuckled harshly. " I believe you are. Yet, if you do not, the island will reject you. Your buildings will crumble. Your beasts will sicken. You yourselves will die . . . if you remain."

" I do not believe it ! " Rus burst out suddenly.

The elder Druid peered at him. " Do you not ? Eh, heh, heh, it is not a pleasant picture, is it ? Reject it if you like. But be very sure that the island will afterwards reject you." He turned to his companion. " Let us go now. We have wasted too much time on these poor fools who despise the ancient wisdom. We will leave them to choose their victim for the sacrifice. That will not be so easy, will it ? Perhaps in the end they will decide to go. There are other isles, you know, chicken-hearted Christians. Leave heroism to the wicked Druids. They set more store by wisdom than by human life, you know. Why, how frightened they all look, don't they ? Heh, heh, heh ! "

They could hear him wheezing with laughter till his emaciated figure was hidden by the sand-dunes ; but the sound had nothing in common with the laughter that they knew. It was harsh with malice and all uncharitableness : it creaked from his withered spirit like the branch of a dead tree in a gale. Anxiously they crossed themselves, turning for reassurance to their leader who had been so strangely silent during the older Druid's attack.

" Father Columba," cried Rus, " is there any truth in this ? " They crowded round as he spoke, their happy confidence shaken by superstitious dread. " Surely it was no more than a tale invented to get rid of us ? " said the herdsman Torannan.

Columba looked round the circle of apprehensive faces. If he made little of the threat they might believe him at first, but if anything went wrong later they would not only lose faith in their enterprise, but also in him. The Druid had chosen his threat well ; for the tradition of securing the stability of a building or settlement by means of human sacrifice was ancient and widely known both in Erin and all the islands of the west. They might not consciously remember, but the tradition ran darkly in their blood.

" He did not invent the tale," Columba said deliberately. " But he misunderstood it, as such a man would. To offer himself as a sacrifice, it is not merely necessary that a Christian's body shall die. His life may be offered, as yours have been. Consider that, my children, and begin your work again."

They obeyed him, but reluctantly. They were not satisfied. Something seemed lacking now from the warmth of the sun, the purity of the sands, the vivid colours of sea and sky. A film of fear seemed to hang between them and the island which had at first appeared to welcome them. They carried their loads with solemn faces, and shook at the sudden cry of a bird. As they passed and re-passed each other on the path their feet had already trodden through the young grass of the pasture that sloped down to the sea, they averted their eyes, each fearful that the look on a comrade's face might mean that he had seen death shadowing their own. They expected to receive scolding and reassurance from Columba, who was usually so ready to exhort and encourage them. But Columba for once was silent. They were accustomed to find him ready to take even more than his share of the drudgery of the communal work, to swing the heaviest burden on his own broad shoulders. But as they made the preparations for rigging up the rudimentary hut which would serve as a church, and another which would offer them all shelter, he still sat motionless, with Oran at his feet, gazing out over the sea. It was Rus who supervised the collection of stones which in that

bleak land must take the place of the timber with which they were
accustomed to build their huts. It was Lugaid who decided that
they must eat, after they had carried enough stones for the
foundations of the huts, Cobtach who took out the coracle and
brought back fish. While they worked, calling nervously to each
other from time to time, Columba sat still on the beach, his face
expressionless, his eyes blank and his spirit preoccupied with
urgent intercessory prayer.

When Lugaid came to him and asked for a blessing on their
food he rose at last, with Oran following him, and took his place
at the head of the board which they had improvised from usefully
placed rocks. As they ate, little groups of islanders, led by Urdan,
came closer to look at them, concealing themselves prudently
behind boulders in case the strangers' magic might not always be
benevolent, apt as easily to strike a man silent as to loosen a lad's
tongue. When the meal was over the monks gathered about the
foundations of the little church of unmortared stones that they
were about to raise, and as the people crept inquisitively closer,
Columba began to chant in Latin the Psalm which had been his
favourite since the day he had first heard it at the oratory as a
small boy, newly dedicated to the service of the Church in Erin.
Now, standing beside the foundations of the first Christian
church in the pagan island of the magicians, he seemed to hear
again the voices of his first friends as they translated it at the old
priest's knee.

" The Lord is my shepherd : I shall not want. He maketh me
to lie down in green pastures : he leadeth me beside the still
waters . . ."

As they sang, the anxiety went from their faces, little by little,
as the familiar words brought to each of them some picture of his
home. But Oran stood a little apart from them, gripping a
boulder with desperate hands as he tried to combat the waves of
deadly sickness that swept over him. He felt, in that secret
struggle, very much alone. The others all came from Erin, had
some background in common, but he was a Briton whose parents
had migrated westward during his childhood and died soon
afterwards, leaving him alone. He was a stranger, and yet bound
to these comrades by the ties of shared adventure which seem
sometimes stronger than those of blood. He had come to love
these men, who had accepted him so unquestioningly as one of
their number. Yet his sickness on the voyage had made him feel
helpless and wretched, a mere drag on them all. It had not been
till the Druid had jeered at their terror of human sacrifice that
he had suddenly seen what he could do. Now, as they sang on,

he was seeking courage with which to do it, so that he, whose flesh shrank already from the gross darkness in the valley of the shadow of death, might now approach it willingly if his going should give security to his friends.

When the noon office was over he made his way shakily forward and knelt at Columba's feet. " Father, I have a request to make."

" What is it, my son ? "

For the last time Oran struggled with the instinctive longing for life which urged him to demand the careful tending, shelter and medicine which would give him the chance of physical survival for which his sick body craved. Then suddenly, the struggle was over, and he saw his purpose clear before him as a straight road beneath the morning sun. Thus, and thus alone could he in his turn give to his comrades the hope and courage which their acceptance of him into their company, lonely and alien as he was, had given to him.

" I ask that you will let me offer this sickness that is on me for the life of the community," whispered Oran. " I heard what the stranger priest said, and I know that he hoped so to divide us from one another, because each of us feared that he might be the one chosen to die. But because I am sick, let me take that duty upon me, Father, so that the others in their strength may all go free——"

Columba held out his hands, enclosing Oran's limp fingers in his tremendous clasp. " So you, whom I would not burden, are willing to take up the heaviest burden of all, Oran ? "

" Most willing, Father."

Awed, incredulous, ashamed, the others crowded about them. They had treated Oran as one of themselves because brotherhood was their ideal, their obligation. But they had never thought much of him. He had always been puny, though willing, and when they had to finish the tasks which were too heavy for him, he had irked them with his anguished apology. Now, as he drew to himself the task from which they had all recoiled, they saw him with clearer eyes, as already a spirit whose brightness blossomed from his very infirmity.

" Very well, my son," Columba said.

Oran lifted his arms. " Strike, then . . ." he cried. " Let my blood be sprinkled on these foundations and my body go into the ground."

But Columba shook his head. " Such responsibility is too heavy for me," he said. " My son, God alone can be asked to accept or refuse such a sacrifice. We will build a hut for you where you will be tended by your brothers night and by day. If your sacrifice be accepted, you can be sure that the community will be blessed by the courage and devotion which prompted it. And if it is refused it will be because God does not seek another Isaac, but has provided again a ram caught in the thicket by its horns. Come, Oran, and let us make a couch where you may lie and watch the buildings rise about you. We shall need your prayers."

Awed and obedient, the monks returned to their work, the superstitious terror purged out of them by Oran's intervention, the hordes of demons which their fancy pictured held at bay by the love and pity of one sick man. Now Columba worked with them ; directing, digging, and placing the stones in position. Steadily the walls of the little beehive church rose, and after it the hut for Columba as Abbot, a few rough shelters for the members of the community, as well as necessary buildings such as stores, granary, and mill.

And Oran lay on his couch of heather, through the lengthening summer days, trying to conceal the cough that racked him and nausea that came over him in increasingly deadly waves. He was oddly content as the noise and bustle of building flowed about him. It was not till the longest day of the year that he died.

CHAPTER XIII

LUGAID sighed as he picked up a tottering pile of earthen platters from the floor of the lean-to shed which adjoined the newly built refectory and served him as a cooking place and store.

" I could sometimes wish," he grumbled, " that our Father Columba had not seen fit to release your tongue, Urdan. I doubt if it has ever stopped wagging since. Even in sleep you rouse the brethren."

" But Lugaid, there is so much to say after a silence of seven years," protested Urdan, staggering back from the refectory with a stack of porridge bowls which reached to his chin. " I am so happy to be here instead of at the fishing village. I have to keep on saying so or I should burst. Oh, Lugaid, I am so happy ! Rus has promised to show me how to blow up the fire for his forge. He is going to dip the bell he has made for our Father Columba in bronze that will seal the cracks so that it will have a clear tone and the Abbot will not have to raise his voice to summon us to the church. And Torannan wants me to go to the mainland with him to drive back the cattle he is buying for the monastery. And Cobtach says I may go with him to the seal island, and Eochaidh is going to show me how to use a sickle in the harvest field . . ."

" I can see," said Lugaid glumly, " that I am to do without a kitchen-lad."

" No, indeed," said Urdan, shifting his weight from one bare foot to the other, " I will find time for all between dawn and darkness. Ah, Lugaid, when you have been alone a long time it is a happy thing to have all at once so many brothers as this."

" Huh," said Lugaid, smiling unwillingly at the boy's excited face. " If you rush about like that you will break half the dishes that remain to us after what happened yesterday."

" I will try to be sober," said Urdan penitently. " But how was I to know that the stool stood in my way as I bore the dishes ? "

" By carrying less and looking where you go," said Lugaid, as he laid the flat stone for baking the day's batch of barley bannocks across the other stones which enclosed the hearth fire. " Now I shall need more driftwood to get up the heat."

" I'll get it," said Urdan at once.

" But mind how you go," scolded Lugaid. " Can it be thought

suitable that a lay-brother should skip like a young kid ? It is not as if you were still a child. You are a great lad now, and you might meet with our Father Columba."

" It wouldn't matter if I did." Urdan spoke confidently. " I fell flat at his feet only yesterday when I was fetching Cobtach's creel from the boat. He just picked me up and laughed." Urdan ran round the corner of the hut, where, in seclusion, he relieved his feelings by putting out his tongue.

For Urdan already knew instinctively that he need never be afraid of Columba. The affectionate gratitude he felt for the man who had rescued him from bondage and silence was enhanced by a boy's awed admiration for Columba's strength and skill, his mastery of all manly crafts and his willingness to share his monks' labours, for the absolute justice of his decisions and the humour that so often lit the Abbot's candid grey eyes.

Columba had needed all his gifts during the two years that had followed the community's arrival on the island. They had been hard years for every one but hardest of all for Columba, to whom everybody else turned in their difficulties, who must advise, command, encourage, reassure, make peace, and understand every aspect of the work in hand. Urdan well remembered how their leader had never spared himself, but gone tirelessly about the settlement from dawn to dusk, pausing to offer criticism to the men digging or building, considering the quality of the soil which the wooden ploughshares were turning up in the fields, running a fistful of it through his fingers with thoughtfully pursed lips while the sunburned young men looked on, greeting the little huddle of islanders who collected daily outside the enclosure, whispering and pointing at the vigorous workers, gaping in astonishment at the steadily rising walls. Columba welcomed the islanders to the church, still roofless though it was, in which the monks sang the daily offices, and a small crowd habitually gathered before Vespers, filling the open space about the church in the translucent northern summer evenings, when the cloudless sky that arched over them was like pale glass, and the voices of the monks sounded far across the scarcely ruffled sea.

During these first years on the island Columba had no time to spare for the Scots on the mainland of Alba, though reports of their hardships came frequently to the island from his cousin Conall, their King. He was too able an organiser to venture to think of conducting a campaign against a distant objective until he had made his base secure. His first task was to establish the monastery and to receive as many converts as possible from among the islanders.

Urdan himself, delighted by the honour, was the first to be baptised. The rest of the islanders were still wary. They maintained that the two Druids, whose magic had once ruled them, and who had now retired to the rocky fastnesses to the west of the island, were preparing spells against the Christians. But if Urdan survived, they argued, perhaps the Christians were stronger, after all. And since nothing disastrous happened to Urdan in consequence of his baptism, and the creed of such obviously competent and contented men as Columba's monks made an increasingly strong appeal to their romantic natures, they also ventured, one by one.

The Druids, on the other hand, obstinately refused all further contact with the Christians. They withdrew into seclusion, with a few adherents, making their headquarters a small collection of beehive huts which looked out across the western sea from a high meadow encircled by great rocks. Here they occupied themselves after their own fashion, studying the movements of the stars, the comings and goings of the tides and the structure of the rocks, speculating on the past and on the future, preserving in their ageing memories the exclusive tradition whose grandeur was to be so little appreciated by later ages because their rule insisted on verbal instruction, forbidding any priest familiar with the alphabet to write his knowledge down. So, when they died, their knowledge died with them, and in due course two cairns built by their few remaining followers remained as memorials to these victims of the gnostic avidity of man.

The settlement, on the other hand, grew rapidly. It had already become an organised monastic community whose members were given work according to their abilities, and in which they were supervised by the members of the original company who acted as instructors and guides.

A small group of older, studious men, who had come to the island from the mainland, became known as the Seniors. They were in most cases not strong enough to undertake manual work, but were glad to make new copies of the Gospels and Psalms as required. They possessed both erudition and spirituality, and the island offered them a refuge for which they were profoundly grateful, revering Columba as their heaven-sent benefactor. It was one such scholar from turbulent Alba who first gave the island that name which was afterwards to become famous. Was not the Latin word for dove Columba ? In the Hebrew it was Jonah, or Iona. And since the island's name was already I or Hy in the Gaelic, therefore, only a small melodious addition was needed to offer an appropriate tribute to their patron and future saint.

The main body of the monks were known as Working Brethren. They had taken their vows and were permanent members of the community, but their gifts ran to husbandry rather than scholarship. Their duties were extensive ; with the Seniors they sang the offices, managed the sheep and cattle, of which the monastery had a fair number, worked in the fields, caught fish, repaired or added to the monastic buildings, worked at various trades or went on voyages of conversion or discovery among the surrounding isles.

The Juniors or Novices, who came to the monastery in great numbers, were those still receiving instruction prior to the taking of their final vows. From the month of Columba's arrival the island had begun to receive many such applications for membership, besides seekers for advice or consolation, and a vast indefinite, inquisitive, sight-seeing multitude whose motives were often not clear, even to themselves. Columba had given orders that the guest-house was to be provided with all the comfort his own austere cell lacked, and the brothers in charge of it had instructions to receive each guest with as much reverence as they received the Eucharist. Hospitality was now a sacred duty on Iona. " Often, often, often," Columba would remind them, " goes the Christ in a stranger's guise."

Each guest was greeted with courtesy, but special ceremony, on account of worldly eminence, was shown to none. The chieftain might find himself waiting his turn while the brother in charge of the guest-house washed the feet of a vagrant, and if such treatment made him call for his cloak and swirl out, bracelets clashing and weapons swinging with indignant pride, the attendant brothers merely smiled. It must be hard for those who had achieved importance on earth to realise that such importance was unlikely to gain them priority in heaven.

Columba received each suppliant with attentive kindliness, though the expression in the wide, grey eyes he turned on strangers often gave them the uneasy idea that he did not merely see what was visible to other men. The monks had ceased to be surprised when he received an unpromising applicant without question, sent what seemed a likely candidate to work out a long penance on the probationary settlement on Tiree, told one chieftain to return to his worldly splendours and another to put on the monastic habit of undyed wool that very day.

It was characteristic of Columba that he never attempted to force Christianity on those who were not yet ready for it in order to gain more souls for the new faith. He was too wise for that, now, though through the dreams which sometimes came to him during the brief period of rest he allowed himself each night there toiled the same symbolic procession of armed men, stumbling painfully up a rocky hillside. Some of their faces were lit as if the morning sun were on them, but others were still dim as the deep shadow that filled the valley through which the blood-gorged stream ran. Night by night the sunlight spread from face to face, but from the shadows other death-pale faces rose, so that Columba woke and wept, remembering the dead men of Culdremne and all that remained for him to do before he might return home. Meanwhile, he worked on. He had already become a legendary figure among the islands. Respect was due to a priest who could sail a boat as well as any fisherman, who passed unscathed through tempests and laughed among waves beneath which most men would have drowned. It was even said that the winds obeyed him, sea-monsters fled from him, mortal diseases were cured by him, and angels walked with him unawares. But Columba became very angry when incautious monks spoke of such things.

" I have nothing to do with such wonders. See that you give God alone the glory, my sons."

Columba neither sought glory for himself nor permitted his monks to exalt themselves by complaining of their fellows. Among the Juniors he often encountered such jealousies, thinly disguised by zealous words, though by the time they came to take their final vows, most monks had realised the futility of such attempts.

" Father," an anxious-minded monk asked him one day, " as we go about our duties the women of the villages plague us out of curiosity. Ought we not to dismiss them, so that our work is not hindered in this way ? "

Columba's smile was shrewd, but his voice was kind as he laid a hand on the young man's shoulder.

" Beware of jealousy, Melban. I know how the women linger round Dolbar, whose face reminds them of their own children's innocence, as he herds the cows with you. In your anxiety I believe you would have me banish even the cows from the island, saying that where there are cows there are women and where there are women there is sin. Is that not so ? "

" Indeed, Father . . ." Melban's thin face was darkened by a blotchy, unbecoming flush.

" Indeed, Melban, if they had talked more with you and less with Dolbar, I think I should have had no complaints. Am I not right ? "

" Perhaps," the young man admitted huskily.

"It is hard to work with one as fair of face as Dolbar," Columba said frankly. "But it would be less painful, perhaps, if you went to the church and thanked God for such beauty. Your own face would be fairer for its gratitude, since it is not the smooth skin or the bright colour that causes admiration, but the glimpse these things convey of a sweet spirit."

"Then are all fair-faced folk holy and do all the ill-favoured sin?" asked Melban sulkily.

"No, indeed. The most beautiful face may be ruined by a disagreeable nature, and the plainest made noble if great love is within. Love more, Melban. The source of all beauty lies there."

"Yes, Father." The young man turned away, and Columba smiled to himself as he watched him trudge off towards the church, where, as his Abbot had instructed him, he would thank God for Dolbar's beautiful face, hoping perhaps, poor child, that his obedience might bring to his own some magical beauty in return. How hard it was to prevent beginners from bargaining with God, Columba reminded himself. He sighed. So many roads led heavenward, and so many people walked them backwards because they grudged other people heaven's generosity. Melban, he guessed, would remember little of the interview except what he wanted to remember. If he quoted his Abbot at all it would be as saying that where there were cows there were women and where there were women there was sin.

Columba smiled ruefully as he walked on between the huts of the monks towards the track which led to the fields from which the stones had been cleared in preparation for the new sowing. Melban's preoccupation with women had not surprised him. It was almost inevitable among young celibates who had not yet learned how to redirect their perfectly normal energy towards a different level of being, where it would come more consciously under the control of the disciplined and dedicated will. Thus directed, nothing need be lost or unwholesomely suppressed, but only changed, as the angle of a boat's sail is changed when the boat is to be driven along another course by mean of the momentum offered by the same strong wind.

He himself treated the women who flocked about him for instruction with the kindly courtesy he would have shown to his mother or the equally courteous wariness which his early experiences with Maeve had taught him long ago. Good women, silly women, tired, sick or suffering women were entirely comprehensible. But bad women still puzzled him. He remembered Maeve with an involuntary shudder of revulsion. It was their unnecessary falsity to a pattern which should have been beautiful

which alienated him. The minds of such women were dark ;
he could not understand their distress, though he knew it to be
often genuine where so much else was false and vain. With such
women, he was prepared to admit, he was sometimes over-severe,
because he was also impatient and afraid.

As he walked across the island Columba was no longer
thinking of Melban and his difficulties, but of the missionary
campaign which he was now ready to begin. He had recently
received word that his old friends Kenneth and Comgall were
to come to the island that spring, and he intended to ask them
to share the exceptionally difficult mission to the court of the
Pictish king, Brude. He had come to agree with his cousin Conall
that the strenuous Pictish opposition to the Scottish colonists from
Erin was based at least in part on religious grounds. Kenneth and
Comgall belonged to that branch of the Pictish tribe which had
long ago settled in Erin and their consequent knowledge of the
Pictish form of Gaelic would be invaluable.

It was said by those who visited his dominions that King
Brude was an extremely superstitious man, whose weakness had
been well used by a formidable fraternity of magic-working
priests, similar to those by whom Columba had been confronted
when he first arrived on Iona. Then, he had not been ready,
but now, with the monastery well established and his old
companions once more by his side, the strategic moment to
strike at the persecutors of his countrymen in Alba seemed to
have arrived.

Impatient as ever to be off, anxious for the first glimpse of the
boat which was bringing his two friends from Erin, Columba set
out on one of his periodic inspections of the community's outlying
fields. The whole saddle of fertile land that ran across the island
had been brought under cultivation now, and Columba made
his way from east to west by a rough track which wound among
the knuckles of rock that showed through the sheep-cropped turf
like the bones of a tightly clenched fist. Once at the centre of the
island the meadows slid away towards the sickle-shaped western
bay with its curves of pale sand and banks of vivid shingle
from which the monks obtained the foul-smelling kelp with
which they manured the land.

From a commanding hillock Columba surveyed the progress
made since his last visit, noting each thrifty little field reclaimed,
its sandy soil dunged for greater fertility and ploughed in hope.
He smiled as he watched the young man who was now casting
the seed with the same wide, sweeping gestures which had been
ancient when the Gospels were written, and must have been

greeted, then as now, by a cloud of birds whose wings seemed to take a man's heart with them as they soared, white against the clear sky.

They had done well, these children, Columba thought. It would be pleasant to show the companions of his own novitiate how quickly the enterprise of his exile had grown. Once again he looked across the fields to the waters of the Sound which lay, milkily hazed, on the horizon. If only they would come . . . he was ashamed of the eagerness with which he awaited their arrival. Until he had heard they were coming he had told himself that he was content with his life on Iona, that he asked nothing more. But with the news of them a wave of longing had swept over him for the sight of any living creature from Erin, prompting him to the same overwhelming love as he had felt for the exhausted, migrating crane which his monks had tended for three days on his instructions, because it, too, came from Erin. Now, with his friends so near, he could hardly keep his attention on the Psalm he was transcribing, or answer a question till it had been repeated twice. Dismayed at such weakness, he had forced himself to further fasting, longer vigils and more urgent prayers.

But when at last the small sail appeared, far away to the south, a sudden calm came over him as if he had himself regained a peaceful harbour after the alternate buffetings of hope and fear. He had scarcely dared to believe that he would be permitted to see the beloved faces of his friends again. Now, as the distant sail grew from a speck to a blur, and from a blur to the spread of a bird's wing, he forced himself to walk slowly back to the breakwater which the monks had built out into the Sound at the southern end of the tiny natural harbour, and there to wait, motionless, for the clumsy boat to reach land.

Soon they saw him, and hardly had the boatman made his craft fast before Kenneth was ashore, with Comgall barely a couple of paces behind him. Columba's first forlorn thought was : " how direly they have changed in these few years." His second responded to the reassurance of their well-known voices : " No. They have not changed at all." Gaunt as he was, Kenneth looked stronger, at forty-five than he had ever done, but his gentleness had always had a core of rock to it, as Columba knew. Comgall had grizzled a good deal about the temples, but his short, wiry frame was resilient as ever. Kenneth was still pale from sea-sickness, but Comgall's humorous face, with the creases at the corners of his eyes that came from staring, like Brendan, towards the colours of far distances, was deeply tanned already, in the springtime of the year.

Columba held out his arms to them, his voice suddenly shaken. " My friends . . . my dear, dear friends . . ."

Each took a hand, clasping it in both their own. Tears stood in Kenneth's dark eyes, and Comgall gave him a twisted smile. " Columba . . . how good it is to see you . . . Have these years seemed long ?"

" Erin has been the dimmer without you, Columba," Comgall said. " Surely the light has followed you here," He stood looking about him, his artist's eyes wide as he glanced from sea to sky, at the isle lying like a rough-cut jewel between. " I did not dream of such beauty outside heaven. It is something in the light, not the land . . . impossible to catch it with any pigments known . . . to paint such a light a man must needs dip his brush in the glory of God . . . Columba, what poems have you written ? Do they hold the colour of the sky ? I will write them out so fair for you that——"

Columba shook his head, laughing. " I have other work for you both. Harder work, Comgall, than copying manuscripts. A journey by land, Kenneth. It should be easier for you to bear."

" I will go anywhere, provided it is not so far by sea again."

" What is this journey of yours ? Have we ended one only for another to begin ? " said Comgall.

" Come to the guest-house. I will tell you more when you have dined," said Columba, leading them towards the monastery, where, according to custom, he himself washed their feet while the brothers in charge of the guest-house prepared their meal.

It was not until after Vespers that Columba told his guests of his intention to visit King Brude in his stronghold on the far side of the Alban mountains, beyond the inland water called Loch Ness. He spoke of the Pictish king's persecution of their countrymen, his magic-working Druids, his threats to the Scots from Erin. " I suggest that we three, who have faced so many ordeals together in the old days, shall visit him and see if we can persuade him to leave them in peace. You, Kenneth and Comgall, speak the Pictish tongue, and can soon teach me the way of it. If we succeed, life will be very different for our countrymen. And if we fail——"

" We shall not fail," said Kenneth confidently.

Columba brought his hand down on his friend's shoulder with such amiable violence that he staggered. " Kenneth, you are the same as ever you were. Mild as milk till the urge for martyrdom is on you, and then like a burn in spate. How I have longed for you. And for you too, Comgall, though you sit there and say nothing. Just now I saw you reach for your staff and grope with your foot for the shoe you had laid by."

"Indeed, you two shall not go without me," Comgall agreed.

Once this had been decided, it was not long before they were ready to set out. Columba had already arranged to hand over his duties as Abbot to his deputy, the three friends made no provision for the journey beyond slinging their Gospel satchels on their backs and taking stout staves in their hands. Dermot, the reticent young lay-brother who had recently become Columba's personal attendant, providently took however, both bread and water-skin in case the reverend fathers had interpreted the scriptural command too literally. A Pictish lad, who had been one of their most recent converts, asked for the opportunity of seeing his own people again, and at the last moment Urdan begged so hard to be allowed to carry Kenneth's supply of medicines, ointments and bandages that Columba agreed to take them too, for Urdan was a big lad now, almost seventeen, strong, intelligent, and willing to make himself useful in any way.

Every one of the community, which now consisted of several score monks, assembled at the harbour to bid them godspeed after Prime on that May morning, so that Columba's last impression of the island was of its dark rocks and the monk's white habits, and the great surge of singing that followed them across the mist-hushed sea.

Their journey followed the route which was later to be known as the Pilgrims' Way, and to be marked in years to come by tall white stones. But in these early days the journey through the great glens was wild and desolate as anything Columba had yet attempted, through solitude which seemed to brood like a presence upon the boulder-strewn hillsides below strangely terraced peaks, from which an occasional eagle sailed superbly, on the watch for an unwary rabbit or a straying, bewildered lamb.

The Pictish lad, Gondal, who was to act as guide, was used to finding his way through the mountains, so that Columba and his companions had only to follow him as he plodded with a deliberation which irked Columba's impatient spirit, along faint tracks worn on the hillsides by the coming and goings of innumerable sheep.

Kenneth teased him. " Still the same Columba, who would like to reach his objective in a single stride ? "

"Indeed, yes," said Columba. " If only it had seemed advisable to the Lord to endow his servants with wings ! While we trudge, the fire seems to leave my spirit, like a brand that has

smouldered so long that when the time comes for it to blaze it
has been burnt out."

"These things do not trouble me," Kenneth said. "Perhaps
my spirit is one which is intended to smoulder like a clod of
turf, not to blaze like a kindled brand."

"Heaven can use both turf and brand, no doubt," said
Comgall, trudging stoically on. "I have no wish to kindle,
even to glow. I would rather be a quiet pool that reflects all
the beauty that passes across it, from the summer butterfly to
the winter's snow. It is always in my mind that I—I—Comgall
the scribe—must subdue my spirit's conflict utterly if it is to show
that earth can reflect even a little of the beauty that is in heaven."

The others listened to him in surprise. It was seldom that
Comgall spoke of himself and afterwards they walked on in
thoughtful silence. Then Columba, noticing that Kenneth had
begun to limp and even the boys seemed oppressed by the prodigious solitudes about them, began to sing, and at once their
feet began to move more freely, and their arms to swing again.

"Long is the journey, huge are the mountains,
Cruel are the rocks to my dust-whitened feet.
Sweet face of Mary, smile for my solace,
Jesus, the shepherd, be thou my guide.

Strange is the journey : go thou before me,
Shine through the mist that wraps corrie and ben.
Strong arm of Michael, save me from stumbling,
Jesus, the shepherd, still be my guide.

Dark is the journey : weary my heart now,
Steep, steep the way to the fortress of heaven.
Hungry the wolves are, slinking like shadows,
Loud are the torrents that rage through the glen.
Fearless among them walks heaven's foster-mother,
Bride of the angels, the milk-maiden Bride,
Bright sword of Michael, lighten the gloaming,
Jesus, the shepherd, lead home thy child."

It was not till dusk came down that they felt weary again,
ready to search among the boulders which lay everywhere for a
sheltered nook in which to spend the night.

"Tell me again, Comgall," said Columba, when they had
eaten some of the bread that Dermot carried, "how you left
Erin ? Time seems to have stretched itself out of all reason since

I sailed away from Derry, so that I can no longer reach back to see how the hills tower above the oak trees, or watch the smoke from the cooking fires rise high into the air. Do the colours change still in springtime, as they change on a pigeon's breast when it stands preening itself in the sun?"

"When you talk of Derry," Kenneth said, "there is a look in your eyes as if you spoke of heaven."

"Why, yes," said Columba, "if heaven is not at least as fair as Derry of the oaks I shall be cheated indeed. But tell me of Erin, meanwhile, Kenneth and Comgall. You have brought me greetings from my parents and made me happy because my mother is well. But now, tell me of the lesser things, which mean so much. Tell me how the fishermen are prospering. Are their old boats weathering the spring tides? How are the young woods looking where we planted new trees for those that we cut down? I want to know the progress of each hawthorn, each rosette of primroses beside the monastery walls, Leave heaven for a while, Kenneth. Tell me of Erin, Comgall."

Next day they rose with the first light and journeyed on, and the day after, and the day after that, new glens opening before them, and the stags bounding away into the mists, with here a pass to be negotiated and there an easier few miles by the side of a rocky-bedded burn, till at last the waters of Loch Ness opened before them and they were able to take to the boat for which Columba had bartered a sheath-knife and his own hooded cloak.

"But the wind is against you if you are to sail up the loch to-day," the boatman said.

Columba laughed. "Then we shall sail into the wind, my friend."

"Are you magicians, then?" said the boatman sourly.

"No, merely islanders who must learn to use a sail when the wind is contrary as well as at other times."

But the boatman, whose knowledge of sailing that narrow inland water was confined to running before a favourable breeze, continued to shake his head and mutter. Columba and his companions must undoubtedly be magicians. With their long habits of undyed wool, their unfamiliar tonsures, their strange tongue and their air of majesty, they reminded him of the magicians he had once seen when he visited the king's headquarters at a time of great rejoicing some years ago. These magicians had been terrible people, able to make cliffs answer them and men run mad and clouds darken the air. It would be as well not to offend these strangers. Who knew what might happen if he were rash enough to contradict them? So he let them go and stood for a

long time watching them tack uncannily up the loch into the wind
He shrugged. Magicians, undoubtedly. But there was, he hoped,
nothing magical about the knife and the hooded cloak for which
he had parted with his leaky old boat. Suspiciously he felt the
stuff between finger and thumb, trying the knife-edge on the bark
of a tree. He was relieved to find that they seemed earthly
enough. After all, he had not done so badly against the magicians,
since it would probably be magical indeed if the boat did not
sink long before they reached the far end of the loch.

So Kenneth was just saying, as Columba set the sail for the
new course, while Comgall and the lads cupped their hands and
baled. But Columba only laughed, and the wind carried the
great rolling sound up the loch ahead of them. For the wind was
coming round. Soon it was necessary to tack no longer and they
were flying up the loch on a straight course, their wake spreading
behind them, the parted water creaming half-way up the prow.
Then Comgall tore a strip off his already ragged habit and stuffed
it into the hole through which the water had been bubbling.

" That plug of cloth will never hold," groaned Kenneth, who
was not at his best on journeys by water, though the respite was
a blessed one for his badly blistered heel. Columba had advised
him to go barefoot as he did himself, but Kenneth's feet never
seemed to have the toughness of other people's. Journeys were
irksome to him. He did not complain, but the sandals that
protected his feet had also blistered his heel.

" It will hold like a limpet on a rock," roared Columba,
whose spirits had been rising as their journey neared its end.
Once more they were faced with drama, danger, the need for
rapid thought and decisive action, all the things which came more
easily to him than the patient endurance of a pedestrian's way.
" It will hold indeed, if you but brace your foot against it,
Comgall ! "

CHAPTER XIV

So THE THREE friends surged down the grey waters of the long narrow loch, alternately drenched by piercing showers of spring rain and blessed by briefly exquisite bursts of sunshine which minimised the fearful threat of the surrounding mountain ranges. Meanwhile, on either side of the loch, rumour outstripped them, rumour which travelled at the breakneck speed common among primitive peoples who have been driven to perfect their intelligence system by urgent necessity.

To the three priests the wilderness through which they had been journeying had seemed uninhabited except by the herds of deer that fled from them into the pine forests which swept up the foothills towards the crags where last winter's snow still lay deep. But they had been watched ever since they entered Pictish territory by silently moving men who paced beside them through the forests, peered at them as they paused to drink at the mountain-shadowed fords in the deep glens which the sunlight scarcely pierced before noon, crept to their encampments to whisper with the Pictish lad, Gondal, when his masters were at their devotions and Urdan and Dermot slept, and at last, watched them, open-mouthed, when they sailed off down the loch, as it seemed, into the very wind's eye.

Startled reports went ahead of them, reaching the Pictish headquarters before the little boat was half-way down the loch. With them requests for instructions. Did the commander of the king's forces wish them to be killed immediately, before landing, to be put to death as soon as they approached the fortress-capital, or to be saved alive for questioning?

The Pictish leaders met in conference. The arrival of the strangers was not altogether unexpected. It had been known that the Scots, who had persistently clung to the western isles and only been driven back foot by foot from that area of the mainland which they had occupied, worshipped gods of their own. The Druids, who had taken advantage of King Brude's morbid terrors to establish a religious dictatorship over the Picts he ruled, had always expressed the most violent hostility both towards the Scots and their creed, but the Druidic influence over the King had come to irk the military leaders increasingly as it deprived them of the right to marshal their spearsmen for battles of their own choice. Consequently, their attitude was temperate. They were unwilling to massacre at the magicians' whim.

" These men, I hear, are also magic-workers," said the governor of King Brude's fortress-capital. " To my mind, therefore, we cannot do better than set them at Broichan and his Druids, leaving them to fight it out, warlock against warlock, spell for spell."

" But surely," objected a nervous provincial commander, " if we let the magicians loose against each other, the strongest magic will win and we shall be more bound than ever, whichever the victor may be."

The governor of the capital snapped his fingers, " Rubbish, man ! The whole thing is against all common sense. What we want is a chance of showing King Brude that his precious Broichan is, quite simply, a fraud. If these magicians from the west can expose him, so much the better. Once Broichan is discredited the strangers can go home again. We will take charge."

" And if they fail ? " said the sceptical warrior who had seen six tired, unarmed men toiling along a mountain track in the teeth of a gale. The Druids always travelled in state ; their litters were borne by relays of sweating servants, their sacred persons shielded from any threat of rain or wind. How could three humble priests, whose magic could not even save them a drenching, compete against all the thunders of the Druids, who gave judgment in fearsome ceremony, with the fire of heaven ready to leap from their hands ?

" If they fail ? Then we shall be no worse off, shall we ? " said the governor. He leaned forward across the council table and wagged a bony finger at the younger man. " The trouble with you people is that you won't use your brains. You fight well enough, I grant you, as long as it's merely a matter of dealing with enemies who can be split apart with one stroke of your sword. But when it comes to an enemy who rules you by fear of the powers that can strike you dumb or twitch your good sword from your hand altogether, your knees knock like an old woman's. Can't you see that it's better to let those strangers do the fighting for us ? They have their own spells, no doubt. Let them use them against Broichan and the rest while we sit in council and wait and see who wins."

" Well . . . maybe . . . "

" I have never set much store by Broichan, as you all know," said the old commander boldly. " I would have challenged him personally for fraud more than once if there had been an opportunity. Rumours keep reaching me. I hear a good deal from the servants' quarters in the Arch-Druidical establishment, you know. I'm ready to swear that most of Broichan's power is based on sheer trickery. But—well, you know how it is—a man doesn't much like to try conclusions with someone who says he can turn you into a toad or a viper or something equally unpleasant if he should be too much provoked. The trouble is "—he spread out his hands in an eloquent gesture—" the old fraud might—just possibly might—be able to do what he says. It's not the sort of thing one cares to risk."

A heartfelt murmur of agreement rose from all sides.

" But what does it matter to us if he changes these strangers into vermin ? He can spirit them away altogether, for all I care. And at least, if he does not, we can be pretty sure that it will be because, after all, he simply has not got the gifts he claims. Well, what about it, my friends ? Shall we give these strangers all the assistance in our power to cross swords with Broichan and save us the necessity of doing it ourselves ? "

Again they agreed. They were cordial, even optimistic now.

" Very well. As you know, Broichan has been taking it upon himself recently to give various orders in the name of the king. But I will also give mine "—he chuckled—" in my own."

The council of commanders dispersed ; tall, ponderous men, whose hair, dark or red, fell on to the leather cuirasses reinforced with iron bands, the style of which owed something to the Romans whom their forefathers had defeated. Some wore also leg-coverings of cross-gartered cloth or leather, others merely an undertunic which left most of their brightly tattooed thighs bare· They were fine-looking soldiers, fanatically brave in battle, but like the other Celtic races imaginative enough to fall easy victims to any man who threatened them with supernatural power. A people who lived, as they did, in surroundings of such awful grandeur could not fail to be aware of much that could not be seen or heard by bodily eyes and ears. As they left the timbered guard-room beside the main gate of the fortress in which the conference had been held their faces were still haggard with superstitious terrors, and they did not look each other in the eyes. But the governor himself was humming a tune as he strode off to have a word with the men in charge of the main gate.

Meanwhile, the boat was still holding together, though the water now covered the travellers' feet as it neared the landing-stage. Once ashore, they followed the course of the wide river which left the mountains behind as it flowed between outcropping hills towards the wide firth which bit into Alba's eastern coast. Long before they reached the Pictish fortress on its abrupt, flat-topped crag, the place was visible as they trudged down the valley through which the river now wound. Not a human being was to be seen. Only the forests and hills looked down on them through the clear light of a calm spring day. There was evidently some sort of a settlement nearby, for a haze of smoke rose from behind the fortress which defended that part of Pictish territory from attack by sea or land. Within the inimical stronghold itself, Gondal told them, King Brude and his retinue, already warned of their coming, would now be waiting for them to arrive.

" Will they send no one to greet us ? " Kenneth wondered. " It is a strange reception, neither friendly nor hostile. What does this indifference mean ? "

" I think," said Gondal nervously, " it means that they first want to see what you can do."

" Do ? " said Comgall, puzzled.

" The Druids rule this country," Gondal reminded them. " Here they are not likely to withdraw from the conflict, as they did on Iona, because we were too many for them. These men are mighty magicians. Even I——" He crossed himself. " Forgive me, Father Columba, I am a good Christian, I swear, but this is my native country and all the old fears, once more, run coldly down my spine."

Columba's confident laughter made him shiver. And even Kenneth and Comgall were grave, the phlegmatic Dermot edged a little closer to his master and young Urdan was wide-eyed. Columba alone was as happy as a bridegroom on the way to his wedding. Girding his habit, which was ragged and dingy now after their weeks of journeying, he picked up his staff. " Come then, son, I will show you something that will warm that spine of yours. Give me my satchel. Stand on my right side, Kenneth, and on my left, Comgall. Follow us boldly, Dermot, Urdan and Gondal. No harm shall come to any one of you. My friends, remember that to us all things are possible." He made the sign of the cross. " Let us take thought only for this moment. The future lies in the hands of God. *In nomine Jesu Christi . . .*"

Together they began to climb the steeply winding track that led to the fortress which brooded over them in an appalling silence, a silence only broken by the sound of Kenneth's sandals scraping occasionally on an underlying rock. Snuffling apprehensively, Gondal walked almost on Columba's heels, while Dermot and Urdan followed closely behind Kenneth and Comgall.

From the fortress their approach had been observed by the sentries posted to give warning. By the instructions of Briochan, the Arch-Druid, the great gates had been closed and the bolts shot home. On either side a group of soldiers waited, according to the orders of the governor. Men also stood along the walls and in the corner-towers, The king and his court had assembled in the main courtyard within the gates, wearing robes of state and attended by Broichan, the Arch-Druid and all his priests, white-robed and garlanded. On either side of the priests who stood round the king's chair were the military commanders. They bore weapons and looked either grim, uncertain or indifferent. But the governor who sat on the king's right hand was stroking away an almost impish smile as he twisted his long grey moustache. King Brude himself, a tall, gaunt man near middle-age, with the protuberant eyes of a startled hare, glanced apprehensively from the soldiers to the priests, and the heavily ringed hands which should have been crossed in his lap were continually restless, now fidgeting with the gold collar at his neck, now adjusting the brooch of the ceremonial robe which was heavy on his shoulders, now nervously scratching thigh or nose or ear. The royal diadem bit into his forehead, but more irksome still was the continual, crippling sense of inadequacy, which he had carried as long as he could remember, ever since, as his mother's eldest son, he had known that he must be king of a nation which wor-shipped physical strength and beauty and would be sure to despise him for his stammer and his nervous fears.

Broichan, the Arch-Druid, had said he need fear nothing. All the difficulties of kingship would disappear, he promised, if Brude did just what his priestly advisers said. He need not worry about his stammer. It would go too, because they would tell him just exactly what to say. And so they had. But things were no better. On the contrary, they were worse. Broichan was standing behind him now. Brude could feel his presence like an iron vice which clamped his spirit, supporting him, admittedly, but constricting him also, almost more than he could bear. He moved restlessly in the chair of state which was so much too big for his wasted limbs. What new demonstration of Broichan's tiresome magic was coming now?

A soldier came up to the governor and made a report.

" What's that ? " demanded the Arch-Druid.

The governor raised his grizzled eyebrows. Ignoring Broichan, he spoke to the king. " I hear that the strangers are at the gates. Is it your pleasure that we admit them, sir ? "

" No," said King Brude. Broichan had told him to say that. He didn't want to say it at all. He would have been glad to greet the strangers kindly. New things and people interested him. But the trouble was that only as long as he said what Briochan had told him to say did it seem possible to speak at all. If he gave orders of his own he always stammered, feeling as helpless as if he had stepped from solid ground into a bog from which he had to struggle to extricate each foot with agonising efforts which so exhausted him that he was ready to give it up and sink into silence as into the bottomless ooze. When Broichan told him what to say it was different. He seemed to be impelled across the bog, from tussock to tussock, by the power of a vastly stronger will. It was as if he had been taken forcibly by the nape of the neck and borne along. He himself was no stronger for Broichan's presence. Strength was merely imposed on him from outside. It wasn't really what he wanted. He wanted to be helped to be strong, taught to express his own thoughts, to be free of the compulsion that held him, to give orders to his people as a king should.

"You refuse them admittance, then?" said the governor.

"I do," said King Brude in a strangled, unhappy voice.

"Very well," said the governor. "The king refuses admittance to the strangers," he shouted, adding in an undertone : "let us see what happens now."

King Brude was never very sure, afterwards, what actually did happen. He could hear the soldiers on the ramparts taking up the governor's proclamation, so that the words went rolling over the vitrified walls and ancient earthworks, across the waters of the firth towards the distant peaks beyond. "The king refuses admittance . . . the king refuses admittance . . . refuses admittance to the strangers . . . to the strangers . . ." The defiant words echoed and re-echoed till the clamour seemed to roll round and round inside his aching head.

Then another voice answered from outside the walls. The stranger was apparently speaking in some unknown language, for Brude had never heard any of the words before. But what struck him was the strength, the beauty and the certainty of the voice itself. In some strange way, it seemed to be associated with light ; it had the sort of momentous astonishment of a lightning-flash as it seared its way across his dark spirit. Then there was silence again. Every one waited, while the governor, smiling in an odd way, turned again to the king.

"You still refuse them admittance, sir?"

Behind the unhappy king's chair Broichan frowned thunderously ; his white beard jutted forward, his long-fingered hands were curved, tense as the talons of some predatory bird.

"Y-y-y-y-yes," said King Brude.

"The king refuses admittance . . . refuses admittance . . . refuses admittance . . ." The soldiers on the ramparts took up the governor's shout once more. Then, from the far side of the great gates the stranger spoke again, and this time his voice seemed actually to reach King Brude's shrinking body and touched the lonely heart within. He half rose from his chair, struggling desperately to speak, not the words that Briochan wanted him to say, but those which were prompted by his own rebellious, doggedly struggling, inarticulate desire.

" L-l-l-let th-th-them c-c-c . . ." He fought the words as if they were enemies, his face scarlet with anguish, his mouth distorted with the effort to compel his recalcitrant muscles to obey his will. The sounds he made were barely coherent ; only his inchoate intention reached out towards the unknown man who demanded admittance, to be beaten back by the Arch-Druid's shout.

" No ! "

Brude could feel Broichan's murderous will assaulting his own as if a vast, black bird had buried its talons in his neck and was hammering at his undefended skull with its iron beak. He sank back in his chair, exhausted. Around him nobody moved. Nor, as far as he could see, did any of the soldiers who were standing about the gates.

But the gates themselves flew open. With a noise like rock struck by a hammer the great bolts, thick as a man's arm, shot back in their sockets, and the gates swung apart so violently that they shuddered against the walls. Brude saw the eastern firth lying like a sword flung down among the mountains that towered beyond it, snow crowning their summits and the pine forests running up into their arms. Against the tremendous background of mountains and sea stood three men, smiling. And round their shoulders peered three astonished lads.

" Treachery, treachery," shouted Broichan, crimson-faced. He had stepped out of his place to scold the astounded courtiers, his fists clenched above his head, his voice see-sawing up and down, alternately raucous and shrill as he tried furiously to counteract the impression which this astounding development had made on the assembled noblemen and soldiers. " It is treachery, I tell you ! The king's command has been disobeyed," he thundered, thrusting his angry face forward till his clenched teeth threatened the governor like those of an enraged wild beast.

" Who has disobeyed the king's command, Broichan ? " said the governor mildly. " From where I stood the gates seemed to open of their own accord, with no man near them. I should have called it magic rather then treachery, most venerable Arch-Druid."

" Magic ? Trickery, I tell you ! These men are vagrant

tricksters. To us alone has belonged the knowledge of magic since time began. These ignorant creatures have gained admittance by fraud."

"Fraud, Broichan?" said the governor politely. "Surely the strangers' magic is not fraudulent merely because in this instance it seems to have been stronger than your own?"

"It is no magic, I tell you," roared Broichan. "It is mere vulgar trickery. Or else some of your soldiers have had a hand in it. Perhaps they opened the gates. Out of my way. I mean to look at the bolts. They have been tampered with. They must have been . . ."

But the governor, obstinately polite, sidled to and fro, obstructing him. "Surely it is more important to greet the strangers, now they have gained admittance, rather than alienate them by refusing to suppose that they opened the gates in that remarkable way? Look, here they come . . ."

Columba, with Kenneth on one side of him and Comgall on the other, was already approaching the king, through a lane of whispering soldiers and fisher-folk who were pushing and peering and gaping at the strangers with faces of terror and awe. King Brude had already risen to greet them, his own face like that of a man who scarcely dares to believe what he sees, in whom new hope struggles against a lifetime of inadequacy and despair. He spoke, and spoke clearly.

"You are welcome, strangers."

Though Columba did not understand the words, everything else was evident. He saw the wide, distraught eyes, the beginnings of hope, the marks of mortal fear. He saw the tall figure of Broichan, brooding and resentful, loom up behind the king. He felt the struggle, the domination, the plea for help. It was the plea that he answered, speaking with such gentleness, such warmth that the unfamiliarity of the words scarcely mattered, and King Brude smiled like a child awakening from the terrors of a bad dream.

"Christ bless you, King Brude," said Columba. "We meet here as friends, you and I. When I have learned your language we will talk together. Meanwhile my companions here who are of your kin can speak for me, delivering our respectful greeting to the king."

Kenneth stepped forward, while Gondal, still appalled by the miraculous way in which the gates had swung open as his master Columba had made the sign of the cross, watched, trembling in the background. He was much more alarmed than Dermot or Urdan, for he knew that the sullen Druids who were

glaring at Columba were also magicians, that there would
presently be a trial of strength in which the weapons were not
homely blades which lesser men might dodge, but unearthly
shafts of power which would fly invisibly between them and
perhaps catch unwary people like himself on the way. He
wished he had fled when the gates flung wide. He wished he had
never seen Iona, never left his home, never had anything to do
with magic-mongers. He sniffed dismally, his fears only partly
allayed when Kenneth asked for the privilege of speaking to the
king in private, a suggestion to which Brude agreed at once, so
that the three priests and their followers from Iona were being
escorted into the king's private apartments while the governor,
with hands on hips, was still obstructing the furiously gesticulating
Broichan who was trying to make his way through the hubbub
of excited soldiers and fisher-folk, in order to inspect the gates.

In the king's own house it was quiet, for the narrow window-
slits looked out on the distant snows and the noise made by all
the people in the courtyard only reached them faintly and from
far below. King Brude, growing bolder with each moment, had
given orders that they were not to be interrupted on any pretext
whatsoever. The doors of the private apartments were for the
first time barred to the Arch-Druid himself. Stammering when
he began, little by little King Brude gained confidence. His
uncertain tongue steadied itself. Though he spoke to Kenneth
and Comgall his wide, startled-hare's eyes flickered continually
towards Columba's strong, compassionate face.

" A-a-are you greater magicians than the Druids ? " he asked.
" I h-h-hope you are, for I am tired of d-d-doing only what they
say. They h-h-hold me in bondage——"

" We do not seek to hold any one in bondage, King
Brude."

" Do you not ? " asked Brude, rolling his large eyes. " You
do not know what it has been like here since Broichan said he
would cure my s-s-stammer. He has never left me in peace for
a moment. He has terrorised the whole c-c-country. He alone
gives orders. Even the warriors have been afraid. He has done
dreadful things, like turning people into rats or pigs or seagulls."

Columba listened patiently while the king's words were
interpreted. Then he looked about him with interest. " Who
has been changed into a rat or a pig or a seagull by Broichan's
magic ? " he asked in his practical way. " Have you ever, with
your own eyes, King Brude, seen such a change take place ?
It is one thing for a man to disappear and for Broichan to say
that he is now a certain pig or bird. But have you yourself, seen

the man become the pig? That, to my mind, is the crux of the matter."

"Truly, I have never seen anybody being changed in my presence," King Brude admitted, rolling his wild eyes. "But Broichan has done such fearful things that I would not have cared to see that happen, even if I had had the chance. After all, he is not a man to be trifled with. He has raised storms on the loch in order to drown people who have defied him, and brought others out in blotches with a single spell. Yes, and he has called down the lightning to strike men dead. So when he says he has changed people into rats or gulls or pigs I would rather take his word for it than watch him do it, Columba. He might have enough magic left over to change me into something unpleasant, too."

Columba's shout of laughter made King Brude's apprehensive eyes almost start from his head, but he grew calm at the touch of Columba's reassuring hand. "Listen, my friend," said Columba. "There is no reason for you to be so afraid. Because Broichan can do a few strange things, that is not to say he can do whatever he likes. He can have no power whatsoever over you unless you give him that power through your own fear. All things of the spirit are in the gift of God, and the first fruits of his gifting are love and joy and peace. Never fear the power of man. Power carries a blessing only while it is used for the glory of God. No blessing goes with it when it is used, as Broichan uses it, to terrorise the people and increase the glory for himself. Such power is tainted, and can only dominate men who are afraid. Forget the pretensions of Broichan the Druid of darkness and terror, King Brude, and listen while I tell you of the young Druid of heaven, Christ the Prince of Glory who came down to guide men home . . ."

He had long since outdistanced Kenneth's interpretation and forgotten to wait for it, but though his words might be incomprehensible, something in the warmth and conviction with which he spoke conveyed itself to the king, who sat watching rather than listening to him, a tentative, wondering smile beginning to chase the apprehension from his face. As Kenneth, stumbling hastily through Columba's prolonged burst of eloquence, managed to reach the last few words, Brude rose and knelt at Columba's feet with the simplicity of a grateful child.

"Truth is in your eyes, Columba, and in your voice, and in the grasp of your hands. What your words are I cannot yet tell, for your language is strange to me. But where so much is true I cannot think your words are otherwise. Learn our language quickly, Columba. I wish to hear more of the God who sends such messengers."

Columba made the sign of the cross above Brude's bowed head. " ' *Cognoscetis veritatem*,' " he said gently. " ' *Et veritas vos in libertatem vindicabit.*' "

The shouts of the excited people in the courtyard came below faintly up to them, as they clamoured for the workers of magic. but Brude did not hear them. Instead, he seemed to hear the sound of a door opening, a door which had so long been held against him by men who used the infirmity of his fear for their own ends. Now, across the shadowed floor of his prison a narrow beam of sunlight fell, fanning out and illuminating it as Kenneth's gentle voice translated the promise of St. John. " ' You shall know the truth, and the truth shall make you free . . .' "

CHAPTER XV

THE CONVERSION of King Brude was the beginning of Columba's greatest and most far-reaching achievement, as a diplomat as well as a priest. With Broichan's final defeat the immensely powerful hierachy of paganism would receive its death blow in northern Alba, and, since all its influence had been consistently directed against the Christian Scots from Erin it might reasonably be hoped that under a Christian government the Picts would react towards friendship with those whose kinsman had freed their country from the worst excesses of priestly dictatorship. Once set in motion, the consequences of Columba's Pictish mission reached still further, into that future which none of the missionaries could hope to live to see, of which even the seer Columba only received occasional glimpses, when the tribes of Alba would no longer war against each other but be united into a single kingdom, bearing the name of those very Scots whose destiny Columba's exile from Erin had so dramatically changed.

None of these things were, however, immediately evident. The three friends had to fight for every inch of progress, against the malignantly hostile members of Druid priesthood, whose interests were all vested in their country's paganism, and therefore opposed the newcomers with every weapon and subterfuge they could devise. While Columba had still to depend on the services of an interpreter, his dynamic personality was leashed and his eloquence thwarted, but he was soon able to make himself understood in the dialect which was not, actually, so very different from his own. For his friends, too, there were other points of contact. Comgall became the centre of a group of potential converts whenever he picked up a stick of charcoal and began to draw recognisable likenesses of his enraptured audience on any boulder or flat stone. Kenneth's skill with salves and bandages gained converts before he had begun to speak of religion, and a group of hopeful people tended to follow Columba wherever he went in delighted expectation of further miracles, even before he could speak their dialect sufficiently to explain what he was doing in their country at all.

The warriors were respectful, and the governor friendly in a rather conspiratorial way, Columba liked him, and as his knowledge of the Pictish Gaelic improved, they would often sit together in the sunny courtyard, talking of old campaigns and the long-dead heroes they each revered. He reminded Columba of Tombul, though the grizzled old Pictish commander was more astute than his dead friend had ever been. But they had the same way of assessing a newcomer, measuring him up by certain standards, and if he showed up well enough, accepting him without further ado. To Columba, inherently a diplomat, obliged by the increasing responsibilities of his great position to deal with every sort of elaborate and self-interested deception, the contrasting directness of the old soldier's attitude made an increasingly strong appeal. He also recognised that permanent conversion of the soldiers was essential. At present they supported him enthusiastically in his task of discrediting the Druids, but Columba knew that he must achieve a profounder modification of their ideals if there was not to be a reaction towards the old tribal ferocity once his personal influence had been withdrawn.

So he spent a good deal of time with the governor of the capital's fortress, as much from genuine interest as from diplomatic reasons. At first, however, he found his purpose frustrated by that old campaigner's frank and friendly cynicism.

"Of course I welcome the Christian religion. Anything would be better than the domination of the Druids," the governor said. "Not that it makes all that difference, as far as I can see, what a man believes. Let him have what gods take his fancy, provided they make him a better soldier and a braver man. The Druids did people no good. They made them jumpy, if you know what I mean. Your people seem more wholesome. You don't take so much on yourselves. It's more homely. I couldn't sit here on a bench with one of those Druids, not just talking, you know, like this. I'd soon begin wondering what he was after, whether he'd any spells up his sleeve, if I was feeling quite as well as I did. I don't care for sorcery."

"We are not sorcerers," said Columba, stooping to pat the dog which had come to sit beside him on the sun-warmed sand. "Broichan uses magic to terrify : we accept miracles as proof of the existence of the greater laws of God."

"Miracles, yes, well, we don't set too much store by them either, do we ? " grinned the governor. "Those gates, now. It looked very well, didn't it, to see them fly open ? I thought that little bit of mystification answered your purpose nicely. Gave you a chance of taking the place by storm, didn't it ? But don't let's talk of miracles." He winked. "Not just between ourselves."

"My friend," said Columba smiling, "no miracle breaks

God's laws. It merely fulfils them in a way which may not be evident to man. If God used your ingenuity to help to gain admission for his priests at a time when admission seemed impossible, then I would say the miracle was that your consenting spirit should offer the ground for such intervention, so that in their amazement, the people received it as a token of God's will. Why should I ask for more?"

"Hum," said the governor, stroking his long chin. "I must say that way of looking at it had not occurred to me. Then—you really believe what you tell the people about God, and the love for man which brought his son down from heaven?"

"If I did not," said Columba, smoothing the dog's silky ear as it laid a long snout on his knee, "why should I be here?"

"I don't know," said the governor. "You don't look like a fool, and I can't see what you get anything out of it. You accept no power, you own no lands, you don't even eat enough to keep that dog on its feet. What in this world——"

"Nothing in this world," said Columba. "And only the vision of another, a kingdom still to come, could make reasonable men cease to give priority to the things of the world here and now. Is that not so?"

"Yes," said the governor. "But still, all this——" he waved his arms to indicate the courtyard and the wide-flung gates and circling hills "——seems to be substance, doesn't it, while yours at best is shadow? Why not then enjoy what this world offers, at least meanwhile?"

"As to which is substance, and which is shadow, there may be more than one opinion," said Columba placidly. "But tell me, would you allow your men to swill themselves blind drunk on the eve of a mortal encounter? Would you let them eat like beasts and sleep without watching?"

"I would not."

"But why?"

"Why? Because they would be fit for nothing when the crisis came in the morning."

Columba nodded. "Exactly. And for the same reason we deny ourselves our fill of the good things of earth lest after we had stuffed ourselves with them death might find us too gross for the world to come. Bread is good, but it is written that man shall not live by bread alone."

The governor looked at him closely. "Yes, it is strange. Undoubtedly you believe what you say."

"I would be proud," said Columba, "to be offered the chance of dying to prove that, my friend."

The old soldier did not speak again for some time. His blue eyes, under the heavy brows, seemed to be surveying the flight of an eagle which soared high above the nearest peak into the illimitable vault of cloudless sky. " Perhaps . . ." he said, in a reluctant, almost shamefaced voice, " I shall ask you to speak to me further of these things one day. I cannot brush aside a conviction that so possesses a man, any more than I can despise a cause which makes a hero less careful of his life than of his sword. Meanwhile . . ." He rose, nodded, and tramped away. Columba, looking after him, smiled. He was well pleased. But he was in no hurry. The truth made all men free. If he could succeed in freeing these people from the terrors of paganism his time would have been well spent, however prolonged the struggle might be. So he thought, schooling himself to further patience as he played with the dog's limp ears, glad of the brief respite from the duels of wit and skill which constantly beset the Christian priests. If Columba intended to sail across the firth, Broichan would undertake to raise a storm or make the wind contrary, so that Columba had to use all his seamanship to tack against the gales which often rose at that time of year, whether caused by magical intervention or not. If Broichan declared that the water of a certain spring had diabolic properties so that it was liable to unsettle the wits of all who drank it, Columba would bless the well and drink the water, promising that it would now possess healing qualities in all time to come.

Columba never invited these encounters, but he knew that to refuse them would be to lose the faith of the people. So he endured them, taking every opportunity to demonstrate the Christian creed in action rather then to preach its theory. He knew that the new faith was steadily gaining ground. But progress was slow and patience one of Columba's most hardly won virtues. He would have liked to accomplish his purpose so fast that he would be able to return to Iona in a few months, but it was now evident that if the new faith were to be firmly established before his departure he must be prepared to remain in Pictish territory for several years. The work was essential, and he meant to complete it if it took the rest of his life, but he was thinking rather wistfully of the peace and seclusion of Iona as he sat twisting the dog's silky ears in the sunny courtyard. Then a shadow fell across the sand, and looking up he saw the young man Urdan before him, obviously anxious to speak. Columba's grey eyes smiled up at him.

" Proceed then, Urdan," he said.

But the young man's face remained troubled as he knelt at

Columba's feet. Now the moment had come he was silent, scrabbling in the soft sand and patting the dog's head, which still lay blissfully across Columba's knee.

"Strange," Columba helped him, "to realise that you are a man now, Urdan. It seems only yesterday that we found you on the shore. We shall have to be thinking of your future. Is it of that future you want to talk about now?"

"Yes, Father," said Urdan. "I—I—would you think it a mortal sin if I no longer felt able to join the community as I once promised to do?"

"Scarcely, my son." Columba's attentive gravity was very kind.

"You see, I had meant to dedicate my life to the priesthood," Urdan said ruefully, "in gratitude for the miracle that gave me back my speech. It seemed the finest life in the world. I asked nothing better than to serve the community all my days——"

"And what," asked Columba thoughtfully, "has now made you change your mind?"

"Something that—that has happened to me since we came here," said Urdan uncomfortably. "I—I don't know what you'll think."

Columba's lips twitched, but his voice remained steady as he looked at Urdan with laughter and love in his eyes. "Child," he said, "the love of a man for a woman may be the most beautiful thing in the world, and born by providence of God."

"How—how did you know?" gasped Urdan.

"Never mind," said Columba, "but tell me about her, now. When can you marry her?"

"That's just the whole trouble," said Urdan, eloquent now. "You see, Father, she's a slave."

"Christians can have no slaves," said Columba. "She must at once be set free."

"But she's Broichan's slave, Father, and he isn't a Christian," said Urdan urgently. "He has enslaved her, too, without right. Her people were free-born, but she was orphaned, as I was, in a raid. So Broichan took her for a kitchen slave. But she's been baptised. It was at one of our services I met her. Her name is Lorne and she loves me, but we don't know what to do. Broichan won't set her free."

Columba laid a reassuring hand on Urdan's shoulder. "Leave that," he said, "to me."

He was glad to have the opportunity of facing Broichan on a straightforward issue. Here was something about which there could be no equivocation. The girl was free-born and a Christian. Broichan had made her a slave. If he set the girl free, at his request, well and good. If he refused, Columba was inclined to think, so much the better. It was time matters came to a head.

As Columba set off for Broichan's house, a quiet, disciplined anger burned within him, an emotion very different from the ungoverned rages which had once dominated him. He was now in complete possession of himself and knew just what he must do. Sweeping aside the Druid priests who were in attendance in the ante-chamber of the largest wooden building in the cluster set apart for the Druids, he marched into the inner room where Broichan sat before a table covered with scrolls and documents. The Arch-Druid scarcely raised his head at Columba's entrance. Waving away the unwelcome interruption, he continued to murmur and to reckon from the scroll in his hand.

" I am told," said Columba, " that you have among your slaves a free-born Christian girl, whose name is Lorne. Is that a fact, Arch-Druid ? "

" If it is, what of it ? " said Broichan indifferently.

" You know the law as well as I do. She is free-born, though a stranger. Further, she is a Christian, baptised by me."

" She is an excellent cook. That is all I care about," said Broichan, his quill spattering across the parchment before him. " I intend to retain her in my household. If I forbid her to leave it she will obey me. Out of respect, my friend."

" Out of mortal fear——"

Broichan reached out for a long rod with which he began carefully to join certain points on his diagram with faultlessly neat lines.

" Fear or respect, it is all one to me. She remains my slave," he said.

" I demand," said Columba, " that you set her free."

" Indeed ? " said Broichan. He appeared uninterested. Enough prestige had been lost when he allowed his rage to bring him into open conflict with the Christians. He did not intend to allow Columba to make him angry again. He was, he fancied, in a sufficiently strong position to hold his ground and let Columba attack in vain. The girl was shut up in the slaves' quarters, prostrate with weeping. It had been easy to break down the first brave defiance of her conversion. Oh, yes, very easy indeed. Just a few tricks that were known to any apprentice in the art of magic.

" To save you further trouble," he said coldly, " let me tell

you now, and finally, that I refuse to set free either this girl or
any of my household whom you may later seek to wheedle from
their duties. Now perhaps you will leave me. I have work to
do."

Columba had so far done his utmost to avoid anything which
might be considered competitive magic, allowing the sorceries
of the Druids to break against the wholesome scepticism of his
followers. The Christian belief in a supernatural order of
reality was too soundly based on their acceptance of the natural
order which underlay it on earth for them to be impressed
by any jugglery by which natural laws might appear to be
capriciously displaced.

To Columba the spiritual universe was the essential reality,
within which the lesser reality of the natural world was cherished
and by which it was sustained. Even now, as he summoned to
his aid all the celestial powers in whose existence he believed as
firmly as in his own, it was not in order that Broichan might be
struck down by magic, but in order that the superstitious fear of
magic which he had so often used against other people might be
turned against himself with consequences which might well seem
magical, though the weapon used would merely be the terror in
the victim's magic-obsessed soul.

Drawing himself to his full height, Columba let his deep voice
roll out, beating down on Broichan, clearly audible in the ante-
room beyond. " Then, by the great God I worship, I curse and
condemn you, most presumptuous man. For the sake of this
creature you have tormented and enslaved, you shall be yourself
ten-fold tormented and enslaved by mortal fear. You shall be
brought into imminent danger of death, yes, to the point of death
itself, confronting the most awful enemy in your own person, in
sudden and deadly sickness, sweating and misery, in cramps and
vomiting, in racked limbs and dimmed eyes, in pains intolerable
of head and heart and bowels, in breath drawn in agony as if
pierced with swords, in darkness and unutterable torment of the
spirit until you set this prisoner free."

Broichan, assaulted by the full blast of Columba's suggestive
tirade, struggled desperately to withstand its force. His face
remained expressionless, but the knuckles of his talon-like
hands were white as he gripped the table's edge. At last, when
Columba paused for breath, he was able to force his face into
a sneer, croaking defiance in spite of the unpleasant dry-
ness in his mouth, and the heaviness which made it hard to speak
at all.

" Well cursed, Columba, upon my word," he said. " But I

fear you've wasted your breath, my friend. I will not set the girl free. Now, will you go ? "

"I will," said Columba. "But soon you will send for me."

Broichan's laugh was as discordant as the cry of a jay in the summer woods. Columba, with the strange transport of his recent malediction still upon him, turned and walked out through the silent groups of Druids who stared from the corners of the ante-room. As his tall figure disappeared Broichan furtively wiped the sweat from his face and neck, shook his narrow head as if to dislodge unwelcome thoughts, then turned to his scrolls again.

Columba went to the conference chamber in the fortress where he was due to be received by the king and his chief advisers who had met to discuss the possibility of improving the relations between the Picts and the Scots, the two tribes of northern Alba which had now accepted Christianity, and between whom, therefore, further conflict was undesirable. It had been a prolonged and controversial conference, for the question was a difficult one. The military leaders admittedly preferred theoretical Christianity to Druidical magic, but they were still reluctant to accept its implications and abandon the old and convincing methods of settling any difficulties by the sword. As Columba had guessed, all his persuasive gifts were going to be required to convince them that the benefits of a peaceful trading agreement with the neighbour kingdom of Erin would outweigh the advantages of the pillage and violence on which they habitually relied. The matter was still in the balance when an unexpected diversion occurred. An agitated officer asked permission to admit an envoy from Broichan on immediate business with Columba, and when this had been given a terrified young Druid ran across the council chamber to collapse at Columba's feet.

"Master of magic," he cried, "undo your spell ! Broichan has been taken with mortal sickness, and even now, vomiting and convulsed with cramps, he is ready to die."

Columba looked grimly at the young man who knelt before him. "And will he set the Christian girl free ? "

"She—she—she has been set free already," the young man babbled. "We could not get her out of the house quickly enough. She is waiting outside now, as I speak."

"Bring her in," said Columba. The instinct for drama which he had inherited from every ancestor in his dynamically artistic race, as well as the diplomatic genius which was all his own, made him take delight in this new development of the Broichan incident, recognising it as one which might be used to further his dynastic ends. But his own natural unstudied compassion was responsible for the gentleness with which he received the bewildered girl.

" Well, my child, so they have let you go. Have they hurt you at all ? "

Mutely, she shook her head. She scarcely dared look up at him, or at the nobles who stood around.

" By all the gods," protested the young Druid, " except for a few stripes such as any disobedient girl might receive from her own parents, she is entirely unharmed."

" That is well," said Columba sternly. Then raising his voice he asked : " Is Urdan here ? "

" Yes, indeed, Father." The young man hurried in.

" Give me your hand. And give me yours too, my child," he added, turning to the girl. " Lorne, you are free now to choose your way of life. Is this man your choice ? "

She raised her head now and smiled, not shyly, nor at Columba, but deep into Urdan's eyes. " Yes, Father, he is."

" Urdan," said Columba. " I entrust her to you, now and for ever. Take, I command you, good care of your bride."

" Master of magic," implored the young Druid as Urdan led Lorne away, " I implore you now to undo the spell you worked against him, or Broichan, the Arch-Druid, will die."

Columba smiled as he looked for some material object by means of which he might present a counter-suggestion to a magic-ridden mind. Stooping down, he dislodged an ordinary amber bead which had been trodden at some time into the earthen floor. Prising it out with a thumb-nail and tossed it to the young Druid. " Let this pebble be dropped into a vessel of water," he said. " It will float. Give the vessel with the pebble floating in it to Broichan and let him sip from it until he revives. That is all." With a gesture of dismissal he turned back to the appalled circle of councillors. " Well then, my lords, shall we consider again this question of better relationship with my kinsfolk, the Scots ? "

Considerably shaken, the council resumed its deliberations. The question of the projected alliance had taken on a new urgency, for after Broichan's extremely public defeat there seemed no further doubt that the Christian God could on occasion, endow his servants with supernatural power. Admittedly, there might be some who would maintain that Broichan's indisposition had been no more than a violent attack of colic brought on by unwise eating, while others would hint that the girl he had pressed into his service had co-operated with Columba by slipping something poisonous into the Arch-Druid's next meal. But few of the councillors believed these sceptics. The shock of Broichan's surrender was enough finally to discredit the Druids as magicians, and to create, even in the cynical nobility, a healthy respect for the new faith. Among the soldiers, perhaps an even greater impetus to its adoption was presently given by the action of the governor, who soon afterwards asked to be baptised.

Columba's task, in essentials, had now been accomplished, but it was not until the new faith had been given long enough to establish itself in the daily life of the people, and his first converts trained for the priesthood so that they could be trusted to carry out the work he had begun that he considered himself free to return to Iona by way of the western capital of Scottish Dalriada, from which Kenneth and Comgall would set out for Erin.

Gondal, who had seen enough of the land of his birth to be only anxious to leave it, returned with them ; Dermot, taciturn and devoted, did not care where he went, provided he could serve Columba ; Urdan and his wife were to make a home on Iona, near the monastery. These two were exuberant with delight, sometimes racing ahead and sometimes dawdling far behind the rest of the party. The world might have been as empty as Eden as far as they were concerned : they wandered through the wilderness singing, amazed by all sorts of unsuspected beauty, laughing at shared secrets, hand in hand.

And Columba, striding along the path that led westward, took pleasure in the sheer rhythm of the swing pace that swallowed up the miles, in the gleams of sunshine, the drenching autumn showers, the sharply scented wind. He too was aware of their happiness and blessed them for it. Then, suddenly, all was changed. He came on them, one morning, standing by the western coast they had just reached like two scared children, tremulous with dismay. Urdan's hand was at his throat, he was making strange, uncouth noises, and his eyes were appalled.

" Father Columba . . . Father Columba . . . he can't speak ! " Lorne cried.

But Columba nodded understandingly as he looked at Urdan. " So it was here ? " he said. " Here that they burned your home and murdered your parents . . . ? "

Urdan nodded, his finger sketching the outline of the remembered bay, his whole body shaking convulsively as he pointed at an almost obliterated mound.

Columba put his arm round the rigid shoulders. " My son," he said. " See, the past has buried its dead. Where your home

stood are now sea-pinks and willow-herbs. There is no more pain
here for the dead. They have entered into the peace of those our
Lord loves. But your wife is frightened. Remember, it is your
privilege and your joy to care for her now."

"Yes, Father," Urdan said. And his voice rang clear as a
bronze-tongued bell, as Columba made the sign of the cross over
the blown sand.

"Let us go on in peace," Columba said.

By the end of the next day they had reached the capital of
Scottish Dalriada, where both Columba and his news of the
Pictish conversion were most joyfully received. But he himself
saw the work he had already accomplished, great as it was, only
as part of an immensely greater whole. His dynastic imagination
was already reaching far ahead towards the union of the peoples
of Alba into one nation, ruled by one king, worshipping one God.
Towards this ideal, the first step had now been taken as the
northern Picts, emerging from paganism, prepared to accept the
presence of the Christian Scots. Next came the alliance with the
southern Picts beyond the Grampians, who had been, like the
Britons of the south-west, already instructed by the great Ninian
of Candida Casa. Once the Britons had been included, only the
pagan Angles of the south-east would remain in darkness, alienated
from the rest of the young country. And in due course, if it
pleased heaven, Iona would provide for them also another kindling
brand.

So, while he spoke of peace to the King of Dalriada,
Columba saw in imagination the promise of the future break
like a dawn over the shadowed land. As he listened to
the tremulous gratitude of his ageing cousin Conall, his mind
was already reaching forward towards that other hour in which
Conall should die, and his sorrowful courtiers come to Iona,
asking him as its Abbot to consecrate their chosen successor to
the throne of Scottish Dalriada, a successor from whose line,
centuries later, the first king of a united Scotland would be born.
But the face of that successor he could not yet see.

The question of the Dalriadic succession did not arise for
nearly ten years. Busy years they were during which Columba
travelled continually among the western islands, often to the
mainland of Alba, several times to the Pictish country, once to
visit the great saint, Mungo, on the river which was afterwards
called Clyde. Wherever he went, legends gathered like a nimbus
about him, and centres of Christianity sprang up, as much from
a sort of contagion of goodness, as from his most careful
instruction. Wherever he went, enthusiastically reverent crowds

greeted him, and even though much of the enthusiasm afterwards subsided as fast as a blaze in the gorse, there were always some in whom the new ideas burned with a steadier flame, who banded themselves into communities and built churches all over the west country in the name of Colum-Cille.

The recurrent dream that had haunted the years of his exile still came to him, but now most of the faces of the men from Culdremne were no longer shadowed, for the light of the rising sun was on them, and as they went, they smiled. Soon, soon, it would be time for him to return to Erin, Columba knew, but the summons had not yet come. He must wait, wait a little longer, be patient yet again, while the monastery at Iona came all the pilgrims from the mainland and the western isles, following the track he had himself taken on the first of his many missionary journeys, the track which had now indeed become the Pilgrims' Way. The guest-house at Iona was seldom empty, and in his bare little cell Columba received a constant stream of troubled men and women, who came to him in search of guidance, hope and consolation, bowed or broken by the burdens of the world. Their importunities often kept him from study, transcription or prayer. But whatever the cost might be to himself, no creature in need was ever refused. Then, one day, inevitably when least expected, the crisis he had foreseen ten years before in Dalriada, broke through the peaceful sequence of the daily routine.

Columba had been spending a few days in retreat from the monastery on a small rocky island where his meditations would not be interrupted by the usual demands. There he had been visited for three nights in succession by a dream in which an angel showed him a shining book in which was written the name of the next king of Scottish Dalriada after his cousin Conall's death. Columba was surprised, for the name was not that of the young man he himself would have chosen. Nor did he seem likely to be the people's choice. But the dream came again, and yet again. And when Columba returned to Iona the deputation from Dalriada was waiting to tell him of Conall's death.

" We have also come," said the spokesman, " to ask you to give your blessing to our newly chosen king."

" We will go to the church," Columba said. He rang the bell which was the signal for the monks to assemble in emergency, and led the way to the larger and more beautiful building which had now replaced the humble original. As he stood before the altar, hands outstretched in supplication, the scabbards of many swords clanked on the flagstones as the nobles of

Dalriada knelt among the still breathless monks in preliminary prayer.

"And now," said Columba, "where is your future king?"

"Here, Father Columba," said Conall's chief counsellor, leading forward a tall, swarthy boy. "We have chosen Eogan from among King Conall's kinsmen, and now ask you to consecrate him according to the law."

But Columba looked sadly at Eogan. His name had not been written in the angel's book. He himself had always been fond of the lad. Eogan would, he admitted, have been his own choice, but for the thrice-repeated dream. And as he looked at Eogan, he now realised that such a choice would have been disastrous. The boy's bearing as he waited for the ceremony to begin revealed to Columba more than Eogan knew.

"Will you not now give him your blessing, Father Columba?" asked the chief counsellor, puzzled by the delay.

"I cannot," said Columba unexpectedly. "Eogan is not the man heaven has chosen to be your future king."

A movement of consternation swept over the assembly. The nobles turned to look at each other, protesting, murmuring. Below his dark brows Eogan shot at Columba a sudden, malignant glare.

"But—Father Columba——" protested the chief counsellor. "Eogan is the choice of the entire nobility——"

"He would have to reign," said Columba, "over the common people. How well would he care for them?"

"Surely he could care for us all, Columba."

"If he is to be your king, it must be without the blessing of God, in search of which you have come to Iona," Columba said.

They began to murmur in protest, the murmurs became a sullen, grumbling roar, in which first one voice, then another, could be distinctly heard.

"Eogan is our king . . . We will have no other . . . do not listen to him . . . We will have Eogan . . . Eogan . . . why should our choice be overruled . . . we will have Eogan . . . Eogan . . ."

Hands were actually laid to sword-hilts. The monks, making the sign of the cross, huddled together, whey-faced with fear. Would these men venture to threaten their Abbot, the holy father, Columba? Then Columba's voice, raised in thunder, easily dominated the uproar.

"People of Dalriada," he said impressively, "listen to me. I have been visited three nights in succession by a dream in which an angel showed me the name of the man who should next reign over Dalriada. When the dream came the third time I returned to Iona and found you already here. The man you ask me to bless is not the man God has chosen. If you choose him, it must be without a blessing. If you value the blessing, you must permit me to choose another man. What is your will, counsellors of Dalriada? Take time to consider. For your country this is a moment of fate. I will await your answer, and meanwhile the community of Iona will pray that heaven will guide you all."

In the quiet church the monks obediently knelt ; shabby, unworldly men, in their working habits of undyed wool, some with sleeves still rolled high, others in aprons. As a hush fell on the church, the counsellors of Dalriada began to whisper together, while the young man, Eogan, stood sulkily apart, scowling and pricking patterns in the dust that had filtered between the flag-stones with the point of his sword. At last the chief counsellor approached Columba. Deferential again, he knelt.

" Father Columba, we cannot forget all that you, under God, have done for us. Without the peace that your intervention secured we should still be persecuted by our neighbours. We do not believe it right for us to choose a king you cannot bless. Choose therefore for us, Father Columba, so that on our king may rest the blessing of God."

Columba looked over the kneeling man's head at the assembled company. " Does your leader speak for you all ? " he demanded.

Back came the answer, deep-throated. " He speaks for us all."

" Then," said Columba, " I will do as I have been bidden."

Stepping down into the crowd of nobles and courtiers he moved slowly among them, his eyes lowered, his hands outstretched before him in the groping gesture of a man unwilling to trust his eyes alone. Step by step they fell back before him, silent now, so that in the stillness of the church the scream of the gulls on the rocks below beat frenziedly about them, and even the whisper and thud of the waves on the white sands seemed loud. At last Columba paused in front of a slight, plainly dressed young man.

" Give me your hand, Aidan," he said. " For heaven has chosen you to succeed your kinsman as King of Dalriada. Come with me, my son."

The young man's thin face flushed darkly, then the colour faded again till it was ashen, but he held his head high as he followed Columba, to stand with him before the altar, facing the motionless crowd as the Abbot of Iona began the ritual inaugura-tion of the newly-chosen king, a ceremonial which was, in parts, older than Christianity, with roots that drove deep into Erin's legendary past.

At last the solemn, prolonged ceremony was over, and Columba gave his blessing to the new king and the representatives of Dalriada. Aidan was stripped of his royal robes and stood once more in his plain, dark tunic, while the officer in charge of the proceedings complacently folded up the gorgeous garments which were worn at the inauguration ceremony only, and afterwards became the property of himself and his heirs.

" Now, go, my children," said Columba. " I wish to speak to your king alone."

Slowly they filed out through the narrow doorway, scuffling a little as various nobles asserted their right to precede others, elbowing their way through the crowd, eyes threatening, heads high, hands moving easily towards the hilt of dagger or sword. At last the church was empty. Columba turned to the young man who stood there, his thin shoulders bowed a little as if the burden of the royal robes still weighed him down. Smiling, the Abbot of Iona held out his strong hands.

" Courage, my son," he said. " God has given you a great destiny."

" It is because it is so great, Father," said Aidan humbly, " that I am afraid."

" You need fear nothing," Columba reassured him, " for no adversary will be able to resist you and the people of Dalriada, unless you and your people break faith with me and mine. Warn them therefore, Aidan, your people and afterwards the sons that shall be born to you, and their sons who will follow them in their turn. For Dalriada shall prosper, as long as its people remember, in their new-found freedom, all they owe to their kinsmen, the people of Erin, and honour the oath which has been taken here."

" I shall never forget these things," Aidan said.

" Then the future of your kingdom is assured," said Columba. " Now go, Aidan, leave the monastery where you hoped to spend your days in peace for the troubled destiny that has led you instead up the steps of your country's throne. And may the blessing of heaven, the peace of this holy island, and the hope of the fairer world to come be with you, newly consecrated king."

" We—we shall meet again, Father Columba ? " Aidan's voice faltered, and he moved unwillingly towards the open door through which could be glimpsed the newly-painted, flower-wreathed boats, the brightly dressed oarsmen, the excited crowds

of his people who had followed his retinue from the mainland.
" We shall certainly meet again," Columba said.

For as the young man had knelt to receive his blessing the
mists had lifted again from the mountain-peaks of the future,
and he had seen that the time of his return to Erin was now
very near. He had also seen that when he returned, it would be
in such triumph as must unsettle the wits of all but the most
truly humble, for he was to be received with the homage given
only to a few earthly conquerors, as he came home to Erin, leading
Aidan, King of Dalriada, by the hand.

CHAPTER XVI

IN THE CELL on Iona which had become the focus-point of so many activities, both sacred and secular, Columba awaited the summons to set out with the new King of Dalriada for the synod or assembly of the greatest men in Erin, which was to be held during the coming year at Drumceatt. It was a meeting-place which had been familiar from his first years of gospelling, quite near his much loved Derry, poised on the knoll above the river from which it looked out on meadowland so beautiful that the very angels themselves must linger there.

But Columba's offer to bring Aidan to Drumceatt was not merely prompted by his desire to see Derry again. He was diplomat as well as priest, and the passion of his life had become the union of the warring tribes of Alba, that farouche land of his adoption, into the Christian nation of his vision. Much, he knew, had already been accomplished. The Northern Picts, under King Brude, had not relapsed into paganism, and though their Christianity was still at times superficial, he had been very hopeful when he had last returned from the fortress which had once been so ineffectively barred against him. But more, much more remained to be done, and it was at the synod of Drumceatt that Columba hoped to see the next step taken. For the young kingdom of the Scots was not yet independent. Yearly tribute was exacted by the High King of Erin, nominally in return for his defence of the people of Dalriada against the enemies they themselves might be unable to repel. But in practice, Scottish Dalriada had long been left to defend herself, and the tribute exacted in terms of ships and war service by her overlord in Erin merely prevented her from becoming part of the new and independent nation which Columba wished to see.

Accordingly, he had arranged to present Aidan at the next synod, demanding freedom for his kingdom on the grounds that it had now outgrown the need for assistance and would indeed do better on its own. It was an occasion which called for all his diplomatic gifts if he were to succeed in convincing the leaders of Erin that such a concession was to their advantage also, and, in order to give weight to his appeal, Columba had agreed to be escorted with the ceremony appropriate to a great spiritual lord. But the pomp and formality of such occasions always irked Columba's candid soul.

" Alas, Kenneth," he said ruefully, tired of approving lengthy lists of those to walk before him and those to walk behind him, and those to bear the canopy above his head, " alas for the old days when you and Comgall and I kilted our habits and strode across the mountains, barefoot. That was the better way. I am fretted to death with this talk of canopies and pole-bearers and banners and fringes and robes. Scarcely a day passes without a deputation arriving from Dalriada on some ridiculous business of precedence or vestments or ritual. Who shall go first, the bearer of the king's sceptre or the man who carries my pastoral staff? As if I cared! Am I never to be left alone for an instant? I have been six days on the transcription of this single chapter and the work is not done yet."

" It is the company of heaven that they honour, Columba, in your person," said Kenneth peaceably. " Yet I sympathise. How long is it before you set out? "

" The messenger is expected at any hour. Yet every day holds but the same hubbub of deacons and students, bishops and priests, assembled here till there seems scarcely room to set foot on the island without casting one of them into the sea."

" And what of the new king? Is he shaping well? "

" Very well," Columba admitted. " He is working all day with his counsellors, organising the country's affairs as if no journey were to come. The angel of the Lord was indeed wiser than I. They say that Eogan, the cousin we all fancied, thinks of nothing now but riding the life out of his horses and beating his hunting dogs. Disappointment has soured him as it often sours unworthy men. Well, heaven alone saved the country from his kingship. I was as taken with him as all the rest. Ah, but how I weary for us to be gone! "

" Still the same Columba," teased Kenneth, as he had done on the first journey across Alba, years before.

" It is good to hear you laugh at me, old friend," said Columba wryly. " I grow afraid when too many praise me instead. Only my old friends here on earth recognise me as the sorry creature I am known to be in heaven. Yes, I do lack patience, Kenneth. I pray for it with tears, night and day, yet something still burns within me when I watch the bungling of fools. Heaven grant me more humility. But look—is that a sail on the far horizon now? "

The messenger came at last, bearing not only the summons to the synod, but the news of Phelim's death to sadden Columba with many memories and make him grieve for his mother's loneliness. He sent Eithne an immediate messenger, promising to visit her as soon as his work was done. Then, at last, they set out. The king's retinue was exactly equalled by Columba's escort, which consisted of twenty bishops, fifty priests, fifty deacons and fifty students, in their episcopal robes or white habits of ceremony ; with croziers, psalters or staves in their hands. The fleet which left Iona seemed to cover the face of the sea with a patch-work of bleached or tawny sails, which leant on the favourable wind as they scudded towards the west. Kenneth, who was sailing with them, heard Columba's voice raised in thanksgiving so heart-felt that he wept. For the joy of Columba's homecoming revealed what the anguish of his exile must have been.

But to Columba it seemed at last so natural to sweep past the wooded meadows of Lough Foyle that he could scarcely believe this return to be different from all the other times he had returned in his homesick dreams. Twelve years ago he had rowed sadly down the same estuary, taking only a dozen men. Now he was returning with nearly two hundred ; a king and all his retinue. Ahead of them, as they rounded the last bend, piercing-white against the young green of early summer woods, flew like an omen a string of three wild swans. Already the crowds had gathered by the familiar landing-stage to welcome him, who had left as an exile, and now returned like a conqueror. Seated at the tiller of the leading boat, Columba shaded his eyes with his hand. He had sung in triumph as they left Iona. Now he could scarcely speak. As the sail ran down, and the boat jolted gently against the timbers of the landing-stage, he still sat there, grasping the tiller, as if the solid wood's reality were the only thing, in that instant of overwhelming emotion, in which he dared believe.

His anxious attendant, Dermot, made his way between the rowers' benches to his side. " Father Columba, they are all waiting. Are you not well ? "

He rose then, and stepped ashore, moving shakily, his face blank with sheer awe as he stood on the landing-stage, looking about him, a huge man in his middle fifties, with a face so deeply tanned that the large grey eyes seemed larger than ever and bright as a lad's, though the closely curling hair beyond the frontal tonsure already showed many strands of grey. A hush fell on the murmuring crowd, while Aidan and his retinue waited, forgotten, off-shore. Then, in the distance, a child's excited voice rose high. " Mother, mother, look ! There stands the blessed Columba, with a shining angel on either side . . ."

Columba raised his hands, half in benediction, half in appeal. " My people . . . my country . . ." he said incoherently. Like a suddenly subsiding wave the great company knelt to receive his blessing.

"Heaven bless you too, Columba," cried an old woman, "you that come bringing the holy angels of God to Erin again."

Columba smiled down at them, at the gentle countryside, where the great oaks stood like symbols of eternity in the green pastures of the psalmist's vision, and the hawthorn trees, creamy with blossom, seemed poised like the angels who found Derry a second heaven. As he turned to give his hand to King Aidan and beckon his retinue ashore, Columba knew that throughout the hubbub of business and diplomatic preoccupations which would fill most of his time at Drumceatt, the memory of his homecoming would shine among the leaden clouds of controversy like a morning star. Meanwhile, the procession of his assiduous followers formed behind him, the bishops complaining of the damage done to their ceremonial robes by sun and sea water, the bearers of the canopy hurrying the children aside, the priests, deacons and students pushing into their places, and the king's retinue shouting for their attendants to bring cloaks, banners or weapons from the boats. But Columba, remote from it all, stood smiling to himself, content. In his mind's eye was printed the memory of green pastures that sloped down to still waters, a burnished surface mirroring the beauty of three flying swans.

Slowly the ponderous machinery of the national assembly moved into action. Processions like their own wound their way towards Drumceatt, where another High King, elected since the day of Columba's censure, was soon to receive the representatives of Church and State. Like that of all the other men of importance, Columba's encampment was beseiged by suppliants who wished to have their causes put forward by any noble or churchman with a good chance of being heard. Columba's tremendous reputation as priest, miracle-worker, and diplomat made so many people wish to enlist his help that his attendants spent most of their time turning away suppliants who insisted, sometimes with violence, that if they could but speak with the blessed Columba for an instant, he would recognise their cause as one which he could not deny. In vain they protested that Columba had come to Erin for only one purpose, that of placing Scottish Dalriada's claim for independence before the High King. The petitioners would not listen ; from morning till night, sometimes even all night through, a crowd of querulous people surged round the group of huts which housed the party from Iona. Columba, always ready to preach, to heal, to comfort all those in trouble,

had no wish to be involved in mere legal controversies. He was
a priest, not a man of law : if they wanted justice they must go
elsewhere. Only on one occasion did he relax his rule, and that
was when Kenneth unexpectedly interrupted his meditations by
arriving in Columba's hut early one morning with two men at
his heels. One was shaggy and unkempt as an ancient peasant,
the other elegant but distraught. His hand was shaking so
that a continual tremor of sound came from the little bells on the
golden branch he held.

"These men," said Kenneth apologetically, " are both ollave
poets, Columba, and it seems they knew you well as a child.
They are in great trouble, so I thought you would see them,"
he added rather apprehensively. Kenneth was too soft-hearted
to be an efficient guardian of Columba's privacy, but on this
occasion his leniency had not been misplaced. Columba ignored
the elegant poet with the golden branch but he went towards
the disreputable old vagrant with welcoming arms spread wide.

"Gemman ! My most honoured teacher, how good it is to
see you after all these years. What help can you want ? Is it
possible that you, who are able to summon all the beauty of the
world to your harp-strings, need anything from me ? Shall I not
remain your merest apprentice till I die ? "

" Er—the fact of the matter is—well, of course—we need
nothing for ourselves," twittered Olim from the background. " I
am, as you may remember, a court poet. The question touches
the honour due to our order. This has been most—er—ignobly
threatened. So——"

Gemman brushed aside the interruption with the gesture of
an amiable bear as he clasped Columba's hand and began at once
to state his business as if they were meeting again after a trivial
absence of a few days. " The trouble is," he said, " that people
will no longer stand the airs that certain poets assume. They
object to the number of attendants that the poets take with them
when they tour noble houses, reading poems and exacting
presents. There has been quite a rebellion." He grinned mis-
chievously. " A request is to be made at this very synod to have
the order of poets dissolved. That's what it comes to, my son.
It's a pretty drastic remedy. But the question is, is there another
way of getting rid of the trash without losing the good stuff
too ? " His little, twinkling eyes, almost lost in the tangle of
white hair which fell about his creased, berry-brown face,
swivelled in the direction of the elegant, agitated Olim. Clearly
it amused him to find himself defending the honour of his
profession in such odd company.

"I agree with the rebels," said Columba. "The court poets were living like lice on the body of Erin even while I was a child."

"Our pride was not for ourselves, but for our ancient order," Olim bleated. The little bells in his hand trembled with fear and rage.

"It was into your own coffers that the jewels went," said Columba. "People were afraid of the venom on poets' tongues. Unless they paid all you asked, housed your monstrous retinues, propitiated you with presents, they knew you would publish the foulest satires against which they had no redress. Why should I oppose any one who seeks to put an end to these things?"

"If you do not, we shall starve," whimpered the court poet. "The making of verses is our only skill."

"It is a foul thing as you have used it," said Columba. "You have turned the bright torch of your art into the club of an extortionist who has fattened on other men's fears. Why should I ask for mercy?"

"I . . . I do not know," said Olim miserably.

"I can think of a reason," Gemman said. He had been watching appreciatively while Columba's anger seared the vanity from the complacent courtier. But now, on behalf of the order of poets, he intervened.

"We are all poets here, Colum-Cille," he said slowly. "He and you and I, beside all the rest. Some of us have used our art one way, I grant you, while some have used it in another. But the art remains greater—to my mind—than us all. If the name of poet is to be taken from us it will also be taken from Erin, for the poets have been in the past the keepers of her fairest treasure. The keepers may be ignoble, but the treasure is one we can ill afford to lose."

Columba looked darkly at him. "Do you ask mercy for this—this fop who has despised you as a vagrant, and huckstered his art like a travelling bagman?" he asked.

Gemman grinned. "I do not care about him, one way or another. His contempt is as welcome as his praise. But I care a great deal about the making of poetry."

"And how shall that cause be best served?"

"By your intervention, I think," said Gemman. "That is why I am here."

"You are still my master, Gemman," said Columba. "What do you want me to do?"

"Your name is known to all Erin," said Gemman slowly, "as one who has returned to us mantled with the glory of great achievements, conversions, miracles performed in the name of

Christ. The reverence accorded to you is like that accorded to
the saints of heaven. I ask you to take up the cause of your
country's poets at the synod which is being held here. Deplore
their excesses as you will, demand what reforms you must, but
ask, I beg you, that there shall still be an order of bards in Erin.
When membership offers nothing in the way of earthly splendour,
then those who join our order will join for the art alone. Is that
not so ? "

"Surely," said Columba. "What do you say, Olim ? "

The little bells on the golden branch shivered, and the court
poet's downcast eyes inspected his threadbare sleeve. "I suppose,"
he said disagreeably, "that beggary will be somewhat eased if
obscurity be not added besides."

Gemman chuckled. "That is the best you can hope for,
anyway. And I have never found beggary disagreeable. After
all, is it not the only state of complete freedom ? It will be
interesting to see if this is an idea you can share."

Olim shuddered.

"If you will make such a plea, Colum-Cille," Gemman said,
"that is all we need ask of you. Our order has been dying of a
surfeit. After such drastic purging it may live."

"I will do what you ask," Columba said.

"Then, for the present, I will say good-bye."

Casual, serene as ever, Gemman turned to go, with Olim
trailing wretchedly behind him, dismally conscious that the
interview had not turned out too well.

On the following day the first meeting of the synod was held
in a great pavilion specially built for the occasion by all the
craftsmen for many miles round. They had felled great trees,
comandeered teams of horses, and worked from dawn till dusk
for many months. Now the pavilion, hung with the banners of
the greatest men of Erin, was ranked with benches on which the
representatives of church and state took their appointed places
on either side of the High King's throne, ready to debate all
those urgent questions connected with the future government of
Erin, which would in former years have been brought to ancient,
pagan Tara, from which the glory had departed so that the
national assemblies met elsewhere, according to the wish and
local associations of the presiding king.

It had been at Tara, nearly fifteen years ago, that Columba
had heard judgment given against him, judgment against which
in arrogant fury he had rebelled. Now he was reverentially
placed among his peers, the bishops and nobles of Erin ; and
Aidan, on his introduction, had been given his place among the

kings. Quiet fell on the assembly whenever Columba rose to
speak, though indeed in all the company there were few who
remembered the earlier humiliating scene. Aedh, who was now
High King, had only reigned a couple of years, and most of the
faces of the lesser kings were also strange to Columba. Among
the churchmen, he only knew his own contemporaries, so that
he might well have found an excuse for forgetting his humiliation.
It would have been easy to take the acclamation as his due. But
Columba himself had changed. The years of voluntary exile,
the discipline of hardship and penance, the inexorable schooling
of experience and responsibility, had scarred and seared and
purged his personality into the humility of a man so absorbed in
his work as to be quite unaware of himself, a state so rare in
that arrogant assembly as to command immediate, astonished
respect.

When he rose to put a proposition before the company, men
were impelled to listen, not because of the violence with which
he pleaded, but because of the skill with which he presented his
demands. For Columba no longer attempted to dominate
opposition by the strength of his own will, but set about under-
mining the ground from which that opposition grew. Few of
those present, watching him, knew the cost of the patience he
imposed upon himself, as he dealt with each hostile critic.
But Kenneth, from his place among the other priests, knew the
cost of that forbearance and loved him for it even more than he
admired him for his skill.

Columba's appeals were largely successful. The synod
granted independence to the kingdom of Scottish Dalriada. A
narrow majority also agreed to accept Columba's plea for the
ancient order of bards, though the long and bitter struggle was
considerably exacerbated by King Aehd's natural indignation
at the presumption of the chief court poet, who had recently
demanded to be given the royal wheel brooch in fee for a single
laudatory poem. At Columba's further suggestion, however, the
order was shorn of most of its privileges and the number of each
poet's followers drastically curtailed. The decision was received
with joy by those poets who had been scandalised by their
companions' excesses, and with relief by the noblemen on whom
the poets had battened. But the poets who had, like Olim,
abused their privileges greeted the verdict with fury and
dismay.

Tired, but content, Columba relaxed his attention from the
affairs of the synod. His plea for certain political prisoners had
met with less success, but it was a question which he had only

agreed to press at the last moment out of friendship for one of his father's former comrades. His failure could not compare with his success, and the gratitude of the contingent from Dalriada was even greater than the delight of the reprieved poets. Aidan and his nobles surrounded Columba as he left the hall, imploring him to accept rich presents for which he had no use, as well as the privileges for his community which he was glad to receive. The poets, too, crowded about him, praising, thanking, and promising odes in his honour, at the idea of which he smiled.

He was glad when they left him at last, all the noisy nobles and eloquent poets who had crowded his encampment and insisted on kneeling to kiss his hands, buzzing and circling round him till he wanted to flap them away like a cloud of importunate gnats. He wished to see young King Aidan alone, in order to give him the counsel and encouragement he needed from his confessor. And he wanted to have a few minutes with Gemman, who was still chuckling over Olim's outraged disgust.

Such interviews were a respite from the general hubbub, though the freedom of solitude, which he had in his later years now come so much to value, no longer seemed obtainable. Even when it was time to leave Drumceatt and set out on the tour of inspection of the much loved monasteries he had founded before leaving Erin, his followers insisted on escorting him, with psalm-singing and jubilation, from one monastery to the next. And Columba, meekly tramping the winding tracks in the cloud of dust raised by their eager feet, smiled to himself as he submitted. Were they not all the children of his ministry, and must children not be allowed to show their pride and love ?

He had kept Derry to the last, in order that he might look forward to the special welcome he would receive from the monks of his beloved foundation in the place of oaks. But just as he was thankfully preparing to set out on that final journey, a summons arrived which he felt it impossible to ignore. It was from his mother, asking him to come immediately to Gartan, since Maeve had been taken with a sudden sickness and now lay at what seemed the point of death. " But I believe that you, my son, even now, could save her," Eithne had told the messenger to say. Columba received the news as he came out of the chapel after saying his evening office, with the intention of lying down for a few hours' sleep before setting out for Derry at dawn.

" I will come at once," he said.

He took only Dermot, his personal attendant, arranged for somone to be sent to Derry to explain the delay, and set off to walk through the night across the mountains which lay about the dun in which he had been born. Even after a long day's work he was scarcely aware of physical fatigue, for it was so restful, by contrast with the weeks during which he had been surrounded by acclamation and importunities, by so many shifting, clamorous and emotional crowds, to walk, almost alone, through the quiet obscurity of the summer night. He knew the way so well that he had left the messenger behind to get some rest, and Dermot was content to plod unobtrusively at his heels. For the first time in what seemed an eternity of conspicuous living, he was making a journey on which he was free to accept the consolation of the quiet hills about him, to let their peace and steadfastness bless his parched spirit like dew.

He reached Gartan before sunrise, when the loughs still lay beneath mist-banks out of which the tops of the tallest trees rose like heather besoms up-ended in snow. His way down the hill took him past the ruins of the little oratory, long since deserted, where birds built and strayed sheep sheltered in what remained of the wattle-and-daub huts where he had spent seven of his most formative years. He made the sign of the cross as he passed, murmuring a blessing on the scattered members of that former community, wherever they might be. And the memory of that first hour spent in the chapel, as an awed, uncomprehending child, came over him so strongly that he seemed actually to have become that child again, to feel the very roughness of the mud floor, his own breath warm on the fingertips of his obediently folded hands.

" *Ego sum pastor ille bonus, et agnosco meas, et agnoscor a meis . . .*"

Once again the voices of the children answered the old priest out of the luminous obscurity of the hour before dawn.

" ' I am the good shepherd. I know my sheep and am known of mine . . .' "

Columba would have liked to say his morning office there, among the whispering memories, but while someone lay at the point of death he had not the right to linger by the way. He would say it as he went. His Lord, who understood all things, would surely not take it amiss that on this as on other urgent occasions, he did not say it on his knees.

He reached the dun before many people were stirring. It wanted some little time yet before sunrise, and smoke twined up from only a few cooking fires. Unrecognised by the few people busy round them, Columba made his way to his father's house. Here, every one was awake, and the men had vacated their sleeping-places already, not caring to be within doors at the moment of the strange visitation of death. They stood about, wrapped in their cloaks against the dawn chill, or huddled about the reluctant, smoky fire. At the sight of Columba's tall figure, famous now throughout Erin, they fell back respectfully. Greeting them with a gesture, Columba passed on.

As he entered the timbered hall the past seemed to surge towards him, a past made up of glimpses so conflicting and so clamorous that it tinkled about him like a vessel shattered into fragments too numerous to be identified. Gemman's voice, Maeve's sneer, his mother's anxious eyes, his father's restless hands, old Nalda's arms, Tombul's great laugh . . . the memories rose thick about him as birds from a stubble field. Then the leather curtain at the far end was drawn back and his mother appeared. At the sight of him some of the weariness that burdened her thin shoulders seemed to leave her. " I knew you would not fail me, son," she said.

Gently, Columba kissed her. She felt as frail as thistle-down. " How is she now ? " he asked.

" Fighting with untold terrors," Eithne said. " I cannot comfort her, for all my prayers. But now——"

" Take me to her," Columba said.

Maeve had been propped up against a pile of sheepskins, since that was the only position in which she could get her breath. She was sitting bolt upright, her shoulders high about her ears from the effort of breathing, her hands clenched on the coverlet placed over her. Her thin face, framed in the startling pathos of darkly-dyed hair greying at the roots where the dye had not been renewed, was turned sideways, and her wide eyes stared out at the mist which was shredding now away from the loughside trees. Columba, who had only seen her once since the battle at Culdremne, was overwhelmed with pity at the change in her. She was fighting her own last battle now, in all the desperation of lonely, uncomprehending fear. She did not notice when he took a stool beside her, but when he laid a hand on hers she slowly turned her head.

" Why, it's . . . Colum-Cille," she said faintly. A ghost of her old smile curled her cracked lips. " So you've come to watch me . . . die."

" I have come to bid you godspeed on your journey home," Columba said.

" Home ? I wonder . . ." The old sneer was still in Maeve's voice, though Columba fancied that a certain wistfulness tempered it. " Do you remember . . ." she went on, " the day you tried to kill me ? Here . . ."

" For that I ask your forgiveness."

" Mine ? Don't be a hypocrite . . . Colum. I . . . goaded
you . . . and you know it. If it is a question of forgiveness . . ."
she grimaced as the words came with difficulty " . . . I must
ask yours. I meant . . . to ruin you."

" Why ? " asked Columba gently. She was speaking the truth,
he knew."

" I was jealous . . ." said Maeve. " Of the way people
loved you. You had a way with them that irked me . . . I was
too proud to . . . seek their love . . . so I had to make do
with . . . lust instead. It's a poor substitute, Colum-Cille . . ."

Columba nodded.

" Give me some . . . wine . . ." Maeve said. " Don't try
to stop me talking, Eithne. I shall be quiet enough . . . when
I'm dead . . . give me that wine . . ."

Columba held the drinking-horn that Eithne brought to
Maeve's lips. She gulped at it greedily. Then she made a wry
face. " Poor stuff . . . it's water . . . and I wanted wine. Well,
it makes talking . . . easier. Colum-Cille . . . I'm frightened.
I don't want to die . . ."

" Why not ? " said Columba quietly.

" All the things I've done . . . not the wrong things so
much . . . but the cruel ones . . . the unkind things I've said
. . . I can feel them clinging about me like the water-weeds . . .
I nearly drowned in them once . . . if death is a river, as they
say . . . then I shall drown forever this time . . . the weeds are
so thick, Colum . . . they're dragging me down . . ."

" Tell me what is troubling you," Columba said. His
thunderous voice was very gentle now.

" I . . . can't . . ."

" Why not ? "

Her lips had drawn back from her teeth in a grimace which
was almost a rigor. " It . . . hurts . . ."

" It only hurts your pride. You, you yourself want to be rid
of the memories that are drowning you . . ."

" Yes . . ."

" Speak then."

" Why should you . . . listen ? "

" I am Christ's priest."

" You'll condemn me . . ."

" How should I condemn, where my master did not ? "

" Did not ? "

" He said : ' neither do I condemn thee . . . Go and sin no
more.' "

" Tell me . . . what else he said . . ."

Once again Columba remembered the oratory, the kneeling children, the calm-faced old priest, the first Gospel words he had ever heard. "He also said : ' I am the good shepherd . . .'"

"Go on . . ." Maeve whispered.

"He thought more of the needs of one terrified lost sheep than of the safety of ninety-nine who had never butted their obstinate way out of the fold . . ."

"Go on, please . . ." The words were barely audible, just flickering on a shallow breath.

"He followed that sheep," said Columba, "across the mountains and chasms of the dark. And when he bore it back, all the songs of heaven welcomed it home . . ."

All that day Columba sat beside her. He had neither eaten nor slept for nearly thirty-six hours, but he showed no trace of weariness as he fought for the liberation of that terror-bound soul. Sometimes Maeve lay listening quietly, and sometimes, with a sudden twist of her old irony, she would rasp some satirically barbed comment from twisted lips. But little by little her defiance yielded, and with it went her fear. Her fingers ceased to clutch, the lines between her brows relaxed. As the day wore on she told Columba many things he had already guessed, others which he had never suspected. She still mocked, but at herself now, and the tears spilled from her half-closed eyes as he at last pronounced absolution. "Read me something . . . from that book . . . of yours," she said. "I don't mind if it's in Latin. I like the comfortable sound . . ."

Columba's Gospel book fell open at the fourteenth chapter of St. John. A mist of fatigue was beginning to close down on him now, as the evening mists were closing down once more upon the dun, but he knew that the conflict had been won at last. As Maeve's fingers relaxed their grip on his he began to read aloud.

" *Ne turbator cor vestrum. Creditis in Deum* ; *etiam in me credite . . . Dicit ei Jesus* : '*ego sum via illa, et illa veritas, et vita illa . . .*'"

He looked at Maeve's face, from which the years now seemed to be lifting, line by line, their burdens and their sorrows and their sins, till only the peace of a child slipping contentedly over the verge of sleep remained. As he raised his hand to make the sign of the cross over that homeward-turning soul he smiled up at his mother and the silent company now standing about the bed.

"Let not your hearts be troubled," he translated softly. " Ye believe in God, believe also in me . . ."

IV

Vespers

"*Ego sum Alpha et Omega, principium et finis,
dicit Dominus, qui est, et qui erat, et qui venturus est.*"

JOANNIS THEOLOGI APOCALYPSIS.

CHAPTER XVII

THE ISLAND lay in the autumnal darkness as if in the maw of a great beast intent on shaking the life out of it with ravening gusts of fury that swept across the rock-strewn pastures and whirled about the clustered buildings on the eastern shore, tearing at the stone-weighted thatch with almost vindictive ferocity, snatching at a pile of sacks which had been left in the lee of the refectory and sending them sailing high in the air to thud against door or window-shutter like the body of some unearthly visitant. Latches shuddered and timbers creaked till the waking monks evoked the protection of the blessed saints against the demons whose laughter they seemed to hear above the yelling of the seagulls and the pounding of the sea.

But soon the darkness that gripped the island between the pale fangs of the furious waves was pricked here and there by scattered points of light. Figures bearing lanterns struggled out of the huts and toward the church to which they had been summoned by the handbell on whose small, familiar note the gale had immediately pounced, bearing it far out across the raging waters of the Sound.

Inside the church it was so suddenly quiet that the men who had been leaning against the wind in the wake of the small, bobbing pools of light from their lanterns almost fell forward as they entered the area of blessed stillness provided by the squat building that shouldered off the howling darkness of the sky.

The candles on the altar hollowed out a little cave of brightness at the east end of the church, and as the members of the community gathered so the brightness grew, each lantern adding its small quota. All the monks were present at the dawn office except those in the infirmary and the brothers who had charge of them. They stood before the altar, rank by rank, Seniors, Working Brethren, and Juniors, in lines that reached back from the steps of the altar to the west door. The island community, which had consisted of a dozen men on its arrival, now numbered over two hundred.

They wore their winter habits of undyed wool, shorn, carded and woven from their own sheep, covered by the hooded cloaks that were lined, for extra warmth, with the skins of the seals whose welfare was so zealously watched over by the monks as the providers, not only of winter clothing but oil for their lanterns and flesh for their ceremonial feasts.

237

The office was read by Baithene, that quiet scholar who was already Abbot-elect and accustomed to deputise for Columba on these occasions when his superior's work took him, as it still so often did, overseas to Alba or Erin or one of the western isles. It was part of Columba's deliberate policy that even the members of his own community at Iona, the Family of which he spoke with such immense and understanding love, should not come to count on him, or on any mortal man, too much. He knew the danger that they might seek to invest him with more splendour than he could bear, yet at the same time he understood their need to offer him the veneration which he must not receive in his own person, but only as the priest whose humanity reached towards heaven, offering itself as a bridge across which the worship of ordinary men might pass towards the less comprehensible fellowship of the saints and the infinite glory of God.

So when they knelt to him, he neither attempted to reprove them nor to retain their homage for himself. Behind their reverence for the man he recognised their worship of the God to whom their imagination scarcely dared aspire. But during the twenty years the community had now been on Iona, he had never, after the first two, hesitated to leave them in the charge of others. So, he hoped, they would learn the truth of something he had often tried to explain ; for the privilege of his office lay less in its authority than in its stewardship. Seeking heaven, they must not come to rest in him.

And yet, because it was so easy to gift a beloved earthly leader with all the attributes of the heavenly Father, it was inevitable that they should, to some extent, disobey him, as they groped through the obscurity of their misconceptions towards a stranger splendour than anything they had ever known. Inevitably, too, as they gathered in the church while Baithene read the dawn office, those who had known him best were wondering when Columba would return to them, thinking that in these later years since the Synod of Drumceatt he seemed to be more than ever in demand elsewhere, resentfully telling themselves that he seemed scarcely to spend any time with them at all now. And then, with his return at last expected, had come this murderous gale. As Baithene read their lips moved obediently, making the appropriate responses. But they were listening, also, to the pounding of the waves, aware that even in the massively built church little flickering tongues of air were whipping here and there, blowing the flames of the altar candles aslant, tweaking at their cloaks, ruffling their thinning hair.

Twenty years had passed over the men who had been, like

Columba, in their early forties, when they landed with him at the southern bay which now bore his name. They stood among the ranks of the working brethren, changed by the passage of time, yet recognisable, since the years had merely emphasised the qualities already inherent in each. Rus, the smith, towered above the men on either side of him, massive now that fat had begun to infiltrate muscle, with the traces of charcoal grime emphasising the lines of effort traced on neck and jowl by each day's work. Under his tuition his two assistants, Scandal and Carnan, had each become expert smiths. Lesser men than Rus, grumbling a little under his leadership because he drove them sometimes too hardly, they still did all the metalwork for the entire community's increasing needs.

Torannan, the first herd, had found his responsibilities many times doubled as the community's flocks and herds grew. But he seemed, at sixty-five, as plump and serene as ever, for his work contented him. He loved animals with a sort of humorous, understanding affection to which they responded instinctively. Setting his lantern on the floor at his feet, he had tucked his cold hands into his wide sleeves as he sang the well-known words in his warm bass. Cobtach, reeking slightly of the fish which he handled continually, was wondering about Macculthan, who had not been able to help him with the community's fisheries since he broke his leg in the spring. Cobtach's deeply sunburned face was anxious as he listened to the wind and wondered if the boats had all been drawn far enough up the beach to be out of reach of this phenomenal tide. He did not care for the sole responsibility of directing the willing but unskilled Juniors sent to learn his craft, He hoped, as he sang the responses through his nose, that Macculthan's leg would soon mend.

Beside him stood the directors of husbandry, Grellan and Eochaidh. Catan had once worked with them, but he had overstrained himself carrying sheaves one harvest, and now spent his time transcribing texts in his cell, work which gave him great and unexpected joy. His was the only one of Columba's initial appointments which had ever been altered, except that of Ernaan, who now ruled the community on a nearby isle. The men Columba had selected for certain work usually retained their positions against all comers with unshakable tenacity, accepting the help of the younger members of the community with the dignity which was to be expected from those on whom Father Columba's first choice had come. Even Lugaid, gaunt and dyspeptic, apt to be short-tempered with those who worked under him in consequence, never considered for an

instant the expediency of giving up his office to the younger men
who were only too obviously anxious to replace him. Lines of
pain had folded themselves about his thin-lipped mouth and he
was getting a little short-sighted as the years went by, so that
sometimes the special dishes he prepared for the community on
feast days were not quite such a treat as they were intended to
be. But he still regarded himself as the man chosen by the
blessed Columba twenty years ago to cook for the community,
and in spite of the gentle but frequent suggestions made by his
contemporaries, and the almost incessant annoyance caused him
by the clumsy Juniors sent to him as kitchen boys, he merely
drew down the corners of his mouth into the obdurate expression
which the lay brothers most dreaded and told himself that
whatever stomach-aches beset him and whatever annoyances
exasperated him, he must not fail the blessed Columba, who had
given him the task for which he had been most fitted twenty years
before.

Throughout the service the haggard, storm-stressed light had
steadily grown, till now, as they sang the final psalm, the candle-
light that had warmed the faces of the men grouped round the
altar was daunted by the cold clarity of the dawn which
spared no trace, in fallen jowl or sunken socket, sallow cheek or
whitened hair, of the passage of each day of twenty years.
Baithene, slight and anxious-faced, seemed to be hunching his
shoulders as much under responsibility as against the morning's
chill; Kenneth, who had come to the monastery the night before
now stood listening to the sound of the wind as if in a dream;
Rus had the desperate look of a hungry man battling with
tantalising visions of savoury food; Lugaid's slightly twitching
nose indicated his anxiety that the porridge, left to simmer in the
great cauldrons hung above the smoored peat, might be singeing
if the wind had fanned the peat into an unexpected blaze. Cobtach's eyes were screwed shut as he tried to remember where he
had personally seen that each boat of the community's little fleet
had been made secure; Eochaidh was reckoning how many
sacks of barley must be set aside for the spring sowing and how
many might be sent to the mill. Torannan's wide mouth was
pursed with concern as he worried about the straying members of
his precious flocks.

" May peace, faith and charity . . . be with you all . . ."

The familiar words of the benediction gathered their wandering thoughts like one of Torannan's own shepherding cries, and
presented in that instant of their recollection each man's cares
and preoccupations to the transfiguring illumination of prayer,

from which, if only for that instant, the dedicative purpose of each was rekindled in response, and the clogging ash of petty, self-gratifying importance blown away. Lugaid's expression relaxed as he remembered a recipe that might tempt the appetite of one of the sick men in the infirmary, Torannan's mind dwelt with affection on his safely-folded sheep. Rus thought of a way to adjust his bellows so that Scandal would gasp less when he blew up the forge fire, and Cobtach thankfully remembered the mooring-rope that he had wedged securely round a spike of rock.

The community filed out of the church towards the refectory, where in due course the Seniors and Working Brethren would break their fast while the Juniors served them and awaited their turn. The sun had risen now, and with it so much of the menace of the gale seemed to be dispelled that the monks were positively light-hearted as they sat down to the wooden bowls of porridge which the Juniors put before them on the bare boards of the trestle tables which ran the length of the refectory.

At the Abbot's table at the far end Kenneth was glad to sink down on the hard wooden bench and wait for his food. He had only come to the island the day before, after an arduous journey from the capital of the northern Picts. He had been recently sent to Alba in order to comfort and bid god-speed to the dying Brude, whose thirty-year reign was evidently coming to an end. Brude had indeed died, soon after Kenneth's arrival, and the Christian party had at first felt a good deal of anxiety in case the election of his successor should not fulfil Columba's hope. But Kenneth had been able to exert a certain amount of influence, and he considered that the people had eventually chosen well. Gartnaidh, son of Domelch, was a Southern Pict, so that his accession united the two branches of north and south and extended the scope of the Scottish alliance. The new reign promised well, Kenneth thought, as he tramped behind the litter which bore the remains of the dead king on its rough journey westward to embark on the last stage of the pilgrimage to Iona, where Brude had asked that his body should lie.

Strange, Kenneth was thinking, as he kicked off the shoe that irked his blistered foot, and remembered how Columba had teased him in the old days about his tender heels, strange how the gale had sprung up almost as soon as the cortege had landed on Iona. Almost as if hosts of malignant demons were venting on the island community their rage at being defrauded of that once vulnerable soul. Yes, they owed that defeat, like so many others, to Columba, Kenneth reflected, laying down his spoon as he pondered over the disaster of Culdremne, which had once seemed certain not only to wreck Columba's life-work, but also to drag down after him, in despairing disillusionment, all those who had seen the promise of heaven reflected in their leader's eyes.

Yet it had been from that very disaster that Columba's greatest achievement had sprung. Strange . . . strange were the ways of God, thought Kenneth, remembering that journey from Tara, when he himself had clung to Columba's arm, imploring him to turn from his insensate purpose. He need not have been afraid, Kenneth thought, smiling. God was not mocked nor was he to be defrauded of the valour of his saints. And yet, at that time of crisis, surely Columba himself had been in mortal danger? Had he chosen wrongly, refused to accept the exile and defeat that seemed to be the end of all his hopes, the crowning achievement of his life would never have emerged from the mists that hung over Alba. Columba had only reached the summit of his life's purpose by following a path that seemed to lead directly away from it, into the quaking morass of utter defeat. Strange, it had been. Yes, strange . . .

Columba's hour of greatest danger had also been the hour of greatest blessing. How futile were the judgments of men, who stood, as it were, in a deep valley and reckoned the whole world according to the compass of their eyes. Columba sought the mountain-peaks, even if it had been from such a peak that he had been compelled to turn his back on his life's work. Kenneth guessed that he had found it hard indeed to obey such a command. He had been in great danger then. In danger . . . danger . . . danger . . . How the word clanged through his brain . . . it was like the summons of a bell . . . giving him no peace till he had obeyed. Columba had been in danger after Culdremne . . . he knew that : it was all over now, thank heaven. Or . . . was it . . . ?

Kenneth gripped the edge of the table with both hands. He saw no vision, heard no voice, but he was suddenly overwhelmed by a greater certainty than could have been conveyed merely by eyes or ears. Columba was in danger . . . now. Not then, not twenty years ago, but now, at this instant. Now, now, now. Columba was in danger, mortal, urgent danger. Now.

At last he understood. Without taking time to shuffle his foot back into the discarded shoe, he rose abruptly from his place beside the astonished Baithene, crying out an incoherent explanation which nobody understood. Blankly, uncomprehendingly, they turned their heads to watch him go.

Kenneth butted his way, head down, against the gale, gasping for breath as he limped towards the empty church, wrenched the door open, ran the length of the aisle and threw himself down before the altar, to pray aloud, with all the passionate urgency of his loving spirit, for the immediate deliverance of his dearest friend from a mortal danger, though he knew not what.

He had no idea of how long he lay there, for the zeal of his entreaty so exhausted him that at last he fell asleep, only to be roused by the entry of the Seniors who had come to say the office of Terce.

" The wind . . ." Kenneth said, as they helped him to his feet. " The wind . . ."

" The wind has quite died down, brother," a gentle, peering Senior said.

Kenneth seemed to be looking far beyond the little group of inquiring monks as he murmured his thanks. Then, bringing his attention back to them, he smiled.

" Are you saying the office with us, brother ? " Baithene asked.

" No." Kenneth's eyes were still dreamy, but his voice was as definite as if he were reciting explicit instructions. " I must go to the harbour now," he said.

They drew aside to let him pass, heads turning, necks craning, eyebrows lifting as they peered inquisitively after him, speculation sharply rippling the placid surface of minds which were habitually more occupied with the minutiae of Gospel allusions and the three-hourly repetition of the day's offices than with the actual comings and goings of the present time and the substantial world. Mildly curious, they whispered together, and from the whisperings a legend began to grow.

" Why was Kenneth in the church between the offices ? "

" He must have been summoned . . ."

" Yes," nodded the old man who had been sitting opposite Kenneth in the refectory, " he received a summons. From heaven. Yes, indeed . . ."

" From an angel ? "

" The sand on the refectory floor was whirled together at the end of the abbot's table . . ."

" As if by folded wings . . ."

" A vessel of milk went over, though no man touched it . . ."

Undoubtedly, it seemed, an angel had spoken to Kenneth. The old man who had been sitting opposite raised his voice again, anxious that his testimony should not be overlooked.

" Yes, indeed, it was an angel so bright that my eyes were dazzled. Do they not still blink from it ? "

" They always do," murmured a sceptic in the background. But already, irresistibly, the legend was taking possession of their

imagination. The aged brother indignantly repudiated the idea
that it had been merely a ray of sunshine which had fallen on
him through the nearest window of the refectory as the gale blew
the sky clear.

"Nothing of the sort. The light was unearthly, angelic.
Had my eyes been younger I would have been able to describe
the angel's face. But it was so strong . . . so strong . . . I had
to blink. And when I looked again . . ."

"What did you see, brother?"

"Oh, an angel, undoubtedly. A spirit that was majestically
tall . . . with features, well, no, I could not presume to describe
them . . . not in detail . . ."

"In general, then . . ." they pressed him, as avid for a
marvel with which to illuminate the dim path of routine duty
as children for sweet stuff which would relieve the monotony of
nourishing but unexciting food. It was easy to yield, pleasant
to see them crowding round, eyes wide, mouths agape, to find
himself the focus of their eager awe, instead of being the one to
be forgotten, pushed aside, disdained.

"I did not see enough to be quite sure. But . . ."

"Yes . . . yes . . . ?"

"Tell us . . ."

"How did he look?"

"It was a fine, beardless face," said the old man at last.
"Beardless, yes. Terrible, yet gracious, the lips parted in speech
as they smiled. The eyes . . ."

"I thought that your own eyes had failed you, brother?"
complained the sceptic. "Now they seem to have served you
only too well."

"I received an impression . . . of course it was no more . . .
but such as it was . . ."

"It has grown like the gospel's mustard seed as we questioned
him . . ."

"Let him be," said a kindlier voice. "Who knows what
presence the old man felt to be near him? His faith may be
holier than our derision. Perhaps he cannot say what his eyes
have seen . . ."

"I tell you, I saw an angel speaking to Kenneth."

"Who are we to deny that Kenneth was commanded by an
angel?"

"Yet that was not what the old man said at first."

"Tell us, brother . . ."

"I will only tell you what I choose. I saw an angel," said
the old man fretfully. He had forgotten his first tentative sug-

gestions, for opposition had made him cling obstinately to the vision of which they now seemed to want to deprive him. The earlier scatter of impressions which had reached his tired brain in the instant Kenneth had leaped to his feet had now been fused together by the heat of controversy into the visible, tangible shape of a mighty angel, white and glorious and blinding bright, with wings so immense that the lowest pinions swept the sand of the refectory floor and the uppermost were bent aside by the beam of the roof. In his anxiety the old man found himself babbling that he had seen the exact spot at which the topmost quill was pressed aside. " Just by the knot in the wood that is above the end of the table, brothers. Just by the knot in the wood . . ."

" We shall soon be hearing that the angel shed a feather with which our brother here intends to write the fairest text that ever came from Iona," said an elderly scholar whose taste ran less towards the miraculous than towards the textually accurate. But the old man's ears were still keen, though some might consider themselves unable to trust the evidence of such very rheumy eyes.

" At least an angel's feather would be unlikely to fall into your hands, brother," he said sharply. " Heavenly messengers would know better than to cast such a pearl before——"

" Brethren, brethren, shall we proceed to say the office ? " suggested the mildly authoritative voice of Baithene.

Kenneth walked down to the harbour through the October sunshine. He was conscious of such beauty about him that his responsive spirit was awed almost to tears. The wind had swept the sky clear of every cloud, then dropped to a mere sighing breath, so that, though the waves still towered, the air was almost as quiet and warm as if it had been a morning in June. The working brethren had already dispersed to the fields or to their special duties in smithy or capenter's shop, mill, granary, tannery, weaver's shed, kitchen, or threshing-floor. Only the fishing brothers, inspecting the boats and nets under Cobtach's supervision, saw Kenneth going towards the harbout with something of the obsessed urgency of a man walking in his sleep.

" Surely he can never mean to take a boat out with the sea that's running ? " Cobtach grumbled. " He may be our blessed Columba's dearest friend and we all know him for a saint in the making, yet there is no man I would care less to entrust with a boat, no, not in the whole world."

But Kenneth made no attempt to launch any of the carefully secured boats which were so dear to Cobtach's anxious heart. He merely stood on the shoreward end of the rough breakwater with which the monks had completed the natural harbour, shading his eyes with his hand and looking far out across the crests and troughs of the tumultuous, indigo-dark sea.

Cobtach, still uneasy, shook his head at him. " I hope to heaven he is mistaken if he expects that a boat will try to land on Iona," he muttered to the lay brother who was helping him to patch up a rent in the side of a coracle with a carefully chosen piece of hide. " With a swell like this it would take St. Peter himself to guide a stranger past the rocks. If he expects any more pilgrims for the funeral of King Brude it is to be hoped they have already made their peace before embarking. They'll never arrive."

" He's right, Cobtach, all the same," said the lay brother. " Look—a sail."

" Tch, tch," said Cobtach, screwing up his eyes. " I don't think so. Who would be such a fool . . . H'm, yes, I believe you're right, though. I see it. Coming from Erin, too. They must have been at sea all night. The blessed St. Peter took pity on them indeed or they could never have ridden out such a storm as we had at the hour of Prime."

He moved behind a rock on which he could rest his elbows, cupping his hands round his eyes to exclude the brilliant sunshine and peered past Kenneth's tall, expectant figure towards the horizon on which a defiant tawny sail could now be clearly seen.

" A rare battering they've taken," he said, reluctantly admiring. " The mast's been spliced, the sail's in rags, they're baling steadily. Three of them," he added, as the boat came nearer, tossing between the wave-crests, her torn sail just filled by the gentle breeze which was all that remained of the morning's gale.

" It's one of our own boats," shouted the lay brother. " I know the rig."

Cobtach continued to peer and mutter. " Why . . . heaven be praised for the deliverance . . . it's our blessed father, Columba," he announced at last. I might have known . . . I might have known. No one else could have ridden out such a storm. Wake up there, lad. Be ready to greet him. Take ropes. haul down that boat and launch it in the lee of the breakwater. Get out the oars. Take two men with you. That boat of his may founder yet. From the way she's labouring she might go down before our very eyes in the midst of the Sound. Get along with you. Cast off that rope, haul out the boat, pick up the oars. Don't stand there with your knees weak and your mouth wide."

Kenneth waited quietly on the breakwater while all the hub-

bub of preparation went on about him. Word went round all the
brothers who were working on the shore that Columba's boat was
returning, that it was damaged, that he had barely survived the
night of storm. Another boat was launched, manned, and nosed
to the end of the breakwater in case it was needed. But Columba's
own boat came steadily on, while Cobtach paced the breakwater,
complaining that it was impossible she should remain afloat
another instant, that now, now, now she must surely go down,
that she could never weather this patch of current, that towering
wave. But still the battered boat came on, till Kenneth could
see the exhausted faces of the crew who were guiding her towards
the harbour, and Cobtach groaned at the sight of the splintered
mast, the sagging, tattered sail, the gaping seams.

At the tiller, Columba seemed serene as ever, but as the lay
brothers leaned out from the breakwater to make the shattered
hulk fast, he looked up at Kenneth with the old, familiar, almost
impish smile, in which the wisdom of a man of over sixty seemed
strangely blended with a zest so young. And his casual greeting
instantly dispelled the memory of recent danger with a bright
shaft of laughter.

"Yes, Kenneth," he said as he climbed ashore, "perhaps it
was as well you didn't wait to put on that other shoe."

CHAPTER XVIII

As THEY WALKED from the harbour towards the refectory, to which Columba had already despatched his exhausted crew, Kenneth heard something of the desperate ordeal which had lasted all night.

" Surely we must have had all the hosts of hell against us," said Columba wearily. " And though dawn came like a blessing from heaven, the gale seemed to gather as much strength from it as we did ourselves. I suppose it was soon after Prime that the mast went. It stunned me in its fall, and for a time the poor lads thought we were done for."

Kenneth nodded silently, the memory of that strange moment of knowledge in the refectory strong upon him. But Columba had paused, resting a tired hand on his friend's arm.

" How good it is to be here, Kenneth," he said. He stood looking about him from the entrance to the monastery at the summit of the gentle slope behind the harbour, now laid out in little thrifty fields, already shorn and being ploughed for next year's crop. Loads of peat cut from the moss to the north of the monastery were being carted in and stacked against the winter in the lee of the refectory wall. Smoke rose from the curing-sheds in which fish were being kippered for the wild days when no boat could put to sea, the rhythmic clang of hammer on anvil came from the smithy, the rasp of a saw from the carpenter's shop, and the thud of flails from the threshing-floor. Under them all boomed the deep-voiced chanting of the Seniors, now concluding the office of Terce, and from the shore rose the unceasing counterpoint of the pagan gulls, that interminable outcry which seemed to weave its way through every other sound on Iona by day or by night, whether the great birds circled the head of the ploughman, were flung high above streaming rocks in a gust of spray, or cruised, as they were doing now, with scarcely a wing-beat, against a sky of cloudless, unfathomable blue.

" How good it is to be here, Kenneth," Columba said again. His voice was that of a man almost at the end of his strength. " After such a night there seems so little between this isle and heaven. All these years I suppose I've looked on Iona, in my heart, as the place of my exile. Now it seems very near home."

" Nearer than Erin ? " Kenneth reproached him.

" My mother died five days ago," Columba said slowly.

" And her death has turned me astray upon the world. I did not know how much the departure of one very old, very tired woman could mean. We met so seldom, and her eyes had grown too dim to see my face, yet while she lived her spirit seemed to call mine back to Erin. Now she beckons me on——"

" Not yet, not yet, Columba," said Kenneth, his own voice sharp with fear.

" Oh, no," Columba said. " My work is not yet done. But I must look forward now, not over my shoulder, like a man who has put unworthy hands to heaven's plough."

" Perhaps Alba will claim you yet," said Kenneth.

Columba sighed. " Perhaps it will. Yes, there is still much to be done there before darkness comes down on the west . . ."

" Darkness ? In the west ? What do you mean ? "

" Never mind what I mean, Kenneth. It will not come yet. My mother wished that her body should lie within sight of Iona. I have arranged for this." He paused, brushing the tips of his long fingers across his forehead as if to clear away a web of painful memories. He looked gaunt and strained, so unlike himself that Kenneth was alarmed.

" Come, Columba. You must rest and eat. You are faint from want of food."

" Fasting should be nothing new to me," said Columba with a wry smile. " And yet it is true enough. My wits are all astray. Perhaps, yes, perhaps I will take a little food before settling down to work. I have seen many Christians die, Kenneth, and never a fairer company of angels than those who came to take my mother home. Yet her going leaves the world empty . . ." He felt un-expectedly forlorn as he spoke, and his voice faltered as he turned again to Kenneth. " You must forgive me. I am ashamed of such weakness . . ."

" You need not be," said Kenneth gently. Together they went slowly towards the entrance of the monastery, as he sought for words with which to comfort his friend. The news of Columba's return seemed to have preceeded them, so that monks were emerging from every shed and workshop, their faces showing a whole series of emotions, as they realised the danger which must so recently have threatened their Abbot at the same instant that they saw he was safe.

" See how these need you," said Kenneth at last. " And their need is that of the whole world."

Columba smiled, his tired face regaining life at the sight of their eager welcome. Rus had run to the doorway of the smithy, the sleeves of his habit rolled high, his leather apron girt about

him, charcoal dust and sweat masking him to the verge of his
tonsured grey hair. Eochaidh, just back from the mill, clapped
his flour-dusted hands together so that he stood in a small cloud.
Urdan and his eldest son, who had brought a present of fish for
the monastery, pulled off their caps and knelt. Dermot, who
had been unable to make the journey with Columba because of
a fever that had kept him in the infirmary, came running up,
his usual taciturnity overwhelmed by unexpected joy. Even
Lugaid, ladle in hand, peered from the doorway of the refectory
as the rumour reached him, frowning and grumbling still. At
the sight of Columba in the distance, however, he hurried back
to prepare an immediate meal for the Abbot who had been so
miraculously restored to them, sweeping his assistants indignantly
aside.

" Out of my way now," he scolded. " Here's the blessed man
back and never a scrape of porridge left to offer him after you
great loons have run your fingers round the pots when my back
was turned. Let me get to the fire. Blow the peats, you, instead
of wasting your breath in whistling. He can have eggs and milk
and bannocks. What a thing . . . out in that storm all night
. . . it was like to have been the end of him and what in all the
world would we have done then ? There now, he's coming. I can
hear them calling to each other outside that the Abbot's safe.
Don't stand there gaping. Fetch trenchers and salt and take the
fresh bannocks out of the ashes. Tch, tch, did ever man have as
much to put up with ? " he grumbled, turning from the fire to
scold the kitchen boys for standing idle behind him. But the
kitchen was empty, and his scolding had been wasted on heedless
air. The two young monks had run out with the rest to welcome
their Abbot home.

It was evident, as Columba entered the refectory with Kenneth,
how deeply the community's greeting had touched him. He had
made many other journeys and been joyfully received on his
return. But on this occasion circumstances seemed to have
combined to give the welcome a very special significance.

Eithne's death might only have strengthened the essential
bond between her and her son by freeing from the restrictions
of physical existence a relationship which had long outworn
them. But it had also finally loosened Columba's association
with the place of his birth. His second brother had been the
ruler of the dun ever since his father's death. His brothers'
families had long ago taken possession of the familiar homestead
and made it clear to him that the distinction of having as a relation
a man revered throughout Erin might also be regarded, from

another angle, as an embarrassment. Columba was used to that. But when he had left Gartan for the last time his mother had no longer been standing in the doorway to bless his departure, and with her going his former home had lost the last of its significance. All that the word stood for had now passed to the island of his adoption, and his family consisted of the community which called him Father.

So, while they sat in the empty refectory, waiting for Lugaid to bring the Abbot's frugal meal, Kenneth was aware not only of his friend's physical exhaustion, but also of the beginning of a subtler change, a suggestion that old age had begun to touch even Columba, who had seemed throughout their association, to bear upon him the blessing of perpetual youth. Kenneth, with his compassionate longing to alleviate pain, had always been a student of physical disabilities and nearly as much of his life had been devoted to the care of stricken bodies as to the illumination of darkened souls. He knew how often men who had come triumphantly through all the trials of an active and exacting life rebelled against the final ordeal of old age. It was so hard to believe that the subjection of the body by helpless weakness must be the preliminary to the spirit's ultimate freedom. He himself had been for some years aware of the waning strength of his limbs, the dulling of his vision, the increasing burden of habitual weariness. But he received such intimations, if not with joy, at least with the fortitude of a traveller who is aware that the path is at its steepest when the journey is nearly done. Detachment had long been so habitual with him that when the time came it would be as natural to relinquish the life of the body as for a future winged creature to submit to the death of its earth-bound prototype and enter the chrysalis which is its grave.

But, for Columba, the impetuous, the unresting, the superbly strong, how would age come? Might it not bring with it a passionate struggle to maintain the vehemence of youth, the force of maturity, a struggle doomed in its failure to drag the spirit down with the defeated body into the terrible pathos of a second childhood which, in the absence of all repose or dignity, merely parodied the first? Old age, he thought, must inevitably be hard for Columba, whose strength had made him the leader in every dangerous enterprise, as his keen brain had enabled him to grasp the essential conditions for the future greatness of his adopted country, and his spiritual gifts equipped him to guide the peoples of Alba towards it. Could he, whose whole nature had expressed itself in active, dominant leadership, make, when the time came, the immense renunciation which would be necessary if he were merely to inspire while others led ?

" Well, Kenneth," said Columba with disconcerting suddenness, " you are looking at me as you looked before the battle of Culdremne. What blunder are you expecting me to make now ? "

" Why . . . none, indeed," said Kenneth in confusion.

" None ? " Columba's grey eyes were disconcertingly direct. " Unless . . . at least . . ."

" Kenneth," said Columba, resting his elbows on the scrubbed board in front of him and bringing his jutting, white brows together in a thoughtful frown, " you are lying to me, I'm afraid."

" No . . ." said Kenneth.

" Why ? " Columba persisted.

" Because . . . I am afraid," said Kenneth unhappily.

" That is the truth now," said Columba. " Of what are you afraid ? "

" Of the hardness of . . . growing old," said Kenneth slowly.

" You, my friend ? " said Columba in astonishment. " I had always thought you were one of the poor in spirit whom this world could not retain."

" I was not concerned with myself," said Kenneth in distress. " What does that matter ? I was thinking of you. It—it does not seem right that you should be old, Columba," he said in a tone of such personal injury that it sounded unexpectedly absurd. For a moment Columba looked at him gravely, though his eyebrows twitched. Then he began to laugh, not loudly, but shaking all over, his eyes creasing and the tears brimming them so that they streaked down his face and he had to wipe them away with the back of his hand, so that Kenneth began to laugh himself from sheer infection, without knowing what there was to laugh about.

It was at this moment that Lugaid came in with Columba's belated meal, carrying a dish of eggs baked in the embers, some barley bannocks and a pitcher of milk. At the sight of his seniors he paused in the doorway, the corners of his thin mouth turned down, eyebrows arched, eyes raised as if in appeal for tolerance of such an unseemly thing as mirth. At the sign of his obvious dismay Columba, grave again, sighed.

" Why, Lugaid, you look as if you had found us committing one of the more deadly sins instead of sharing a joke. Come in, man, come away in. I shall be glad of the food you bring me as long as your disapproval of our laughter has not soured that excellent milk. But tell me, also, why should you have been so displeased ? "

" It is not for me to say, Father Columba," mumbled Lugaid dourly. " Whatever you do, is done well."

" Indeed it is not," said Columba emphatically. " Many things are done exceedingly ill. But this is not one of them. You should laugh more, Lugaid."

" I have little cause, Father Columba."

" I am sorry to hear it. Are we working you too hard ? "

" I am glad of hard work."

" But not of the laughter that lightens it, eh ? "

Lugaid sighed. " I see little occasion for laughter in this world of sin."

" Perhaps," said Columba, " it might be more like heaven, Lugaid, if we laughed more."

" Heaven ? " Lugaid's long face was a mask of consternation.

" Yes, indeed. Shall there not be laughter as well as praise in heaven, Lugaid ? "

Lugaid put down the food and the pitcher of milk before Columba with a hand that shook, but he made no attempt to answer his Abbot's question. The idea seemed to rebound from him as if his spirit rejected it with the violence of a man rejecting blasphemy.

" Well, Kenneth, what do you say ? " Columba asked.

" Why, surely," Kenneth agreed after a moment's thought. " If we are to become as little children in order to gain admission, we must also be prepared to share their laughter, Lugaid."

Columba began to eat. " Have you broken your fast this day ? " he asked Lugaid.

" I—I scarcely know," Lugaid admitted uneasily. " There was so much to do, and the porridge barely went round, Father Columba . . ."

" Bring yourself a pitcher of milk and some bannocks and eat them here with me," Columba commanded. And when Lugaid had reluctantly returned and taken the place beside Kenneth which the Abbot indicated, he went on, with a shrewd smile : " You and I, Lugaid, are not as young as we once were— are we, Kenneth ? " His wide, grey eyes beamed appreciatively at his friend. " And we must not think we are able to achieve as much as we did when we came to the island together. Sit still and eat, Lugaid. I am talking as your brother, not as your Abbot now."

" Why, Father Columba, I should be at my work in the kitchen," said Lugaid unhappily. " The Juniors ought to be preparing the fire to bake the day's bannocks now. And there are fish to be cleaned and cooked——"

"We shall have to learn to leave something to the young, Lugaid. Or so I am told," he added, one quizzical eyebrow raised. "That is something new for us, but something we must both learn, you and I. We are getting old——"

"You, Father Columba? Why—the world must be coming to an end if you are calling yourself old."

"Better I should say it than leave other people to tell me," said Columba cheerfully. "There is no harm in it, no harm at all, Lugaid."

"No harm?"

"Only in refusing the experience it offers. Is that not what you had in mind just now, Kenneth?" he asked suddenly, the abruptness of the question softened by the amusement in his eyes.

"Yes . . . it . . . it was just that, Columba," Kenneth admitted. He felt unexpectedly humbled by this new aspect in his friend. Columba the fighter, the brawler, the rebel, he had once known only too well. Columba the leader, the statesman, the organiser, he had come to revere, but Columba the philosopher, who accepted the limitations of old age, not merely with resignation but with laughter, this was something new. For Columba, as Kenneth had guessed, it would be harder to meet the challenge of weakness, weariness and pain than to confront at once all the dangers of flood or tempest, battle, lightning, malignant demons or evil men. Columba's courage had always been the gift of God, but it had been received by a man whose superb body never yet failed to meet the demands he had made upon it. But now, Columba contemplated a darker battlefield, the prospect of being forsaken even by his own strength, and he was still unafraid. Kenneth, that gentle creature, who revered the courage of others, and was quite unaware of his own, loved Columba for that new quality, and tears stood in his eyes as he listened to what he was saying to Lugaid.

"There is nothing wrong in growing old, Lugaid," Columba was telling the keeper of the community's kitchen, while Lugaid facing him across the bare board, crumbled the bannock he had been offered and looked at his Abbot with the distressed eyes of a sick hound, furiously bewildered and resentful of the chains laid upon him by his stiffening limbs.

"But surely, Father Columba, disease and death are among the sorest evils on earth? Are we not then bound to fight them off as long as we may?"

"'Ne obsistite improbo,'" said Columba thoughtfully. "Have we not been expressly commanded not to resist evil, Lugaid?"

"What, are we then to allow ourselves to be overcome?"

" Is the field of barley overcome when it bows before the wind ? "

" Perhaps not, Father Columba. Yet——"

" Lugaid, Lugaid," said Columba, " you are sitting there agreeing with me because I am your Abbot and you must pay attention to what I say. But in your heart you are telling yourself that you are not in the least like a field of barley, and that though it may be seemly for the grass of the field to bow it is more seemly for men to stand upright, Is that not so ? "

The deeply marked creases which had been seared down Lugaid's face by years of obstinate disapproval, by the pangs of indigestion and ill-temper, could not be eradicated by a moment's laughter. But a convulsion passed across them as an unfamiliar expression was superimposed. A sort of cross-hatching began to be visible on Lugaid's leathery cheeks. Reluctantly, awkwardly, almost resentfully, he smiled.

" That . . . is so, Father Columba," he admitted.

Columba shook a mockingly indignant finger at him. " Yes, indeed. You are less like the field of barley which yields to circumstances and takes no harm in consequence than like the pine tree on the exposed hillside which will not yield an inch and is torn up by the roots. There is no shame in yielding, Lugaid, if it is pride and not necessity which is urging you to stand fast."

Lugaid's long face, after that one brief flash of illumination, had resumed its habitually shuttered expression. The corners of his mouth turned down again as he swept the crumbs of his bannock thriftily together and looked at Columba from under drooping lids. His voice rasped with suspicion as he asked :

" Why are you telling me all this, Father Columba ? "

" Because," said Columba serenely, " I have recognised that I am getting old."

" Then I too must be getting old," said Lugaid defensively. " But I do not feel it. I am as well as ever I was. The years have brought me experience that I can offer the community. I have more skill now than I had as a young man. I can save expenditure in a thousand ways. I know just how much is needed of this and that. I measure by the pinch where a young fool would toss in a handful. All my life has gone to obtain the knowledge of the preparation of food which is my contribution to our life here on Iona." He twisted his rheumatic hands together as he spoke, and his voice rose higher, harsh with distress. " You do not understand me, Father Columba, if you think like all the others that I am just a bad-tempered, niggardly old man who scolds the Juniors who come to me for instruction because he must always have his own way. We who came with you to the island, long ago, were each given our work for the community, work of which we shall be expected to render an account on the last day. Rus, there, is an older man than I, yet he still rules the smithy."

"Younger men swing the hammers now," Columba said.

"Torannan has still charge of the flocks, Cobtach of the boats, Eochaidh of the crops. Am I to be the only one to fail in my charge?"

"At this moment you are the only one who still seeks to do all the work with his own hands."

Lugaid's face crumpled with misery. "Father Columba, if you take my work, you might as well take my life away, too."

For a moment, watching Columba, Kenneth thought that the Abbot was about to break into one of the stormy denunciations which had been so typical of him in the early days, but instead he sat silent, eyes closed as if in supreme effort of concentration. And when he spoke at last his voice was gentler than Kenneth had ever heard it. It was as if, Kenneth thought, such gentleness had long been inherent in Columba, but concealed by the energetic burgeoning of his dramatic achievements as the true form of a great tree may be concealed by the brief profusion of the leaves. Then, as the leaves begin to fall from it, the essential, beauty of its nature is laid bare. Just so, it seemed, might age, which took away so much, actually serve to complete the development of his lifelong friend.

"My son," Columba was saying to Lugaid, "it is not for me to take any man's work away. But it may be for him to decide that the time has come to lay it down."

Lugaid gripped the edge of the board with desperately clutching fingers. "I cannot . . . I cannot . . . if I had nothing to do I should be no more than a drag on the community. They need me now, because I prepare their food. If I did nothing for them they would only want to be rid of me . . ."

"That is surely untrue, Lugaid."

"No—no—it is not. I have never had any time to make friends among the brethren. I have always had my work. If you take my work from me I have nothing, only to sit idle among the shadows till I die."

"If that is how you feel, Lugaid," said Columba sadly, "then it is I who have failed."

"You, Father Columba?"

"Such wild talk means that I have taught in vain. Lugaid, a man's work may either be done for his own glory or to the greater glory of God. If he has worked for his own glory, when that work is taken from him he is left in the dark indeed. But if he has given the glory into safer keeping, then it will shine like a star above him to guide him home at the end."

Lugaid shook his head. He had not been listening. He was too tired, too frightened to take in new ideas. He clung to his original instructions with the obstinacy of a man whose brain's receptivity has been exhausted. " I must work on, Father Columba. I must still work on," he mumbled. " I cannot live without my work."

Columba rose from the table, making the sign of the cross above the remains of the meal. " Lugaid," he said, " come here."

Obediently Lugaid knelt before him. It was no longer an informal discussion between brothers. The Abbot was about to issue his commands. But still he was patient. " Lugaid," Columba said, " I will never seek to impress any truth on you by force. But I command you to consider what I have said. Go to the church and read there the twelfth chapter of the Gospel of St. John, especially the twenty-fifth verse, considering its application to the work which you call your life. ' *Qui amat animam suam, perdet eam,*' " he quoted in his sonorous voice. " Think well whether you are loving that life of yours so well that you are in danger of losing it, Lugaid."

" But Father Columba, I should be cooking the fish," Lugaid lamented, " and not reading the Gospels."

Then indeed Kenneth saw the old fire flash out in Columba. " Tell the lay brothers to cook the fish for you," he thundered. " Is the fish that will fill our bellies to be considered before the welfare of your immortal soul ? Do what I tell you. Now."

For a moment Lugaid still knelt, his appalled face imploring Columba in vain. Then, bowing his head in reluctant obedience, he rose and trudged sadly away.

Columba turned to Kenneth with a rueful smile. " Well, my friend, I am grateful to you for your warning. It was timely, very timely indeed."

" My warning, Columba ? " said Kenneth. " From the way you spoke, it was evident that you needed none."

" Oh, yes, I did," said Columba calmly. " It is harder to put my own words into practice than to rebuke poor Lugaid. What will he do, I wonder ? Is he too tired to learn something new, so that he can do no more than plod along the same old path ? Heaven help him and lighten his load."

" I hear," Kenneth said, " that the unfortunate man is getting so short-sighted that he cannot tell the contents of one pitcher from those of the next, so that when the Juniors put them back in the wrong places, as Juniors so often do, we are all liable to be poisoned by the concoctions that are produced."

" Tch, tch," said Columba. " Yes, I had already heard that before I left for Erin. If he will not surrender his office it looks as if I shall be obliged to take it from him, but it would be so much better for Lugaid if he could lay it down of his own free will. I think we must take the risk a little longer. After all, nothing harmful should ever be kept in the kitchen, whether the chief cook is short-sighted or not."

" There may be nothing harmful in the kitchen," said Kenneth mildly, " but there are certain proportions which are usually observed in cookery. It is not pleasant when Lugaid means to put in a handful of flour and puts in a handful of salt instead."

Columba merely smiled. " Suffer him a little longer, Kenneth. Did the ninety-and-nine obedient sheep grudge the shepherd's inattention when he gave so much extra care to the one that had strayed ? "

" It is not so much the attention, but the thirst that troubles me," Kenneth said. " You know that your own rule obliges us to eat all of whatever is on our plates."

Columba waved aside the protest as they left the refectory together. " At least there is no shortage of water at present, and no rule which forbids you to use it in order to quench such a thirst. Do not make difficulties."

Kenneth looked at his friend with wry amusement. " Life is a strange thing, Columba. Just as I come to tell myself that you have changed and grown so that I can no longer keep up with you, I realise how much of my boyhood's friend, thank heaven, remains."

They stood together in the doorway of the refectory, looking out across the thatched roofs of the monastery buildings and the slope of carefully cultivated fields, now dotted with the figures of monks in their white habits returning to the monastery for the noon meal, towards the still ruffled Sound and the rose-red coast of Mull. Between the jade-green water and the inverted bowl of cloudless, wind-swept blue the island seemed to float, neither in water nor in air, but in living, vibrant light. The peace about them was as much an actual part of their surroundings as the visible world itself, all but palpable, almost to be enclosed between widespread arms and folded to the heart.

"I should have gained but a poor sort of wisdom," said Columba at last, " if it were to make me a stranger to my earliest friends."

CHAPTER XIX

DERMOT, importantly aware of his responsibilities, was moving about his Abbot's cell with the careful deliberation which was characteristic of him. Before the writing-desk he paused, itemising the fresh sheet of vellum, the Gospel book open at the page midway down which Columba's diligent hand had paused the evening before, the ruler, the sharp-pointed stylus with which the guiding lines were incised, the quills he had just pointed, the ink-horn in the clip that secured it to the right side of the desk. As he made sure that Columba would have everything he needed for the morning's work his face showed all the concentration of an artist surveying an incipient masterpiece or of a worshipper intent before a shrine.

His office of attendance on the Abbot of Iona gave him all he had ever asked from the religious life. Dermot had come to Iona many years ago and been received without question by Columba after a single instant of that piercing scrutiny under which, men said, their very souls lay bare. No one, except perhaps Columba, who had his own ways of knowing things, had much idea of how Dermot's pre-religious life had been spent. There were various rumours, but no certainty that he had ever been a man of great possessions who had sold them all at a divine command and come to Iona to spend the rest of his life there, not as a priest but as a servant. Dermot himself provided no clue, either deliberately or by accident. He was by temperament a grave and silent person whose love for Columba blossomed like a single flower in a landscape that some unknown disaster, people fancied, had blasted into aridity long ago. His care of Columba was entirely unspectacular and unself-seeking. He asked neither recognition nor gratitude, only the privilege of lifting from his Abbot all the minor preoccupations of mundane existence in order that he might so be freed for the more urgent needs that lay beyond. So Dermot, who might once have been a man of substance, was entirely happy as he sharpened quills and ground colours, prepared food and ran errands for Columba, who might have been a king.

In his deliberate way, he found as much satisfaction in preparing a sheaf of the quills which Columba wore down so fast as if he himself had preached one of the sermons with which his

Abbot so kindled the imagination of whole congregations that the very air about them seemed astir with shining spirits and the awed faces overshadowed by the movement of majestic wings. To Columba, Dermot knew, the world invisible was not the subject of a vaguely speculative hope, that hope which lurked in the background of most men's calculations, to be looked for only in the last resort and when all more substantial resources had failed. He knew, without needing, or indeed being able to analyse the nature of such knowledge, that for Columba the balance of life had shifted, so that for him the habitually invisible had now a greater reality than the more ordinary environment of the average man. Though it might still be in the three-dimensional world of sense perception that Columba lived and moved, it was now elsewhere that he had his being.

But Dermot, who had come, as time went by, to know more about his beloved master than perhaps any man alive, as devoted servants do, also did less to satisfy the curiosity of the persistent questioners, both within and without the monastery, who sought to share that knowledge. Since his return from Erin, after the great storm, Columba had been coming, little by little, to spend more of his time at Iona as the years went by, not only because the many demands he had always made on his physical strength were, as Kenneth had realised, at last beginning to exact their toll as he approached the age of seventy, but also because he seemed to be aware of the need for a difference in his way of life. He had begun to seek a less active and more contemplative existence, to enter a phase during which his urgent personality was undergoing a subtle but definite modification, so that he became by degrees less of a fiery cresset streaming aslant the winds of the world than a tall altar candle before whose steady flame men knelt to kindle their own.

Such a change did not pass unnoticed by the members of the community, to whom the behaviour of their Abbot was habitually the subject of eager speculation. Those in search of exceptional manifestations of holiness found in his increasing personal austerity the pretext for much horrified reverence. They vied with each other in curtailing their hours of sleep because it had come to their knowledge that Columba sometimes spent entire nights without sleeping at all. They discarded their bedding because Columba was believed to sleep on a mere shelf of stone. They pursued the unwilling Dermot with inquries and implored Columba himself for severer penances and more strenuous opportunities for self-mortification, which Columba, well aware of the danger of competitive excesses which sought to short-cut the deliberate processes of spiritual evolution, steadily refused to allow.

It was only against his strict instructions that any of his monks inflicted on themselves greater austerities than the ordinary rule of the monastery laid down. If he himself chose to give less time to bodily refreshment and more to meditation and prayer, that was a matter which lay between him and God. One of the things which could still rouse him to anger was to discover that his private meditations had been watched by such over-zealous sensation-mongers, and, though Dermot was not aware of it, as he waited for Columba to begin his work of transcription, it was an instance of such inquisitiveness that had detained him now.

For Columba had announced in the refectory that morning after Prime that he wished to go alone to the western side of the island, as he often did, for meditation and prayer. Dermot, who was used to such retreats, had gone to the Abbot's cell as usual to make preparations for his work there, and the brethren also went about their business, whether in workshop, field or cell. Columba had indicated that he would not be long away, so that Dermot, accustomed to his punctual habits, was astonished when, instead of his Abbot's heavy footsteps, he heard the summons of an angrily shaken bell.

Dermot ran with the rest, for when the Abbot rang his hand-bell in such a way, it meant that the community must immediately assemble, whether for exhortation, corporate action or for prayer. Often in the middle of a winter night such a clanging would rouse them to hurry to the church and pray for some soul in extremity, of whose plight Columba had, in ways available to him alone, become aware, But this, evidently, was not such a summons. It led them to the refectory, not to the church, and Columba, who awaited them there, was looking angrier than most of those present had seen him look for many years. As the last breathless monks came in from the outlying fields he began to speak, in a voice which turned the assembled community pale with fear.

" Did I not," said Columba, " tell you after the morning office that I was going to walk to the west of the island and wished to be left undisturbed ? "

" Yes, Father . . ."

" Yet one of you disobeyed me."

" Surely not, Father," murmured the gentle Baithene, who, as Columba's chosen successor, represented the rest of the community when a spokesman was required. " You made your wishes perfectly clear."

" Yes, so I thought. But I was disobeyed."

" By whom, Father ? " asked Baithene.

" That is for the disobedient one to say," thundered Columba. " Let him stand forward now. I will hear what he has to say."

A ripple of consternation ran through the community. Heads were turned, hands were clasped, shoulders shrugged by monks anxious to make clear that they had no knowledge of the affair. The Seniors stroked their beards or shook their heads. Sandalled feet shuffled with little rasping sounds on the sanded floor. Nobody spoke. And for what seemed a very long time nobody stirred.

" If the disobedient man does not stand forth," said Columba in a dreadful voice, " I will lay upon him the curse of . . ."

With a sound like a sob one of the Juniors broke from his place and flung himself on his knees at Columba's feet. " Forgive me . . . forgive me, Father . . ." he stammered. " I followed you . . ."

" Why ? " asked Columba inexorably.

" It was because . . . I wanted to see the heavenly angels . . ."

" Why did you suppose," said Columba, " that disobeying a man who has asked to be left in peace for an hour would be likely to earn you the privilege of a vision of angels ? "

" Because . . . because every one knows that the holy angels accompany you, Father . . ." babbled the young monk, " and so I thought that if I followed you I might see them too. So I hid myself very carefully in case you should look back and went after you, keeping behind one boulder after another, while you followed the road that leads to the western fields . . ."

" And then ? " said Columba. Only those who knew him well could guess that the sternness of his voice had begun to yield to the pity of which he gave no sign as he continued to frown down at the terrified young man.

" And then you climbed the little mound they call the Fairy Hill . . . and . . . and there you began to talk with the blessed angels that came down to you from heaven . . ."

" Did you see the angels ? " demanded Columba.

" Yes . . . Oh, yes . . ." the young man babbled.

" Did you ? Be careful. I want the truth now," said Columba, who knew very well how much vision-mongering was apt to go on among religious people and objected to such competitive holiness with all the vigour of his uncompromising personality. His annoyance at being followed was quite genuine. Far too much peeping and prying had been going on lately. Whether he had been visited by angels was a matter which concerned him alone.

He now intended to make an example of this inquisitive young man.

" Well . . . yes . . . no . . ."

" Do you mean yes or no ? " said Columba. The young man wavered before the look in his Abbot's steady eyes.

" I don't know, Father. The light was so bright it almost blinded me . . . it . . . it was difficult to see . . . I thought . . ."

" You thought you would satisfy your curiosity, and that of others like you," said Columba sternly, " by bringing back reports of marvels which you had no right to see. There has been too much of·this. Did I not find another inquisitive watcher with his eye against my keyhole the other night when he ought to have been resting in sleep till the bell for Matins roused him ? Let me tell you, this unwholesome seeking after visions must now cease. Do you wish to become like the rootless creatures who followed our Lord through Galilee in search of a sign from heaven ? Except ye see signs and wonders will you too not believe ? Look now at this wretched boy who lies here and remember that blessed are they who have not seen and yet have believed." Then, stooping, he took the young monk by the elbow, and spoke more gently as he helped him to his feet. " What is your work here, my son ? "

" I work in the smithy, Father . . ." the young man admitted miserably.

" And you wish for a more spiritual occupation. Is that it ? "

" Yes, Father."

" Then try and remember that our Lord spent nearly thirty years at such a task," said Columba gravely. " Go back to the smithy and swing your hammer to better purpose for that memory. Be satisfied with the beauty of the sparks that fly from the anvil instead of seeking the less bearable beauty of the angels who visit us from heaven. Those who look too long at the sun will end by blinding themselves. Do you understand ? "

" Yes, Father." The young monk's voice was humble now.

" Then go. And let this be a lesson to you all," said Columba in the voice which seemed to echo round the far end of the refectory like thunder in the hills, though he had hardly raised it, as far as Dermot, who stood close behind him, could tell.

" All this has kept me too long from my work," the Abbot sighed as he left the refectory. " Dermot, is everything prepared ? "

" Everything, Father," said Dermot, as he followed Columba to his cell. Each quill, he knew, had just the supple spring that Columba liked, was cut fine enough, yet not too fine. Columba was particular about his writing materials. There was still a splash of ink on the wall of the cell at which he had flung a quill which had not been cut to his mind. Dermot always grinned as he looked at that mark. It was such a comforting reminder that the blazing temper of the old days had not been entirely dominated by the heavenly serenity which frightened him with the thought that his beloved Abbot might not be required to remain much longer in such an imperfect world. And so, as he walked meekly behind Columba on the way to his cell, he thought with pleasure of the full-blooded wrath with which Columba had scolded the unfortunate young man who had made himself a nuisance with his desire for visions of angels. Surely, Dermot thought, such good earthy indignation meant that they might have a chance of keeping Columba on Iona for a few years more?

It was one of those strangely quiet autumnal mornings when the stillness seemed almost like a weight that burdened the air so that the very birds did not care to fly. The gulls stood about on the wet sands which their splayed feet had covered with leaf-like patterns, or rocked gently on the water that showed scarcely the trace of a wave as its margin crept across the white sands with a whisper hardly louder than the sigh of a child in its sleep. Such quiet was almost uncanny, and Dermot was quite glad to reach Columba's cell, though Columba himself seemed cheerfully unaware of any oppression as he twisted his cloak off his shoulders and let it fall across Dermot's outstretched arm.

" So everything is ready as it always is. I hope these preparations did not take too much time from your own devotions? "

" Oh, no, Father," Dermot said. It was difficult to explain in what way such preparations were devotional, but Columba, it seemed, understood.

" Your care of me is something you may well offer to God, my son. There is never a day that I do not thank heaven for it. Yet if at any time you feel that more time is needful, you will not hesitate to ask for greater freedom from these tasks of mine? "

" I need no greater freedom, Father," Dermot said. He hung Columba's cloak in its corner, looked to see that the freshly ground colours were where the Abbot could reach them, that flint and tinder were beside him, as well as a couple of rushlights in case the light should grow still dimmer on this mist-hung day. Columba sat down before the desk and picked up a quill, trying it absent-mindedly against his thumb, his mind already reaching out towards the strangely different world of which St. John had written, and in which the greatest drama of eternity had been played out in space and time. The cosmopolitan bustle of

Jerusalem and Jericho were so far removed from the quiet of Iona on that windless autumn morning that it seemed impossible that they could both find a place in the same world. Yet Columba, it seemed, passed easily from one to the other in the instant of taking up his quill.

" *Adhuc multa habeo quae vobis dicam, sed nunc non potestis portare* . . ." Columba wrote. And Dermot, waiting till he was sure that his Abbot had all he required, heard him afterwards murmuring the phrase in his native Gaelic, as his lifelong habit had been.

" I have yet many things to say unto you, but ye cannot bear them now . . ."

The voice might be only that of Columba, Abbot of Iona, but to Dermot, listening humbly in the background with the profound attention of his worshipful love, the words seemed to gain, for an instant, a universal significance, so that they bore something of the original pity with which they had been spoken, not only to the little group of frightened men huddled together on the brink of tragedy in an upper room in Jerusalem, but to all those who were to follow them throughout the world and during all the centuries to come ; who, in spite of all the assistance that intellectual brilliance and natural insight could offer, were still to find all the implications of that revelation so much more than they could bear.

So Dermot stood there wondering, while the autumnal stillness lay heavily upon them and the regular sound of Columba's quill on the page before him sounded louder than the whisper of the tide on the beach below. Dermot watched Columba's left forefinger keep pace with his writing hand across the copy which he himself had placed so carefully before Columba's return, actually daring to sit for a moment in the Abbot's chair, with a murmured apology for his boldness, in order to make sure that the position of both the old and the new versions was correct. He seemed to have judged well, for Columba was now writing steadily, his head moving very slightly, his forefinger following the progress of his quill along the faintly incised line from which each letter hung.

Then, just as Dermot was preparing to creak out of the cell as quietly as possible, a distant shout came faintly but unmistakably across the Sound. Dermot sighed, recognising it for a summons to the ferry from someone who wished to cross to the island. Perhaps if he went to the harbour he could find out the visitor's business, perhaps even persuade him to see Baithene or one of the Seniors and leave the Abbot undisturbed. But Columba, it seemed, had been disturbed already. Shaking his head, he looked up with a wry smile.

"Dermot, keep an eye on that fellow who stands shouting yonder. He may be well-meaning, but the chances are that in his haste he will upset my ink."

"I will not leave him for an instant, Father," Dermot said. He did not pause to consider how Columba knew certain things beforehand, for he was not habitually a speculative person. He only knew that in some way which was naturally quite beyond his own limited understanding, Columba could see certain things which were beyond the sight of ordinary men. The Abbot occasionally, and more or less by accident, dropped such hints of his own wider vision. He would probably not have mentioned his knowledge of their next visitor if he had not been specially anxious to complete the chapter of the Gospel that he was transcribing without spot or mark. And Dermot made up his mind that if his own vigilance could change the course of fate— and surely in so small a matter, a man's directed will could turn its flow aside—Columba's page should be unspoiled.

After the momentary distraction, Columba had returned to his task with his usual profound concentration, so that Dermot knew he would not hear him if he spoke, nor notice if he left the cell. But before going, he made a careful survey, shook the clip in which the ink-horn rested to make sure that it was secure, tested the wooden shutter which was held back by the proper hook, glanced round the legs of the Abbot's stool, the stand of the desk, the position of the ruler. All things were in order, and no accident seemed likely to upset the ink during his absence. On his return with the visitor, all he need do to avert the annoyance which the Abbot had foreseen, Dermot told himself, was to take the ink-horn away.

Carefully he shut the cell door behind him, shaking it to make certain that the latch had dropped into place so that no unexpected gust of wind which might suddenly arise even on this windless morning could swing the door wide and scatter Columba's writing-materials, so that in an effort to save them he might upset the ink himself.

Prophecy, Dermot knew, was a strange thing. He had sometimes tried to stop such premonitory glimpses from coming true before, and failed, though whether his failure had been due to the very anxiety which made him run straight at the situation he had been trying to avoid, Dermot was not subtle enough to decide. On this occasion, however, he considered that his own credit was at stake. He would be a poor creature if he could not cheat fate in the matter of an ink-horn about which he had already been warned.

His honest, anxious face was creased with concentration as he walked down to the harbour, from which a boat had put out in answer to the persistent bellowing from the far side of the Sound. Dermot, aware of the malignancy of the minor demons who might be expected to do their best to distract his attention, stood at the end of the breakwater, watching every movement of the oars, and refusing to be interested by the high voices of Urdan's two small grandsons who were building a miniature village from wet white sand as they waited for their father's return from the fishing-grounds. Unable to understand the reason for Dermot's unusual aloofness, they were all the more determined to obtain his help.

" And this is the monastery . . . Dermot, we can't get the church right . . ."

" Huh," said Dermot absently. The boat had reached the far side of the Sound. A stranger was getting in. The boat had turned. It was setting out for the island, its wake spreading in a fan of ripples like the ornamental pattern on a warrior's spear-head.

" This is meant to be the Abbot's cell, Dermot. But it's all gone funny . . ."

" Look, I'll make a wee man out of seaweed and put it inside. Then we'll know . . ."

Dermot's concentration wavered. It could scarcely be considered respectful to represent the holy Father Columba by a strip of seaweed. And the piece the small boy was waving so triumphantly was undoubtedly grotesque. " If you make the sand into a better shape and thatch it properly you won't need any bits of seaweed at all," he said severely.

" We can't. Not unless you show us how," they squeaked in triumph.

With their reproachful eyes upon him, Dermot hesitated. " Not just now," he said. The boat was coming nearer. It would soon be at the land. The two little boys danced round him imploringly. " Oh, please, Dermot, please. Nobody builds things in sand like you do. If you won't help us we'll get it all wrong. And then you'll be cross because we've been rude to the Holy Father by pretending he looks like a piece of seaweed."

Dermot glanced down at the half-finished group of sand buildings, carefully placed in approximately their proper relationship to each other, and surrounded, as in reality, by a turf wall and ditch scooped out of the pleasantly moist sand. " If we can't

get it done soon it will be all spoilt," the elder boy said beseech-
ingly. " The tide's coming in."

" You should have built it above high-water mark," Dermot
said.

The boat was approaching the breakwater. He could see the
man who had come across in it. He looked like a merchant.
His clothes were not ornate enough for a noble, but the fur cloak
and hood were not those of a peasant. He was fat and shifty-eyed,
Dermot thought, and he clutched nervously at the boatman as
he stumbled ashore. Assuming all the dignity of the Abbot's
personal representative, he stepped forward to greet the visitor
to the island, while the small boys sat back on their heels, dusting
their sand-covered hands together as they watched.

" Have you come to see the Abbot ? " asked Dermot. " If so,"
he went on hastily, " I am afraid he is working, and cannot be
disturbed."

" Of course not, of course not," said the stranger effusively.
" As a matter of fact, I have come to see the man in charge of the
kitchen, as regards a little matter of seal-oil. Just a little matter
. . . not of the first importance, naturally. But I should be glad
to see him. Lugaid is the name, I believe . . ."

Dermot looked relieved. Evidently it was a false alarm. The
fat man didn't even want to see Columba. As for Lugaid . . .
Dermont hesitated. Relations between himself and the monastery's
chief cook were not of the best, since in his capacity of personal
attendant to the blessed Columba Dermot considered he was
entitled not only to supervise the preparation of his food, but also
to offer it to the Abbot with his own hands. This Lugaid denied,
and though Columba, when asked to decide between their
claims, had settled the matter in his characteristic way by commanding that his food should be brought to him by the least
important Junior serving at that time in the kitchen, Dermot and
Lugaid were now ostentatiously distant in their bearing towards
each other, and never met save when they must.

" I've been here before," said the merchant blandly. " I
can find my own way."

" Well . . ." Dermot said uncertainly. The Abbot's instructions had been explicit. But it seemed that either the Abbot
had been mistaken for once, or that the visitor who would spill
his ink had not yet come. If this fellow knew the way to the
kitchen, why should he not be left to go there ? He himself
would surely be better occupied watching in case another visitor
should unobtrusively cross the Sound. " The kitchen," said
Dermot, " lies at the back of the refectory, which is the large

building on the far side of the enclosure. Turn to the right at the
entrance. You can see the smoke of the cooking-fire rising far
into the sky."

"I see it, I see it," the stranger said. He smiled obsequiously,
showing large yellow teeth. "You I suppose, are the blessed
man's deputy?"

"No," Dermot said briefly. He heard the small boys snigger,
and turned to silence them with a glare.

"I am his servant," he said carefully.

The fat man's smile became odious in its patronage.

"Quite so, quite so. He keeps you busy, I'm sure. I shall not
ask you to come with me to Lugaid. The kitchen is at the back of
the refectory . . . I remember quite well . . . Lugaid is an old
friend of mine, you know . . ."

He bustled off, while Dermot looked after him with distaste.
Surely he need take no more trouble about one of Lugaid's
huckstering acquaintances, who had come to see if he could drive
a better bargain, no doubt, for the seal-oil that the monastery
could ill spare, since the Abbot never wished more of the seals
on their little seal-farm to be killed than was strictly necessary to
provide for their own needs. He liked the creatures. But, of
course, Lugaid . . .

"Dermot, Dermot, show us how to put the roof on Father
Columba's cell . . ."

"Look, we've got the church all wrong . . ."

"Dermot, please do this bit for us before the tide comes
in . . ."

For a few moments Dermot, forgetting to be cross, also forgot
everything except the children's importunities. Crouching beside
them, he took the wet sand in his hands, slapping it skilfully into
more familiar shapes, enjoying himself as he always did when he
had the chance of making things.

"That funny man's still watching you, Dermot," one of the
small boys said.

Abruptly Dermot looked up. The fat man in the fur cloak
had turned at the entrance to the monastery and was looking
back towards the harbour. Then, having satisfied himself that
Dermot had not followed him, he went on again. But inside the
entrance he was turning, not to the right, but to the left, to set
off briskly towards the closed door of Columba's cell.

Scattering sand in all directions, Dermot rose and fled up the
path from the harbour, pursued by a wail of indignant protest.
Too late he realised the folly of having taken the man at his word
when he said he wished to see Lugaid. Only the foolish resent-

ment which made him anxious to avoid an encounter with a man he disliked, thought Dermot penitently, could have made him so credulous. Did he not already know how cunning the pilgrims were when they wanted to see Columba? They would do anything, anything, thought Dermot, as he pounded up the slope, to avoid the vigilance of the monks who occasionally wished to ensure a little peace for their hard-worked Abbot. He ought never to have left him, never to have been tempted by the pleasure of playing with the children. Now . . . if he did not hurry . . . he would be too late.

The shifty-eyed stranger heard the sound of Dermot's hasty feet, just as he turned away from the refectory. He himself was no runner, but he began to trundle along at a jog-trot which kept him far enough ahead of his pursuer to be able to lift his hand to the latch just as Dermot, too breathless to shout, turned the corner behind him. Crimson-faced, Dermot put on a frantic spurt of speed, wretchedly aware of being too late to avert the accident which Columba had predicted, and which now seemed, to his inflamed imagination, momentous and inevitable as the hidden instant of his own death.

He reached the door of the cell in time to see the stranger thud down on his knees beside Columba's desk, hands clasped and raised in emotional treaty, little round eyes wide with a blend of triumph and alarm, as Columba's quill reached the end of a line and paused and Dermot, aghast in the doorway, tried to break through the sense of helpless frustration which seemed to nail him where he stood.

Dermot's arrival, Columba's abstracted greeting, the sweeping gesture with which the stranger caught the tip of the ink-horn with the edge of his cloak as he surged forward to kiss Columba's hand ; all these things hardly occupied a couple of heart-beats, but to the helpless Dermot they appeared isolated by great tracts of time. After what seemed like centuries he was still staring at a great pool of ink which was slowly spreading across the page that Columba had just covered with his beautiful writing, too wretched to raise his eyes and meet his Abbot's crooked smile.

" Well, Dermot," said Columba mildly, " the next time I give you such a warning I hope you will act on it, my son."

CHAPTER XX

THE YEARS as they passed over the island, had begun to mean less to Columba now. Time silted about him, blurring all trivial and recent memories as the white sand blurred the patterning of the innumerable rabbits' footprints when the south-west wind sent it flying high above the dunes. Imperceptible as the fine particles, the instants as they passed were unnoticed as his own heart-beats, yet like the sand that drifted into the folds of the cloak which was his only extra covering during the nights he sometimes spent alone in prayer upon the beach, their accumulation laid an increasingly heavy burden upon him unawares.

The only difference, thought Columba, as he walked slowly along the shore one summer's evening, was that one could rid oneself of the burdening sand merely by shaking out the cloak, while the burdens that time imposed upon a man were of a more durable sort. Year by year the accumulation of time had added its quota of fatigue to the load which he would not be able to shake from him till he died. It had become necessary to abandon, one by one, all his active pursuits in order to conserve the energy he needed for the duties which remained. Columba had already chosen Baithene as his successor. Before he went Baithene must be fully trained, capable not only of administering the great complex of religious activities which had their hub in Iona, of directing the various departments of the monastery itself, but of loving and understanding, rebuking or guiding each individual man of the community, as well as all the remoter multitudes of men and women who came to Iona because they needed help.

And so, little by little, Columba was himself beginning to withdraw from the active supervision of each aspect of the community's life, realising that he would do his beloved family a greater service by freeing them from their habit of turning to him for instructions at all times and over all problems than by allowing them to continue to rely upon him, until they were utterly disrupted by the catastrophe of his death.

This process of resignation had proved to be the hardest thing he had ever been called to do in all his life. As he deliberately withdrew from his position of supreme authority he was already fighting, in silence and solitude, the awful and ultimate battle with his own unregenerate self-will which in many men is only completed at the instant of their death, while others are carried still

271

tragically fighting into the unknown. Kenneth had been right when he had said it would be hard, Columba often told himself now. He, Columba, had known what it meant to be a great administrator, to hold between his hands the destiny of a nation not yet conscious of its identity, to shape the first stages of that destiny in obedience to his inner inspiration, always with love, soon with understanding and at last with patience. He had known the responsive exaltation of multitudes, the awed delight of seeing his visions of man's Christ-inspired brotherhood translated into the rough-hewn shapes of monastery and church, the hubbub of their building expressing in diligence the prayers that were not less ardent than those offered with bended knees and meekly folded hands. He had trudged, preached, built, organised, taught, sailed and prayed without respite during these early days. But these things had not been hard.

Many enthusiasts had spoken of the arduousness of the life he led ; or distressed him by over-vehemently praising his energy and fortitude, exaggerating the efforts needed for the long journeys across Alba, up and down Erin, and those tempestuous or idyllic voyages among the western isles. They had been mistaken. These things had not been hard. They came natural to him. His arduous work had also been his joy. Oh no, that had not been hard, not hard as the struggle he was facing now, Columba told himself wryly, that struggle of which no living creature except Kenneth (now far away and over-burdened with problems of his own) had ever been aware. It had never been hard to preach, to kindle, to love, to govern, to give from the abundance with which he had been blessed, to those who needed the things that he could give. But it was hard, it was not only hard, but agonising, to retreat, to resign, to lay down ; to bear the strange, unfamiliar burden of weariness, that daily increasing load which threatened to overwhelm his spirit as it defeated his body.

He was coming to spend more time in his cell now that he could not take his turn with the others at the oars or in the harvest-fields. If he could no longer toil with his brethren at least he could pray for them as they worked, and though his limbs were failing he could still transcribe the Gospels and Psalms which he knew so well that it mattered less that his sight was dimmer now. Even the rheumatism which distorted his hands did not prevent him from making the meticulous transcription which was in itself a thing of beauty, at which Dermot, as he brought fresh rushlights, peered in admiring awe.

Columba found, too, that he was beginning to write purely

personal verses again, an indulgence he had found little time for during the active years when the only composition he had allowed himself had been specifically religious, chiefly hymns for the daily services of the monastery. Now the desire to express himself more personally began to stir within him more strongly than it had ever done since as a mere boy he had spent with Gemman those months of decision which had come between the intellectual intoxication of Moville and the great illuminative experience of Clonard.

The writing of secular verses had been something he had denied himself during his middle years, in order to devote all his energy to his work as a priest. The poet might kindle the priest, as old Gemman had taught him, long ago, but the priest must guide the poet, and the result of such guidance had been, in his case, that the poet had merged his offering in the priest's life work, though from time to time, even since he had come to Iona, there had been occasions on which joy had irresistibly overflowed into the rhythmic shapes of praise and prayer. But now, as the activity ebbed from his daily routine, as he forced himself, day by day, to lay a little more of his personal authority down, Columba found all the old urgency upon him as it had not been since the sunrise time before Clonard.

With his habitual austerity, Columba allowed himself, even now, only a little time for verse-making, compelling himself to complete his quota of transcription before he yielded to the nostalgia which was coming so strongly upon him during these latter days. Through the open door of his cell as evening approached, he watched the shadows spreading eastwards from the rocky outcrops between which ran the rough road that the monks would take on their return from the harvest fields beyond. Columba remembered the parched, yet contented weariness of those late summer evenings so vividly that he, too, might almost have been tramping homewards, a great sheaf across his shoulder and the ripe grain whispering in his ear. With the memory, his love for them all overflowed and reached out towards the toiling company who must be at that moment almost half-way back to the monastery, each bearing a sheaf on his back to be finally dried on the beams of the kiln. Dreamily, lovingly, he thought of them, each man by name, sending out towards them all the fervour of his released spirit as the wings of his imagination lifted it and he began to write.

" I am weary and earth seems strange to me,
    Bear me away, strong arms of angels.

A prodigal son is astray and athirst
For the home of his heart and the welcome of heaven . . ."

A group of the older monks trudged homeward in the mellow
light that lay like a blessing on the land which had at first seemed
so bare and forbidding when they arrived as strangers, more
than thirty years ago. At the crest of the rise, where the road
turned between boulders to wind down to the eastern shore, they
paused within sight of the thatched roofs of the monastery
buildings and the milky expanse of the quiet sea. They were the
last of the harvesters to return, for the younger brethren,
hungrier and more nimble, had already crossed the ridge and
were striding down the slope towards the granary where they
would deposit their sheaves.

Pausing where the road turned downwards, Eochaidh swung
the burden from his shoulders and waited for the little party of
slowly-moving, elderly men to catch up with him.

"There's something strange," he said, "about this place.
I'm just a plain, labouring man, and I've never been one of the
holy ones here, as you know. But it's been the same every evening
since harvest started. Just here, always just here . . ."

Torannan, who had left his flocks to help with the harvest,
nodded. "Yes, I've noticed it, too."

Rus, bulky, white-haired and sweating, had let his smithy-fire
die down while he joined the rest of the community, with his
assistants, Scandal and Carnan, in the urgent task of getting the
harvest home while the fine spell lasted. Surprisingly, he agreed
with a brief nod.

Grellan smiled rather complacently at Cobtach and Macculthan, weary after a day's work away from their boats. As a
husbandman, accustomed to work all the year round in the
fields, he could sympathise with the aches due to the unfamiliar
movements of harvesting, a communal activity for which even
fishermen, smiths, leather-workers, carpenters or weavers were
expected to leave their trades. Cobtach, too, added his comment,
however.

"This is not my work," he said. "I find it back-breaking.
Yet every evening, just at this place, all fatigue seems to leave
me. I could walk like those youngsters who have gone singing
ahead of us down the road to the granary with the sheaves light
on their backs as thistledown."

Catan, who had changed over to a scribe's work after over-
straining himself in the fields, still helped at harvest-time by
gleaning behind the reapers and carrying a light load home. Now

he said eagerly : " not only do I forget my weariness just at this point in the way, but I feel the fragrance of all the flowers in the world sweet round me. Roses, such as I have not seen since we left Erin seem to bloom here, among these rocks . . ."

" It is like a fire," said Rus. " Not fierce, but as welcome, even on a summer's day, as the fire in my smithy on a raw winter's morning."

Baithene, Abbot-elect, stood among them, panting no longer, not even troubling to lower the sheaf from his slight shoulders, but standing upright under it, as if he scarcely noticed now the weight of the burden that had bent him nearly double all the way up the farther slope. Now, he seemed ready to bear that greater burden which would soon be laid upon him, the leadership of the community, and looking at him, his companions were aware of strength which went far beyond the capacity of one small, middle-aged man. He had about him a quality which they all recognised. Instinctively they turned to him now.

" Tell us, Father Baithene," asked Eochaidh, " have you noticed anything here during recent days ? "

" Indeed, I have," said Baithene.

" What does it mean ? " The question came from Rus, the downright, practical man who disliked to be mystified.

Baithene looked round the group of elderly monks. Here was the nucleus of the monastery, the men who had been there from its beginning, on whom so much depended now. He knew that no vague hints of hallowed ground or harvest blessing would satisfy them. He spoke simply, offering his own impressions for their acceptance or refusal, without making any claim for their dogmatic truth.

" I think," he said slowly, " that it is the spirit of our blessed Father Columba, which he sends forth, now that he is no longer able to work with us in person. His love and blessing greets us at this spot because it is the farthest point on our homeward journey which, as he sits in his cell, he can see."

" Yes," they all said. " Yes, that must be what it is. Our blessed Father Columba . . . that is just what he would do . . ."

They stood for a little while, smiling, as they looked down the slope towards the cell which their eyes were no longer keen enough to pick out from the rest of the monastery buildings. Then, swinging their sheaves back across their shoulders, they set off downhill, entering the shadow cast by the rocks of the summit as they went.

Only Rus, the smith, lingered by Baithene, and his face was

anxious as he expressed the thought that was troubling all their minds.

" Father Baithene, do you think this means that the blessed Columba is shortly going to leave us ? "

" I do not know, my son," said Baithene.

" He has looked as frail, these last months, as an eggshell which I could crush in my fist. Yet he ails nothing . . ."

" His spirit," said Baithene, " seems to have burnt his body to a shell so fine that the light within streams through. Sometimes at night, Rus, when I have been wakeful, I have risen from my bed before the bell called us to Matins and seen such light shine from the window-slits of the church as could surely never have come from any rushlight. And when I entered, blinking at the glory, I found our Father Columba there already, at his prayers."

Rus shook his head. " It is all very strange, Father Baithene. What is body then, and what is spirit ? "

" How should I know, my son ? "

" Fire is bright and warm," said Rus in his persistent way. " Iron is dull and cold. Yet the dull metal can be so changed that it glows like the sun and runs like water. I am not a man of ideas, Father, being a man of my hands instead. But I have sometimes wondered, working at my forge, whether the change that God works in us through the action of his Spirit is something like the change that fire works on a lifeless lump of iron. Yet it is not lasting, as regards iron and fire. When the fire is withdrawn the iron will lapse again."

" So will the greatest saint who no longer seeks the grace of the Spirit."

" That is true," said Rus. " Yet if the action of the Holy Spirit be continued it will soon be no more possible to detain our Father Columba among the things of this world, than white-hot iron can be held in a wooden bowl."

" I agree," said Baithene. " But say no word of this to the others. It will break their hearts."

" I will say nothing," promised Rus. But his broad, grime-creased face was sad as they trudged homeward. And Baithene himself was silent, for the magnitude of his task had been further revealed to him by the reverent faces of the monks as he spoke of Columba's care. Now, in spite of the strength which had been given him on the summit, he was dismayed. Who was he, how could he hope to follow this great man ?

Rus, trying to check the instinctive, spontaneous distress which the thought of losing his leader inevitably caused him, kept his promise to Baithene and said nothing of his fears. But his thoughts did not need to be explicitly shaped into words to pass from one member of the community to another. And so, all that winter, the fear of Columba's death crept about the monastery like a November fog, till, as the year turned, the island was grey with it. It was not possible to keep the prevailing mood of the community from Columba himself, who, when he became aware of their apprehension, chose to scatter it, as if by an east wind, by speaking calmly and cheerfully, at every convenient opportunity, of his coming death. It was Dermot who took it most hardly, and Columba who comforted him.

" Harness the pony to the cart, Dermot," the Abbot said one morning, unexpectedly laying down his quill. " I wish you to drive me to the western fields to greet the brethren who are working there at the spring sowing."

" Very well, Father Columba," said Dermot doubtfully. " But are you wise to go to-day, Father ? The wind is still keen."

" Did I come to any harm," said Columba cheerfully, " the last time I drove in that cart, though the wheel might have come off at any moment because someone whom Rus is still chasing with wrath forgot to renew the lynch-pin ? "

" You came to no harm, Father, praise be to heaven."

" Then if my guardian angel can keep an unsupported wheel from coming off no doubt he can also see that I survive the effects of a pleasant spring breeze. I shall be sent for, Dermot, when I am wanted. Meanwhile I need fear nothing. My work is not yet done."

" Indeed, indeed, it can never be done while this sinful world remains, Father Columba," cried Dermot with frank grief. " We ask nothing more than that you should stay with us, Father. Without you we must all go astray——"

" Nay, then, it is high time I left you if you feel like that, Dermot," said Columba sternly. " You will not get far on your journey home if you insist on following another benighted wayfarer like yourself, equipped only with a flickering lantern, when you might have been guided by the Wise Men's star."

But Dermot only flung himself on his knees at the Abbot's feet, tears spilling from eyes that were wide with terror and despair. " But you—you are our star, Father Columba. Do not leave us, do not leave us. The world is so dark . . ." He hid his face in his hands and his shoulders shook.

" Child, child," said Columba more gently, touched by the sight of such grief from the usually stoical Dermot, " you do not know what you ask. I shall have been here thirty-four years at Pentecost, instead of the thirty years that were ordained for me. I am seventy-seven already, and several years ago I might have left you——"

" I remember," murmured Dermot, " the time you were ill. And we all prayed . . ."

Columba sighed. "Yes, you all prayed. But soon, Dermot, the messengers will come again to guide me home. It would be courteous, would it, to send the angels away empty-handed once more ? I will tell you the truth, Dermot. I am very tired. I long to go home. You would not seek to keep me here against heaven's will and mine ? "

" No," Dermot whispered penitently. " No . . ."

" I have been with you for the festivities at Easter and during the forty joyous days that follow, I shall remain," Columba said.

" And then ? "

" Do not pull such a miserably long face, Dermot," said Columba, pretending to lose patience. " I have prayed that we might all spend Easter together, but if you insist on behaving as if I were dead already I shall be sorry I did not ask to go home during Lent."

" Indeed . . . I will try to be gay," faltered Dermot.

" As a beginning," commanded Columba, " go and harness the pony and take me out."

Twisting his tear-streaked face into a dubious, valiant smile, hunching his strong shoulders against the misery of anticipation that lay on him like a great weight, Dermot did as he was told. And Columba, swinging the cloak about him with a gesture almost like that of a young warrior in its eagerness, was waiting in the doorway when Dermot returned, driving the community's old grey pony in the clumsy lurching cart.

" Now, Dermot," said the Abbot, as he clambered over the wheel and sat down heavily on the plank which was laid across the cart from side to side, " drive on."

The cart was used for many purposes besides the conveyance of passengers ; a sort of vaguely composite flavour lingered from the loads of manure, seed-bags, meal-sacks, peat, driftwood, fish or kelp which it had from time to time contained, and the harness which the leather-workers had made for the sedate old pony was patched and stained with sweat. Obeying Columba's instructions, Dermot flapped the reins on the pony's back and it moved off at that deliberate pace which it considered suitable for all expeditions, and never varied in any circumstances. As they rocked up the uneven track Dermot began to talk in a dogged, desperate way, chosing his subject at random in order to fight back the unfamiliar surge of tears.

" Father, do you remember the man who would give you no peace till you told him what would be the cause of his death ? "

" Your mind seems to be running along a single track this morning, like a good hound on the trail," said Columba, with a chuckle. " Yes, I remember the poor fellow. He was in a sad state, and though I did not wish to answer him, he pestered me till I told him that the cause of his death would not be any enemy, but his constant companion, of whom he had no suspicion at all. Well, what of it ? "

" He has died, Father. Suddenly, after months spent in solitude because he dared not trust even his wife or his oldest friends."

" May it be a lesson to those who seek to peer into the future in search of that which in mercy is hid from them," Columba said. " I would have pacified him and sent him home to his prayers. But he would not listen. Did you hear the manner of his death ? "

" Yes, Father. It was very strange. Climbing a bank, he fell on his own hunting-knife which he was carrying unsheathed for fear of attack. And because he was alone he bled there till he died."

" Killed indeed by his constant companion, of whom he had no suspicion at all," said Columba rather grimly. " May the blessed angels receive his soul and guide him in wiser ways. May I, too, be forgiven my impatience with a man whose inquisitiveness wearied me. Dermot, I have never seen the island looking more beautiful. So it was when we first landed, long ago, at this very time of year, yes, even almost at the same day and hour. Yet, if I remember rightly," he went on, talking half to himself, " it was not its beauty that I first saw, though now, as I look about me, I can see nothing else, no, not in the midst of winter or in the wildest storm. Strange, strange are the ways by which we are led home."

Dermot looked round him at the steep, rock-studded sheep pastures through which the track they were following wound. He was not an imaginative or articulate man, but his love for his Abbot he reached beyond the limitations of his own personality trying to see what Columba must have seen on that far-off day.

" I can believe," he agreed, " that a man coming for the first time to this island that we love might see it as a strange, bleak place, with little hope for husbandry."

Columba nodded. " It is always bleak to the critical stranger. So is the Christian faith. In Iona, as in Palestine, perhaps, a man must kneel if he is to see the beauty of a million tiny flowers."

He was smiling as he looked about him, serene in the knowledge that this was the last official inspection of the community's
outlying fields that he would ever make, enjoying each aspect of
the familiar territory because the last sight of things much loved
holds, when recognised, all the enchantment of the first. It was
startling, yet oddly satisfactory to his poet's mind, to see the
island now almost exactly as he had seen it on his arrival thirty-
four years ago. Once again the spears of the wild yellow iris,
crowned with the first brave blossoms, were mustered in every
moist hollow and ranked like a silent host on both sides of their
way. Once again every fold in the rocks held its splash of
primroses, like paler sunshine, while in the thyme-sweet turf of
the heights already the tiny flowers of milkwort, eye-bright,
tormentil and red-rattle had begun to unfold. Once again, as
they moved towards the centre of the island, the harsh complaint
of the gulls dwindled in the distance and the sweeter voices of
skylarks took their place. The slow, jogging process was very
pleasant. The sun's warmth fell comfortably on Columba's
bowed back as he sat looking serenely about him, his hands
lying, palms downwards, on his knees. The hood of undyed wool
had fallen back from his head, but even Dermot had come to
realise that to a man who had so evidently come to the verge of
another world, the over-careful attentions of those still preoccupied with bodily existence could only irk him. So, while the
light airs ruffled the thick white hair that fell back from the
frontal tonsure, he did not venture to protest.

" Stop the cart now, Dermot," Columba said at last. But the
old pony knew the ways of its masters almost as well as their
Abbot himself. Before Dermot had tightened the reins its
deliberately shambling feet had come to a standstill at the side
of the field in which the brethren were toiling, stooping and rising,
stooping and rising, in the back-breaking business of stoning a
newly reclaimed area for the first crop of corn.

At the sight of the cart first one and then another paused,
till all were staring in astonishment at the unexpected sight of
Columba, whom they had imagined to be resting within doors.
Then, as if drawn by the instinctive compulsion which leads a
child to its parent, turns a plant to the sun, they left their half-
filled baskets and hurried across the furrows to receive the
blessing of their Abbot who had not for many months been able
to travel so far.

" It is Columba . . . the blessed Father has come to see our
work . . . Columba . . . Columba himself is out again . . ."

Excited, murmuring, they crowded round the cart, sturdy

men with habits kilted and sleeves rolled high for field labour,
their faces and tonsured heads already tanned by the strengthen-
ing sun. As Columba made the sign of the cross above them,
standing in the cart, while Dermot anxiously held the unmoving
pony's head, they knelt.

"My children," said Columba, "here for the last time, I
bless these fields and you who work in them. Do not grieve,
because your Abbot will soon go home. If heaven is nearer to
the glory of our Lord it must surely, too, be near the children
whom He also loves. Do not be afraid when you see me no more.
Wherever I may be, in heaven or on earth, I will bear the love
of all at Iona always in my heart."

"Father Columba," they whispered, "pray for us . . ."

" Pray for us, blessed Columba . . ."

"Pray for us, we beseech you . . ."

"Wherever I may be," said Columba again, "my prayers
for you all will rise towards the infinite mercy of God. And
while you live as brothers, after the pattern and in the humility
of Christ, the love of God shall be as sunshine about you, and
no poisonous creature shall mar for you the Eden of this little
land. Pray for me also, who am awaiting the welcome summons . . ."

"We pray for you also, Father Columba . . ."

"The blessing of God be upon you . . ."

"God speed you, holy Father Columba . . ."

Then Columba turned to Dermot. "Set the pony's head
towards home, my son."

The monks stood for a long time watching the lurching cart
diminish in the distance, then reluctantly turned back to the
task of removing the stones which many could not see clearly
for their tears. Stooping and rising, stooping and rising, the
rhythmic movements of the labouring monks began again.

But from that day an air of expectancy hung about the
monastery. In obedience to their Abbot's command the monks
tried to check their grief, even to share the exaltation that transfigured Columba's whole being, as if, in some odd way, the
long-desired journey homewards had already begun. According
to his wishes, the routine of the monastery went steadily forward
under Baithene's active direction, while Columba spent most of
the time he was not celebrating the daily Mass or taking part in
the regular offices, in his cell, tranquilly proceeding with a new
and faultless copy of the Psalms.

It was not until the Saturday of the week which had begun
with his expedition in the pony-cart that Columba summoned

Dermot to go with him, this time about the monastery itself.
Leaning on Dermot's arm, he walked very slowly, with frequent
pauses, round the workshops of the monastery, where men knelt,
with the tools still in their hands, among shavings or old iron or
piled hides, or newly cured fish, to receive Columba's blessing
and look with amazement at his radiant face. Near the harbour
they met Urdan, middle-aged now, but swarthy and strong as a
tree as he trudged, fishing-creel on his back, beside his eldest son,
while his two small grandsons bounced excitedly beside them as
they returned from meeting Urdan's home-coming boat.

"I need hardly ask if life is treating you kindly, Urdan," said
Columba, smiling at his first convert on Iona, who was trying
to stop the two small boys from playing with the knots on the
Abbot's girdle-cord.

"No, Father. Nor, I think, need I ask you," said Urdan gently.

"Heaven has given you understanding in your happiness,
my son," Columba said. He blessed them all, laying his hands on
the restless heads of the little boys, who scuffled their feet as they
knelt, just as the other little boys had done at the oratory in the
mountains near Gartan, seventy years ago.

"*Ego sum pastor ille bonus, et agnosco meas, et agnoscor a meis* . . ."
Once more the words went whispering through his mind.

"It is strange," thought Columba aloud, as they went on to
inspect the granary, "how clear these earliest memories have
become. Almost as if the shape of a man's life is not like a straight
or crooked line left by his footsteps across untrodden snow, but
like a complete circle in which apparent extremes meet. A circle
. . . beginning and ending in God. '*Ego sum Alpha et Omega,
principium et finis, dicit Dominus, qui est, et qui erat, et qui venturus est.*'
Eh, Dermot ?"

"I have but little Latin, Father," said Dermot humbly.

Columba's voice was dreamily content as he translated. "'I
am Alpha and Omega, the beginning and the ending, saith the
Lord, which is, and was, and is to come . . .'"

After they had been to the granary Columba paused. "Let
us sit down for a moment. After I have found my strength again
we will climb the little hill before us from which I can see the
whole monastery, once and for all."

"Yes, Father," Dermot said. But as the old grey pony came
shambling towards them he rose again, thankful for the chance
of relieving his feelings by chasing the beast away. But Columba
checked him.

"Leave it alone," he said. "The creature is fond of me.
Let it be."

The old grey pony laid his head on Columba's shoulder and remained there, motionless, except for the occasional movement of its tail with which it switched away the first summer flies. To Dermot's astonished eyes it seemed to weep, and certainly it sighed. Columba lifted his hands and began to comfort it. Knowingly, soothingly, the movements taking the place of words, his thumb and fingers rubbed the base of its ears, touched the sleek muzzle, endured its gusty breathing on his neck.

" You, Dermot, may be a man with a rational soul," he said. " Yet something has been revealed to this beast that you would not have known had I not told you. It knows, in whatever way God has chosen to reveal the truth to it, that I am going away. And like you, it is sad." Gently, reassuringly, he stroked the soft muzzle which wrinkled as if anticipating a titbit, under his hand. " Heaven bless you, too, old friend," he said. " Be comforted. The God who made us both will not take me far from those I love. Now, Dermot," he added, as the old pony, lifting its head almost as if it had understood what had been said to it, moved away, " help me to the summit of this knoll."

" Father, surely you have done enough ? "

" When I have done enough," said Columba placidly, " I shall be able to do no more. Give me your arm."

Together they went slowly up the slope, Columba smiling to himself at the memory of the former impatience which would once have driven him to the top of the hillock in a few great bounds. Now he must curb his spirit to match the tedious, shuffling paces of an old man whose body could only be compelled to serve him for a few hours more. From the summit he looked down on the cluster of buildings ; the church, the refectory, the cells of the brethren, inside the protecting wall ; and the utilitarian work-shops, granary, and mill outside. In their keeping were thirty-four years of his life. Lifting up his hands in a movement which gathered the people of Iona, monks, lay-brothers, workers of every skill, fishermen and pilgrims, within the protective circle of his arms, he blessed the island and its community in a prophetic farewell.

" To this place, small and mean though it be, shall not only the kings of Alba and Erin bring their peoples, but multitudes shall come here in all ages from many strange and foreign lands. And the peace of this place shall come upon them from God."

Dermot stood ready to support Columba as he swayed. His face was grave with the knowledge of the responsibility that had come upon him, who was never a man of nimble wit. Here he was, alone with the blessed Columba, only recipient of the final messages of their great Abbot. Anxiously he prayed that he would remember exactly what words Columba used and be able to repeat them when questioned. He was, he knew, most unworthy of so great an honour. He could only do his best. Carefully, rather out of breath, he bore the increasing weight of the Abbot's arm about his shoulders as they returned to Columba's cell.

" Now, Father, will you rest a little ? "

" Not yet, my son. Give me my inkhorn and point a quill for me. I will go on transcribing the thirty-fourth psalm from where I stopped at noon."

He took the quill and began to write. For the rest of the day he worked steadily on, pausing only to sip a little of the broth that Dermot brought him instead of going to the refectory for supper, and to attend the evening office at dusk. On their return, he called for lights, and Dermot kindled a couple of tapers with flint and steel. Standing behind the Abbot, he watched the progress of Columba's hand, which formed, slowly, and yet more slowly, word after word, line after line. At last, as he reached the end of the sheet of vellum which had been prepared for his day's work, Columba laid the quill down.

" Here I must cease . . ." he said. In his voice was all the anguish of that conflict which he had thought resolved long since, which now came back on him, in this hour of complete exhaustion, with renewed violence. For an instant, the last vestiges of his authority seemed sweet, too sweet to be laid down. Then, with a supreme effort of renunciation, he resisted the temptation to call for another sheet of vellum, to insist at least on completing the transcription of one psalm. Instead, he proclaimed in a steady voice the surrender of his last earthly task.

" What follows . . . Baithene must write."

" Will you lie down for a little, Father, now ? "

Columba allowed himself to be supported to the stone shelf on which he usually slept. But though he lay still, he was wakeful and wide-eyed. Now and again he murmured, so low that Dermot had to put his head close to the lips to hear : " Children . . . love one another . . . Life . . . is no more than this . . ."

When the bell, rung by Baithene, sounded for Matins, Dermot was dozing, overcome by fatigue and grief. Staggering to his feet at a sudden sound he looked wildly round for Columba, his sleep-hazed eyed bemused by a blaze of light which seemed to have its focus, not in the rushlights, now burnt almost to their sockets, but in the Abbot's poised figure, vital as a young tree in spring, his transfigured face lit as no earthly candle could light it, his backward-streaming hair like pale flame. For an instant Columba stood there, arms outstretched as if in welcome, his lips parted in the smile of a child called home. Then he swung on his heel and was gone . . . Outside Dermot could hear the sound of his hasty feet running, running, like the feet of an eager lad. But . . . the blessed Columba had been hardly able to stand. How could he, then, run ?

Frantically Dermot plunged after him. It was near the end of May and scarcely dark outside, so that he caught a glimpse of the pale blur of Columba's habit disappearing towards the church, while from the various cells other shadows followed, unaware that anything unusual had happened, moving deliberately to attend the midnight office, with lanterns in their hands.

Inside the church it was dark again, and Dermot, without a lantern was at a loss. His distraught voice echoed through the empty building.

" Father . . . Father Columba . . . where are you ? "

But there was no answer. Sobbing wildly, Dermot groped his way towards the altar, encountered a limp body on the steps and gently lifted Columba's head on to his knee.

" Bring lights . . ." he cried. " Bring lights . . ."

They crowded in, raising their lanterns so that the beams fell on Dermot as he crouched on the altar steps with the Abbot's body in his arms. And Dermot, speechless, looked back at the members of the community, at those men, now shouldering their way forward, who had been Columba's first companions and who now stood together round his body, their faces ennobled in the uncertain light, as if grief, in drawing them together again, had also purged their alienating faults away. Lugaid, sorrowfully cadaverous, seemed no longer mean but only faithful over very little things ; Rus, the strong man, was silently weeping ; Torannan's plump face had puckered like a child's ; Eochaidh's wide mouth was twisted with distress ; Cobtach and Macculthan stood side by side, their faces swarthy from the sea winds. Grellan, Scandal and Carnan huddled together, awed and tearless ; little Catan the scribe was shaking his sad, bald head. Then, as if by common consent, Columba's companions and all the others who had followed him to Iona during thirty-four years drew aside to let the new Abbot go by.

" Is it well with our blessed Columba ? " asked Baithene.

" It is very well," said Dermot steadily. " In this same hour he has gone home to Christ."

As he spoke a great groan came from the assembled

company, a groan which was taken up by the first gusts of the suddenly rising wind. The gale blew for the next three days and nights, flailing shutters, pounding the coast-line with great breakers that sent sheets of spray flying far inland, making all communication with the mainland impossible, so that no stranger whether from Erin or Alba or any of the more distant lands out of which pilgrims had ever come, was able to be present at the ceremonies with which the monks of Iona bade their first Abbot farewell.

Palled in fair linen, watched by candles, Columba's body lay in state while the monks, in the white habits of high festival, sang his requiem. Rank upon rank of Seniors, Working Brethren and Juniors filled the church to its very doors, and most of their pale, strained faces showed only too clearly their tragic awareness of immediate and heartbreaking loss. Yet, here and there, into the eyes of those who had most unobtrusively and sincerely loved Columba, came, as they sang, a very different look, an expression that was strangely like his own in its hour of transfiguration, so that among the shadowed sorrowing faces some were lit with a sort of wonder, an air of uncomprehending, almost unearthly joy.

THE END

BIBLIOGRAPHY

ADAMNAN, *Vita S. Columbae* (Latin text w. notes) Reeves. Dublin University Press.

ADAMNAN, *Vita S. Columbae* (Trans. w. notes) Fowler. Oxford University Press.

ANDERSON, J., *Scotland in Early Christian Times.* Hamilton.

BRYANT, S., *Celtic Ireland.* Kegan Paul.

CARMICHAEL, A., *Carmina Gadelica* (4 vols.) Stewart, Edinburgh.

DUKE, J. A., *The Columban Church.* Oxford University Press.

DOWDEN, J., *The Celtic Church in Scotland.* S.P.C.K.

HANNAN, *Iona and Some Satellites.* Chambers.

HUME BROWN, *History of Scotland.* Oliver.

KEATING, G., *History of Ireland,* tr. Dinneen 3 vols. Irish Texts Society.

KENDRICK, T. D., *The Druids.* Methuen.

JOYCE, P. W., *Social History of Ancient Ireland.* Longman Green.

MACALISTER, R. A. S., *The Archaeology of Ireland.* Methuen.

MCCLINTOCK, H. F., *Old Irish and Highland Dress.* Dundelgan Press.

MACNEILL, E., *Celtic Ireland.* Parsons.

MENZIES, L., *St. Columba.* Dent.

NORRIS, H., *Costume and Fashion.* Dent.

O'GRADY, S., *History of Ireland : the Heroic Period.* Samson Low.

RITCHIE, A. & E., *Iona : Past and Present.* Stewart.

SKENE, W.F., *Celtic Scotland : a History of Ancient Alban.* 2 vols. Edinburgh.

STOKES, G. T., *Ireland and the Celtic Church.* Hodder & Stoughton.

TRENHOLM, *The Story of Iona.* Douglas.

WARREN, *Liturgy and Ritual of the Celtic Church.* Oxford University Press.